Rebecca Winters lives in Salt Lake City, Utah. With canyons and high alpine meadows full of wildflowers, she never runs out of places to explore. They, plus her favourite holiday spots in Europe, often end up as backgrounds for her romance novels—because writing is her passion, along with her family and her church. Rebecca loves to hear from readers. If you wish to email her, please visit her website at rebeccawinters.net

Lynne Marshall used to worry she had a serious problem with daydreaming, and then she discovered she was supposed to write those stories down! A late bloomer, she came to fiction writing after her children were nearly grown. Now she battles the empty nest by writing romantic stories about life, love and happy endings. She's a proud mother and grandmother who loves babies, dogs, books, music and travelling.

Also by Rebecca Winters

The Princess Brides
The Princess's New Year Wedding
The Prince's Forbidden Bride
How to Propose to a Princess

Escape to Provence
Falling for Her French Tycoon
Falling for His Unlikely Cinderella

Secrets of a Billionaire
The Greek's Secret Heir

Also by Lynne Marshall

Cooking Up Romance
Forever a Father
Soldier, Handyman, Family Man
Reunited with the Sheriff
Her Perfect Proposal
A Doctor for Keeps
The Medic's Homecoming
Courting His Favourite Nurse

Discover more at millsandboon.co.uk

UNMASKING THE SECRET PRINCE

REBECCA WINTERS

RUNAWAY GROOM

LYNNE MARSHALL

MILLS & BOON

First Published in Great Britain 2021
by Mills & Boon, an imprint of HarperCollins*Publishers* Ltd
1 London Bridge Street, London, SE1 9GF

www.harpercollins.co.uk

HarperCollins*Publishers*
1st Floor, Watermarque Building,
Ringsend Road, Dublin 4, Ireland

Unmasking the Secret Prince © 2021 Rebecca Winters
Runaway Groom © 2021 by Harlequin Books S.A..

Special thanks and acknowledgement are given to Lynne Marshall for her contribution to *The Fortunes of Texas: The Hotel Fortune* series.

ISBN: 978-0-263-29953-3

0321

MIX
Paper from
responsible sources
FSC™ C007454

This book is produced from independently certified FSC™ paper to ensure responsible forest management.

For more information visit: www.harpercollins.co.uk/green

Printed and bound in Spain
by CPI, Barcelona

UNMASKING THE SECRET PRINCE

REBECCA WINTERS

Dedicated to my four wonderful children,
who've always been my Champions.

PROLOGUE

"ALEX? WE HAVE a new lead. You're to leave for Rome at three. When you get there, take a taxi to the Jupiter Hotel, where you're already booked in. Rigas will come to your room tomorrow morning and fill you in on what we've found out."

Alex smothered a moan. "I can't leave yet, Uncle Zikos." Though he really wasn't his uncle, Alex loved him like one.

"You mean because of Giannina."

"She's my life. I've made plans to spend the weekend with her before she goes back to Greece next week." In an hour he would be picking her up at her apartment.

"I'm sorry, but you'll have to cancel them. This is too important."

Alex closed his eyes tightly, not wanting to hear it though he knew Zikos was right. But how to say goodbye to Giannina? It was already tearing him apart.

At thirteen, Alex had met eleven-year-old Giannina Angelis the year before his parents, the king and queen of Hellenia, had been killed. Her father had come to

Hellenia, an island kingdom in the Aegean near Greece, to discuss shipping business with the king.

She'd run around the palatial estate with him chasing after his dog. They'd laughed and had eaten some treats in the little summerhouse. She'd been more fun than any girl he'd ever met. When she'd had to leave, they'd shared a chaste kiss.

A year later, the men who'd murdered Alex's parents had been hunting for him. Zikos had rescued him from certain death and had taken him to Croatia. He'd fashioned an elaborate disguise for Alex so he could hide in plain sight, and he was given the name Philip Dimas. To this day Giannina didn't know his true identity or that they'd met years ago.

The situation had to stay that way for her safety as well as his. Alex's whole mission in life hinged on finding those monsters and forcing them to pay for their crimes. But until they were captured and arrested, he couldn't settle down and marry the woman he loved.

He shouldn't have allowed his relationship with Giannina to grow at all, but he hadn't been able to help himself. In case the enemy saw through his disguise, it could mean danger or even death to her too. If anything happened to her because of him, he wouldn't be able to bear it.

Alex had been in London for the last month working on a story for the *Daily Courier* as a freelance journalist. It provided cover for what he was really doing here. He could never have dreamed that the young girl he'd met years earlier outside the palace had grown into the breathtaking woman who came to a night lecture sponsored by the newspaper.

She'd approached him after it was over, telling him she'd even heard him speak at her high school four years earlier in Salonica, Greece. But she'd been too nervous to approach him. Now she was doing an internship at the London School of Journalism. One of her teachers announced a night lecture that featured the noted journalist Philip Dimas and she'd decided to come.

Remembering how delightful she'd been as a girl, he was enamored with her immediately and asked her out for drinks so they could get to know each other better. By the time the evening was over, he realized he'd met the woman for him. His whole world changed that night, and he'd spent every possible free moment with her when he wasn't running down leads.

But he hated it that he couldn't tell her about his mission and reveal his identity. Worse, when the time came that he'd be able to be truthful with her, he had the gut feeling she'd never forgive him for lying to her.

She had to be the most gorgeous woman he'd ever met. The stunning brunette beauty with her warm, light brown eyes had stood out from every woman he'd ever met. She thrilled him with her native intelligence. Her natural charm and femininity would haunt his dreams until he could claim her for his wife. But he feared that day wouldn't be coming anytime soon.

"Alex? Are you still there?"

"Of course. I'll be on the flight at three." It meant

he had to get to the airport at least an hour ahead. That didn't leave him any extra time.

"I'm sorry, Alex. I hope you realize that."

"I do." Zikos was a saint. Alex owed him his life and everything else. "I'll call you from Rome."

After he hung up, he grabbed his suitcase and hurried out of the apartment to his rental car. Giannina would be waiting for him to pick her up. They'd planned a day in the country.

When he reached her apartment building, he rang for her to let him come up.

She'd left her door open. The glorious sight of her in what looked like a new pair of white pants and a lemon ice silk blouse took his breath.

"Philip—" She launched herself into his arms, covering his mouth with her own. Her hunger matched his. For a few minutes he forgot everything else and gave in to his feverish desire for her, clinging to her curvaceous body.

He loved her wavy brown hair that cascaded down her back like liquid chocolate. She'd left it loose and flowing so he could tangle his fingers in it. The scent of her peach shampoo stirred his senses. Everything about her entranced him, but he had to let her go.

"Agapi mou," he murmured, putting her gently away from him. "Something has happened I need to tell you about."

She cupped his face in her hands. "You sound so serious."

"I'm afraid it is. When we first met, I told you that

if another story came up, I would have to take off immediately to cover it."

Pain filled her eyes. "You don't mean now—"

"I'm afraid so. We've been lucky I haven't had to leave before today. I just had a phone call and must get to the airport ASAP."

"Philip—" She moaned his name.

"I wish it weren't true, but I have to investigate a potentially explosive story for the *Forum Chronicle* in Italy and time is of the essence. The last thing I want to do is leave you."

She looked fragmented. "But I hoped you'd fly to Greece with me next week when I returned home. I want you to meet my family. There's so much I want to show you and do wi—"

"I'm sure I would have loved all of it," he broke in, crushing her against him once more. Since meeting her, he'd wanted to take her away and make love to her for weeks on end. But he would never do it without them being married first and the time wasn't right for that. Not yet...

"I can't believe you have to go." She was heartbroken. So was he. Talk about agony. At this point tears gushed down her cheeks. He kissed them away.

"Surely you know I never want to be separated from you. I don't want to go anywhere without you, but I have a job to do. One day I'll explain all the reasons why I have to go alone. Sweetheart, I promise I'll write to you all the time so you won't forget me."

"As if I could." The words came out in choking sobs.

"I love you, Giannina Angelis. One day we'll be together forever. Remember that."

"Philip—" She half sobbed his name. "Don't go—" The pain on her lovely face, the anguish in her voice, was killing him.

"I'll be back. I swear it!" After another long deep kiss, he broke free of her and left the apartment before he couldn't. His only solace was that in tearing himself away, he was removing the danger to her. Alex was glad she'd be going back to Greece, where she'd be safe until he could claim her.

CHAPTER ONE

Three years later, Salonica/Thessalonika, Greece

"Boss?"

Twenty-six-year-old Giannina Angelis had been drinking coffee at her desk when the managing editor entered the office without warning. She looked up from the latest draft of the financial section of the newspaper she needed to approve. "What is it, Khloe?"

The forty-two-year-old married woman who'd become the managing editor of the Angelis family-owned *Halkidiki News* in Thessolonika, Greece, had never appeared so excited.

"Excuse me for bursting in, but you're going to be astounded when you hear who just called the newspaper. The secretary routed it through to me first. This man is in Salonica and is asking to meet with the editor-in-chief ASAP!"

Giannina had held that position for the last ten months. Prior to her promotion as head of the influential newspaper that covered northern Greece, she'd been the managing editor for a brief period of time.

"Take a deep breath first," Giannina teased.

She rolled her amber eyes. "He's only *the* most famous journalist in Europe, and so handsome from the photographs I've seen, it hurts!"

Gianinna's body lurched. She knew exactly to whom Khloe was referring. In all the world there could be only one man who filled those descriptions hands down, but she let out a disdainful laugh. "Are you telling me that the award-winning, prize-winning, sensational Philip Dimas of all people has actually arrived on *our* Aegean doorstep?"

Khloe's smile broadened. "Yes. I am. I almost fell over my keyboard when he introduced himself on the phone. He has this fabulous vibrant voice I can still feel."

So could Giannina. Just the thought of the man who'd enslaved Gianinna's heart before draining it dry three years ago caused her to struggle for breath. She sat back in the chair refusing to believe it was true. He hadn't come near her in all that time. "I'm afraid it could be a joke being played on me, Khloe."

"Are you serious?"

Giannina nodded. "Remember my uncle?"

"You mean the guy who blamed you for the fake story he'd had printed in the paper about Prince Alexandros being alive?"

She nodded. "I have every reason to believe he's the one responsible for that phone call."

In her mind Ari had always been repugnant to her, even though he was a member of the Angelis family through his marriage to her aunt. As such, he knew about Philip Dimas, the man Giannina had fallen in love with in London. He'd heard of Philip's abandonment of her. If nothing else, he'd used Philip's name today in the hope of tormenting her.

It *had* to be her cruel uncle Ari Hatzi, a citizen of both Greece and Hellenia, who was trying to hurt her again, this time in an excruciating way. When she'd been an editor working under him while he'd been managing editor, he'd made up a colossal, impossible lie about the missing prince of the island country of Hellenia having been found alive on Mount Athos.

The whole world had had been looking for him, but there'd been no news of the prince since the king and queen had been murdered years earlier. Everyone at that time believed young Prince Alexandros had either been killed secretly or had disappeared never to be seen again. There was no proof he existed anywhere.

Her uncle had attributed the flagrant lie of a headline to Giannina in order to embarrass and ruin her so the board would have her removed or fired. Of course, there was no evidence of wrongdoing on her part, but she knew the reason for his hatred.

She'd made the mistake of criticizing the present dictator of Hellenia in front of her uncle and some other newspaper staff. Her political opinions about the man she called an evil, underworld tyrant had infuriated Ari and he'd rebuked her for it in a humiliating way.

Gianinna's father, Estefen Angelis, was also infuriated, but for a different reason. He'd conducted a thorough investigation of the incident. Not only had he made certain the paper printed a retraction of the lie Ari had perpetrated, her father had fired her uncle and installed *her* as editor-in-chief. He'd also sued Ari for damages to the paper's credibility.

During that period, her aunt Olga started divorce proceedings against Ari, who had disappeared. Gianinna's brother, Nico, had gone looking for him with the Grecian police to arrest him until his trial, but to this day Ari hadn't been found.

"Tell him to come at one this afternoon. We'll soon find out what's going on."

"I'll phone him back right now. This is so exciting if he turns out to be the famous journalist! I can't wait to meet him in person." The starstruck editor wheeled around and left the office, acting like a teenager rather than a mature woman.

Giannina slowly drank the rest of her coffee. She doubted anyone would show up at one o'clock and continued poring over the draft in front of her. To her chagrin, she found herself reading the same copy again and again.

Her mind went back to the year she'd finished her university studies in Paris at the Sorbonne School of Journalism. After graduation she'd done a year's internship at the London School of Journalism. It was there she'd met Philip Dimas. The gorgeous, dark blond, blue-eyed journalist born in Portugal had given a night lecture for the *Daily Courier* and the public had been invited.

Once it was over, she'd approached him and told him she remembered when he'd come to an evening symposium for parents and students at her high school in

Greece four years earlier. While they talked, she found herself captivated by everything about him. He asked her to have a drink with him and that was it.

Her whole world changed that night and they spent every spare moment of those four weeks together. She'd fallen so deeply in love with the tall, handsome journalist, and she went into shock when he'd suddenly had to leave for Italy on a story of extreme importance.

Though he hadn't taken her to bed or proposed, he'd told her he was in love with her. After insisting that she was the only woman for him and one day they'd be together forever, she'd assumed he'd meant marriage and that it would be soon.

A week later he'd sent her a postcard from Rome, telling her he loved and missed her. But there was no return address or mention of meeting up with her or future plans for them to be together. She'd thought, of course, he would ask her to travel to Portugal with him so she could meet his aunt and uncle.

Giannina had learned his mother had died in childbirth, and his father, a military man, had been killed on active duty. That left his father's brother and wife to raise him. She'd longed to meet them and their children, and for Philip to get to know her parents and family, but it never happened.

Over the last three years, she'd received hundreds of postcards from him at her address at the newspaper. He never signed them and simply told her he was on a story. One day he would come for her. On every card he added that he would always love her.

What a fool she'd been to believe him. Devastated to

realize his career ambitions were greater than any love he'd had for her, she no longer looked for those postcards. After a few months, she determined to forget him.

Too bad she kept seeing his name in the news for writing prize-winning stories that exposed fraud and corruption in various governments. No one would question he was the best at what he did. The meaningless postcards kept coming, always declaring his love. She'd stopped reading them. His words meant nothing to her.

She took the advice she'd once given her brother about moving on and she started to date other men. Giannina refused to be like Nico, who'd spent his life mourning his first love, whom he believed hadn't loved him after all. Even if in the end a miracle had happened to her brother, *she* didn't believe in them.

Alex left his newly rented apartment on Nikis Avenue and walked through Aristotelous Square in the center of Salonica. A combination of dread because he'd lied to the woman he loved, plus excitement because he was about to see her again, gripped him. He approached the *Halkidiki News* building a block away more nervous than he'd ever been in his life.

After three years separation, he was about to lay eyes on his breathtaking Giannina, who'd enamored him first as a young girl, and later as a woman. It had pained him that he'd met her too soon in London for them to be married. But that wasn't the case now.

The joyous news that General Ruiz and his junta had just been arrested along with one of the two assassins of Alex's parents meant the nightmare haunting him was over. No more threats of danger. Tonight he would be witness to the other killer's arrest. He needed to tell Giannina the news before she heard it from anyone else since it involved her uncle.

That was only part of the reason why he was in Salonica. The other part would be the fulfillment of his dream to marry her. If all went as planned, he would soon sit on the throne of the Aegean island kingdom. And if his prayers were granted, she would agree to be his bride.

But it meant revealing himself as twenty-eight-year-old Prince Alexandros Pisistratus of Hellenia, the young prince she'd once met and played with in the palace grounds. All this time he'd lived a lie and hadn't trusted her with the truth. Philip broke out in a cold sweat knowing it would take a miracle for her to forgive him, let alone be his wife. She wouldn't listen to his reasons. Who would? That's what terrified him.

Through an infallible source he learned that Giannina wasn't seriously involved with another man yet. But he had zero hope she would fall into his arms when they came together in a few minutes. In order for that to happen, he needed time to build her trust again, but he feared it was far too late. He'd broken her heart.

Alex knew all about that devastating feeling. He'd been the walking wounded after having to fly away from her for her own safety. Life had lost its savor since then. It frightened him that if he couldn't win back her love, he'd never be truly happy again.

Because of his love for Giannina, she would have

been the one unknown factor who could have prevented him from carrying out his plans to get rid of the dictator who'd taken over his country in the wake of his parents' murders, General Ruiz. Even in his disguise as Philip Dimas, he hadn't dared allowed that to happen. Her safety had meant everything to him.

After his parents' deaths when he was fourteen, Zikos Novak had whisked him away to Dubrovnik. That was the home of the vastly wealthy Novak family on his mother's side dating back three hundred years with an estate and a fortune in oil. Zikos had developed a plan for Alex to win back the throne once the general and his henchmen were captured and arrested.

Alex owed *his* life to Zikos, the man who'd rescued him from Hellenia after the murders. Zikos, also Hellenian, had been chief adviser and best friend to Alex's father. He'd given him the fictitious name Philip Dimas to hide his true identity.

To make the transformation complete, his black hair and brows were dyed dark blond and his black eyes were covered by blue contact lenses. As he grew older, he had to shave every day without fail. So far his disguise had worked perfectly.

While he attended the university in Dubrovnik and became a journalist, Alex never gave up on his quest to avenge his parents' murders and restore the throne to his family. After graduation he left Croatia to establish his journalism career while he surreptitiously hunted down his parents' killers to bring them to justice.

Still on the hunt for the assassins, ten days ago Alex got the surprise of his life through the Hellenian underground. He made the gut-wrenching discovery that Gianinna's uncle Ari Hatzi, of all people on earth, had been identified as one of them. Alex couldn't believe that the woman he adored and had wanted to protect was his enemy's actual niece.

To think that all the time he'd been searching for the killers, her uncle had been a member of Gianinna's family, trying to track down Alex. Hatzi had once been the managing editor of the Halkidiki newspaper. Now he was wanted by the Greek police for blaming a false news story on Giannina, who'd been put in as editor-in-chief.

Alex had read her father's retraction and knew that she and her family had no love for Hatzi. He also knew that when he brought her this news it would be earth-shaking. But she was the only person who had the right to know everything before the rest of the world heard about it.

He entered the newspaper office wearing a business suit and was shown to the editor-in-chief's office on the third floor. A charming woman introduced herself as Khloe Paulos, the managing editor, and told him to go on through.

His heart thudded as he walked into Gianinna's impressive private office and found her working at her desk, dressed in a chic tan and white short-sleeved summer suit.

Between her classic features and passionate mouth, plus the mold of her five-foot-seven body, she looked even more exquisite than he'd remembered. She wore her brunette hair in a side part that reached her shoulders. Gone were the long tresses. Those light brown eyes he'd stared into so many times studied him without blinking or warmth. The expression *persona non grata* came to mind as he drew closer.

"Senhor Dimas—" She spoke in the Portuguese accent he'd once taught her and felt gratified she'd remembered. "So it *was* you who phoned. I gave up on seeing you a long time ago. As for those pitiful postcards…"

A groan escaped when he realized how much damage he'd done. Alex had felt searing hurt coming from her and was reeling in pain himself. He sat in one of the chairs placed before her desk. It took all the mental fortitude he possessed not to reach out and beg her forgiveness before explaining anything.

"I didn't know how else to keep reminding you that you were the only woman for me, and still are." If she only knew she was his whole life!

"I lost count a long time ago."

He deserved her contempt and so much more. "Believe it or not, those postcards have always conveyed my love for you, but my life was forced to go in a different direction. I couldn't make the plans with you I'd hoped we could make at the time." He'd promised he'd be back, but she didn't want to hear it now.

Giannina cocked her head. "It doesn't matter, Philip. We've all had our flings, but that time in England was over ages ago. No harm done. Since London you've become even more famous all over Europe. Your accomplishments precede you."

He cleared his throat. "Not without a lot of help."

* * *

"Don't be modest. The latest stories of uncovering the money laundering in France and the failed assassination attempt of the prime minister in Germany have put you and you alone right at the top of your game."

It was clear Giannina had done her research and was pretending their relationship in London belonged to ancient history. But he could see a nerve throbbing in the base of her delectable throat that told him this meeting had disturbed her as much as it did him. Could he dare believe it gave him a modicum of hope?

"If anyone is at the top of their game, it's the brilliant editor-in-chief of the *Halkidiki News*. I knew you'd be exceptional when you took over the reins."

She shook her head, dismissing the compliment. "Why don't you get to the point. Since I know I'm not the reason, what has brought you to Greece?"

More and more he feared he'd truly lost her. This was agony, but it was past time she knew the truth. "My love for you, Giannina," he said forcefully. "But I realize you don't want to hear that because you don't believe it."

"You're right. What's the real reason?"

Unbearable as this was, he needed to go on. "I've come with incredible news. General Ruiz and his junta have just been arrested and Hellenia is now a free country again."

A soft cry of surprise escaped her lips. "I can't believe it."

"It hasn't been leaked to the media yet, and there's more news. I've been investigating a related story, but you're the only person who has the right to it. I'm afraid it has to do with your uncle Ari Hatzi."

At those words, lines marred her beautiful features. "*He's* the latest story you're after?" She sounded angry. "His outrageous antics have already been covered. He was fired for it and has disappeared."

"I'm talking about the unspeakable crime he committed a long time ago."

A frown marred her features. "What else has that despicable man done besides run away before signing the divorce papers my aunt filed?"

"I remember you telling me that you never cared for him, but you didn't want to hurt your aunt by letting her know."

"That's right, but you're talking in riddles. What are you trying to say?"

She sat back in the chair. "I'm waiting for your news on my hateful uncle."

He dreaded telling her the truth about something for which she could never be prepared. It would hurt her, but it had to be said. Tragically, Alex knew she'd never accept comfort from him.

"A few days ago, I learned through my sources in the Hellenian underground that an eyewitness has named Ari Hatzi as one of the two assassins of the king and queen of Hellenia."

CHAPTER TWO

"WHAT DID YOU SAY?"

Giannina's face paled and she looked so stunned, Alex wanted to take her in his arms and never let her go. How would he ever be able to make her understand the reason for his deception and get her to fall in love with him again? Right now he couldn't see a way. The knowledge shattered him.

"It's true. As you said, he's been in hiding. The last sighting of him has led a contingent of loyal Hellenian patriots to Mount Athos, where he's been living and impersonating a monk."

A cry escaped her lips. "You're talking about the Ari Hatzi who married *my* aunt? The uncle who blamed me for a false story printed in the newspaper about the prince of Hellenia being alive on Mount Athos?"

He nodded. "The very one. I'm on my way there now to witness his arrest. It's going to happen tonight."

She stirred in the chair. "What newspaper has sent you on this story?" came the biting question.

Alex shook his head. "No one sent me. I've given

up journalism. This is my last story, but only you have the rights to it because I love you, Giannina. You can choose to publish it or not."

"Love?" She mocked the word. "Don't insult me with that excuse." In the next breath she got to her feet and paced the floor for a moment.

He knew this news had rocked her underpinnings, but her rejection of him was killing him. This was so much worse than what he'd imagined.

"Before it becomes public and he's exposed by the world media, no one has more right to know what your uncle has done than you and your family. Even though the assassination of the royal family happened a long time ago, it wounds me that your family will bear some of the scrutiny when the news breaks. I wanted you to be warned and wish to heaven there were a way to protect you from it."

Giannina turned to him, her expression tortured. "My uncle really helped kill them?"

"I'd give anything if it weren't true, but there's irrefutable proof," he murmured.

She let out a moan. "It was a horrible, ghastly tragedy and gave me nightmares for a long time. Our family feared for the prince. No one knew if he was dead or alive." She looked away. "I've wanted to believe he's still living out there somewhere. Unless my uncle did something to him too. I hope he's still alive."

Alex struggled for breath, knowing how badly he was going to pay for this sin of omission.

"Do you know I met the prince when I was eleven? My father took me with him when he had business talks with the king in Hellenia. The prince had a dog and we played together. It was fun."

It was more than fun for Alex. Moved to the core by what she'd just told him, he said, "You actually remember it?" The subject of the royal family of Hellenia had never come up when they'd been in London. They been so enamored of each other, and it was old news.

"Yes. After the murders, there was news the next day that the prince had been killed too. Some stories said he'd been dragged from his bed in the dead of night and tortured. The possibilities were endless."

He hadn't expected all these thoughts from her. Thanks to Zikos, who'd found Alex asleep and taken him to safety in Croatia with no one aware of what had happened until it was too late to find him.

"I told you about my aunt Olga." Giannina kept talking. "She made a scrapbook devoted to the royal family because Ari was Hellenian. He had to become a Greek citizen in order to marry her. I remember poring over those early newspaper clippings with pictures of the prince," Giannina continued.

"My aunt followed the news that went on in his country. When the tragedy happened, my aunt never got over it or her fear for the welfare of the prince. I'm afraid I didn't either after having met him." She shuddered. "To think my uncle was responsible is incomprehensible to me." Her voice shook.

"I'm afraid your uncle used your aunt for many reasons, including Salonica's close proximity to Hellenia. You're only two hundred miles from Hellenia's capital city of Loria. The country held certain exclusive trade relations with Salonica, including a valuable partnership with your family's shipping line, which General Ruiz tried to maintain without success."

Alex was now in possession of all the details about Gianinna's uncle who'd inveigled himself into the Angelis family.

"Becoming your aunt's husband gave him entrée to one day use your newspaper to support the dictator's ideology. But your uncle was stopped in time. You got in his way and became editor-in-chief. That's why he was cruel to you. For my own satisfaction I want to see that monster arrested."

She turned to him with a pained look. "Are you absolutely certain this man impersonating a monk is *my* uncle? You believe he's living on Mount Athos?" With her guard down for a moment, the Giannina he'd fallen in love with came out, making him desire her more intensely.

"I'm positive. Otherwise I wouldn't be here risking everything to approach you when I know how much you must despise me."

After a pause, "When will you be leaving?"

"Tonight at seven. I've hired a boat."

He heard her sharp intake of breath. "Since you came to me with this story, it's mine to do with as I like. Is that what you said?"

Philip could hear her mind working. "You know I did."

"Then I'm coming with you to see him for myself and take a picture."

His heart leaped. That sounded like his Giannina,

who had an adventurous streak. Nothing could have thrilled Alex more. It meant he could be with her for a little longer.

"There's just one problem. If women were allowed to go there, I would have asked you to come with me so we could witness his arrest together."

She smiled. "I'm not worried about the rules forbidding women on Mount Athos. I'll accompany you on your boat as far as the dock at Ouranoupoli, where women *are* allowed. After the arrest is made, can't the police bring him on board? I have a few choice words to say to my uncle."

"You and the Hellenian people. I'll arrange it."

Her bold determination defined the woman Alex was crazy about. She'd get no argument out of him. He walked over to the desk and wrote down his cell phone number on a notepad. After heading for the door, he turned to her.

"If you change your mind, give me a call. Otherwise I'll come by at seven for you."

"I need to talk to my brother first. I may not be able to reach him until later tonight."

"I'm afraid we have to leave at seven so I can be on time for the arrest." By tomorrow she would know the truth of everything. "For what it's worth, Giannina, thank you for seeing me when you have every reason to tell me to go to hell."

His greatest fear now was that she would wish him on the other side of the universe.

Her eyes narrowed. "I did consign you there a long time ago."

"That comes as no surprise to me. If my life hadn't had to go in a different direction and I'd been given my wish, I would have kidnapped you from London and never let you go."

Then why didn't you? Gianinna's soul cried out as she watched his tall, well-honed physique leave her office.

Left witless by Philip's parting words, she sat down at her desk in a daze. There'd been a time when she wouldn't have let him go without running into his arms first and smothering him with kisses.

When they'd been in London, every moment became a struggle when it came time to say good-night. That month neither of them got enough asleep because it was so hard to disentangle themselves. Just now she'd almost called to him to stay with her. To her surprise, her desire for him hadn't abated. It proved she was close to being out of her mind.

Once he'd gone, Khloe hurried into her office with an enormous smile. "Oh, Giannina—if I were younger and not married…"

She averted her eyes. "You and a million other women, Khloe. Now I need to make a call."

"Of course."

After the door clicked shut, Giannina struggled to get a grip on herself before she phoned Nico. Her pulse raced off the charts. How could she still want and desire Philip? He'd broken her heart in such a cruel way, she'd thought she was completely over him. Yet she'd just told him she wanted to go with him. It proved he still had a stranglehold on her heart.

Giannina had never needed her brother's advice more. She hated bothering him when he was the busy CEO of the Angelis Shipping Lines and had become a new daddy a month ago. He and Alexa had named their little boy Nico and they were so crazy about him, she hated to bother him.

But she needed her brilliant sibling to help her make sense of Philip's claim about Ari, let alone his unprecedented visit. She'd never imagined hearing from him again, let alone that he would approach her on anything as shocking as the news he'd brought.

It took a half hour before Nico was able to call her back. "Giannina? What's going on?"

"Forgive me for asking your assistant to track you down. I need advice and you're the only one who can help me."

"You can always call me. You know that. What is it? You sound upset."

She bit her lip. "I'm not sure what I am, Nico. But here's what I know. This morning I had a visit from Philip Dimas." Her brother knew everything about her former relationship with the famous journalist who'd broken her heart.

After a silence, "What's it been? Three years and a ton of postcards with no return address? He actually came to see you?"

"Yes." Her voice shook. She swallowed hard. "When he walked into my office, I'm afraid I had the same reaction as you did after you saw Alexa for the first time in seventeen years."

"He has uncommon courage to face you after what

he did. I'll give him that. Has he asked for your forgiveness?"

"No. His reason for coming to my office has shocked me to the core. He brought news no one knows about yet. General Ruiz and the junta have been arrested along with one of the assassins of the king and queen of Hellenia. Philip says Hellenia is now free."

"You're right. I'm shocked and didn't think we'd ever see this day."

"Neither did I. That's the good news. But there's bad news too. You're not going to believe what I have to tell you, Nico."

"Don't keep me in suspense any longer."

"He has information from his Hellenian news sources that our uncle Ari was the other assassin responsible for the deaths of the royal family."

An eerie silence followed. She knew her brother had heard her clearly and was attempting to deal with what she'd just told him.

"No matter how deeply Philip broke my heart, Nico, I do believe his claim must have legs, otherwise he wouldn't have dared face me after all this time."

"It's possible he's speaking the truth," Nico murmured at last. "Ari had a dark side we all suspected. After what he did to you at the paper, somehow the news that he could be a killer doesn't shock me nearly as much."

"He's an awful man, but I didn't think he'd go that far."

"Philip had to be aware of the false news planted in the paper about the prince and blaming you. No doubt he's aware our notorious uncle disappeared once he was fired."

"He knows a lot, Nico. That's why he's so good at what he does. There's more." For the next few minutes she told him of Philip's plan to go to Mount Athos to witness his arrest. "He told me he'd brought the story to me, no one else. Apparently he's no longer a journalist." *He also claimed that he has always loved me,* her heart nagged at her.

"Does he mean for you to publish it?"

"If I want to."

"Along with the capture of the general, it will be the story of the century, but that's up to you."

"I know. I told Philip I wanted to go with him as far as the village dock. I need to know if it's really our uncle. He's going to pick me up at seven."

"Why doesn't that surprise me," her brother muttered.

"You think I'm insane?"

"Of course not. Even if the man hiding on Mount Athos doesn't turn out to be our uncle, it was an honorable thing Philip did to tell you before it became world news." Giannina had to admit it was honorable. "But there's no question the man has put you in a difficult spot emotionally. You know exactly what I mean, so enough said about the pain he has put you through. When will you be talking to him again?"

"He'll come for me at seven unless I tell him otherwise."

"Then why not go with him and see Ari for yourself. But I caution you to be careful."

She knew what her brother was saying. He worried about her getting hurt again. "I will. Nico? You think Uncle Ari is the killer, don't you? I hear it in your voice."

"I'm afraid so. Now that I think about it, his fury when you criticized the general's ideology explains what was going on inside him."

"I agree." She bit her lip. "Thank you so much, Nico. I love you."

"I love you too. Say nothing to the family yet."

"I won't. Only you. Give little Nico a kiss from me."

After they hung up, her conversation with Philip came back to her. *I'm afraid we have to leave at seven so I can be on time for the arrest.* He was right about acting immediately.

What amazed her was that her brother was willing to give Philip the benefit of the doubt. Nico knew how he'd hurt Giannina by toying with her love for the last three years. Yet he'd given Philip credit for being honorable.

Maybe she was crazy, but a part of her wanted to believe in Philip. What on earth was wrong with her? She couldn't still be in love with him. She just couldn't be! Those heavenly days were long gone.

Alex stood on the balcony of his hotel room that overlooked Salonica. He drank the coffee he'd ordered with an early dinner. Giannina hadn't phoned, but he was still worried that she could change her mind because she didn't trust him. He was a fool to think otherwise.

From the moment he'd entered her office earlier, the

urge to crush her in his arms had dominated every moment they'd been together. But for that nerve throbbing in her throat, she'd remained so cool he could hardly believe it was the same Giannina who'd taken over his heart and had never let it go.

After seeing her again, looking more beautiful than he could ever have imagined, he hadn't been able to settle down. Part of the day he'd talked with Zikos, who'd had a *diamoneterion* rushed through. Alex wouldn't be allowed on Mount Athos without the official permit.

They discussed details of their plan for him to be there when Hatzi was arrested and brought on board. He wanted Giannina there to identify her uncle. She needed to be provided the absolute proof of his identity in order to share the information with her family.

In the late afternoon, he loaded his cabin cruiser with supplies, then returned to his hotel. A group of men loyal to the throne would join him in a second boat. They would dock at Ouranoupoli, the seaside gateway village to the holy mountain.

If Giannina changed her mind, Alex could never blame her for shutting him out of her life forever, not after the cruel way he'd left their relationship hanging. But a part of him was praying her need for truth was greater than her dislike and distrust of him.

Much as he wanted to walk over to her office and intrude on her unannounced, he didn't dare. Once again, he checked his watch. Six thirty. He'd told her time was of the essence. As a newspaper woman, she knew the wisdom in acting fast on a tip. She hadn't phoned him yet. Maybe a miracle was still in store for him.

As he gathered the last few things to take with him, his phone rang. He pulled it out of his pocket and checked the caller ID. Giannina Angelis. Just seeing her name caused his spirits to plunge. He clicked on, dreading to hear she wouldn't be coming with him after all. "Giannina?"

"Philip?" He didn't hear any breathlessness in her voice. "I talked to my brother. He's thankful you're giving our family the chance to know about our uncle before anyone else."

Thank heaven. He let out the breath he'd been holding.

"Just so you know, there'll be a night watchman at the entrance to let you in. He'll show you to the private elevator."

"I'm glad someone's keeping watch over you. I'll be there soon." He hung up, not only elated that her brother had gone along with this plan, but that she hadn't let the pain Alex had caused prevent her from coming with him.

Never had he loved this woman more than he did now. Galvanized into action, he phoned Zikos, who would give the men working for him the signal to meet him at the Salonica dock. They discussed last-minute plans. Alex would join them later that night.

He left the hotel in his rental car and headed for her office, vowing to win her around no matter how long it took, be it weeks, months or, heaven help him, years. Once Hatzi was arrested, Alex would end his deception. Whether she knew it or not, they were in this together now. If she could ever forgive him after she heard the truth, they would never have to be separated again.

The night watchman saw him coming and ushered him inside the lobby to one of the elevators. When he reached the third floor and entered her office, she stood up, still dressed in the same outfit as earlier.

Maybe it was the lighting, but she looked a little flushed. He could hope it was a sign that she was a little excited to see him. If he got closer to her, she'd hear the hammering of his heart.

"I'm ready to leave the office, but we'll have to drop by my apartment for a few things."

"Of course. On the drive over, there's something else you need to know about your uncle."

She stared hard at him. "You speak with such authority, I have a feeling you know a lot more than you've revealed."

"You're a journalist, Giannina. No one understands better than you the need for a great deal of information about a target if you want to cover the news and get the whole truth."

She frowned. "Don't patronize me, Philip."

"That's the last thing I'm trying to do. I love you. My hope is that you'll start believing in me."

Her eyes looked away. "I want to believe you for the sake of our family and my poor aunt Olga, who has yet to know what's going on."

"It won't be long now. Have you ever been to Ouranoupoli village?"

"Several times with Nico."

"When we get there, maybe you'd prefer to stay at

a hotel while you wait for me. Or you can remain on the cruiser while I meet with the men and bring your uncle to you. I can't give you a timeline, but if all goes as I hope, you'll soon be able to meet him face-to-face."

Giannina lifted her head. "That moment can't come soon enough."

"I don't foresee any problems, but in case there are, you'll need to leave your managing editor in charge. There'll be a bedroom for you on the cruiser and food. Pack enough clothes to last a day or two. I have no idea how long this will take. Now's the time to tell me if you've decided not to come with me."

His heart raced in double time while he waited for her answer. "What do you say?" he challenged her. "Are you with me?"

"Yes," Giannina murmured at last. It brought a subtle smile to Philip's compelling mouth, intriguing her.

She grabbed her purse and went down the private elevator with Philip. The confined space meant their arms brushed against each other, arousing her senses. Giannina couldn't believe she was going with him and feared he could feel the rapid beat of her heart.

They left the building and he helped her into the rental car. She gave him directions to her apartment. The interior was redolent of the soap he'd used in the shower. Its scent flooded her with memories of being in his arms while they'd kissed each other, unable to get enough.

"What else haven't you told me about my uncle?"

It took only a few minutes to reach her apartment.

He shut off the engine before turning to her with a solemn expression. "After committing the double murders fourteen years ago with the other assassin, Hatzi's mission in life was to hunt for the prince and eliminate him."

Gianinna's gasp over the unexpected news about her uncle's underlying agenda reverberated in the car. "He admitted as much?"

Alex reached for her hand and squeezed it like he used to do to comfort her when she was upset about something. "In truth, your uncle has been leading a double life for years as a recruit of the general. His whole plan was to marry your aunt to get access to the Angelis fortune and influence. Killing the prince was his next priority."

"I just can't believe it."

Alex pulled her to him and kissed her temple. "I know you're sickened by this, but it's better you hear everything from me before the news leaks out."

She was confused by their closeness that felt so wonderful. Yet she was reeling from this latest news and had to find the strength to pull away from him. "I'm glad you told me."

"Come on. Let's go inside."

They took the elevator to her apartment on the fourth floor. She refused to meet those blue eyes burning with emotion. "While I get my suitcase and pack, you're welcome to anything from the fridge. I think there's a cola."

"That sounds good."

Excitement she shouldn't be feeling consumed her

to be with him again. While he went to the kitchen, she hurried into her bedroom and threw a few items into a small overnight bag. She also packed her camera to get pictures of her uncle to show the family.

Before she forgot, she called Khloe and put her in charge until her return without telling her the end date or the reason why. Any emergency and she could phone Nico. Then she changed into jeans and a short-sleeved, leaf-green top.

After freshening up in the bathroom, she caught her hair back with a clip and rejoined him in the kitchen, where he was just finishing his soda. She reached for a ham roll and ate it, followed by a cola.

His gaze fused with hers. It played over her, missing nothing, causing her legs to tremble. "You look terrific as always."

So did he, also dressed in jeans that molded his powerful thighs. She had to suppress an inward moan. The dark blue pullover suited his rock-hard physique. Giannina needed to stop looking at him and washed her hands. "If you've grown a few gray hairs in three years, I can't tell." Not when he was a dark blond.

He chuckled. "I'll take that as a compliment." He reached for her suitcase. "Shall we go?"

"I'm ready." She fought not to sound too eager. They left and went down to the car. He stashed her bag in back and started the engine. Before long they reached a dock where a number of boats were moored. How strange it felt to be alone with him again like this, yet not in his arms.

"Have you ever been on Mount Athos, Philip?"

"Yes. One time."

"What was it like for you? My brother went there with our father when he was about ten, but I don't remember what he told me."

"It's a fantastical place with giant monasteries. There are twenty of them built on the slopes of the mountain. A few are found along the coast."

"Do the monks live together?"

"Not all. Some of them isolate themselves in caves called *sketes* and have their food lifted to them in baskets on pulleys."

"You're kidding!"

"When I went there with my uncle a couple of years ago, we slept in a dormitory."

She felt a twinge of pain. *A couple of years ago?* That meant he'd been only seventy kilometers away from her while she'd been working in Salonica.

"How long were you there?"

"Overnight. I found it fascinating. No newspapers."

"No women," she added, putting on a fake smile when her heart was breaking over the knowledge that he hadn't tried to get in touch with her.

"You were close by, Giannina. I would have given anything to see you again, but I was doing an investigation and couldn't risk it at the time."

Of course not. "Did you find what you were looking for?"

"No. But it was good to be with my uncle Zikos. We hadn't been together for a long time."

She heard genuine love in his voice. "I'm sure it was."

They reached the pier and parked. He shut off the

engine. "I can see the officers' patrol boats offshore. They're flashing their lights to signal me. The arrest is about to take place. Let's go."

Something was wrong with her. For a moment she'd forgotten why they were here. Being with Philip again had brought back all her old feelings for him that seemed to be stronger than ever.

CHAPTER THREE

ONCE PHILIP HAD grabbed her overnight bag, he held her arm as they walked along to the dock that led to his cruiser. Had he chartered it, or bought it? There was so much she didn't know about him.

As he helped her on board, she felt his touch invade her body, exciting her.

"Are you all right?" he whispered against her cheek.

She could hardly breathe. "Yes."

"I felt you tremble. Don't be frightened. I won't let anything happen to you." He sounded like the old Philip she'd loved so terribly. At that moment it came to her she still did and always would!

"I kn-know that." Her voice faltered.

"Thank heaven you at least believe in me that much."

It was a surprise to her too, but judging from what he'd just said, he sounded as if he'd suffered, as well. She had a hard time realizing that he was here in Greece at last. After three long painful years without him, they were together again, and alone.

No stranger to boats or yachts, she reached for a life jacket and waited for him to untie the ropes. Once she'd sat across from the controls, he jumped on board and slid into the chair to start the engine. His agility had never been more in evidence. She loved everything about him. It felt so right to be with him again. *Philip, Philip.*

Soon they idled out to open water. Giannina glanced at the sky. It would be dark by the time they reached their destination an hour away. The warm June night intoxicated her, reminding her of nights with him in London when they took long walks and kissed every step of the way. During that time they were together, they couldn't stay out of each other's arms. Since then her life had been a wilderness of pain.

He turned the boat toward Mount Athos and shot her a glance. "You have no idea how many times I've dreamed of being with you like this. I've missed you more than you will ever know."

Philip didn't know the half of it.

Oh, Giannina. Don't let him get to you. What if he goes away again?

"Those were halcyon days, no question about it. But they couldn't go on forever and now you're here for me to witness my uncle's arrest. Philip, I appreciate your giving me and our family the news about Ari before anyone else knows. It means everything to me that you wanted to protect us. Thank you."

An odd expression broke out on his handsome features. He leaned over and gently kissed her cheek. It wasn't the hungry kind of kiss she would have imagined him giving her. There was a subtle change in his mood that made her heart flutter. "I'm thankful that you trusted me enough to come with me." With a sudden acceleration, they moved across the calm sea.

She took a quick breath. "You have an impeccable reputation as a journalist that makes me want to trust you. I have to concede that my uncle is a dreadful creature who should be locked up for good. When I think of what he did and has been trying to do—" Her voice caught.

This time he threaded his fingers through hers and kept hold. His touch sent waves of electricity through her. The old magic was there. In truth it had never gone. She didn't want it to go away but was afraid to trust her feelings for him again in case this was just the rush of the moment for him.

"His power is now over," came Philip's deep voice.

"Wouldn't it be wonderful if the prince is alive and could run Hellenia again?"

Philip pressed her fingers a little harder. "He really is special to you, isn't he?"

Warmth filled her cheeks. "I've thought about that day with him more than once. If he's put on the throne, there won't be another news story to top it."

"I can think of one," he murmured, "but I'll share it with you later."

Giannina couldn't understand what he meant by that. "I'm sure you think me silly for saying that."

"Not at all. I've had certain dreams too. They've all had to do with you. Every time I had to cover a new story, I wanted you with me. I craved to hold and taste you." His throbbing voice sent a shiver through her body. When he talked like that, it hurt too much because she felt the same way.

By now they were approaching Ouranoupoli and he let go of her hand. Mount Athos loomed large.

He slowed them down and pulled into a reserved slip. After shutting off the engine, he stood up. "Stay here for a moment. Two of the priests are coming on board to meet us."

She took off her life jacket as the robed, bearded priests approached her. Philip made the introductions. "The Angelis family has agreed to let me bring Kyria Angelis with me this far. We'd appreciate your blessing."

"You already have it," the oldest one spoke. Giannina recognized him. His picture had been taken with her *baba* a year ago. "This troubling business has disturbed everyone. We are thankful it's going to be over soon. Give my best to your father, Kyria Angelis."

"He'll be very pleased to know I've met you."

The priest turned to Philip. "We pray all will go well with this arrest."

"That means a great deal to everyone."

"We must not keep you."

Giannina watched them leave the cruiser. Philip rejoined her. "Come below with me and I'll show you around."

"Don't you want me to help you tie up?"

"That other boat following us holds the men coming with me. They'll take care of everything. Rigas, one of the men, will stay here and guard you while I'm gone. I promise you'll be safe."

Her breath caught. "You're leaving already?"

"I have to."

She reached for her overnight bag and went down the steps to the galley. They passed an office. "Use it anytime you like."

"Thank you." She followed him to the end cabin. "The bathroom is between this one and mine. There's plenty of food and drink in the kitchen. Do you have any questions?"

"How long will you be gone?"

"I can't tell you. Hopefully I'll be back soon."

"With my uncle."

"That's the plan," he murmured. "What else would you like to ask me before I go?"

"I've a thousand questions, but they'll have to keep."

"Wish me luck." In the next instant he gave her a brief kiss, this time on the lips, but she wanted much more. Her desire for him was growing out of control. He had to know it before he turned and raced toward the stairway.

With pounding heart, she hurried to the top deck to watch him leave. For three years there'd been nothing between them. Now all of a sudden, the touching and kisses had thrown her off course. She pressed her fingers to her lips. He could have no idea how much she'd suffered after he'd abandoned her. Giannina couldn't bear to go through that kind of pain again, yet here she was, dying for his embrace.

Her eyes tracked his incredible male physique as he joined the group of men on shore. Darkness made it difficult to see their movements, but his dark blond hair stood out. Before long they disappeared.

The tough-looking man named Rigas had planted himself on the dock next to the cruiser. He was dressed like a local fisherman, but Giannina had no doubt he could take care of anything or one if he had to. He nodded to her, making her feel perfectly safe.

For the next two hours she stood at the rear of the cruiser, reliving that month with him. Much of the time he'd taken her for a meal and a drive had followed. They'd park by a lake and reach for each other, trying to make the most of every moment together.

Now things were different because *he* was different. He said he still loved her, but what were his future plans? How long could she count on him to stay in Greece? She was also nervous for what could happen where the arrest was concerned. No matter how carefully he'd planned, he could be in danger if something went wrong.

Beyond the twinkling lights of the village, Philip was out there on the mountain to watch the downfall of her uncle. Her thoughts drifted to her aunt and how she would take the news that her estranged husband was a killer. Better not to think.

It was near midnight before she heaved a sigh and went below to get ready for bed. But when she came out of the bathroom, she changed her mind about sleeping in the cabin. In fact, she didn't think she'd be able to sleep at all.

Still dressed in the same clothes, she reached for her pillow and blanket, then went back on deck. In a minute she'd fashioned a makeshift bed on one of the padded seats. Next, she pulled out her small digital camera and got it set so she could capture pictures the moment Philip returned.

She planned to take pictures of her uncle so her family would have the proof. Those photos would go along with the breaking story she'd been planning out in her mind to publish.

The water lapped against the cruiser, rocking it in a gentle rhythm. A wondrous star-studded sky filled her vision. With the air like velvet, her body ached for the man who'd caused this trembling with that last kiss. She didn't understand him. All she knew was that after tonight she'd never be the same again.

For so long she'd managed to live her life without him. But being with him now had broken down her defenses. This was what Nico had warned her about. Be careful, he'd said. Though she'd tried to harden herself, Philip had this way of infiltrating her heart and body until all she wanted was to be with him.

He'd reentered her world. For how long she didn't know. She was a fool but being with Philip again made her feel alive for the first time in three years. No man was like him. She hadn't been able to get interested in anyone else.

He had that unmatchable power to excite her mind and touch her in a way that ignited her passion. Philip Dimas owned her heart. He should have been wearing a warning sign from the beginning. Caution: to love this man could cause you heartache forever.

At some point Giannina lay back and pulled the

blanket over her. She'd set the camera beyond her pillow so she could reach for it at a moment's notice. After
a few minutes, she turned on her side facing the dock
to get comfortable and closed her eyes. Her thoughts
went back to that time in England when Philip had set
her on fire. She'd loved him so terribly.

When she came awake later, her pillow was wet,
and she heard muffled voices on the dock. She sat up
to hear better but couldn't make out words. The next
thing she knew a male figure came on board. Her heart
throbbed in her throat.

"Philip?" she called out.

"Giannina—what are you doing on deck?" Her
watch registered 5:30 a.m. Relieved he was back, she
threw off the blanket and got to her feet. "I couldn't
sleep and was waiting for you."

He'd come alone. She watched him slide in the cap-
tain's chair and turn on the engine. She sat across from
him once more, trying to make out his striking features
in the early light.

"What happened? Where's my uncle?"

He grimaced. "We were too late. I'm afraid his
friends had already helped him escape in one of those
baskets bringing him food. They've made their way to
a forested inlet up the coast. That's where we're going
and will catch up with him."

Philip had warned her time was of the essence and
had to be bitterly disappointed. So was Giannina, for
his sake as well as her own.

She knew the inlet he'd talked about. Earlier in her
life she'd gone there diving with friends where the

water was deep. It was only a few minutes away on the other side of Mount Athos. But unlike the holy mountain, it wasn't forbidden to women. When Philip went ashore this time, she'd be able to go with him and take pictures.

"What can I get you? Coffee? A soda?"

"Water, if you don't mind."

"That sounds good to me too. I'll grab us both a bottle." She went below and retrieved two from the fridge before hurrying back to him. "Here you go."

"You're a lifesaver." He removed the cap to drink. She watched his throat as he emptied the bottle without taking a breath. "That tasted good."

She took the empty bottle from him. "Just so you know, I'm planning to go ashore with you this time and take pictures."

"That's exactly what I want you to do."

His surprising remark robbed her of the fight she'd planned to wage if he told her she had to stay on the cruiser. "What aren't you telling me?"

"Only that you need to stay right next to me when we leave the boat. My job is to protect you to the death, so promise you'll do as I say and ask no questions."

This was a new side of Philip she'd never seen before. His fierceness silenced her.

Mount Athos was silhouetted against a lavender sky. Morning had come to this glorious part of the Aegean with the man at the throttle she'd thought she would never see again. Once they caught up with her uncle, maybe today would be all she'd have of Philip before he left Greece. He'd promised that one day they'd be together forever, but were they just words? She didn't know.

Don't think beyond today, Giannina. Just don't.

During the few minutes it took to reach the inlet, she grabbed the bedding and went below. It was time to freshen up and apply fresh lipstick. Once back on deck, she put the camera in her case and looped it around her neck. Philip's intense gaze swept over her. "Do you have any idea how beautiful you look this early in the morning?"

He sounded so sincere, but a compliment at this late stage only brought back the pain. After this adventure was over, she feared he'd leave her again.

With expertise, he drove the cruiser to the inlet, where several other boats were moored. He shut off the engine and got to his feet. "Let's go," he urged. "I'll help you."

Philip put a strong arm around her waist and lifted her over the side into shallow water like she weighed nothing. She could tell he was in a hurry. He grasped her hand and together they rushed onto the bit of sand before entering the lush greenery of the forest.

Farther ahead, Rigas waved to them and led the way. Before long they came to a little clearing where she saw six armed men surrounding a pup tent. One of the guards walked over to lift the flap of the tent. With her pulse racing, Giannina pulled the camera out of her case in preparation for the first glimpse of her uncle.

In seconds a scruffy-looking man maybe in his early fifties—hunched over and grizzled—emerged in hand-cuffs and a blindfold. He wore black-tunic-type clothing like a medieval monk. His silhouette didn't remind her of her uncle, but she hadn't seen his face.

She darted Philip a searching glance, but he was fixated on the man with a frightening expression on his features she'd never seen before. The savage look in his eyes astonished her.

Giannina didn't understand. His set jaw told her at a glance he was barely holding on to his control. One of the guards removed the blindfold.

"Uncle Ari!" she gasped at the same time she snapped his picture. *It really was her uncle!* The camera slid from her hands and fell to the underbrush.

One of the guards turned to Giannina. "Kyria Angelis? You need to be informed that your uncle Ari Hatzi is arrested for involvement in the murder of the royal family of Hellenia. He's wanted by the Greek police for fleeing arrest, but more importantly by the Hellenian patriots."

She took a step closer to the man who'd been married to her aunt for years, the man who'd caused such pain and trouble for the entire Angelis household. "To think it was you who helped to kill the king and queen."

He'd lowered his head, refusing to talk.

Her rage grew. "All these years you've lived with my aunt, you've had blood on your hands!"

"Don't be so melodramatic."

How many times had he said that to her over the years, disparaging everything she ever said or did. He hated their family and her interference at the newspaper. Talk about sinister...

"And you've been stalking the prince too, all these

years!" Her cry rang throughout the forest. She threw her head back and stared at Philip, who picked up her camera so she could put it in her case.

"Let's go, Giannina."

After grasping her hand, he walked her through the forest to the sand. The next thing she knew they'd reached the cruiser. He lowered her to the deck. Once on board, he carried her in his arms and took her below to the bedroom he'd designated for her.

Alex knew this was a traumatic moment for her. It was one thing to have disliked her uncle, but another to learn he was a killer.

He sat down on the end of the bed with her in his arms and rocked her. "Forgive me for putting you through this, Giannina," he murmured into her hair. "But I knew you'd never quite believe this of your uncle until you saw him."

The heaving sobs coming out of her shook him to the deepest regions of his soul. "It's my aunt I'm crying for, Philip." For the next while, all he could do was hold her close and let her give way to her sorrow.

When she grew quiet, he got up with her and laid her out on the bed. Needing her warmth, he slid next to her and pulled her into his arms with her face against his chest. Soon the tears started again, soaking the front of his pullover.

"I always despised him," she spoke at last. "Nico felt the same way. When Ari married my aunt, and my father let them take up residence in the west wing of the villa, a change came over our whole household. Because he came from Hellenia and had no home of his own in Salonica, my parents made him welcome. Baba gave him a job at the newspaper. There's no one kinder than my parents or aunt, who opened their hearts to him."

Alex kissed her forehead. "I'm so sorry this had to happen to your family, Giannina."

She lifted wounded, wet brown eyes to look at him. "I could feel his resentment of me and my brother from the moment he moved in. He had a mocking attitude none of us could stand. It still astounds me that my aunt could have fallen in love with him. But she admitted those feelings wore off once they were married."

"Chemistry draws people together, even someone like the man she thought she loved."

"He never loved her!" she cried. "She was the means to an end. I'm glad he's been caught. The worst is over for her now."

At this point, she rose up. "He used to watch me at the newspaper with those icy eyes, wishing I were nowhere around."

He pulled her close once more. "You need never worry he'll torment you or your family again."

"I'm so thankful he's been caught."

So was Alex. With Hatzi's capture, Alex prayed she would accept him when she learned who he really was. A new nightmare had begun. With reluctance, he let her go and rolled off the bed.

"Why don't you freshen up while I fix us something to eat. We both need food and coffee."

She made a slight nod.

Euphoric over Hatzi's capture, he got busy in the

galley to give her privacy. Before long she joined him and sat down at the table.

"I just talked to Nico."

That didn't surprise Alex. She'd once told him her brother was her rock. He believed it. Pleased to see she'd started to recover, he said, "Do you think the news shocked him?"

She stared at him over the rim of her coffee mug. "You mean that Ari's a cold-blooded murderer? No. Nico said he thought Ari was capable of anything. He couldn't be happier to know our uncle has finally met his deserved end. My brother will tell our parents and find a way to inform our aunt."

"That's good. Hatzi will be held in a Greek jail until the Hellenian authorities have him extradited to Loria. Your brother can arrange for him to sign those divorce papers before he's transferred."

"You're right." She took a bite of sandwich. Alex was glad to see she could eat. He'd been afraid she might have been too upset. "Mmm. This is good. I didn't know you were a cordon bleu chef as well as a journalist."

"My lifestyle means I've learned how to stay alive on my own cooking." His gaze studied her features. "I need to fly back to my uncle who has helped me all these years and tell him what's happened. Will you come with me? We'll fly in his private jet. It'll only take a half hour."

Her eyes lit up, thrilling him. "I'd love to come. But if we have to travel all the way to Lisbon, that'll take much longer tha—"

"My uncle hasn't lived there for a long time," Alex interrupted.

"I don't understand."

No. There was so much she didn't know yet, but soon.

"Uncle Zikos is a very wealthy man with residences in half a dozen countries. We lived in Portugal for a time, but these days he's been staying at his home in Dubrovnik, Croatia, where his family's oil reserves are located. With contacts all over, he'll have heard of the arrest and much more."

She went quiet, but he could hear those wheels turning in her head.

"I'm afraid I've overloaded you with too much information, Giannina."

"Not at all," she murmured. "It's just surprising to learn things about you I never knew before."

"For your safety I wasn't free to tell you everything when we met in London. After today's revelation about Ari, you're my only concern. But maybe you'd rather be with your family and get back to work on the story. We can fly to my uncle's another time."

"Philip—" she blurted, shaking her head. "I'm fine. Honestly. I've always wanted to meet the family that raised you."

"Before we get there, I want to fill you in on my uncle's situation. My aunt died of pneumonia last year."

Another surprising revelation. "I'm sorry. I'd hoped to meet her."

"It's very sad you can't. You would have liked her. As for my two cousins, both are married now with children and live away, so there's only my uncle at home."

"Then he must miss you very much when you're gone."

"That works both ways." He flicked her a glance. "You'll like him a lot. He's been anxious to meet you too, believe me. I don't think he has a single enemy, except for those factions in our world who bring hate and chaos."

"He sounds like my father. Baba's not only well loved, but a fighter for freedom. When he learns the whole truth about what Ari did, I'm sure he won't be surprised. You have no idea how good he was to my uncle, who harbored an obsessive jealousy of him and everything he stood for."

"Some men are beyond redemption and need a miracle to intercede for them."

"He had my angel aunt Olga, but he was too filled with malice to know it."

His blue eyes pled with her. "Let's forget him and enjoy this time together."

"There's nothing I want more."

"Neither do I." Grateful that she didn't hate his guts yet, he got up from the table, admiring her indomitable spirit. "I'll be waiting for you on deck."

CHAPTER FOUR

PHILIP'S INVITATION WAS what Giannina had hoped for three years ago! It had finally happened. She couldn't wait for him to take her on a tour of the city and show her where he'd gone to school. What were his favorite haunts? Was there a certain bistro he loved? A favorite place?

To guard her heart, maybe she shouldn't be going, but she couldn't help herself. She'd never fallen out of love with Philip, and a lot of things about him were starting to make sense. He'd been hiding things from her. Now was her chance to find out what they were so there'd be no secrets between them.

Philip had the backing of a wealthy uncle so he could go where he wanted, when he wanted, in pursuit of a news story. For now, he had an apartment in the posh section of Salonica and had access to this sleek cruiser to get him around.

Dazed by all this, Giannina got busy and did the dishes. Her next task was to gather her overnight bag and camera case. She straightened the bedding on the bed she hadn't slept in and went up on deck.

He'd been watching for her and handed her a life jacket, which she put on. After handing it to her, his hands slid up her arms in the old familiar way. But suddenly he let her go. When he didn't follow through with another kiss, she wandered over to the side of cruiser, having to pretend it hadn't affected her. She wanted him so badly it was torture.

Soon they were speeding past Mount Athos. There was no sign of the other two boats. Though the scenery was magnificent, her gaze fell on Philip, the most attractive man she'd ever met or known. He'd shaved and changed into an open-necked sport shirt. Was it any wonder Khloe had practically fainted at the sight of him back at the office?

Giannina touched fingers to her lips where he'd kissed her earlier. She could still feel the sensation that had swept through her. Yet oddly enough she didn't need to recall her brother's sage advice. He'd warned her this could be a dangerous situation if she allowed Philip to take advantage of her. Yes, he'd invited her to meet his uncle. But what Nico didn't know was that she had no idea what the future held where Philip was concerned.

While they'd been on the bed in the cabin, he'd held and comforted her, nothing more. She'd wanted him to make passionate love to her and didn't know what to make of his behavior. It disturbed her that she still loved him so terribly.

If he'd felt the same way about her three years ago, they'd have been married by now. Though he insisted that he'd always loved her, the fact that he'd never taken her to bed puzzled her more than ever.

Today she'd learned some surprising things about his past where his wealthy uncle was concerned. She suspected she didn't know half of what Philip was all about. Talk about him being an enigma! The only way to get through this situation was to be patient and hope for more. A few brief kisses and touches weren't enough.

She looked out over the water, watching some sailboats in the distance. Truly no more magical place existed than this part of the Aegean. She'd love to go sailing with him. She'd love to do anything with him!

A full sun shone on the blue of the water, a blue almost as beautiful as the color of his eyes. Her gaze darted to him. The sun gilded the dark blond tips of his hair. She should have kept her camera case around her neck so she could take more pictures of him when he wasn't looking.

But that was a foolish thought since she probably wouldn't see him again once she returned to work. She'd promised herself to get rid of those postcards, but they remained stashed away in her dresser at home. It really was past time for her to move on and find a love she could depend on.

Philip would go his secret way. He said he'd given up journalism. To do what? Still, it didn't matter. Better not to have any more remembrances of him. While she was deep in thought, he called to her. "Come and sit near me. I want to hear about your life. We have a lot to catch up on."

Her life? How ironic when she didn't know nearly enough about *his*. But she did his bidding and planted herself on the padded seat. "Since you know I've worked at the newspaper since returning from London, there's very little to tell."

"That's not true," he came right back. "I want to hear how many men at the paper are besotted with you."

She rolled her eyes. "Probably several dozen. But we have a rule about fraternizing with the staff, so my ardent suitors are found elsewhere."

"There must have been someone."

"But nothing serious," she answered honestly. Her love for Philip had ruined her for other men. "Like your work, mine has pretty well consumed me."

"It's possible that one of these days soon you'll be busy publishing an amazing new story."

"You mean besides the story on Ari? A bigger one? The one you *won't* be covering?"

He nodded.

Philip was being mysterious again. Frustrated by his behavior, she shifted in place as they sped through the water. "If you don't mind, I'd rather hear about this huge change you've made that has brought your career as a journalist to an end."

Philip flashed her the kind of smile that had captivated her in the beginning. The man was so incredibly attractive, she looked away. Her intense desire for him frightened her.

"I want a family," came his admission. "It means I can't be a journalist who travels around Europe at a moment's notice."

"Some reporters do both," Giannina reasoned while

reacting to what he'd just said. "There's a married man on my staff who makes it work."

"How often is he in Salonica?"

She bit her lip. "Not as much as he'd like to be, I'm sure."

"That's the point. I intend to stay home and take care of my family."

Giannina had no idea he felt that strongly. "I guess my first question is, where will home be to you? In Croatia near your uncle?"

"No." He sat forward. "I have other plans."

She groaned inwardly. "Does that mean you already know what you want to do for a living?"

Their gazes fused. "I know exactly."

"That sounded final."

"It is. But I'm not certain if the woman I want to marry will be happy with my choice." She sucked in her breath and struggled not to reveal the splintering pain his words had inflicted. He grasped her hand. "Surely you know that woman is *you*. It's *always* been you."

"Please, Philip. Don't joke about anything this serious."

"Were those hundreds of postcards a joke?" he demanded.

"But—"

"I meant what I said on them," he broke in on her. "One day we'd be together forever, *if* it was what you wanted too. Why do you think I want to take you to my uncle's? He's been forced to hear me talk about you for three long years. He's delighted I'm finally free to go after the love of my life."

She really was the love of his life?

"I realize I've waited too long to come for you, though there were life-and-death reasons I couldn't reveal to you at the time. I know you loved me once, but I fear you can't forgive me for staying away this long. Not only that, I have other concerns. You've only known me as a journalist. If we were to get married and I worked in government, you might not like it."

She shook her head in disbelief. "You plan to run for a government office?"

"Not run. It would be a case of being a part of one." He flashed her a glance. "Does that surprise you?"

Giannina was trying to take it all in. "I don't know. What government are you planning to work for?"

"A new one."

New? There he went again, not giving her a full answer. "Somehow I don't see you as a bureaucrat."

A faint smile appeared. "You mean the type concerned with procedural correctness at the expense of people's needs?"

"I didn't say that."

"But you implied it, Giannina."

She cocked her head. "What would you do exactly?"

"Help bring about change to better life as we know it. My work over the years has taken me many places. I've seen and written about things no man should have to witness, let alone live through. Now I've had enough of being a bystander. It's time for me to do something fundamental that could make a difference to people."

"I had no idea you felt so passionately about the news you've covered. I admire you for wanting to promote changes in government when it's so hard to do. For you to want to make a difference excites me."

"But would you be able to handle it being married to me, knowing it will be a full-time job?"

When she'd given up hope, Giannina couldn't believe the day she'd been waiting and praying for had finally come. Had he really proposed to her?

"How can you ask me a question like that? I want you to be happy. If that's the job you want, then I want it for you. Unless, of course, you end up neglecting *me*," she teased.

He didn't lighten up and shook his head. "I'm afraid that could happen in any marriage, no matter the kind of work or profession. Sometimes it's the wife who's the workaholic and the husband suffers neglect."

Again his comments astonished her. "Do you think I'm that type?"

"I'm not sure."

"Does it worry you?"

"Maybe."

Philip, Philip. "Are you saying I didn't live for you when we were in London? That I didn't try to drag you back when you left my apartment three years ago?"

"That was different. We weren't married."

"Are you saying I didn't chase after you like some of the women in the audience once you'd given that lecture?"

"You weren't like that."

"I was exactly like that, but I wanted you and didn't dare act like the others in case it turned you off."

"It worked, Giannina," he murmured, but there was

no smile. The knowledge that he'd just proposed marriage to her in the most unorthodox way she could have imagined had stunned her beyond belief.

"What are you thinking, Philip? From what I understand, most husbands don't want a wife who clings to them constantly. Though there are some married couples who work together, I think it would have its own problems."

"I'm sure you're right." He started to slow down the boat. They'd reached the pier in Salonica. Before she knew it, he'd glided the cruiser into the slip with expertise. Rigas waved to them, having come in on the other boat. The police must have brought her uncle on their boat, but she didn't see it. Philip shut off the engine.

"Giannina?" He'd turned to her. "Do you still love me? Can you forgive me for staying away so long?"

The question caught her totally off guard. "How can you ask me that when you *know* you're my whole life!" she cried. "Why am I here now if I haven't forgiven you? No sooner did you come to my office than I told you I wanted to go with you on your boat. Ari had nothing to do with my leaping at the chance to be with you again. If that doesn't tell you everything you want to know…"

He cupped the back of her neck and gave her a kiss to die for. When he let her go, he said, "I'm afraid there's much more I need to tell you about me. It could affect the way you feel."

"Then tell me now," she begged him.

"I'd rather wait until we reach Croatia, where we'll

have total privacy. Will you trust me putting you off just a little longer?"

She pressed an urgent kiss to his lips the way she used to do. "I guess I'm going to have to. Don't keep me waiting too long."

"I swear I won't."

They both got to their feet. She removed the life jacket and put it on the banquette. After grabbing her overnight bag, he cupped her elbow and they stepped onto the dock. While Rigas tied things up, they left for the parking area and got in Philip's car. He put her bag in the back seat and they were off.

"What's going on in that fascinating mind of yours that has made you go quiet?" They were headed for the airport.

"Maybe it's because you've just asked me to marry you."

He grasped her hand. "I wanted to ask you in London."

"Every night we were together I hoped you would propose," she admitted.

"I ached to. Don't you know I love you with every fiber of my being, Giannina?"

"Philip." She half moaned his name. "I feel the same way."

They drove to the small airport where his uncle's private jet stood on the tarmac. It was hard to believe she was finally going to meet the uncle who'd taken care of him once he'd lost his parents.

A steward greeted Giannina as she and Philip climbed inside the luxurious jet. He showed them to the club section, where she sat across from Philip. The fasten-seat-belts sign went on and the private jet taxied to the runway.

He darted her a glance. "Have you phoned your brother to let him know what's going on?"

"I will when we arrive."

"We should be there in thirty minutes. I don't want him to think I've kidnapped you like I wanted to do back in London."

"Can you at least tell me what stopped you from spiriting me away back then, Philip? Please don't tell me it was because you had to cover a story by yourself and couldn't bring me along."

"The truth is I didn't want to put you in dangerous situations. I couldn't let anything happen to you."

"Are you saying your life was in danger covering those stories?"

"Even in London my life was in constant danger." His admission sobered her. "But there was another reason too. You'd just finished your formal schooling and needed to get back home to work on your family's paper. Because of your hard work, you're now editor-in-chief of one of Europe's most widely circulated newspapers. The numbers are growing. Have I told you how proud I am of what you've accomplished already?"

They'd reached cruising speed and the seat belt light went off. "Even if my father owns it?"

"Maybe more so. He would never make you the head if he didn't know his daughter would turn it into a total success. Do you love it?"

She shot him an amused glance. "You mean the way you love being the top celebrated journalist in Europe?"

"Have I ever said I did?"

His question threw her. She leaned forward. "I just assumed as much. Are you saying you don't?"

He quirked one eyebrow. "It has provided me with a living."

"Plus adventures and literary prizes envied by your peers," she added.

"I've been fortunate, but there are other ways to earn my daily bread that I believe will bring me more satisfaction."

He'd told her that his life as a journalist was over, but it still surprised her. "After the life you've led, what will you do to make up for all the adventure you've known?"

"Many things I've longed to tackle for years. But for now I want to know the answer to the question I asked you a few minutes ago. Since you've run the *Halkidiki News* for a while, do you find that you love it?"

No one had ever asked her such a probing question. She had to think about it while the steward served them coffee. "I wouldn't say I love it, but I can't think of anything else that would stimulate me as much. At an early age, I loved reading the paper. Now that I'm in charge of putting one out every day, there's a certain satisfaction in knowing it serves the public in a way nothing else does."

"That answer explains why you captivated me from the beginning. Among everything else, you have an intriguing mind and a vision for what's important."

"Hardly." She might love his compliments, but she

wanted to hear what else he had to tell her. "I can't put out a good newspaper without good reporting. A journalist like you only comes along once in several decades. Now that you've given up your career to do something else, the media is going to mourn the loss."

"You flatter me, Giannina." He got to his feet and returned their coffee cups to the sideboard just as the fasten-seat-belt sign flashed on. "We're almost there. Buckle up."

"I bet you can't wait to see your uncle."

"You're right." That sounded definite. For so long she'd wanted to meet him and learn more about Philip's past. During the time they'd been in London, she'd fallen madly in love. But she hadn't known all of him because he'd held a great deal back from her.

Since he'd come to her office in Salonica, she'd seen sides of him he'd never revealed. Much of his life had been a secret to her. There was more to this man than she would ever have dreamed, including the fact that he'd suddenly given up a sensational career. Too many thoughts bombarded her. But the fact that he'd asked her to marry him would have to satisfy her until she heard the rest.

She kept looking out the window, willing herself to be patient until he was ready to tell her everything. Before long the walled city of sixteenth-century Dubrovnik rose up to meet them. The blue waters of the Adriatic on the Dalmatian Coast dazzled the eye as they drew closer.

After landing, they left the jet and he carried her bag to a black, elegant sedan waiting for them. The delightful temperature had to be in the midseventies. She saw the driver nod to Philip, who smiled at him. This had been his world and she hadn't known a thing about it. He'd kept so much from her and she had to admit it hurt.

Philip got in behind her and closed the door, placing her bag opposite them. After they fastened their seat belts, he spoke Croatian to their driver, Ivan, then turned to her. "I told him to take us directly to Cavtat."

"Is that a suburb?"

"Not exactly. It's the little town where my uncle lives about five minutes from here. His villa on the mountain is surrounded by pines and forests of cypress trees. If we have time, I'll take you to explore Dubrovnik. It all depends on what he has planned for us."

Her eyes fastened hungrily on the landscape that had been deemed a UNESCO world heritage site. "This is the stuff dreams are made of. It's like looking at pictures in a fairy tale. I feel like I'm living in it with you."

He gripped her hand and squeezed it. They followed the tree-lined road near the shore, then climbed into the green vegetation. With the sea below, she couldn't imagine a more picturesque setting. As the car wound around, Giannina let out a cry. Somehow, she hadn't been prepared for what she saw amid the greenery. This was no villa. He'd brought her to a Gothic palace so spectacular, she was close to speechless.

"Philip—when you talked about your uncle, I had no idea."

"The family on his mother's side dates back many centuries."

"It's glorious."

"So is the estate. We'll go down to the stable later and see it on horseback. When we were in London and went riding on Wimbledon Common, I could see what an accomplished rider you were. I've looked forward to the day when I could bring you here. Come on. Let's go in. Uncle Zikos is waiting for us."

He released her hand, then opened the door and got out before helping her. In the periphery she watched a man emerge from the palace.

"Marko," Philip greeted him.

The other man smiled, then reached for her bag while Giannina was ushered inside and up a picture-lined stairway to an ornate salon on the second floor.

They'd barely entered the double doors when a distinguished-looking man who appeared to be in his mid-sixties hurried toward them. Silver streaked his dark hair. He was of average height and had penetrating brown eyes. She saw no resemblance between him and Philip. Either Philip's mother or father had bequeathed him his dark blond coloring and blue eyes.

Judging by his uncle's casual clothes and boots, she imagined he did a lot of riding too. His fit physique indicated he was an active man, and she had to admit he had a presence.

She watched through teary eyes as they embraced, admiring this man for raising his brother's son who'd lost his family at such a vulnerable age.

"Uncle Zikos Novak?" Alex spoke in Greek. "May I present Giannina Angelis, the editor-in-chief of the

Halkidiki News, and the daughter of the famous shipping owner Estefen Angelis."

Zikos released him and reached for Gianinna's hand. "It's a great privilege to meet you at last. Philip has talked of nothing but you since he met you in London." He kissed the back of it.

"I could say the same thing about you. He told me about the time you and he traveled to Mount Athos. He said it was an amazing experience living with the monks, but more amazing being with you."

A smile wreathed his face. "We've had many wonderful adventures together. Unlike my son, Baldo, Philip has a desire to explore life to the fullest. I'm convinced it's what has made him an exceptional journalist. You've heard about people whose minds soak up knowledge like a sponge and act on it. That's Philip. He can't get enough. I have trouble keeping up with him."

"That doesn't surprise me," she murmured. "When I met Philip, he had already gained a sterling reputation as a top journalist. I found him a fascinating lecturer."

"Tomorrow morning I'll let you look at an album of pictures of him growing up with my family. There are photos of his college graduation, but right now I imagine you're tired after the ordeal of your uncle's arrest. You and Philip need to enjoy yourselves for what's left of the rest of the day and evening. Marko will show you to your room, where I've arranged for your dinner to be served."

"I can't thank you enough, Kyrie Novak."

"Call me Zikos. We don't stand on ceremony around here."

She nodded.

"I'll come to your suite in a few minutes," Alex whispered and watched her leave the salon with Marko.

After the door closed, Zikos smiled. "She's a lovely woman. Though I'd seen pictures of her in the newspaper and the photos you showed me, none of them do justice to her in the flesh. How is she bearing up?"

His jaw hardened. "Amazingly well considering what she just learned about Hatzi."

In a low voice Zikos asked, "How much does she know about *you*?"

"Very little. Today I asked her to marry me. Before the night is over, she'll know everything."

"You've waited a long time for this day."

Alex nodded. "She still believes you're my blood uncle. In all honesty, I feel that you are." Emotion poured out of him. He hugged his uncle for a long time. "Remember that I'm naming you my prime minister." Alex drove the point home. "I hope we're clear about that. Father was about to make you his own prime minister until that ghastly night."

Zikos's eyes dimmed for a moment. Clearing his throat, he said, "You and I will convene the old parliament that's ready to serve you. Before long there'll be a coronation. It can't come soon enough for every Hellenian."

Alec swallowed hard. "I couldn't have done anything without you. No man ever had a better friend than you. I owe you my life, Zikos."

"Your father saved mine years ago from a bullet during the war. If he hadn't given me help on the battlefield, I would have died. We became great friends and stood up for each other at our weddings. It was my privilege to take you to safety when General Ruiz swept in. But his days are over."

"After all this time…"

"That's right. Judging by the way you feel about Giannina, I'd say it should have come yesterday."

"Even though I've proposed to her, it's more than possible she'll refuse me when I reveal who I really am. I've known fear, but nothing like I'm experiencing now. I may have lost her for good, Uncle."

"Nonsense. When she learns your reasons for protecting her, I feel certain she'll understand."

He shook his head. "If I don't miss my guess, trust means everything to Giannina. Ari broke her family's trust. I have to admit I'm frightened when she hears that I've broken hers for three long years."

"Have faith, my boy. Your reasons aren't like anyone else's. I'll be in my office in case you need me. Go and enjoy this precious time with her."

Philip gave him another hug and left the salon, breathless to spend time with Giannina. She could have no idea how he'd longed to be rid of the pretense and emerge as his total self. But as he knocked on the door of her suite, fear swept through him again. In London she'd fallen for a journalist named Philip Dimas with dark blond hair and blue eyes. She'd loved him, but she might not like Prince Alexandros, an unknown in every way.

He thought about how he'd feel if their positions were reversed. If she were the one in disguise, she would be breathtaking whether she were a blonde or a redhead with green or blue eyes instead of warm brown. In his gut he knew the transformation wouldn't matter to him, but he couldn't speak for her.

"Come in."

Alex walked in the sitting room. The smell of her shampoo preceded her appearing in a pair of tan pants and a café-au-lait print blouse. When he'd first met her, he'd thought her a miracle of femininity and curves.

She'd left her wavy brunette hair loose to let it dry. Never had she looked more enticing to him than she did right now. "Do you have everything you need?"

Her smile melted him. "Your uncle is very kind. I'm being treated like a queen."

"He knows how much I love you. Just now I told him I asked you to marry me. He heaved an enormous sigh of relief."

She threw her arms around his neck. "So did I."

He laughed. They clung to each other and kissed until they couldn't breathe. With reluctance he relinquished her lips. "Let's eat and take a ride before it gets too dark. When we get back, we'll have that long talk I promised you."

She pressed her lips to his jaw before they walked over to a small dining table where their meal had been placed. He pulled out a chair, touching her hair intentionally as she sat down. It was like pure silk. The need to twine his fingers in it left him with unassuaged longings that were growing out of control.

"My uncle has had a favorite Croatian meal prepared in your honor."

"That's exciting. What's it called?"

"Black risotto because of the squid ink. Since I know you like fish, I think you'll enjoy this. I'll warn you now the seafood flavor is intense. It's made with squid, olive oil, red wine and garlic."

"Squid, huh?" Her soft brown eyes twinkled in amusement.

He watched her take a bite and grinned. "What's the verdict?"

She munched for a minute. "I think it will be an acquired taste, but don't tell your uncle I said that."

Philip chuckled.

Once they'd finished eating apple-cherry strudel, another Croatian delicacy, they left her suite. He walked her down a rear staircase and out the back of the palace. Their arms and hips brushed against each other as they headed for the stables in the distance. Desire licked through him.

"I haven't ridden for ages," Giannina chatted. "I've been too busy at the paper."

"There hasn't been a lot of time for me either. I've chosen a chestnut mare for you named Yasmine. Rolf has everything ready for us. The older man has been in Zikos's employ at least twenty years."

"Then you know him well. How lovely, Philip."

"His loyalty means everything."

She nodded. "Do you have a favorite horse here?"

"Yes. Haj, an Arabian I'm particularly fond of. There he is now."

Rolf had brought their mounts out in the open. Haj neighed when he saw Alex coming.

Giannina had ridden from childhood and walked around to get acquainted with Yasmine. "You're a beauty." The mare nudged her. "Shall we go for a ride?" She took the reins from Rolf and swung herself in the saddle with feminine grace.

Alex mounted his black gelding. "Ready?" Giannina was the beauty he'd loved for so long.

They rode side by side along one of his favorite trails through a grassy meadow of wildflowers. It rose higher and higher. He felt they'd entered another world and needed to treasure this moment before his revelation ruined everything.

CHAPTER FIVE

A WARM BREEZE ruffled Gianinna's hair. When they reached the summit, her eyes took in the small town at the base of the mountain where the land met the sea. The sun had dropped into the ocean, providing a magnificent backdrop for Philip silhouetted astride Haj.

His chiseled jaw and features stood out. No man alive could ever match his sinfully good looks. He had a virile masculinity unique among the men she'd met. But the outward appearance was only a portion of what made him the man Giannina loved. A fire burned inside him combined with intelligence and a certain elegance that set him apart. His instincts, his drive, fascinated her. To think he was going to be her husband!

Giannina knew he'd given up journalism for something else far more challenging to him. That's what he still had to tell her. She couldn't imagine what it was but realized he could do anything if it was what he wanted. Not every man or woman had that remarkable ability. He'd laid claim to her heart a long time ago and she adored him.

"Do we really have to wait for that talk?" She smiled

at him. "I'd hoped during this lovely ride you would open up to me. We're alone at last. You do realize that when you left me in London, you promised that one day you'd disclose all the reasons for your behavior over the last three years. On the boat earlier you said the same thing. Yet here we are and I'm still in the dark."

A troubled look had crossed over his handsome features. "You're right. It's time." There was a solemnity about him that surprised her. "But I'd rather talk to you in your apartment. Let's go."

He'd asked her to give him time. Her heart beat faster in anticipation of what he would tell her. *Just a little longer, Giannina.*

When they reached the stable, she quickly dismounted and handed the reins to Rolf. "Yasmine is a treasure."

"Philip chose her especially for you."

She smiled at the older man, then at Philip. "He has a good eye."

"Indeed he does."

Philip jumped down and accompanied her to the palace. They walked up the back stairs to her suite. When they reached the door, she thought he'd come right in with her. But she'd been wrong.

"Forgive me, Giannina, but I need to freshen up and will join you in a half hour."

"I don't understand. Do you need to talk to your uncle again?"

"No, but what I have to do first is important."

What was going on with him? "How about another kiss before you go."

"There's nothing I want more." He caught her in his arms and gave her a long hungry kiss that wasn't nearly enough.

"Promise you won't leave me like you did three years ago and never come back?"

"I swear I won't be long."

"I'll be waiting for you," she said, struggling not to show her disappointment. "Thank you for the fabulous ride."

His dazzling blue gaze took in every feature. It took everything not to throw her arms around him again.

"Remember how much I love you."

Why would he have said that to her? His parting words filled her with a strange foreboding. What should be the happiest night of her life was turning into something else she couldn't comprehend.

Alex took off for his apartment down the hall. He had everything he needed to transform himself and hurried in the bathroom. After fourteen years he was finally going to be rid of his disguise.

First, he removed his shirt and took out his blue contact lenses. With that accomplished he reached for the permanent black dye. Once he'd put on gloves, he brushed it into his dyed blond hair, saturating it.

During the wait while the black color penetrated to turn his hair back to its original color, he dyed his blond eyebrows black. Then he stepped in the shower to shampoo his hair and brows. He stared in relief as the black residue drained away. Once he'd stepped out, he removed the gloves and reached for a towel to dry his face and hair.

The test came when he looked in the mirror a few minutes later to see the result.

"You're a new man, Alex. The man you're supposed to be. Your enemies won't know you. Neither will Giannina."

Feeling sick to the pit of his stomach as he imagined her reaction, he went in the bedroom and pulled a white linen shirt from the closet. Combined with a pair of stone-gray pants, he finished getting dressed and rolled the sleeves to the elbows. He slipped on well-worn brown leather sandals, ready to meet his fate. This could be the beginning of the end of his dreams if she couldn't forgive him. But it was too late to back out now.

Tonight she'd admitted that she loved him. Her response to his kisses was everything he'd been praying for. But knowing what was coming had brought his deepest fears to the surface—fears that had been plaguing him from the beginning.

Giannina was a brilliant woman in her own right, the head of a renowned newspaper because she deserved to be the editor-in-chief. She was desirable beyond belief. While they'd been apart, it was a miracle she hadn't fallen in love and married another man.

Alex had prayed she'd wait for him, no matter how long it took. Even though she'd admitted on the cruiser that she still loved him, he knew the damage he'd caused. Could she overcome the revelation he still had to tell her?

Though he'd asked her to marry him, there were no plans to make until she'd learned the whole truth about him. He needed to give her all the reasons why it had been necessary to deceive her. But in his gut he knew what was going to happen. The mere thought of her reaction shook him to the core of his being.

With no time to lose, he headed for her apartment.

After freshening up, Giannina waited for Philip on the love seat. She'd texted Nico to let him know about the arrest and that she was in Croatia. But she didn't reveal anything personal about her and Philip yet. That could come later, after their talk.

She'd just finished sending it when she heard a knock on the door. "Come in, Philip."

Giannina looked up expecting to see him walk in the sitting room. Instead, a tall, black-haired stranger stood at the entrance—a drop-dead gorgeous male defying ordinary description. Her breath caught.

Beneath black brows his eyes gleamed like black fires. The phone slipped from her hands. Though at first glance she didn't know who he was, there was something hauntingly familiar about him.

"Giannina?" The deep voice sounded like Philip's, penetrating to her insides. She didn't understand what was happening and started to tremble. "I'm sorry if I alarmed you," he murmured. "You've known me as Philip Dimas for one reason only. I feared you'd be made a target by my family's enemies and I couldn't allow that to happen. Since London I've wanted to introduce myself.

"My real name is Alexandros Cimon Pisistratus. Just so you know, before I was taken to safety, everyone called me Alex. It's the name I told you to call me when we played together in the palace grounds years ago."

If ever Giannina had been the type of person to faint dead away, this would have been the time. Fortunately, she was still seated.

He came inside and shut the doors. Dressed in gray pants and a white shirt open at the throat with sleeves rolled to the elbow, he possessed the raw, sensuous masculine appeal of Philip. But his black hair and eyes brought out another element that turned him into an entirely different person from the one who'd stolen her heart three years ago.

This man appeared bigger than life, possessing a magnetic aura that shouted he was the missing prince of Hellenia. He stood across from her with his hands on his hips in a totally male stance that made him unforgettable. His gaze burned into hers.

While in a stupor over what was happening, her mind recalled the young, black-haired prince she'd met years ago. Even then she'd seen the promise of the magnificent man in the good-looking thirteen-year-old. After having disappeared for years, here he was in the flesh! It couldn't be... It just couldn't!

He didn't say a word while she tried to fathom one pertinent fact. *There was no Philip Dimas!*

All this time he'd been the prince in disguise while the world wondered if he'd died. The spectacular journalist the world had acknowledged and feted for the years following an early college education had never existed. Their relationship had never been real.

Everything had been a *lie*!

As she started to come back to life after being frozen in place, pain such as she'd never known attacked her entire body. It started in her heart and radiated to every extremity, causing her to cry out in agony.

She shot to her feet, incapable of thought except one. "Welcome to the world you were born to, Your Highness. It's now clear that *this* is the story you've been alluding to, the one that puts the arrests of my uncle and the general in the background. Call my managing editor. She'll arrange for an interview with you when you're ready to announce your return to the throne."

The whiteness of Gianinna's face would stay with Alex for as long as he lived. Everything he'd feared and more had come to fruition with nightmarish clarity.

His heart came close to failing him as she dashed into the bedroom. He reached the entry to her room before she could slam the door in his face.

The plight of Odysseus upon coming home from the Trojan War filled his mind. After ten years absence as prince of Ithaca, Odysseus yearned to be with his faithful, beloved wife, Penelope, and returned dressed as a wily beggar she didn't recognize. Yet once he revealed himself to her, she remained cautious, wary of being hurt and deceived. In the end she set him a test that only the true Odysseus could pass.

Alex couldn't help but wonder what test Giannina would set for him so he could regain the love she'd once felt for Philip. Tragically the two men were not the same in her eyes. He would have to win her heart and soul as Alex, but he might not have the luck of Odysseus and lose his reason for being.

She sank down on the side of the bed with her face buried in her hands.

"Giannina?"

She slowly looked up. A light had gone out of her eyes, causing a physical change in her countenance. He'd accomplished the perfect deception, but the revealed truth had done a kind of damage from which they might never recover.

"We have to talk."

"I wanted to talk during our horseback ride," she responded with amazing calm. "Since the moment we met in London, I wanted to tell you that that I'd hoped you would ask me to be your wife. But I was dying to be the wife of Philip Dimas."

He cringed inwardly while he waited for the rest.

"Now I know why you put me off so long. Your transformation has said it all. I appreciate the trouble you went to so I could be there for Ari's arrest and know the truth. He stole your life away from you, and your uncle gave you a new one. Please give that remarkable man my regards and thank him for his hospitality. I'm happy for both of you. Now I'd like you to leave me alone."

Alex couldn't do that until he'd told her everything. "I'll tell him, but you need to know that Zikos isn't my uncle."

She gave a despairing shake of her head. "Of course

he isn't. I kept looking for a family resemblance but couldn't find one."

Her words cut him to the marrow. "He was my father's right-hand man and would have been made prime minister but for the assassination."

Anger shot her cheeks with color. "Next I suppose the home in Portugal and all his residences around the world were sheer fabrication on your part. Small wonder you never took me there to meet him."

He swallowed hard. "Zikos is a Hellenian citizen who'd fought in an earlier war alongside my father when they were young men. He lived in Loria, where he met his wife. In time he became the chief assistant to my father. That happened after my grandfather, the former king, died of pneumonia and my father was crowned king.

"The night my parents were murdered, Zikos brought me here to his mother's family home, where we've been safe from the enemy. He has treated me like a son."

She averted her eyes. "He's a true hero for what he's done, but I've heard enough."

"You haven't heard everything yet."

Giannina hugged her arms to her waist. "Seeing you like this is enough. It's all making sense now. I was amazed you kept dating me after that first night when we had drinks."

Where was she going with this? "What do you mean?"

"You did your research all right. Ari Hatzi was your target and once we started seeing each other, you discovered I was his niece. There was no stopping you because I'd fallen head over heels in love with you. You saw the perfect way to learn more about one of the men you'd been tracking secretly. His relationship with my family was like finding gold, wasn't it?"

His jaw tautened. "You couldn't be more wrong. I only knew his name *after* you told me about him and how mean he'd been to you growing up. But I didn't learn until ten days ago that he'd helped kill my parents."

"You mean it was just a coincidence," she mocked with cutting scorn.

"Yes. An incredible coincidence. You only have to talk to the eyewitness who came forward ten days ago to know I'm telling the truth."

"What naive little fool do you take me for? I couldn't believe you were attracted to me. One of the most famous journalists in Europe had picked me to spend time with out of all the women around."

"That's because there's never been another woman like you, Giannina."

"Naturally not. They didn't have the advantage of being related to the man you were hunting. *I* was the chosen one and told you everything about myself and my family while you wined and dined information out of me." Her eyes blazed. "How can you deny that you used me in the cruelest of ways?"

A groan escaped his lips. "I deny it before God!"

She looked away from him.

"I had a young teenage crush on you years before we met again in London. I knew after our first evening together that I'd fallen irrevocably in love with you. Nothing else mattered to me during the month we were together. That was the happiest time of my life."

She shook her head. "You were so happy, you suddenly left London without telling me your secret. You didn't *trust* me or grant me even a half hour of your time before saying goodbye to me. You insult my intelligence to suggest you ever loved me. Loving someone means *total* trust."

He could see her body shaking. "I agree, but in our case I was terrified to take you with me in case you got killed because of me. If that had happened..." He couldn't finish his thoughts.

"I never saw you for three years," she accused him in pain. "Then two days ago you ventured into my office with my charming managing editor, who was already smitten."

He moved closer to her. "The postcards I sent were—"

"An affront to me!" she broke in on him. "How dare you mention them. You didn't even trust me enough to give me a PO box on the card where I could write back to you. How could that have endangered my life? Couldn't anyone have found them and killed me at the office?"

"But nothing happened to either of us in London. Once you'd gone back to Salonica, no one ever saw me with you again, so your life wasn't in danger. The postcards were my only way to let you know that you were constantly in my heart."

Caustic laughter escaped. "And when you did come to Greece a few days ago, it—"

"It was to protect you and your family before the news came out about your uncle. I wanted you to be there when he was arrested so you'd see the truth of his malevolence for yourself."

He heard a harsh intake of breath. "Please let's not do this, Philip."

"I'm in love with you and always have been. You charmed me as a girl. When we met up again in England, the reality of your beauty and intelligence overpowered me and I've never been the same."

She refused to look at him. "You didn't even make love to me."

"I didn't dare take the risk of getting you pregnant while we were in London. Furthermore, I wanted you to be my wife before I took you to bed for the first time. You're the only woman I'll ever love and want to marry."

Her head reared, causing her shiny hair to flounce. "Well, I have news for you. The man *I* want to marry doesn't exist yet. Maybe never. When or if he ever makes an appearance, he'll trust me with all his heart, might, mind and soul."

"I already do," he fought back. "Asking you to be my bride means you'll be my lover and wife, the mother of our children. If I'm put on the throne, you'll be queen of Hellenia, beloved by everyone."

"Queen?" She stared at him as if he were insane. "That's the last thing on earth I would ever want to be."

"Why do you say that?"

"I can't imagine being a royal." Her words pierced him. "If you'd told me the truth in London, I would have checked myself out of school and flown home that very day."

"Giannina—"

"Please leave."

She was too hurt and angry for him to try to reason with her right now. "I'll go, but I'm not giving up on us. We love each other and we'll find a way."

It was two in the morning as he left her apartment knowing there'd be no sleep for him now. He raced down the hall to the back stairs. Once outside he headed for the swimming pool at the side of the palace. A workout would exhaust him.

But as he found out after reaching his room two hours later, no activity helped relieve his pain. While he was changing clothes, a new fear gripped him. He'd lied to her in the worst possible way a man could hurt the woman he loved, but she wasn't the kind of person who went into hysterics. Instead she would find a way to slip out of the palace without telling him and leave for Salonica.

If he phoned or texted her, she wouldn't answer. With pounding heart, Alex changed clothes and hurried to her apartment. He checked his watch. Quarter to five. He knocked on her door, but there was no answer.

"Giannina? Are you awake?"

He waited. Still no answer. Hoping she would forgive him, he opened the door, but didn't go in. "If you can hear me, let me know. I have to talk to you."

The quiet alarmed him. Something told him she'd gone.

After dashing back to his room for his wallet and

keys, he raced out the door and down the staircase to the foyer. One of the night staff approached him. "Your Highness? I was told by Kyria Angelis to tell you good-bye. She called for a taxi."

He could hardly breathe. "How long ago did she leave?"

"It has been half an hour."

Maybe there was still time to catch up with her. "Thank you, Jakov. Please tell Uncle Zikos I've gone after her and will be in touch with him."

Alex pulled out his phone and asked Ivan to drive around to the entrance to the palace. He needed to leave for the airport immediately.

If she'd phoned her brother to send the Angelis jet, it was possible he might miss her. Then again maybe she didn't want to bother him and had decided to fly com-mercial. Alex's instinct told him the latter was what she'd done.

He stepped outside to wait for Ivan, who arrived in record time. They left for the airport. En route he phoned the pilot to be ready to fly him to Salonica. When they reached the main terminal, Alex told Ivan to wait and rushed inside. The place was packed with tourists.

There was no sign of Giannina. He hurried to the gate for the flight and found her seated while she waited to board. Relieved to realize she hadn't left yet, he walked over to her. She'd dressed in a small black-on-white print sundress and jacket with white sandals to match. He loved her hair cascading to her shoulders. Alex could eat her alive.

When she saw him, she got up from the chair with her overnight bag and walked away to avoid people. "Don't try to stop me," she whispered.

"I swear I wouldn't do that," he spoke softly after catching up to her. "But I brought you to Croatia and I would like to take you back to Salonica. We'll fly there together in my uncle's jet. It will give us the time we need to finish talking."

"There's nothing more to say." She kept her voice low.

"If it's because you don't want to be married to a ruling prince, then I won't accept the throne. You're the most important person in my life. I'll do whatever is necessary to have you for my wife and live a normal life with you."

CHAPTER SIX

GIANNINA COULDN'T BELIEVE what she'd just heard. After a grateful nation wanted to crown him king, he'd give it up for *her*? Her heart was exploding in her chest.

Here they were in a busy airport terminal and Philip had just walked up to her with a declaration that almost made her legs buckle. He *was* the crown prince of Hellenia. She knew in her soul that after all the agony he'd been through over the years, he wouldn't say something like that to her if he didn't mean it.

One glance at the pain coming from those gorgeous black eyes revealed he'd been suffering after telling her the reason for his lie. Admittedly it had taken uncommon courage, as Nico had said.

How could she insist that she never wanted to see him again and just fly away when yesterday she'd cried out her love for him? She at least needed to hear him out before everything ended. Once they landed in Salonica, he would drive her to her apartment. Giannina couldn't think beyond that point.

"I'll come," she murmured and started walking toward the entrance to the terminal. He reached it be-

fore she did and opened the doors for her. The black
sedan stood waiting in a lane close by. She got in the
back without his help. Alex gave Ivan instructions and
slid in next to her.

They reached the small airport and climbed on
board the jet. Giannina strapped herself in and left a
text for her brother that she was returning to Salonica.
Without telling him what had happened, she said she
would have news for him after she landed. He texted
back that he'd meet her at the apartment later.

When they'd achieved cruising speed, the steward
brought them a meal with hot coffee, fortifying her.
It tasted good. Her chaotic emotions had sapped her
of strength, and she realized she needed sustenance.

"We'll be landing soon," Alex spoke after devouring his food. "But I need to ask you a favor. Zikos just
texted me that he's convening an emergency session of
parliament in Loria. He doesn't want anything leaked
out about me yet. The plan is for me to lie low for the
next twelve hours before I return to Hellenia. I'm assuming nothing will go wrong until I can join them,
but better to be safe."

She shook her head. "You shouldn't have come after
me at the airport."

"I'd do anything for you, Giannina. But my unmasking has caused complications. When I take you to your
apartment, will you let me come in with you? Together
we can enter your building through the back. People
will assume I'm one of your boyfriends."

Her pulse raced off the charts. "Couldn't you go to
your own apartment?"

"Someone on the staff there will question what I'm doing in the Dimas apartment. After years of planning for Hellenia to be a free country again, I can't allow anything to go wrong at the last moment. Zikos is depending on me to be careful."

She wanted to refuse him. But he'd risked exposure to come after her. When she thought of the consequences to everything he and Zikos Novak had been planning for his triumphant return to Hellenia, she found she couldn't deny him.

"Just for tonight," she warned him and felt his black gaze burn through her. "I hope you understand that nothing has been resolved between us."

"I'm aware of that. I also know I don't deserve your help. Perhaps now you realize that there's not another woman on earth to match you. I adore you, my love."

The fasten-seat-belts sign went on. They were descending. After the landing, she undid hers and got up to leave the jet. He carried her overnight bag and before long they reached the parking area, where he helped her into his rental car.

Early evening had come to Salonica. Three years ago, she would have given anything to bring Philip home to her apartment. *Stop it. Philip Dimas doesn't exist. In his place is the prince of Hellenia, a man I don't know.*

He drove to her apartment and pulled around the back to park along the access road. They both undid their seat belts. "I see a night watchman near the back entrance."

"He's always there," she murmured.

In the next breath, he put his arm around her and pulled her close. "Let's make this real, shall we?" he spoke against her lips before covering her mouth with his own.

The action was so unexpected, it caught her off guard. She found herself responding to the hunger of his kiss. It grew longer and deeper until she forgot everything but her need of him. He took her back to those evenings in London where they'd gone on long walks and embraced, not able to get enough of each other. Right now, he caressed every inch of her face before his mouth plundered hers again.

"It's been too long, Giannina." She couldn't tell if the moans came from her or from both of them. They weren't close enough. He molded her against him, kissing her neck and hair until she trembled with desire.

Suddenly she realized where this was leading, where she *wanted* it to lead. White-hot heat suffused her face to think she'd lost control and he knew it. She pulled away from him, struggling for breath. "I would imagine we've convinced the night watchman."

A knowing smile appeared on Alex's lips. "Plus the security guards Zikos has sent to guard me."

"They'll be guarding you from now," Giannina murmured. "You're the prince." His whole life had changed.

He got out his side of the car and came around to help her. She reached for her key while he retrieved her bag and one of his from the trunk. Carrying both with one arm, he put his other arm around her shoulders and nibbled the side of her neck as they hurried past the man.

Once she'd unlocked the door, they entered the building. Thankfully no one was around, and they took the elevator to her three-bedroom apartment. After she unlocked the door, he swept them inside. Putting down the bags, he cupped her face in his hands. A light shone from the recesses of those fiery black eyes. "Thanks to you, we've made it in safely."

He lowered his head and kissed her mouth again, as if planning to take up where they'd left off. Fighting for her sanity, she wheeled away from him and carried her bag to the bedroom. While she freshened up, she discovered herself more out of breath than ever.

Once she'd gotten a grip on her emotions, she walked into the living room. Naturally she found him on the phone speaking Croatian while he drank a cola. She sat down on the couch where she'd left her purse and waited for him to hang up.

Her friends would call him the hunk of hunks. When the news came out with his photo, every woman young or old would stop in their tracks and figure out a way to meet the tall, dark, dashing prince of Hellenia.

Giannina had just been thoroughly kissed by him and still felt the upheaval inside her body. Too many unsatisfied longings cried out for the kind of satisfaction she knew only he could give, but he wouldn't let that happen until she became his wife.

A few minutes later she heard Nico's familiar knock on the door. Alex darted her a questioning glance before he went in one of the bedrooms and shut the door.

She hurried across the room to let him in. Her handsome brother rushed inside. "You're home and safe." He hugged her hard. *"Echaristó parádeiso."*

"Thank heaven is right." Giannina kissed his cheek. "And someone else is here with me."

His brows lifted in surprise. "You're talking about Philip?"

She bit her lip. "Actually no." Her heart pounded too hard.

He stared at her from those intelligent dark eyes. "Then who?"

"The prince of Hellenia is in the middle bedroom on the phone."

Nico gripped her arms. "The prince. He's really here?"

"Yes."

"I saw no security."

"He assured me it's there. Why don't I knock on the door and let him know it's okay to come out."

"Wait—where's Philip?"

She took another breath. "That's a long story. The prince will explain."

He frowned. "You're being very mysterious."

"That's my fault."

Another deep male voice reverberated in the living room. They both turned as Alex walked toward them, bigger than life. Every time she looked at him, she could hardly breathe.

"You have to be Nico Angelis, Kyria Angelis's brother. Your fame is legendary, and I'd recognize you anywhere."

She looked searchingly at Nico. "May I introduce

you to Prince Alexandros of Hellenia, *formerly* known to the world as Philip Dimas."

Her brother was a quick study. As comprehension dawned, he stared hard at her before letting out a long whistle. Turning to the prince, he said, "This is an incredible moment for me, Your Highness." The two men shook hands and took their measure of each other.

"For me too." Alex smiled. "I've waited fourteen years for this day. General Ruiz has been arrested and every Hellenian will taste freedom again."

Nico had been given a lot to process and his expression sobered. "It grieves me and Giannina that our uncle was one of the men responsible for the deaths of your parents. What we can say with joy is that the prince of Hellenia will finally serve as the country's new king. It's a great honor to meet you. If there's anything we can do to help, you have only to ask."

Alex's penetrating gaze focused on her. "Your sister has been kind and brave enough to let me hide here tonight. There are reasons I don't want to be seen until my uncle has met with the parliament and they're informed about me. It's happening now, but we'll have to see. If there's a delay, I'll make other plans to stay hidden."

Nico frowned. "That would present a definite problem. It would be better and safer to stay completely out of sight away from the city where your privacy is guaranteed. If you would permit, I'll drive you and Giannina to my office building now."

Giannina wondered what in heaven's name her brother was up to.

"From there we'll fly in my helicopter to my villa overlooking Sarti Beach, where you'll have the best security available. You can stay there for as long as needed and have everything at your disposal until you're ready to get back to Hellenia."

While her heart raced, Alex eyed her brother with genuine warmth. "That's a very generous offer, one I accept on behalf of my nation with the deepest gratitude, Kyrie Angelis."

"Call me Nico."

"I will if you'll call me Alex."

"Agreed."

No, no, no, Giannina cried inwardly. "I don't need to leave Salonica, Nico."

"I'm afraid you do. News has leaked that our uncle is in custody for his crimes. There could be repercussions against our family since he worked at the newspaper all those years."

Her brows furrowed. "Of course."

"It would be better to avoid any unpleasantness until the prince's return is made public."

"Your brother is right, Giannina."

Nico kissed her cheek. "Since the newspaper staff can't explain your absence at this particular time and they're starting to get phone calls about Ari, it's best you stay away a little longer for both your sakes."

Giannina understood his reasoning, but she had other fears. After those soul-destroying kisses Alex had given her out in the car, she'd been shaken all over again by needs she couldn't seem to control.

He wanted to marry her and said he would give up

the throne for her. But could he really do that? What kind of a queen would she make? What if he grew disappointed in her and in time his duties took precedence over her? Or worse, what if he gave up the crown and then regretted it bitterly. She wasn't at all sure she could marry him under such circumstances. She had to make him understand.

While she struggled with her fears, Nico reached in his pocket for his phone. "I'll alert the security guard at my office and let the pilot know that we're on our way."

Alex had already pulled out his cell. "I'm letting Zikos know what's happened. He'll keep my bodyguards informed. One of them will drive the rental car back to my apartment."

While history was taking place, Giannina walked to her bedroom for the overnight bag she hadn't yet unpacked. Alex had accepted Nico's genius plan to get them away from the city. She knew her brother was devastated over what their uncle Ari had done to the royal family and wanted to do anything he could for the prince.

Earlier this evening she'd believed Alex would leave in the morning and get back to Hellenia. Once gone, she would never have to see him again except in the news. Nothing ever turned out as she thought.

The setting of Nico's villa represented a paradise she'd wanted to show him three years ago. She'd dreamed of being there and lying in his arms, but his deception had ended those fantasies. Her only hope rested in Nico. She would prevail on him to stay with them until he felt it was safe for her to fly back to Salonica.

* * *

After a short flight to Sithonia, the helicopter landed at the back of the Angelis villa in the middle of the night. Alex had traveled to the Halkidiki Peninsula on several occasions and loved the scenery. This isolated spot overlooking the sea couldn't have provided a more perfect place for him to stay out of the public eye.

He'd found a powerful ally in Gianinna's protective brother, who'd insisted she come with them. Though the man had every right to feel hostile toward Alex over his lie of omission to Giannina, he'd encouraged her to go to Mount Athos with Alex to witness Hatzi's downfall. Now he'd offered him his home for an indefinite period.

Nothing could have made Alex happier. He needed time to try to win her over and Nico Angelis was the only person who could help make that happen.

Giannina had sat in the back with him during the flight, but she hadn't participated in the conversation with him and Nico. Once they touched ground, Nico helped her out while Alex reached for their bags. He followed them down the path to the stunning white villa located in the greenery. Starlight illuminated it.

In the living room Nico introduced him to Thanos and Anna, the trusted older married couple who looked after the place. "Alex? These two will help you with whatever you want or need. Now I'm afraid I have to get back to home."

"You're leaving?" Giannina cried. Alex heard the anxiety in her voice.

"I promised Alexa I wouldn't stay. Nico has been fussy." He kissed her cheek. "Call me if there's anything else I can do. Alex? If an emergency should arise and you have to get to Hellenia, the helicopter will be at your disposal."

"I'm indebted to you, Nico. In return it will be my privilege to give Giannina my story to be announced in your family's newspaper. I can tell you with absolute authority she's the only person in this world I would trust with the truth."

Nico nodded. "She will never publish a greater story or set of headlines in this century."

The two men smiled at each other before Alex saw her catch hold of her brother's arm. "I'll walk you out."

When they had disappeared, the older woman said, "If you'll follow me, *kyrie*, I'll show you to your room and fix you a meal."

"That's very kind, but I ate earlier." He picked up his suitcase and they walked down a hallway into a guest bedroom that would have a glorious view of the sea by morning.

"The en suite bathroom has all the toiletries you will need. There's a robe hanging on the door. I made coffee in case you and Giannina want it."

"*Efcharisto*, Anna."

"*Parakalo, kyrie. Kalinikta.*"

As soon as she disappeared, he took a shower and shaved. This was heaven to be here alone with Giannina. But he still had to convince her of his love and gain her trust.

He put on a fresh shirt and pants, then walked down the hall past the living room to the kitchen. Overhead he heard the whirr of rotor blades. With Nico leaving, she would be coming back any second. His pulse sped up in anticipation.

Anna had prepared a tray with sugar and cream. He poured both of them a cup of coffee and took it into the dining room off the living room. While he waited, he reached for his phone and left a short message for Zikos.

I'm now with Giannina at the Angelis compound on Sarti Beach. All is well for the moment.

"Alex? I thought you would have gone to bed." Gianinna's eyes played over him, obviously noticing he'd had time to change.

He put the phone back in the pocket of his shirt. "Anna fixed us coffee."

"That was kind of her."

"Did I upset you by telling your brother I'd like you to publish my story? I should have approached you about it first. Forgive me."

She shook her head, causing gold highlights to shimmer among that profusion of brunette hair. "You're a famous journalist and the missing prince of Hellenia. If that's your decision, it will be a real coup for the paper. Every outlet in Europe, let alone the civilized world, would give anything for the privilege."

"I always wanted you to be the one, but I'm aware I've broken your trust and might never get it back."

She clung to the back of one of the chairs. "Even so, our personal history is not important to a world waiting to hear your news. We'd better get started on it soon."

Giannina was a marvel. "Whenever it's good for you."

"Why don't we say after breakfast at nine. It shouldn't take us long."

He could tell she was trying to have as little to do with him as possible. Yet again the nerve throbbing wildly at her throat gave him hope. "I'll plan on nine."

"Once it's done, you'll be able to fly to Hellenia. As Nico told you, the helicopter is at your disposal to get you to the airport."

Except that Alex didn't plan to go anywhere yet. Zikos would be running the timetable for him. For all he knew, their next meeting might not take place in Loria for several days. Right now he needed to be here with the woman he would marry no matter how long it took for her to believe in him.

After taking a long drink of the steaming liquid, he darted her a glance. "Your brother is one of the most intelligent and generous men I've ever known. I can see why he's always been your rock."

"I've been blessed with a wonderful brother."

"I'm glad you've put him on a pedestal. He is probably part of the reason you haven't married yet. The men in your family would be impossible for another man to measure up to. I realize that *I* don't, not after deceiving you all this time.

"That deception was meant to keep you safe. It's

my prayer that if you'll give me time to show you who I really am, maybe a miracle will occur one day, and you'll agree to be my bride."

"Let's not talk about that right now." He thought he heard a little moan come out of her before she turned away from him. "I'm going to bed. If there's anything you need, just pick up the phone by the bed and Anna will answer."

"I'll do that. Sleep well, Giannina."

She rushed out of the dining room, putting distance between them. But he smiled because she would be only as far away as her phone. Once he'd finished his coffee, he turned off the kitchen light and went down the hallway to his bedroom. She was somewhere in the villa, but he hadn't asked her where she slept.

Before long he climbed under the covers, but his adrenaline would keep him awake for a while. Feeling adventurous, he picked up the cell phone and called her. She answered on the second ring.

"Alex?" She sounded anxious. "What's wrong?"

"Nothing that a little conversation with you won't cure."

A sound of frustration escaped. "So...after the coffee, you're wide awake."

He grinned. "Guilty as charged."

"In that case, let's do your story now. Give me a minute to get my tablet and we'll work on it. After we're through, you can sleep in. Tomorrow when you leave, I'll take a picture of you...maybe of you getting in the helicopter. Nothing posed, of course. I know you don't like that."

Giannina... Even though she pretended otherwise, he sensed in his gut she still loved him and there was no question she knew him better than any woman alive.

"The headline will read, 'Prince Alexandros of Hellenia comes out of hiding after fourteen years.' An action photo will make fascinating copy. What do you think?"

Why not? Except that he didn't plan to leave the villa anytime soon. "I love the way you think."

"Give me a second."

"I've got all the time in the world." Wishing she were right here wrapped against him, he turned on his side and waited.

"I'm back," she informed him, "and I've been thinking about what will be the most important thing for the readers. This will be the very first piece of news on you.

"Naturally hundreds of articles in papers and magazines, not to mention live television interviews, will follow. But this story will stand out forever in people's minds around the world, so it needs to capture the very essence of you from a young teen to a man."

His brilliant Giannina knew how to lay out a story and make it appeal. "What do you want to know first?"

"Some of my questions will be painful, Alex."

"I've lived with the pain for years."

"I'm so sorry."

Despite her anger, her compassion moved him. He had to clear his throat. "Go ahead."

"How soon after you were taken to safety did you know what happened to your parents?"

"Three men came into my bedroom at the palace around four in the morning, waking me from sleep. One of them was Zikos, who told me a tragedy had happened and I needed to go with them immediately. I had to leave in my pajamas. They hurried me out to a service truck at the back of the palace. In their haste, my dog, Achilles, had to be left behind."

"Oh, no! Your darling dog. How heartbreaking for you."

She really did understand since she'd played with his dog too. "To this day I don't know what happened to him. We drove to the port and left in a cruiser for Kavala, Greece, where we flew to Dubrovnik, Croatia, on a private plane.

"During the flight Zikos told me my parents had been stabbed and murdered in their beds. He assured me he'd made my father a promise. If anything happened to my family, he'd raise me as his own."

"Which he did!" she cried. Again he was thankful she'd met Zikos.

"He's a saint who had to endure putting up with me. I went through a difficult couple of years complete with counseling to help my depression."

"I can't even imagine it."

"I was in hell for a long time. My family had been so happy. The change from day to night turned me into a different person. I had no siblings, no living relatives. Through Zikos, plus a lot of help, I learned to live with my fear and face an uncertain future with new resolve to get on with my life."

Following his revelation, a long period of silence

ensued. "I don't know how you lived through that. Thank heaven for Zikos." Her words touched his heart.

"Amen."

"I'm not going to print any of those details. Only that Zikos Novak, the closest friend to your father, took you to safety where he kept you hidden and raised you as if you were his son. From him you learned that your parents had been murdered and their killers were hunting for you.

"I won't say anything about your disguise or your identity as Philip Dimas. Until this day I'll indicate that you've lived with Zikos without mentioning the location. I'll say that he has been in touch with the parliament organized by your father and is standing ready to form a new government. How does that sound?"

"I told you in London you have all the right editorial instincts. It's perfect." *She* was perfect.

"Thank you," came her quiet response. "In a few words, will you tell me what your overall thought has been during these years of exile?"

"My mission has been to remove General Ruiz and his regime from power, thus avenging the murder of my parents and making Hellenia free once more."

"Is there anything else you want to add as a final thought?"

"That the goodness in a patriot like Zikos Novak always prevails and takes away the sting of a tyrant like General Ruiz and his ilk. I owe him everything, including my life."

Again it took her a minute to respond. "Do you want me to mention anything about your future?"

"Yes. That soon I plan to be married to Giannina Angelis, the love of my life, *if* she'll say yes. There's a small summerhouse in the woods behind the palace. I'm looking forward to secret picnics with her there and the dog we'll buy. If we're lucky, children will come."

"Dogs and children." She sounded amused. "How many are you imagining?"

"Maybe three or four."

"That many?"

He grinned. "I never had siblings and don't want that fate for our little princes and princesses."

"I think we're getting way off track."

"You're right. That would be putting the cart before the proverbial horse. I told you it's up to you if I accept the throne."

"That's not fair. I wouldn't want that responsibility, and now I think we're done. I'll run off the story and give it to you tomorrow to study and revise as necessary."

"Excellent. I'll see you at breakfast."

"I think we'd better make it lunch to give you time to sleep in."

Sleep was the last thing on his mind. "How about a swim in the ocean after we eat?"

"Do you have a swimming costume in your luggage?"

"If I don't, I'll wear a towel."

"Alex—"

Laughter poured out of him. He hung up before he said something that would embarrass her. Tomorrow couldn't come soon enough. He'd detected a slight thawing. Maybe she was breaking out of that layer of steel until she came running into his arms.

CHAPTER SEVEN

LAST NIGHT IT had felt good and right to have finished Alex's story. This morning she woke up still remembering a dream about a dog and a boat that made little sense. Remnants of her interview with Alex had obviously stayed with her. She feared the heartbreaking details he'd told her about that horrific night and early years would haunt her for a long time.

The fact that he'd known at fourteen he was being hunted by his parents' assassins caused her to ponder what he'd told her. He'd been so young and vulnerable. He'd survived a tragedy of epic proportions. On top of it, he realized he had a target on his back and evil men were looking for him. From that point on, Alex had been forced to get through his life and try to stay alive.

When he'd first tried to explain why he'd kept the truth from her, she'd been too angry and hurt over too many things and had refused to listen. But last night on the phone she finally understood why he couldn't reveal his true identity. He'd had to take on a totally different one. From the moment he'd met her in London, he'd wanted to protect her from being killed.

For the first time since he'd come to Salonica, she understood why he hadn't asked her to marry him in London. He hadn't yet found the people responsible for eliminating his family and knew his life was in constant danger. After his experience as a young teen, he hadn't dared put her in danger. That knowledge changed her entire perspective on his reason for secrecy.

Her thoughts expanded as she thought of his years as a journalist while he hunted for the men hunting him. She shuddered at the horror he'd been living through since being taken to safety, never to see his parents again.

She relived his story as she got in the shower and washed her hair. While it dried, she opened her bag and put on shorts and a blouse. Anna rang to let her know lunch was ready on the patio off the kitchen.

Giannina went to Nico's office and printed the story she'd written. With that accomplished she hurried through the villa to the patio. A hot sun blazed from a blue sky. Such fabulous summer weather should have put her in a vacation mood. But Alex's revelations last night weighed on her heart. To be constantly watching and waiting for something dreadful to happen wasn't a life she could comprehend.

She sat beneath the umbrella shading the table and looked over the story she'd written. So much she'd left out because the details were too private, yet he'd trusted her with the full story.

Since he hadn't come out to the patio yet, no doubt he was still asleep. Anna had poured lemonade for both of them. Giannina drank hers slowly while the older woman brought out fish salad and rolls for them. No sooner had she gone back to the kitchen than he suddenly appeared wearing a fresh shirt and swimming trunks. It took everything not to gasp. He had the build and features of an Adonis.

He sat down opposite her looking more rested than she'd ever seen him. His dazzling smile played havoc with her insides. "Good morning. You look good enough to eat."

She almost told him he did too. "Every woman enjoys hearing that. Have you heard from Zikos yet?"

"Yes. He's been meeting with members of the parliament who've been waiting for this day."

"It's a wonderful one, Alex. What a great moment for you and your country. It's finally happening."

His eyes held a new light. "Soon he'll phone for me to fly to Loria."

That meant he'd probably be leaving right away. She was happy for him. As for herself, she was a mass of emotions still needing to be examined. "I'm glad we did your story last night. Here it is to look over." Giannina handed it to him.

He drank his lemonade while he read. Eventually he said, "There's only one statement missing. After you insert it, I'll give it my seal of approval," he stated in his deep voice.

"I can't believe I left anything out."

He put down his empty glass. "It's the part where the prince plans to marry Giannina Angelis of Salonica as soon as possible."

She sucked in her breath. "Three years ago I was ready to marry Philip Dimas, the journalist who stole my heart. I'd have gone anywhere with him, done anything."

By now he'd tucked into the salad. "Will it help if I get into my disguise? I can do it in a half hour, and you'll have Philip back. Don't you know I'd do anything for you?"

She stopped eating, unable to swallow another bite. "How can you joke about a situation like this?"

His dark head reared. "It's no joke. I'm deadly serious."

"Alex—it isn't your looks. Blond or black haired, you're still the same person I fell in love with. I realize that now. But my problem is that you're heir to the throne of Hellenia."

He eyed her with intensity. "Before anything else, I want to be your husband and will do whatever it takes to live with you and have children. On the cruiser I asked you if you still loved me and you said you did. I'm asking you again. Knowing the truth, have you forgiven me enough to love me now?"

"Of course I love you, but that doesn't mean I can see us married. Are you honestly saying you'd give up the throne to marry *me*? Don't you know the world has been waiting for the favorite son to appear at last and take his rightful place at the head of the country?"

He wiped his mouth with a napkin. "But I don't have to be king. What if that son would rather live his life with the woman he adores? What if all he wants is to make her happy?"

She blinked. "But you said that all these years, your whole purpose—"

"My whole purpose," he cut her off, "has been to avenge the death of my parents and make Hellenia free again from a tyrant like General Ruiz. The free government will choose a ruler from the people. I never said I wanted to be king, only that I hoped to work for the government alongside Zikos."

Giannina shook her head. "That's hard for me to believe."

"Why? When I met you in London, I fell hopelessly in love. So did you."

"I did," she cried, "but how could you imagine I'd ever be happy knowing you'd give up the throne for me? I'll never forget those news photos my aunt kept in the scrapbook of your family. You don't belong anywhere else. Your parents wouldn't want you to do anything but carry on their legacy and traditions."

His gaze fused with hers. "I don't know that and neither do you. I'm not sure if my father even liked being king. As far as I know he felt he had to do his duty, but that doesn't mean he was happy about it. Do you imagine I could be happy ruling the country without you at my side? I couldn't do it."

"Alex… You don't mean that." She looked shocked.

"But I do. While we were on the cruiser, I told you I planned to work in government. I could be a consultant for the new Hellenian monarchy. It would be a full-time job. We could find a villa there. The beauty of it would mean I'd be home in time for dinner every night with my wife and the children I want to have with you."

Heat filled her cheeks. "When we both know the palace is your home, you're not making sense."

"I'm trying to," he said earnestly. "Admit you'd love it if we bought a home in Salonica near *your* family. I could commute by helicopter from Loria. It's obvious you and your brother are close. You could go on being editor-in-chief of the newspaper if that's what you want. Or you could spend more time with your parents and aunt. I know your father isn't as well as he used to be. We'd make it work, darling."

"I can't see you as anything but a royal," she exclaimed.

"Are you saying you won't even try?"

She sat back in the chair. "I've read stories about royals who dared to live a separate life. I've always felt sorry for them. They've suffered for it in many ways because of their decision."

"I'm not one of them, Giannina. For that matter I don't have to work in government. Who knows where I'll end up if I follow my own destiny."

"Or maybe you'll become one of the greatest kings who ever lived," she blurted.

"That's a thought," he teased. "Come on. This glorious day is calling to me. Let's go down to the beach and enjoy each other. What would we have given to fly here for a weekend when we were in London? To have each other and this weather and beach is more than I could ever have asked for."

Troubled because his arguments were getting to her, winning her around, she pushed herself away from the table and stood up. "A swim sounds heavenly."

"Good. I'm glad we agree on that subject anyway." He got to his feet. "Let's hope you brought a bikini with you. I'd hate to have to throw you in the ocean and ruin those shorts."

How differently this day was going. "Aren't you waiting to hear from Zikos?"

"Always, but I'll take my phone with me. I'm counting to twenty. If you haven't returned from your room by then, ready to swim, I'm coming after you."

The gleam in those black eyes assured her he meant every word. She dashed inside and down the hall to her room. Her old blue bikini would have to do. She put it on and grabbed a beach towel from the cupboard.

"Eighteen," she heard him say as she hurried barefooted into the kitchen. "A wife who doesn't keep her husband waiting. What a blessing you're going to be!"

Giannina ignored him and ran down the steps to the road. It led to the beach. She could hear him coming behind her. The sand felt hot beneath her feet. She tossed her beach towel and plunged into the sublime blue water of the Aegean.

He caught up to her and pulled her against him. "Before we do anything else, I need this."

The next thing she knew, he'd covered her mouth with his own, igniting her in ways she didn't know were possible. The feel of his hands and mouth created such ecstasy, she forgot everything as white-hot heat consumed her. This was Philip and Alex all rolled into one, making her feel immortal.

They clung, not able to get enough of each other. She moaned when he eventually carried her back to the sand. After spreading the beach towel, he pulled her down and gathered her into his arms. Their legs entwined and he began devouring her.

"Agapa mou," he cried over and over again. She hadn't heard those words for so long. Those were words she would have died to hear three years ago. "Will you marry me, Giannina? Tell me you love me and want to be my wife. Otherwise my life makes no sense."

She couldn't think. She loved both men, but one would be become king of Hellenia. It was an inescapable fact. He could pretend that it didn't matter, but the day would come when love for his country would take over all else.

Giannina knew in her heart of hearts he'd make a great king. But she couldn't imagine herself being his wife because the life of a royal was anathema to her. He needed a wife who would make a superb queen. The thought of Giannina being that person was laughable.

He was waiting for an answer. She had to give him one, but it wouldn't satisfy him. On a groan, she tore her lips from his and got shakily to her feet. He stared up at her. "Where did you go?"

She sucked in her breath, trying to keep it. "Back to reality. I couldn't marry you and call you Mr. Pisistratus like any normal man who comes home from work at five. You wouldn't last five minutes, and I couldn't handle the guilt I'd feel that you'd given up the throne for me."

He got to his feet. His jaw had tautened. "You can't be positive about that."

"Yes. I can. I'm also positive that I could never

marry you and be your queen. I'm not cut out to be a royal. It isn't in me, Alex. There's a certain logic in royals marrying each other. From birth they're taught their destiny and know what's expected."

"You're a remarkable woman who can handle anything and don't need to be afraid of anything."

"Except for one thing," she challenged him.

"Which is?"

"To hurt you."

His eyes had narrowed. "What in the hell are you talking about?"

"It's not what, but *who*. I've heard the tragic story of the fourteen-year-old boy who has had to make his way through this life carrying a weight no child should ever have to carry. By some miracle and Zikos's love, you've made it this far. So help me but I don't want to be the one person who brings any more sorrow to your heart and soul by being a disappointing queen."

She reached for the towel and started across the sand to the road.

Within seconds he gripped her hips and turned her around. "I refuse to lose you, Giannina," came the fierce avowal. "There's a third possibility in all this. The news isn't out to the public that the prince is alive. My existence can remain a secret. Life will go on in Hellenia with Zikos's guidance."

"It wouldn't work," she insisted.

"Of course it would. We'd be free to do what we wanted. You could resign from the newspaper. We could fly to a different country where no one knows us and get married. I have plenty of money so we could set up a business.

"Do you remember that we talked about how fun it would be to run a restaurant with the kinds of food we loved? We'd build a chalet that serves cheese fondue, the kind they make in Switzerland with Kirsch and gruyere cheese. We'd be the proprietors and even dress the part. It's the food for lovers and would be a total success."

"Stop, Alex," she begged him, not wanting to revisit that month in London where she'd loved him so much anything was possible. "You don't know what you're saying."

He gripped her arms. "I'm fighting for our lives and our love, Giannina. Can you understand that?" He shook her gently, then let go of her. "Maybe I've been wrong, and you have never felt the way I feel. I was so sure of your love, I believed we could overcome anything. I didn't know you could be this afraid." A haunted look crossed over his striking features before he turned and ran back in the ocean.

Giannina stood there devastated as she watched his powerful body swim out to open water. He was right. She *was* afraid.

So deep was her misery, she didn't realize that a phone had been ringing. *His* phone. For how long she didn't know. It came from his shirt pocket lying on the sand. She ran over and pulled it out, assuming it was Zikos, but the ringing had stopped.

She knew it had to be important and called out to Alex, waving her hands. When he didn't acknowledge her, she dropped the towel and ran in the water to catch up to him.

At some point he saw her and started swimming toward her. Within touching distance now, he pulled her against him and kissed her long and hard. "Giannina, darling. I need you more than life itself. Are you ready to tell me that you'll at least consider what I've said?"

He'd misunderstood her actions in swimming out to him. She pressed her hands against his chest. "I'm still thinking about everything, but I swam out here to tell you a phone call came through for you just now. I imagine it's an important one."

His face registered frustration before he released her and swam toward the beach. She tried to keep up with him. He raced for his phone and began speaking in Croatian.

She reached for the beach towel and waited for him. When he finally hung up, he grabbed his shirt and put it on.

"What's happened?"

He turned to her with a grim countenance. "Zikos returned to Croatia. I've been summoned there, but nothing has been settled between you and me. Now I have to leave. Zikos has sent a helicopter to take me to the airport, where the jet is waiting. It should be here within a few minutes."

Her heart lurched. She couldn't bear the reality of his leaving, but she couldn't tell him what he was desperate to hear. She loved and trusted him with all her heart and soul, but to be his queen...

The second Giannina stepped away from him, he

strode swiftly toward the road leading to the villa. She hurried to catch up to him, but he was faster. When they entered the villa, he disappeared into the guest bedroom. Soon he came out with his suitcase wearing the same outfit he'd worn yesterday. The Alex who'd laid his heart at her feet moments ago was nowhere to be found.

"You're free to run the story in your paper anytime now. If you want a picture, better grab your camera. During the flight I'll call your brother to thank him for his hospitality and everything else he's done. It goes without saying that I owe you a great deal for your part in all of this."

She was in so much pain she could hardly function, yet she managed to run to her bedroom and pull the camera out of the case. At the same time, she heard a helicopter landing.

With no time to lose, Giannina flew out the back of the villa to the pad. The helicopter seemed to float down, but the rotors kept going, creating a breeze. A man appeared in the opening and took the suitcase from Alex. They talked for a moment.

"Alex?" she called to him. He turned in time for her to snap his picture as he climbed inside. She kept taking shots until the door closed. Her heart plunged to the ground as the helicopter rose in the air.

Alex, Alex.

Dying inside, she raced back to the villa and phoned Nico.

"Giannina? How are things going?"

"Before I answer any questions, could you send the

helicopter for me right now? Ask the pilot to take me directly to the newspaper."

"Of course. Hold on."

She didn't have to wait long before he came back on the line. "Where's Alex?"

"He just left on a helicopter his uncle Zikos sent for him."

"Finally Hellenia has a king again."

"Yes, Nico." Her voice shook. "I have his story and a picture. As soon as I get back to the office, I'll arrange for this to be the breaking news for tomorrow morning."

"It'll be the most amazing headline anywhere in the world."

"I know," she muttered.

"Hey—are you all right?"

"No, and I never will be again."

"Obviously something's wrong. I'll meet you at your office."

"You don't need to do that."

"I think I do. See you soon."

He hung up before she did. Since the helicopter would be here shortly, she rang Anna on the house phone to tell her Alex had gone and she would be leaving. She thanked the older woman for her help and hurried to the bedroom to pack her things.

The story she'd printed off lay on the kitchen counter. She'd keep it as a souvenir of her time with Alex and put it in her purse. When she heard the sound of the helicopter, she hurried out to the pad carrying her suitcase.

"Thanks for coming, Charon." She knew Nico's pilot well.

"Happy to oblige, Giannina." He made certain she was strapped in before they took off and headed back to Salonica.

"The boss says you have a deadline."

She nodded. "You'll read what it's all about when you see the newspaper in the morning."

He smiled. "Now you've got me real curious. Bad news, or good?"

"Good. The best there could be."

"It's about time."

"Agreed."

The short flight got her back to the city in time for her to say good-night to Khloe before she left for the night.

"Welcome home," her assistant cried. "I've missed you. Can't wait to hear what you've been doing."

"Come in my office and I'll give you a brief version."

"Whoa," Khloe cried out minutes later and rolled her eyes.

Giannina smiled. "Whoa is right. Now tell me how everything is around here."

She chuckled. "Chaotic as usual."

Giannina nodded. "Of course."

"I've left notes on your desk."

"Thank you. You're the best and deserve a bonus. I appreciate your taking over at a moment's notice. I'll see you tomorrow."

Once back at her desk, she called the guys putting out tomorrow's paper and asked them to come up to her office. When they arrived, she said, "You'll have to scrap the front page. We have a new one that takes precedence. I want the layout to be up style, with a noble feel that will stand the test of time. Don't let me down."

The guys stared at her in surprise.

"You're all sworn to secrecy until tomorrow morning when the paper comes out. I've downloaded the story and the picture that goes with it. This is so important it has to be perfect!"

No sooner had they left her office to get started than Nico swept inside. She jumped up to hug him. "Thank you for sending the helicopter. I don't know what I'd do without you." Her voice wobbled.

"Tell me what's wrong."

"Oh, Nico. That's such a loaded question."

"You're a newspaper woman. Just give me the nuts and bolts."

"It's complicated."

Alex flew to Dubrovnik to debrief. Zikos had arrived from Loria earlier in the day. The two of them talked into the night.

When morning came, Marko brought them breakfast and several copies of the *Halkidiki News*.

Alex sat there sipping his coffee while Zikos reached for one and read it. "This story was underplayed and an absolute masterpiece. So is the picture."

"All of it was Gianinna's idea. She wanted action."

"Her excellent taste tells me a great deal more about her. She'll make you an exceptional queen."

On that note Alex got up from the dining chair, so

restless he couldn't sit still. "She doesn't want to be my queen."

Zikos's brows lifted. "But you've already asked her to marry you."

He threw his head back. "I did. She agreed to marry Philip but that man no longer exists."

Zikos lowered his head, no doubt disturbed by everything he'd told him.

"I'm sorry, son. You have to be in terrible pain. This is one time when I feel inadequate and am at a complete loss what to say to you."

Alex took a deep breath and turned to him. "The fact that you've always been here for me and are listening to me now makes me the luckiest of men. As for Giannina, I can't imagine loving another woman and will have to find a way to live with the pain."

He picked up the other copy of the newspaper and looked at the photo she'd taken as he'd climbed in the helicopter. Their conversation on the phone that night would stay with him forever.

Zikos stood up. "Now that the news is out, it'll be all over the media and we're going to be overrun with people. I suggest we pack and drive to the airport. From there we'll fly to Loria and take the royal helicopter directly to the palace. There's a whole staff and government officials loyal to your family waiting to welcome you home. They'll be overjoyed to see you back."

"You're right. Let's do it, Uncle."

Three hours later they landed on the pad to the east of the royal palace. Alex hadn't touched down on Hellenian soil for fourteen years. His emotions were running rampant when he saw a crowd of people waiting to greet him.

Some faces he recognized. The moment became surreal as he jumped down and was besieged with well-wishers shouting in Greek, "Long live Prince Alexandros!"

The hugging went on and on. On his way in to the palace, a man probably Alex's age drew his attention. "You probably don't remember me. I'm Evander, the gardener's son."

Alex nodded. "Of course I do. You and I used to play together."

The other man beamed. "On the day you disappeared, I saw your dog, Achilles, running around outside, barking. He couldn't find you and was upset. I took him home with me and kept him until he died nine years later. We became best friends, but he always looked for you."

For a moment Alex couldn't speak. He put a hand on Evander's shoulder. "You have no idea how grateful and relieved I am to hear this news. All these years I've missed him and wondered what happened to him. Are you a gardener too?"

"I still help my father."

"I remember you were an expert with cars and wanted to work on them one day."

He shook his head. "I've dreamed of working in a body shop, but the general wouldn't allow me to leave the estate."

Alex gritted his teeth. "Are you married?"

"Yes. We have a son."

"Lucky you. I'm indebted to you, Evander, and you'll be rewarded for what you've done."

"That's not important. When you're not busy, I'll be happy to show you where I buried Achilles. The general never knew what I did."

Alex fought not to break down. "Does your father still work here?"

"Yes."

"Then I'll seek him out and get word to you."

"Welcome home, Your Highness."

"Thank you, Evander." He hugged him extra hard. The loyal gardener's son had just given Alex an idea, one he wanted to discuss with Giannina if she would talk to him. "You've made this a homecoming I'll never forget."

CHAPTER EIGHT

GIANNINA WENT TO her parents' home the morning that the newspaper came out. They and her aunt Olga were overjoyed with the news that the prince had been found. Nico and his wife, Alexa, joined them. They brought her grandfather Gavril with them. He'd been a former diplomat for Greece who'd admired the royal family.

Throughout the day they talked about everything, turning it into a celebration, but Giannina was in pain the entire time. She wondered where Alex was now and what he was doing. For once, playing with little Nico didn't help. She envied her brother and his wife for being able to marry and produce such an adorable baby. Alex wanted a family and would make the most wonderful father.

Near the end of the evening she and Nico took their aunt aside and told her about Ari's involvement. Her brother had waited so he and Giannina could tell her together. They needed to do it now because of the leaks and wanted their aunt to hear the news first before the article was run. She handled it amazingly well knowing he'd been arrested.

She grasped their hands and said, "My love for Ari died years ago. He had a great flaw that grew worse with time. God will punish him. You don't have to worry about me. Thank you for telling me the truth."

At nine that night Giannina kissed everyone good-night and drove her car back to her apartment. After being with her loving family, the thought of Alex not being there was too much. Tears streamed down her face. She couldn't imagine how she would get through the rest of her life never seeing him again.

He'd suggested they find a new country and set up their lives there. Intoxicating as that sounded, she knew he'd been desperate to suggest anything so ludicrous. Giannina felt desperate too, and irrational. If she knew where to find him right now, she'd fly to him and beg him to make love to her. If she could lie in his arms forever, she would.

On her way up in the elevator, her cell rang. Alex? Her heart jumped as she pulled it out of her purse and checked the caller ID.

Nico.

She called him back immediately. "What's wrong?"

"That's what I need to ask you. I knew you weren't yourself today. Neither was Alex when he called me earlier. The man's crazy about you. I'm here if you want to talk about it."

"You're the best. He's asked me to marry him."

"But—"

"I—I wouldn't know how to be a queen."

"Does anyone? Chances are he doesn't know how to be a king. If you love him, and I know you do, then be a good wife to him. That's what he wants, right? It'll help him be a good king."

"Oh, Nico. You make so much sense, I'm in awe." Her voice shook.

"I'm glad. I think you're making a mountain out of a mole hill. As I recall you had the same fear when Baba made you editor-in-chief."

"You're right. I was terrified."

"Yet it all worked out. Have faith in yourself, Giannina."

"I'll try."

The last time she'd been inside her apartment, Alex had come with her. She looked around, feeling an intense loneliness she'd never experienced before. He'd changed her to the point she didn't know herself anymore.

Needing noise, anything, she turned on the news in time to see a broadcast with the picture she'd taken of Alex leaving Nico's villa. "His Highness Prince Alexandros is back home today in Loria, Hellenia, after fourteen years of exile. The world is cheering the arrest of the ruthless General Ruiz, who put unbearable burdens on the Hellenian people.

"None of us will forget the brutal murders of the king and queen of Hellenia. Today we can all rejoice in the triumphant return of the prince. I, for one, eagerly await news from His Highness of his plans to restore a kingdom that has been ravaged by virtual civil war."

By now Giannina was in agony and turned it off. The whole world expected him to rule in the place of his father. For him to give that up to marry her because she didn't want to be queen sounded like...like the pout of an incorrigible, spoiled, silly, immature, stupid, out-of-control little girl without the sense she'd been born with.

For some reason she couldn't explain, she'd been destined to meet a man who'd turned out to become a king. It wasn't his fault or hers. They met and fell in love. It happened.

He could never be a government worker like he'd insisted he would do in order to make marriage palatable to her. His country wouldn't stand for it. No— if she wanted to be his wife, she would have to turn herself into a queen, for better or worse. But how did you do that?

Nico had told her to be a good wife and the rest would follow. But it still meant learning about a whole other world and how to act. It meant teaching any children they would have that they'd been given the most unusual role in life any child could have. What if their children didn't want a royal life and rebelled against it? What if she tried, but couldn't handle it? Her questions were endless.

There were other solutions. She could either remain single in life, or eventually marry a man who led an ordinary existence. Their children wouldn't be governed by royal rules. But that was the problem. So far, no man leading an ordinary existence had come along to sweep her off her feet.

Philip had been the only man who'd changed her world. Why couldn't Alex have remained Philip? His unmasking revealed another man who'd lived another life totally foreign to her. Alex had accused her of being afraid. He wasn't a superb journalist for nothing and had found her vulnerability.

She *was* afraid, *terrified* of not being all the things he needed.

An ordinary housewife had its many challenges, but to be his queen meant something else so entirely different… What if she failed him or somehow inhibited his ability to rule? What if she disappointed him and he would have to tolerate her? What if he fell out of love with her?

Giannina knew he admired her skill as a journalist and editor. But what if she couldn't measure up to his vision of how they would be together as rulers of his country? She'd been born a Greek citizen. Would his people accept her nationality? She could apply for Hellenian citizenship, but would she always be viewed as an outsider?

When his country learned that her uncle had been one of the monsters who'd murdered their king and queen, would it change their feelings about the prince's choice of wife? Had Alex even thought about that? Would the parliament try to prevent their marriage? If they did marry, would they demand a dissolution of it in order for him to marry a suitable royal they could be proud of?

So many questions bombarded her until she sobbed into the pillow and drenched it. In this sorry state, her phone rang again. She wasn't up to conversation. The only thing to do was turn off her phone, but it was in her purse in the living room. She slid off the bed to get it, but almost fainted when she saw the name on the caller ID.

Her body trembled as she clicked on. "Alex?"

"Doxa to Theo," he cried in anxiety. "I called your brother to thank him for everything. He told me you'd gone back to your apartment after leaving your parents' home. I was about to call my security people to find out why you didn't answer."

She sank down in the nearest chair, astounded that he'd even called and that he'd sounded so worried. "I had to hunt for my phone."

"Nico told me you've talked with your aunt about Ari Hatzi."

She gripped the phone tighter. "Yes. She took it amazingly well."

"For your sake I'm glad. Giannina—there's something I want to share with you, but it means you'll have to come to Loria. I know nothing's been resolved between us, but this is of vital importance to me."

She couldn't prevent the slight gasp that escaped.

"Tomorrow can you arrange to stay away from your office one more day? I'll send the helicopter to your office building to pick you up at ten. It will land at the side of the royal palace and I'll be there to meet you."

Giannina knew she wanted to be with him, and the urgency in his tone convinced her. "If it's that vital, I'll be ready."

"Wear something casual since we'll be outside most of the time. Sleep well."

As if she'd get any sleep after this phone call that

had shaken her to the core. Once she heard the click, she hung up.

Wear something casual. She appreciated the suggestion since she'd feel like a fool showing up over-dressed and wearing high heels in front of the staff. Being outside meant walking shoes. She had a favorite pair of khaki pants she would tone with a creamy-orange-and-white sleeveless top.

Toss and turn. That described her night. She awakened early and spent time getting ready. Hair, nails, makeup, including a pink lipstick. She left the apartment and walked to work to calm her nerves. After she reached the office, she grabbed a bite of food in the lunchroom before seeking out Khloe.

"Wow!" her assistant remarked. "You look fabulous. Where are you going?"

"I have a ten o'clock appointment and don't know when I'll be back. Would you mind taking over until I return?"

"This wouldn't have to do with that gorgeous Prince Alexandros would it? Until I saw his picture, I didn't think any man was better-looking that Philip Dimas." Her eyes gleamed.

Khloe, Khloe. "He's a hunk, all right."

"You knocked the newspaper out of the ball park with those headlines yesterday. The guys downstairs haven't stopped talking about it and the phone hasn't stopped ringing. I've dozens of calls from other news-papers to return."

"That's good, Khloe, and puts our paper on the map. The guys did a great job on the layout. Be sure to let them know there's a bonus for them and, of course, one for you. I couldn't get along without you."

"Aw, thanks, boss."

Giannina smiled. "Now I have to leave. Talk to you soon."

After years of planning for this day, Alex and Zikos had contractors already on-site for a complete renovation of the three-story palace. They'd arranged for the staff to live elsewhere and paid their salaries until they could return.

It was going to take time, but the result would be worth it. He hardly recognized it for the home he'd once lived in. The last thing he wanted was any evidence that the general had ever occupied it. He'd turned it into a third world compound that had been filled with his cronies and licentious living. Everywhere it reeked of smoke and had deteriorated beyond recognition.

Everything needed to be redone, including a demolition of his parents' spacious apartment at the rear of the palace on the first floor. But he had no idea what to do with that area.

Dressed in jeans and a T-shirt, Alex left the hotel in town where he and Zikos were staying. The large conference rooms could hold the parliament while they made future plans to get the country started again.

One of the first things he'd already done was have the huge spotlights, guard posts, barricades and electronic gates removed from around the palatial estate. He bought a car and drove to the woods at the rear of the estate, wanting to inspect the tiny summerhouse he'd told Giannina about.

By some miracle it hadn't been damaged, but everything else was a disaster.

As Alex walked around the palace surveying the changes he wanted made to the exterior and landscaping, he checked his watch. The helicopter should be arriving any minute.

There'd been little sleep for him last night. Giannina dominated every thought. If she'd changed her mind at the last second and had decided not to come…

It wasn't long until he heard sounds that had him running toward the pad. When the helicopter landed, he opened the door without waiting for the rotors to stop.

"Alex—"

Giannina looked like a vision. He reached out to grip her waist and hugged her to him before lowering her to the ground. "I thought you'd never get here," he whispered into her hair. She'd worn it loose and flowing the way he loved it. "Welcome to Loria."

Her light brown gaze glanced all around. "What's going on?"

"As you can see, the general destroyed everything beautiful about my home, so it's undergoing a face-lift inside and out of gigantic proportions."

"Are you really safe here now?" She looked anxious.

"He's gone forever, and I have bodyguards on me day and night."

"Even so. How awful for you to have to come home to see this!"

"Don't worry. I knew I wouldn't recognize it, but that doesn't matter. It's in the right hands now and one day soon it will be restored to its former glory."

"Obviously you're not staying here."

"Zikos and I have made the Hotel Poseidon our temporary headquarters." He put his arm around her shoulders. "Come on. There's someone I want you to meet."

He led her to the other side of the palace where he found Evander waiting for him. "Giannina Angelis? Let me introduce you to an old friend, Evander Corso. His father was the head gardener in my father's time. He and I pretty well grew up together."

Her eyes glowed. "I was hoping you'd find a friend. How wonderful! It's so nice to meet you, Evander."

His friend stared at her in male admiration. Giannina was a great beauty and had never looked more breathtaking than this morning. "It's my pleasure, Kyria Angelis."

Alex pulled her closer, inhaling the sweet scent of her hair. "Evander has something to show me. Since it's a surprise, I wanted you to be with me."

"That sounds exciting."

"If both of you will follow me." Alex kept his arm around her as Evander led them along a path into the woods. Before long he slowed down. "This is the place."

She saw the two-foot-high white headstone at the same time Alex did. It was inscribed with the likeness of a Posavac hunting dog. The inscription read, "Here rests Achilles, the noble hound of his noble master,

Prince Alexandros. He looks down from heaven, waiting to run with him again one day."

"Oh, Alex—"

Tears streamed down her cheeks. Before he knew it, she'd left him long enough to hug Evander. When she stepped away from him, she said, "This gift has to be Alex's greatest treasure. No man could ever have a better friend than you.

"I love you for doing this for him, Evander. I was only twelve when he disappeared, but I'd been here a year earlier with my father. Alex and I ran around the grounds with him. I always wondered what happened to him."

"He was a special dog."

Her warmth and charm spoke to Alex's heart. Needing her more than ever, he pulled her against him. "Evander found my dog wandering around after I was taken away. He took the dog home and cared for him until he died nine years ago. I'll be indebted to you forever, Evander."

The other man blinked away his tears. "I loved Achilles too."

Alex had to clear his throat to talk. "This gift takes away any pain I felt at coming back to the palace. Thank you, my good friend."

"It's an honor to know you're going to be my king."

"We don't know what the future holds yet, Evander." He'd told Giannina he would work for the government and not be the king if that was what she wanted. Nothing was more important than to go through life with her.

"I do," Evander said in solemn voice. "Not all sons

born to a king will make a good king, let alone a great one. That doesn't apply to you, Your Highness. We all loved you and have lived for the day when you would be found and wear the crown. Now I must leave you and go to work. It's been an honor, Kyria Angelis."

"And mine."

He walked away, leaving them alone. Giannina lifted her face to Alex. "When you told me you had something of vital importance to show me, I never dreamed anything could touch me more. You must be overwhelmed by what he's done for you. What a sweet man. Imagine having such a friend. I meant it when I said I love him for what he did."

"I love him too," Alex murmured. "And I've got a thought how to show him my appreciation."

She knelt in front of the monument to trace the lines of the dog's head. "Is he a gardener too?"

Alex looked down at her. "Not from choice. He and his wife live with his father. The general refused to let him leave the compound. He's married with a child, but he always loved cars and wanted to work in a body shop."

"Maybe you could make it possible for him to get a job in town."

"That's a good idea. Before we do anything else, let's see about it now. After that, I want to take you on a tour of the palace and get your ideas for designing the interior. I'm starting from scratch."

She turned her head to glance at him. "My ideas?"

"You're a woman. I'd value any input you could give me. This is all new to me. But first, our errand."

He walked her along the path and out to his car. "I'm thinking we'll stop by a certain Realtor's office first. I noticed earlier he's still in business since my father's time. Maybe he's got some ideas."

The drive didn't take long. Alex pulled up in front and helped her out.

"Your Highness!" the older owner cried in surprise when they walked in together. It wasn't a surprise to Alex, whose pictures were all over the media since his story had come out. He was glad to see that no one else was around yet. "It *is* you, all grown up! What a great honor. We've waited and waited years for news of you."

"I've waited a long time too. Allow me to present Kyria Angelis."

"A great pleasure, *kyria*."

"Perhaps you can do me a special favor, but it has to remain a secret between the two of us. No one else."

"Anything, Your Highness. Anything! Please, both of you sit down."

"Thank you. There's a man, Evander Corso. He works with cars. In your business you get around and see things. Is there a body shop for sale?"

The Realtor looked through his listings and found three throughout the 2,200-square-mile island of Hellenia.

"Are any in Loria?"

"One." He nodded. "The owner is asking a steep price I fear he won't get."

Alex nodded. "What about houses for sale in that same area?"

The older man spread his hands. "How big?"

"Enough room for a family of four, maybe more." Alex turned to her. "I'm thinking he might want his father with him."

"That would be perfect, Alex."

"I will find what I can."

"Excellent." Alex got to his feet. "I want you to call him at this phone number." He'd written the number of Evander's father on a card. "I've also put my credit card number on there." In an aside to Giannina, he said, "My savings as Philip Dimas come in handy at a time like this."

Her response was an illuminating smile.

He turned to the Realtor. "When you can arrange it, I'd like you to show him everything. If he likes what he sees, give him the keys and inform him the places are his. Put the bill on my card."

Giannina clutched his arm hard, giving him her approval.

"When he asks what's going on, tell him this is repayment for his care of my dog, Achilles. He'll understand. There's a big bonus in this for you too. Remember—this is between us."

While the Realtor stood there in a daze, they went out to the car and left for the palace. "It feels good to do something for a friend as exceptional as Evander."

"You've done something so marvelous, I'm close to speechless."

"I'm glad you were with me, Giannina." He loved her playing a part in everything. Life without her would be incomprehensible. "Now to tackle the palace."

"Do you want to re-create it in the original?"

"Not completely. I'd like to modernize to some extent and make it even more comfortable, especially for children." *Our children, Giannina.*

Once they reached the palace, he gripped her hand and walked with her to one of the side entrances. Workmen filled the interior, but they stopped to stare at Giannina. No man alive could be immune to her feminine allure.

"Come this way." He led her down a hall to a huge extension at the back of the palace. "Let me warn you now. This was my parents' bedroom and suite."

She groaned and hugged his arm tighter. "I can't bear it."

"Neither can I. Something radical has to be done here."

After a minute she started walking, then spun around. "I know. Why don't you open it up and turn this whole area at the back of the palace into a memorial garden? Can their remains be transferred here?"

"Yes."

"Then do it! Visitors can come and pay respect to your parents. The people never got the chance all those years ago. It would be a permanent way to honor them."

A memorial garden? Where did this marvelous woman come from?

He walked over and gripped her upper arms. "I knew I was inspired to ask you to fly here. You've solved my greatest concern and lifted that terrible weight from my heart. I love you, Giannina. You're the most precious person in my life. I can't live without you."

"I love you too," she cried, "but—"

"No *buts*, darling." Cupping her face in his hands, he lowered his head and kissed her luscious mouth, mindless of time and place. "I'm going to ask again. Will you marry me?" His mouth roved over her features, kissing her everywhere. "I promise we'll have a wonderful life. We need each other. You know we do."

She couldn't deny her need of him. She loved him heart, mind and soul, but she couldn't tell him yes. Not yet. Maybe never.

"Will you give me more time to think about it?" she questioned against his lips. "I can't think when you're holding and kissing me like this. You were born a prince and have planned for years what was expected of you. After the way Evander responded to you today, it's clear you're meant to rule. Give me a little more time."

"I will, because we love each other. Like any married couple, we'll make it work. Right now I want to show you the rest of the palace that will be our home once we're married."

CHAPTER NINE

IT WAS IMPOSSIBLE to refuse Alex and so she went on the tour with him. She couldn't believe the damage done by the cruel despot, but she saw the beauty in the bones of the neoclassic structure.

"My apartment is on the second floor." He grasped her hand as they made their way up the grand staircase. "This was my room."

French-pane bay windows looked out on a forest of deep green. Though most of the glass had been shattered and lay scattered on the floor, Giannina loved the design.

"Would you still like this to be your room?"

He stood behind her and wrapped his arms around her waist. "If you mean *our* room, I think we'd be very happy in here. I used to look out these windows for wildlife. A family of red deer would appear once in a while. I left fruit out for them."

She smiled. "Did they find it?"

He kissed her neck. "I'm sure they did because by the next day it had disappeared."

His stories delighted her.

"There are bedrooms on either side of this room for our children. One of them could be made into a nursery adjoining this one. On the third floor you'll find more bedrooms and what used to be a playroom, but I think you'd enjoy seeing the first floor."

He led her down the elegant staircase to the main rooms, where she found more men working.

"We had a music room with a grand piano and an impressive library. All the treasures, furniture, paintings and books were destroyed. Ruiz not only wanted to take over our country, he enjoyed destroying anything owned by the rich monarchists.

"He'd planned the assault on Hellenia for several years with my parents being the initial target. It came one night in a surprise attack that weakened security and virtually the nation."

Giannina shivered.

"The next thing I plan to do will be to organize our security in a way that such an attack can never happen again. The nation needs to feel safe before anything else. Without the proper policing and allies, chaos steps in every time."

Already he was on fire to establish his government. "History has proved as much. You have your work cut out, Alex."

A smile broke out on his handsome face. "But not today. I've wanted you here so you can see the kitchen and other parts of the palace. Then I'll want your feedback."

Incredible that he was talking about decorating a big palace, not an average home in the city. Taking hold of her hand, they continued the tour. So much would need to be done, but he didn't seem daunted. If anything, she found him energized. He hadn't been Europe's venerated journalist for nothing.

"There's one more thing to show you." He kissed her passionately before taking her out the front entrance.

She let out a cry of surprise. Forty steps the width of the palace leading up to the entrance filled her vision. Beyond them, a glimpse of the city of Loria. "How spectacular!"

"Walk down with me."

Excited, they descended together.

"Now turn around."

Giannina did his bidding. "Oh, Alex—" She was breathless from the sight of the exquisite yellow-and-white facade above. This was the only part of the palace that hadn't been ruined.

The second floor had an ornate balustrade that ran the width of the palace along with a colonnade. A fantastic ridge work with a taller centerpiece outlined the third floor and roof. "I've never seen anything so beautiful in my life."

"Neither have I." But he wasn't looking up. His eyes blazed like black fires as he stared at her. She felt their heat to the deepest recesses of her being before he gave her a kiss to die for.

When he finally relinquished her mouth, he said, "We've done enough for today and I've exhausted you. Let's get you back to the helicopter, but I won't make you climb these steps."

Before she knew what was happening, he picked

her up like a bride and carried her up all forty to the entrance without being out of breath. "I've dreamed of doing this with my new wife."

She hid her face in his shoulder while Alex walked them past the workmen. He made for the side entrance that led to the helicopter. The copilot opened the door and helped her climb in the back. Alex followed and took the seat next to her. In a quick move he leaned over to kiss her and fasten her in.

"What are you doing?"

"Coming with you." He gave instructions to the pilot before strapping himself in. "A limo will be waiting for us at Salonica airport and we'll go out for dinner. I feel like celebrating with you as the man I really am."

She frowned. "You'll be mobbed, Alex."

"There's no time like this evening for a trial run. If you marry me, this will be our life from now on. Why not find out what it feels like?"

"But we're not married. Aren't you concerned about being seen with me? Think of all the unnecessary gossip it will generate."

"Giannina—I have news for you. No one will be looking at me. Every male out there will be wishing he could be with the most beautiful woman to come out of the Aegean."

Within seconds the helicopter was once again in motion and they rose in the air. "I wish you'd be serious. This isn't something to joke about and you know it."

He clasped her hand and squeezed it. "I've asked you to come live with me as my wife forever. How can I be more serious than that? I know you're worried about being married to a royal. Have you considered that I might be worried about not measuring up to your expectations?"

The question brought her up short. She jerked her head toward him. "You couldn't be!"

"I'm only human, remember?"

She lowered her head. "You're braver than I am."

"I must be, otherwise I wouldn't have found the courage to propose to the famous beauty who ruined me for other women even as a young girl."

Warmth rushed into her face. "I was equally enamored by you, Alex."

He kissed the palm of her hand. "Why don't we take it one step at a time. This evening will be an experiment as a potential royal couple." Alex had the kind of confidence that made him exceptional. She needed to take Nico's advice and have faith in herself.

She looked out the window in time to see Salonica rush up to meet them. Soon they climbed down from the helicopter and got in the limo waiting for them. Giannina gripped his arm.

"I'm nervous to go out in public with you, Alex. By now, news about the general and my uncle is all over the media. Everyone will know that he helped murder your parents. Being seen with me could prevent the parliament from backing you. You mustn't do anything that could backfire on your dreams at this point."

His black brows furrowed. "You think I haven't considered all that long ago? The parliament will have to take me 'warts and all.' If they don't, then everything's off the table because I refuse to lose you."

On that note, he told the chauffeur to drive them to the Taverna Kaza, a restaurant near the White Tower with a live band.

"I've heard of it, but never been there."

"The concierge at my hotel recommended it to me. We can go dressed as we are. He said it's a favorite place for lovers who want to dance the night away."

That explained why she'd never eaten there. Philip had gotten in the way of every possible relationship. Because of that, Giannina hadn't wanted to be physically close to the men she'd occasionally dated.

"You look gorgeous." He pressed a kiss to her succulent lips. "We haven't been dancing for three years. I need this night with you."

Even on a Wednesday night, crowds filled the streets. It had been a long time since Alex had been able to relax and enjoy a summer night with his heart's desire. There was a festive feel with music coming from several establishments in the area.

He knew Giannina didn't want to be out with him where he could be recognized, but it was necessary. He'd thrown off the shackles of his disguise and she needed to see them function as a normal couple.

The restaurant with its potted flowers and trees had a certain charm. He'd reserved a table under his given name, but no HRH. Once inside, the host snapped his fingers to the waiter who took them to their table and handed them menus. The younger man couldn't take his eyes off Giannina.

"I thought he'd never leave," Alex said after he

walked away. "The same thing happened when we went out to dinner in London. They'd line up to stare at you."

"I'm not listening to this." She studied the menu. "Everything looks good, but I'm in the mood for moussaka."

"That appeals to me too, and their best house wine."

The eager waiter soon came back to take their order, his eyes all over her. Alex could forgive him. The first time he'd seen her at his lecture, he'd probably looked as pathetic as the waiter.

"Alone at last," he muttered after the younger man had gone. "Let's dance. I need to feel your body against mine."

Without giving her a chance to say they'd better not, he walked around the table and drew her out of the chair. Only a few couples were on the dance floor.

Alex pulled her into his arms. The touch of her, the brush of her elegant legs against his, electrified him. Maybe this wasn't such a good idea after all. Once they ate, he wanted to go back to her apartment and love her into oblivion.

"Enjoying yourself?" He kissed her ear and neck.

"I'm trying to."

"Surely you're used to people looking at you. Men particularly."

"Alex—I don't like being stared at, but that isn't what's wrong. Don't you understand that I'm worried?"

"That's why I brought you here, to get used to the water."

"I'm not talking about my first swim in the ocean."

He chuckled and kissed her cheek. "In a way, that's

exactly what we're doing. Taking a dip together where the world can see us. So far nothing disastrous has happened. If you noticed, our meal has arrived. I suggest we enjoy it while it's hot, then I promise we'll get back in the limo."

"Thank goodness."

He danced her off the floor and walked her to their table. Though he enjoyed the food and wine, Giannina struggled. Alex knew this was a new experience for her, but until now he hadn't realized the depth of her fear at the thought of marrying a royal.

What better proof than to be out with her now and feel her wanting to leave the restaurant as soon as they could. Tonight had not turned out to be the celebration he'd hoped for.

Alex told the waiter they wouldn't be ordering dessert. But after paying the bill, he escorted her back to the dance floor and pulled her into him. "I could do this all night. Just close your eyes and pretend we're the only two people on the planet."

"Don't I wish," she whispered against his jaw.

"Hold on to me and never let me go. I need you in my arms."

"I love being in them, Alex."

"But you still want to leave. We'll go." He kissed her quickly, then led her outside the taverna. They had to walk past dozens of people to reach the corner where the limo waited for them.

She hurriedly climbed in the back without his help. He slid in after her and closed the door, giving the chauffeur instructions to her apartment. Once they drove off, he felt the tension leave her body.

"I won't ask you if you had a good time, Giannina."

"I'm sure I ruined it for you. Forgive me for my behavior tonight."

He put his arm around her shoulders. "I forgive you anything. I love you. Our first swim together wasn't so bad."

She swung her head toward him. "I loved being with you, and the Hellenians love you. But they're not going to forgive you for being seen with the niece of Ari Hatzi. It's ludicrous to imagine a marriage after what he did to your parents. Admit it!"

He put his head back with a sigh. "I agree this is something we'll have to wade through. But most people are forgiving and will realize you had nothing to do with the man who married your aunt. Give them time and they'll come around."

"I don't believe that."

Alex knew he wouldn't be winning this argument tonight. He told the driver to pull around the back of her apartment building. "I'm coming in with you to say good-night."

"No, Alex. It would be better to end this now."

That was panic talking loud and clear. "In that case I want one last kiss."

He pulled her into his arms and fought for her mouth until she surrendered. Their passion took over. When neither of them could breathe, he lifted his mouth from hers.

"You know damn well this will never be over, but I'll let you go in alone this time." He reached across her and opened the door for her to get out. "I'm not going to tell you to sleep well since I know I won't. You'll be hearing from me shortly."

Giannina stared at him with a tormented expression. "For your own sake, you mustn't be seen with me. This has to be it." In the next instant, she got out of the car and hurried past the guard at the back entrance.

"Take me to the heliport," Alex told the driver.

By the time he'd arrived at the hotel in Loria, it was after midnight and too late to talk to Zikos. Tomorrow would come soon enough. For the rest of the night he would dream of Giannina.

At seven the next morning Alex rang for breakfast and called Zikos to let him know he was back.

"I'm glad you called. You have trouble."

"Bad?"

"Come to my room and we'll talk."

"I'll be right there."

When he entered the hotel room, he discovered Zikos at a table surrounded with half a dozen newspapers. They glanced at each other. "There's a photo I want to show you from one of the Greek tabloids. Naturally it made the front page and will be on television nonstop."

Alex took the newspaper from him and couldn't miss the picture of him and Giannina outside the entrance of the restaurant. The headline read:

His Royal Highness Prince Alexandros enjoys Salonica's night life with Giannina Angelis, editor-in-chief of the *Halkidiki News*

Beneath the headline it went on to explain she was the niece of Ari Hatzi, the killer recently imprisoned for the murders of the king and queen of Hellenia committed fourteen years ago.

There was more, but he stopped reading.

Zikos looked up at him. "I've had a call from the parliament spokesman wanting an explanation."

"So it has started." Alex wadded the paper in his hands.

"They don't know of your romantic involvement with her. When we've been so careful, it's understandable they want to hear details. A meeting with you is set up for a half hour from now in the hotel conference room."

Alex nodded. He needed to let Giannina know about the news in the tabloid before she heard it from anyone else. But he'd have to phone her after he'd met with them to get a temperature reading. "Any advice, Uncle?"

"Talk from the heart, my son. Be straightforward like you always are and see where it leads."

The time had come. Whatever happened, he and Giannina would never be separated.

"Good morning, boss."

"Thanks for holding down the fort, Khloe."

"Happy to oblige. Hey—you look exhausted."

"That's because I am." She hadn't slept last night and still didn't have the answer Alex wanted to hear.

Her assistant grinned. "I think I know the reason why."

Sometimes Khloe's needling could be a little exasperating. "What are you talking about?"

"This!" She handed her a copy of the *Thessalonika Sentinel*. "It came out this morning. You and the prince make one gorgeous couple."

Gianinna's mouth went dry before she reached for the local tabloid. After reading the whole story, she felt light-headed and dashed to her office to think. Last night he'd told her she'd be hearing from him, but so far he hadn't tried to get in touch with her or shown up at her apartment.

She could phone him now but changed her mind. The story in the tabloid had proved her point. Her mind was made up once and for all. Before the day was out, Alex needed to hear her answer to his proposal in person. A phone call wouldn't do.

Without hesitation she alerted the helicopter pilot she needed to fly to Loria immediately. After arranging for a rental car to meet her at the Loria heliport, she clutched her purse and dashed out of her office to Khloe's.

"I must leave on important business. Sorry to do this to you again, but I have no choice. Call my brother if something comes up you're worried about."

She eyed her curiously. "Sure, boss."

Giannina flew out the door to the elevator that took her to the roof, where the helicopter waited. The pilot opened the door for her.

"Thanks, Gus." She climbed in back and buckled up for the short flight to Loria.

The island country of Hellenia sparkled like a jewel

in the deep blue water. From the air it had always resembled her idea of a dreamy secret land created by Zeus himself. But having seen the desecration of the palace firsthand, that picture had been ruined for her. Her stomach knotted when she contemplated how Alex must have felt after his return from exile.

Pleased that a car stood waiting for her at the Hellenia heliport, she drove into Loria and found the Hotel Poseidon on the car's GPS tracker. It was one of the huge hotels that attracted tourists from all over the world.

Alex had told her that under the general, Hellenia's economy had gone into a recession. But with the civil war over and Alex at the helm, she knew it would start to recover.

One of the men at the front desk smiled at her. "May I help you?"

"I hope so. I'm here to see Prince Alexandros. Would you ring his room to see if he's in?"

Surprise broke out on his face. He had every right to assume this was a joke. "May I tell him who's inquiring?"

"Kyria Angelis of the *Halkidiki News* in Salonica."

"Ah—one moment please." She waited while he rang the room. After a minute he hung up. "I'm sorry. There's no answer."

"Will you leave a message that I'm here and trying to reach him? Tell him I'll go to the palace to wait for him."

"Very good."

"Thank you."

In all probability he'd already gone there earlier that morning. Maybe she'd catch up to him. Since she hadn't eaten, she stopped at a drive-through for a *yeero*, then drove on.

Today when she reached the palace grounds, she noticed that all the barricades and gates had been removed. Thank heaven it no longer resembled an anarchist's compound.

The magnificent facade came into view. She slowed down. To think this had been Alex's home until that horrific night. Her heart sank before she drove around the perimeter to the rear and parked in an area near the woods. Lots of trucks and cars meant the workmen were busy inside. There didn't seem to be any sign of Alex.

He still hadn't tried to reach her. While she waited, she decided to go to the grave of Achilles. That might be the best place to say a final goodbye to Alex.

"Gentlemen?" Alex looked out at the thirty legislators assembled in the conference room. "To answer your questions about the tabloid reports that came out this morning, Giannina Angelis is the woman I'm going to marry. Zikos will attest we met three years ago in London when she was doing her journalism internship. I've been in love with her ever since."

A groundswell of murmuring ensued.

"I swear before God she had nothing to do with Ari Hatzi. There was no blood relationship. Her only sin was her connection to her beloved aunt, the sister of Estefen Angelis, the shipping magnate whom you all know. That poor woman suffered for being married to Hatzi, who used her abominably. Long before anyone knew he was a killer, she divorced him for his cruelty."

Silence filled the room. It could mean anything.

"The fact that the tabloid press printed this news so fast is a good thing. If you don't feel that the country can support me if I marry her, then I hope you find a suitable candidate soon, so you don't waste time putting Hellenia back together. That's the number one priority for all of us."

They nodded.

"Being a prince doesn't automatically make me a king. I love my country and will be happy to serve in any capacity you'll allow. Thank you."

Again, not a sound.

He and Zikos exchanged a quick glance before he left the conference room for his bedroom. Once inside, the red light on the house phone beckoned him.

Maybe it was their spokesman calling to give him news one way or the other. A surge of adrenaline rushed through him. *"Nai?"*

"Your Highness? This is the front desk." His spirits plunged. "A Kyria Angelis came to the hotel to see you an hour ago."

With that news his heart slammed into his throat. *Giannina!* "Is she still here?"

"No. She left about a half hour ago for the palace but wanted you to call her."

Could his prayers have been answered where she was concerned? *"Efcharisto."*

He flew out of the hotel and drove to the palace over the speed limit. En route, Zikos phoned and told him the parliament council would vote and deliver their decision before the end of the day. He'd let him know the outcome.

Alex thanked him and explained that Giannina had flown to Loria. He was looking for her now and would get back to him later.

When he pulled around the rear of the estate, he saw a white rental car parked near the path leading into the woods. Before he explored there, he got out of his car and raced through the palace in case she'd decided to look around.

None of the workmen had seen her.

Now he knew where she'd gone…

Sure enough he found her sitting on the grass by the headstone with her head in her hands. She'd come dressed in a stunning white summer suit with dark blue trim. White sandals adorned her feet. The sun filtered down through the leaves, spotting her glorious brunette hair with steaks of gold.

He could see her body heaving though she made no sound. Alex absorbed what was going on inside her. So much sorrow revealed a level of pain that revealed the reason for her arrival in Loria.

She'd come to say goodbye.

"Giannina?"

At the sound of her name, she lifted her head, exposing a tear-drenched face.

"Don't get up." He sat down next to her. "The front desk told me you'd come by the hotel to talk to me.

You could have phoned me from Salonica, but I have an idea why you didn't."

"What do you mean?"

"I saw that story in the *Sentinel* too. It appears your greatest nightmare has come true. We knew this was coming, but I'd hoped we'd have a few days' breather first."

"I told you it could happen," she cried.

"I know. Unfortunately a hungry journalist had to have been tipped off by a staff worker at the restaurant. All it took was one leak to set off an earthquake. No one knows better than I how that works. For eight years I made my living that way."

She avoided his gaze.

"While you were trying to reach me, members of the parliament met with me and Zikos at the hotel for an explanation of that tabloid story."

The news brought her to her feet. "What did you tell them?"

"That I've asked you to marry me."

"You didn't!" she blurted in despair. In the next breath she walked a way off to get her emotions under control.

"I also explained that if they felt the people couldn't back me because of the family tie to your uncle, then they would have to find another Hellenian to run the country."

"Oh, Alex, no-o-o." She stood with her back toward him.

He got up and moved behind her. "Before I left the

conference room, I offered my help for any job they'd
like me to do."

Her body shivered. He saw and felt it. "I don't understand why you've done this."

Alex put his arms around her waist and pulled her
against him. He buried his face in her hair. "Yes, you
do. I've borne my soul to you. Ever since we met and
fell in love, I've been able to handle anything believing that in the end we'd be together."

She shook her head. "It isn't too late to speak to
them again. All you have to do is let them know we're
not getting married."

"But we *are* because I'll never give up on you, Giannina. If I have to wait four, five or ten years for you,
you're the woman I want."

"You're not listening to me, Alex! Uncle Ari's
crimes can never be washed away for you. Your country has suffered so terribly for what he did. Do you
honestly think they can forgive you for marrying me
when I'll be a constant reminder of Ari? It doesn't matter that I didn't have anything to do with him. It's in
their heads. They'll never let it go."

"Giannina," he murmured, running his hands up
and down her arms. "If anyone has a right to hate him
and never forgive him, I do. But it didn't stop me from
loving you when I found out what he did. I'm depending on the parliament to understand the circumstances
and feel the same way. Before evening I expect to hear
what they've decided."

"I promise that they won't want you to have anything to do with me." Her voice shook.

He whirled her around, staring directly into her eyes. "If that's the case, we'll leave the country as I suggested and start our life somewhere else. I could buy us a failing newspaper. With you as the editor, we could work together and make it great. I can't imagine life without you in it and know in my gut you feel the same way."

"Alex—you're not an ordinary person. Please don't pretend that you are."

"I've been Philip Dimas for fourteen years, an ordinary guy who got a journalism degree. It's the kind of work I know and am pretty good at."

She slid her soft hands against his cheeks. "Yet all this time Prince Alexandros has lived inside you, waiting to get out."

"*Agape mou*—don't you understand? He'll always be inside me, but it's not the sum total of who I am. Don't we want to have children? To watch them grow? Don't we want to experience everything in life? For so long we've been prevented from being together, but that's not the case now."

Alex couldn't take it any longer and started to kiss her, molding her body to his. "You're my life, Giannina." He could feel his desire growing out of control. "I need to take you where no one will bother us."

She pulled away from him in desperation. "Zikos raised you from the age of fourteen. What does he say about everything? How is he advising you where I'm concerned?"

"Zikos isn't the kind of a man to interfere. He's

never tried to influence me in my personal life. Why are you bringing him up?"

He heard her draw in a deep breath. "He's been your second father for years. Has he *ever* steered you wrong?"

"You know the answer to that."

"Do you value his opinion more than anyone else's?"

He cocked his head. "You know the answer to that too. What are you getting at?"

"That you ask him a straightforward question and wait until he gives you his honest answer. If he advises you against marrying me, which I know he will, then promise me you'll honor him and say a final good-bye to me."

His heartbeat tripled. He'd taken risks all his life. This was the biggest one.

"I promise, Giannina. But what if he surprises you and says he's very much in favor of us becoming man and wife no matter the vote of the parliament? Will you promise to honor him and marry me?"

What are you going to say now, my love? "Do *you* promise? Say it."

She averted her eyes. "I promise." But she'd said it so quietly, he'd hardly heard her. "First we have to go to him together and listen to what he has to say, Alex."

"Agreed. He saved me and raised me like I was his son. I owe him my life. I love him."

"I love him too for loving you with such devotion. He faced mortal danger to get you far away from that monster and keep you safe."

He gripped her hand. "We'll go to the hotel in my car and come back for yours later."

"I'd rather drive mine there now. It'll be a lot closer when I have to leave for the heliport."

She thought she'd be flying away in the next little while. He had news for her. "If that's what you want, then I'll follow you." No way would he let her out of his sight, let alone his life.

CHAPTER TEN

ALEX LED HER to her car and gave her a long, passionate kiss before shutting the door. Giannina trembled so hard, it was a miracle she could drive.

Zikos Novak would not be giving his blessing on a marriage to her. He'd consecrated his life for the good of the crown. In acting like a second father, he would make certain Alex followed in the footsteps of his deceased friend and king.

Once Alex knew how the man he loved truly felt about the situation, it would influence him enough to let go of his idea of being her husband. He'd promised her that.

Certain things in life were forbidden and unattainable. Thanks to Ari Hatzi, plus the fact that she was a non-royal, their marriage headed the top of that particular list.

Giannina had fought him ever since he'd shown up in her office, so it made no sense she experienced a guilty thrill that he stayed right behind her all the way to the hotel. After they met with Zikos, she would have to put Alexandros Philip Dimas Cimon Pisistratus away for good.

One day down the road, she'd watch him on the news in all his splendor as the new king of Hellenia. It would kill Giannina to see the bride he chose. She'd already made up her mind that she wouldn't watch his coronation or his wedding.

In fact, she'd arrange to be on vacation when it came time for his nuptials. Maybe Canada. Her sister-in-law, Alexa, had lived in Ottawa for years. She'd urged Giannina to travel there with her and Nico to see her old haunts. That would be the perfect time to put thousands of miles between her and the man she would adore for the rest of her life.

When she turned into the hotel parking, she looked in the rearview mirror. Alex had stayed glued to her. Just the sight of him interfered with her breathing. He'd always had that effect on her.

She'd barely turned off the engine when he opened the door to help her out. But he kissed her first with an almost savage hunger that equaled hers.

"We can't do this out here," she gasped.

"We just did." He put his arm around her waist while they walked in the hotel. "I phoned Zikos on the way. He's been talking to some key members of the parliament in his room, so he'll meet us in mine."

"Did you tell him why I want to be there with you?"

"We didn't have the privacy to talk freely."

They took a private elevator away from the others that rose to the top floor. The doors opened on an elaborate foyer with chandelier. His apartment turned out to be the kind of suite reserved for heads of state or royals. He might like to pretend he was an ordinary person, but the rest of the world didn't view him that way and never would.

He lifted her hair to kiss the side of her neck. "I'll get us something cold to drink while you freshen up. The bathroom is down that hall on the right."

"Thank you."

In a few minutes Zikos would be arriving. What he had to say would change Alex's world and hers. She'd always accused him of being the brave one. This afternoon she would have to put on the greatest performance of her life.

She brushed out her hair and applied fresh lipstick before going back to the elegant sitting room. Her heart jumped when she saw Zikos seated on one of the love seats holding a cola. Alex had brought one for them too.

"It's a pleasure to see you again, Giannina." Zikos got to his feet and came over to kiss her on both cheeks. It surprised her considering the circumstances. He hadn't done that the first time she'd met him.

"I feel the same way. When we left you the first time, I never had the opportunity to thank you in person for everything. I'm sorry."

He waved it off with his hand. "You were in a hurry. Alex tells me it's important that the two of you talk to me while you're still here in Loria."

Zikos didn't mince words.

She sat down on an upholstered chair opposite him. Alex handed her a drink and took his place on the couch.

"Before I ask Alex, tell me what's on your mind, Giannina."

His kindness should have put her at ease, but this was one time when she was jumping out of her skin with stark, cold fear.

"Alex has asked me to marry him and I've turned him down. There's no way this country will forgive him for taking a wife who's the niece of Ari Hatzi. Has the parliament already voted either way about his decision to marry me?"

"Yes."

His simple answer shook her to the foundations. "But you haven't told him the outcome yet."

"No."

That meant she'd been right, or Alex would already know. Fresh pain seized her. "Have they also voted about whether to allow him to be a part of the government, rather than be king?"

"That's correct."

"I see."

"I have one more question, Zikos. You've been his mentor since rescuing him from the palace that tragic night. He loves and reveres you. Your thoughts hold more weight for me than anyone else living. How do you feel about him giving up everything in order to take me to another continent where we can marry and live like ordinary people?"

Zikos sat there calmly. "Let me ask you some questions first. How do you like the idea of leaving everything both of you hold most dear in the hope of living ordinary lives elsewhere? Be careful before you answer."

"I don't need to be careful," she said without looking at Alex. "I already know the answer. It's the last thing I would want."

"And how do you feel about him helping shape the government without being their leader?"

She got to her feet. "It wouldn't work. Another leader wouldn't stand a chance with Alex being a part of parliament. Everyone already defers to him. Everyone's been waiting for him to ascend the throne." The memory of the look in the Realtor's eyes would always stand out in her mind.

"So *you* believe he should be king."

"I do. I believe it's his destiny."

"Do you think he'll make a good one?"

"Surely you're joking. He'll make a great one."

"How do you know this?"

She stared straight into Alex's burning black eyes. "Because of the way he treated Evander Corso at the palace on his first day back. Evander was his boyhood friend and took care of his dog after you rescued him. The love and kindness both men showed each other despite years of separation tells me everything about Alex's humanity. That's the quality needed in an exceptional leader."

Zikos smiled at her and stood up. "Such eloquence. You, my dear, should run for parliament. If I've answered all your questions, I'll leave now. Certain matters of importance are waiting for me."

At this point she was frantic. "You haven't told us about the vote yet!"

"Didn't I?" He scratched his head. "They heard his defense of you and voted unanimously that you should be his queen. The coronation will take place after the palace has been renovated. It's their hope you will marry right away to bring joy to a nation that has suffered.

"That, of course, is my greatest hope, my dear. I never knew a man more in love and can see why. I beg of you to say yes so I can finally get a good night's sleep. It'll be the first one I've had in fourteen years, so have pity."

Giannina couldn't believe her ears.

What had he just said?

She stood there stupefied as he left the suite.

After the door closed, Alex wandered over to her with a new light shining from his eyes. He pulled something out of his pocket and reached for her left hand.

"You promised to marry me if he gave us his approval."

Still in a complete daze, she watched him slide a gold ring with a stunning solitaire diamond onto her ring finger. A perfect fit.

"I—I can't fathom that the parliament has given their consent," she stammered. "What did you say to them in my defense?"

"That your only sin was the connection to your beloved aunt, a woman who suffered anguish for being married to Hatzi and divorced him long before he committed murder."

"Alex—Alex—" She threw her arms around his neck and pressed her mouth and body to his, finally able to tell him what had been in her heart for so many years.

"I love you, my darling. I've loved you since the day

we ran around the palace grounds. I couldn't believe I was playing with a real prince. You were so much fun and made me laugh. When my father said we had to leave, I didn't want to go. After we returned to Salonica, I kept begging him to take me there with him again. He said he would the next time the king needed to talk to him. I waited and waited."

Alex crushed her to him. "I drove my parents crazy asking them to invite you and your father back to the palace. They told me you could come for my father's jubilee, but that day never came."

"Darling—" She buried her face against his shoulder. "I had a secret crush on you. Then Philip Dimas came to my high school to talk about current events, and I developed another crush. You can't imagine how excited I was when years later I learned you were giving a lecture in London."

He cradled her face in his hands. "I almost had a heart attack to realize you were the Giannina Angelis from my boyhood all grown up and so beautiful."

"I fell for you immediately, Alex. It surprised me how strong my feelings were right from that first moment. That's because underneath your disguise lived the prince, my young woman's fantasy of perfection. Don't you know my love for you is beyond comprehension? I want to be queen if it means I can be married to you. Nothing else matters."

"Agapitos," he murmured at the base of her throat. "You've made me the happiest man in existence. There's just one problem. I need to take you in the bedroom and not come out for weeks. But I want us

to be married before I claim you body and soul. Since you heard Zikos say he would like our wedding to take place ASAP, I want it to be tomorrow."

"So do I." She half moaned the words against his marauding mouth.

"Then let's get in my car. I want to show you the church where I'd like us to be married and we'll arrange it with the priest. Shall we say three days from now?"

"What I'd give if that were possible."

"I'm not a king yet and can do what I want. Tonight we'll fly to Salonica. I want to ask your father for your hand and tell your family our news. Zikos is probably phoning his family right now. We'll keep it a small, private affair."

She hugged him harder. "I'm glad for that because I know things will be different for your coronation."

"That won't be for another month. Not until the palace is ready for us. In the meantime, we'll live here at the hotel. As for our wedding, I want you to plan it."

"I'm so happy, I feel like I'm going to burst."

"Now you know how I feel. Come on before I drag you in the other room and we retreat from the world for good."

That evening at the Angelis villa, Gianinna's mother pressed her hands to her mouth. "Three days?"

"I know it's fast, but neither of us can wait any longer. The only people we want to be there are our families."

"I guess being king, Alex can make the rules. That's kind of exciting. It's true you never got over spending time with the young prince. Your story is a true fairy tale."

"I know." Giannina giggled. "Of course, he hasn't been crowned yet."

Her mother caressed her cheek. "Just now you sounded like my little girl. Do you want to know a secret?"

"Always."

"Your father and I talked about it. He has told Alex to make use of the family yacht for your honeymoon. It will give you the privacy you need and keep you close to Hellenia in case something of importance happens."

"No one ever had better parents than you." She hugged her.

"Or a daughter as wonderful as you. I suffered when you came home brokenhearted from London."

"Little did we know Philip would turn out to be the lost prince."

"It's really incredible."

She nodded. "Do you think Baba will be up for the flight to Hellenia?"

"The doctor says he has improved since retiring. I can tell you now he wouldn't dream of missing the wedding of his precious Giannina. Olga is terribly excited. It goes without saying Nico is delighted. To think both of you suffered such heartache for years, and now look at you. He's never been so happy with Alexa and the baby. And you are *beaming*!"

"Oh, Mama. You'll never know how much I love him."

"That's how I feel about your father."

"Of course you do."

Three days later at the church in Loria

"Ooh—this white lace wedding dress is out of this world."

"Mama chose it. Thanks for helping me dress, Alexa. I'm so excited I'm shaking."

"I know the feeling. This is a beautiful church."

"Alex said it's where his family worshipped."

"What a lovely tradition. Nico and I got married at the church at Sarti Beach. He wanted to do it fast. No one knew anything about it since we didn't want to spoil wedding plans for Dimitra and Kristos. I think your husband-to-be has a lot in common with mine."

"They *are* alike in many ways. Handsome, brilliant, brave, adventurous."

"Keep going," Alexa teased her. "You've got it bad."

"I do. I'm so crazy about him I can't think straight."

"What's going to happen to your job at the newspaper?"

"We haven't talked about it yet. For now Khloe is handling everything just fine."

She handed Giannina her bouquet of white roses and stephanotis. "Is there anything else I can do for you before we leave the anteroom to join your father?"

"You've done more than enough. I love you."

"I love you too."

Alexa opened the door for her and they walked out to the vestibule of the small seventeenth-century church, famous for its frescoes. Giannina saw her father seated in his wheelchair. He'd been very handsome like Nico as a younger man. Age had made him more distinguished than ever.

His brown eyes lit up when he saw her. He held out his hand, which she grasped. "If ever there was a vision…"

"Baba…"

The organ music had started. He eyed her. "Ready to go seal your fate?"

"I've been waiting three years."

He chuckled. "Don't I know it."

One of the altar boys opened the doors and they proceeded down the aisle. Only a few chairs had been set up near the front to accommodate their families. She saw her tall, black-haired husband-to-be immediately. Though this was supposed to be an ordinary wedding, at the last minute she'd asked him to wear his royal dress blue uniform.

One day their children would pore over these pictures. When they saw how magnificent he was, they would burst with pride over their father. She felt overcome herself to realize this remarkable man loved her, had always loved her.

Zikos appeared resplendent as well in dark blue. He stood up for Alex. The only people missing were his beloved parents, but Giannina felt they had to be watching.

The priest came in a side door. He'd agreed to perform a very short afternoon ceremony in deference to her father and Alexa's grandfather, both of whom were in wheelchairs.

"Giannina and Alexandros, if you would approach and clasp hands."

Alexa took the bouquet and Zikos stepped back.

Warmth ran through Gianinna's body as Alex took her hand in his. He rubbed his thumb over her palm in a private message that turned her insides to mush.

"Prince Alexandros?" the priest began. "This will be the last time I address you this way. God has sent you back to us a man, heaven be praised. May He bless this union.

"If you will repeat after me, I, Prince Alexandros Cimon Pisistratus, promise to love and cherish this woman through mortality and beyond, through sickness and in health. I will provide for her welfare and worship her with my body."

Giannina listened to Alex's deep voice repeat the words. Then it came her turn. "I, Giannina Panagos Angelis, promise to love and cherish this man through mortality and beyond, through sickness and in health. I will be his comfort and worship him with my body."

The priest smiled at them. "Bless you, my children. In the name of the Father, the Son and the Holy Spirit, I pronounce you husband and wife. You may kiss your bride."

The fire in Alex's eyes caused her to tremble as he gave her a husband's kiss she wanted to last forever.

"Let's go, my love."

They'd planned to forgo a celebration with family. That would come later after the coronation. Their ring ceremony would happen then too. He grasped her hand

and they left the church. A limo stood waiting to take them to the yacht.

Giannina never remembered the drive to the port. The two of them forgot the world as they tried without success to show each other how they felt. Once on board in familiar surroundings, they went straight to the guest suite her father had picked out for them. It had windows overlooking the ocean.

Alex closed and locked the door before turning to her. He took off his suit jacket and tossed it on a chair. His gaze roved over her, not missing an inch, before he reached in her hair to remove her short veil. "Never has there been a more beautiful bride. I can't believe we're married and that I have you all to myself at last for as long as we live."

"I never dreamed this day would come," she whispered. "I still feel I'm dreaming."

He reached around to unfasten the back of her dress and slid it off her shoulders. While she stepped out of it, he disappeared into the bathroom. He came out a moment later wearing a robe and laid her dress on the love seat. In the next breath he picked her up in his arms and carried her over to the bed.

She clung to him as he lowered her to the mattress and began kissing the daylights out of her. Each sensual kiss grew longer, filling her with desire she'd never known. Wrapped in each other's arms had to be one of the greatest joys in life as they sought to give each other pleasure.

His hands and mouth brought an ecstasy she didn't know was possible. With their legs entangled, she'd never experienced such rapture and forgot the time, let alone her surroundings. Darkness filled the room before she had cognizance of anything but loving and being loved. Her lover had taken her to the heights and she never wanted him to stop.

"Alex?" She smoothed her hand over his chest. "I love you too much."

A deep male laugh came out of him. "Explain *too much*."

"If anything happened to you, I'd die. When I think—"

But his mouth stopped her there. "No thinking, my love. I've done too much of that over the last three years worrying about you, wondering what you were doing, what men you were attracted to, the ones you were kissing."

She rose up and half lay on him. "There's never been another man but you. A young prince captured my heart. It's been yours ever since."

"Darling—"

"I'm afraid you ruined me for all time, Alex."

"That day we played on the palace grounds sealed my fate too. You stole *my* heart and I never forgot you." He rolled her over and began kissing her again. "You've been my obsession and you haven't made it easy on me."

She covered his face with kisses. "I'm so sorry. You know I love you more than life."

"I'll forgive you if you'll order us some food. After it arrives, I'll tell you how you can make my pain go away."

She did his bidding, then put the phone receiver

back and turned to him. "Just so you know, I wasn't too thrilled with those tiny epistles you sent that left no address or phone number."

"Those cards were a form of code."

"Code?"

"Yes." He kissed her earlobe. "You were supposed to read between the lines and know how I felt."

"Obviously they kind of worked because I'm now your wife."

"Indeed you are. In every possible way. Do you know you remind me of the gorgeous Penelope who had many ardent suitors?"

"You mean the adored wife of Odysseus, king of Ithaca?"

"The very one. It's our story, Giannina. When he got back from the Trojan War, he was disguised as a beggar. She didn't recognize her husband or welcome him right away. It hurt him terribly. He had to prove to her that he was her husband so she'd take him back."

"I forget how long he was gone."

"Ten years."

"Well, that explains quite a lot, especially if he didn't write her any postcards at all. But as I recall, she forgave him in time, and they lived happily ever after."

"They couldn't be as happy as we are."

"No one could be," she whispered before kissing him again and again. Eventually a knock sounded.

"Our food is here. I'll get it."

"Just a minute, sweetheart. I told them to leave it outside the door. I know you're hungry, but there's something I want to tell you first. I hope it will make you happy."

He looked down at her. "What is it?"

"Nico gave me some advice that I know is right. When I told him I was nervous about being queen, he told me that all I needed to do was be a good wife. The rest would follow. So I'm afraid you're stuck with a clingy wife who's so crazy about you, I'm going to be an embarrassment."

"Thank heaven!"

EPILOGUE

"THE NEWS IS very good," Alex announced to his cabinet assembled at the palace. "After a year, the economy has started to recover, and job growth has skyrocketed. We've opened trade relations with dozens of countries and tourism has risen three hundred percent."

Alex was gratified by the clapping and cheers coming from the government officials. They were responsible for the dramatic changes since the evil regime had been eradicated.

Zikos got to his feet. "You've left out the most important piece of news, Your Highness." He turned to the others. "In the first year of our new government, the king and queen have produced an heir, which ensures the continuation of the Pisistratus royal line. Hail to the king of Hellenia!"

The others sprang to their feet to offer their congratulations. Pleased as Alex was by their response, the mention of their five-week-old baby daughter put thoughts of the nation out of his mind. He flashed Zikos a private smile.

When the noise quieted down, Alex said, "I appreciate your continued support and enthusiasm. Thank you for your sacrifice to our country. Nothing could have happened without all of you pulling together. Now I'm afraid I have to be excused and help my wife do the really important work of the day."

As the room filled with good-natured laughter, he left the conference room through a back door and hurried down the hall to the grand staircase. Taking the steps two at a time, he raced up to their bedroom on the second floor.

There was no sign of Giannina or Zoe. Where would they be at four thirty in the afternoon?

He asked the guard in the hall if he'd seen her. "Yes, Your Highness. She said to tell you she was going out to the summerhouse and would wait for you there."

Excited about that, Alex went back to the bedroom to change out of his suit into casual clothes. Then he took off for the tiny summerhouse he'd had renovated.

Giannina said that the first time she saw it, she'd thought of it as the little house in the forest where Goldilocks met the three bears. He'd made certain it resembled the drawing in the book. They stole out there when they wanted to get away from the palace. Soon it would be a playhouse for their children.

When he walked in, he discovered both of them on the double bed in the corner next to a little table. Their precious Zoe with her brunette hair lay on her back sound asleep. No doubt Giannina had been nursing her, and now his exhausted wife had fallen into a light sleep too.

At the foot of the bed lay their dog, a replica of

Achilles. The beautiful sight of the three of them touched his heart. Giannina had wanted to name him Neoptolemus after the son of Achilles. They called him Toly for short. The dog saw him come in and jumped off the bed to greet him. Alex hunkered down to play with him.

This was the kind of life with Giannina he'd dreamed of years ago. How long it could go on like this, no one knew, but he thanked God for this happiness and the most adorable wife imaginable.

Stealing across the room, he lay down on the bed. He curled his arm around her and pulled her close to him, careful not to disturb Zoe.

"I've been waiting for you to come," she whispered against his jaw. "I thought we'd have a celebration in here."

His heart thudded. "Celebration?"

"I had a checkup with the doctor earlier today. He's given me a clean bill of health, so…"

"But what about Zoe?"

She flashed him a beguiling smile. "Clista is outside to take care of the baby for a few hours. I asked her to bring the leash so she can take Toly with her."

"Giannina—"

Her arms crept around his neck. "I wish parenthood could be an experience for every woman or man wanting a baby. But you need to know how much I've been dying to make love with you since she was born. She's just been fed, and I can't wait any longer."

"Neither can I."

He rolled off the bed and walked around to pick up

his precious daughter. Toly followed him. A second later he opened the door to hand her to Clista.

"I'll take care of both of them, Your Highness."

"I know you will."

Alex kissed his daughter's cheek, fastened the leash to Toly's collar, then closed the door and hurried back inside to his wife. She'd let her hair grow longer. It splayed on the pillow. She'd never looked more exquisite to him.

"Love me," she cried softly. "Your shameless wife is back."

"So is your shameless husband who couldn't leave the conference room fast enough to be with you."

"I'm so proud of you and all you've accomplished, darling."

He pulled her on top of him. "Zikos reminded them that our daughter is our greatest accomplishment."

"She is, so far... But who can say what this evening will bring?"

"I know one thing," he murmured against her lips. "You've made me the happiest man alive. Work your magic, Giannina."

* * * * *

RUNAWAY GROOM

LYNNE MARSHALL

This one is for Sweet William.

And sincere thanks to Susan for giving me the opportunity to write a Fortune story.

Prologue

Mark Mendoza shuffled the cards and groused to his brothers. "I can't believe Rodrigo isn't here tonight." Here being the tasting room at the family winery in Austin, Texas.

"He's stubborn, you know that," Carlo, his older brother, didn't waste a beat to reply.

This was how Mark wanted to spend his last night as a bachelor, playing poker with the guys he loved and trusted most in the world, his brothers Chaz, Carlo, Rodrigo and Stefan. But Rodrigo had refused to come tonight, and more unbelievably, to his wedding tomorrow. It hurt.

He dealt, but before he picked up his cards, he

took another drink of thirty-year-old whiskey, compliments of Chaz. Smooth, smoky, with just the right amount of heat as it went down. Then he reached for the lit Dominican cigar Stefan had provided and took a puff, enjoying the full-bodied aroma while he studied his cards. It struck him as ironic that winemakers who preferred clean air were sitting in a confined space beneath a cloud of smoke. But, hey, it was a bachelor party for a thirty-five-year-old guy who had finally realized how much he wanted to get married and have a family, and this was exactly how he wanted to spend it—man time with his *hermanos*.

"He thinks I'm making a mistake, but I've thought everything through," Mark said, determined more than ever to convince his brothers that he didn't want to make the same mistakes his parents had made—marry for love and passion, drive each other crazy with jealousy, then slip into infidelity, making each other miserable until they finally divorced.

"He doesn't agree with your plan, that's all," Chaz said, starting off this hand of the card game with a mediocre bid.

"Says you've made it more like a business deal," Stefan added, as he passed.

Mark held cards in one hand, and the cigar in the other. "And I ask, is that such a bad idea?" he said as he raised the stakes.

"Nothing beats love," Carlo said as he took his turn. Married to Schuyler, he thought he was an expert.

The game continued around the table.

Mark had figured out the best way to choose a good woman to spend the rest of his life with, and it had nothing to do with love or a matchmaking website. Like a fine cigar, a marriage was something you developed a taste for.

"Let's use Rodrigo's example, then, and think of marriage as a successful business deal. Each party knows exactly what is expected of them and they follow through on the plans." He lifted his brow when Carlo raised his bet, then Mark called but didn't miss a beat with his explanation. Because it mattered to him that his brothers understood. That, and the fact he didn't want to give away his great hand. "The key is being honest," he touted before demonstrating with a huge grin as he laid down his full house.

But victory was brief when Carlo showed his four of a kind. "Don't forget you have a tell, little brother," Carlo teased. "You sniffed and scratched above your eyebrow when you made your bet. I knew you weren't as positive as you pretended to be."

"Yeah," Stefan said. "I noticed earlier you sniffed when you mentioned how excited you are to marry Brianna, too."

"Guys, this is not how a bachelor party is supposed to go. You're supposed to be happy for me, support me, let me win."

They shared a group laugh on the last part. Still, the secret message about his tell and having used it when talking about Brianna tore at his confidence about doing marriage his way with logic and reason. Love would come later. Wouldn't it?

He liked Brianna a lot and had no illusions about how she felt about him. She wanted someone to take care of her—someone stable and with a steady job. Mark wasn't dumb, he knew "steady" was code for lucrative, and he'd keep his end of the bargain there. He was part owner of the family winery, with a marketing side business breaking into new venues every week. They had also agreed on having a family as soon as possible. His practical approach to achieving a mindful marriage would ensure a stable home for their future kids, which he hoped would be many. Brianna was as excited as he was to have a big family, too. He'd seen plenty of passionate romances crash and burn, so, in Mark's view, friends with benefits was the only way to go.

Carlo claimed the poker pot. "What if this approach to marriage backfires?"

"Oh, now I see you've been talking to Rodrigo, who you may have noticed *is not here*." He didn't try to hide his frustration or impatience.

His younger brother Rodrigo had begged him to

reconsider, but Mark insisted he knew what he was doing. Bottom line, he didn't want to wait much longer to start that big family.

"Maybe he's right," Stefan posed.

"He's just ticked off I'm beating him to the altar. And now you guys are trying to ruin my last night as a single man. Are we playing poker or what?" Mark lifted his glass for Chaz to give him a refill and took another puff of the cigar. His brothers nodded. "Then let's shut up and deal. Okay?"

An hour later, having lost the card game and developed a coughing spasm from smoking the "fine" cigar, which had begun to taste like wet acidic tobacco in his mouth, Mark let more doubt seep in. Rather than spend the night tossing and turning, he'd make a plan. Another plan. Who cared if they said it was bad luck for the groom to see the bride before the wedding? He didn't believe in luck, he believed in plans. Besides, they weren't getting married for the usual reason—love—so why follow tradition. Theirs would be a solid untraditional approach to happily-ever-after. Just like in marketing where you followed the accepted steps to success and got results. This was his plan, and he was excited to get married and start the next phase of his life—together with his bride.

To put an end to the doubt his brothers had stoked with their stogies and whiskey and cards night, he'd sneak off to see his bride before the wedding tomorrow afternoon. He'd surprise Brianna and make one final analysis on the marital collaboration, to confirm that they were still on the same page about their marriage and family deal.

It was a simple plan that was bound to reassure him his unique strategy was the only way to go.

Chapter One

Ashley Fortune glanced around the busy restaurant and smiled. Saturday nights at Provisions in Rambling Rose had been booked solid for the entire month and nothing could make her and her other two triplet sisters happier. But her smile faded as her line of vision stumbled across the entrance and over the man standing there looking like the walking dead. He wore a tux with the jacket and vest both unbuttoned, and the silk bow tie loosened around his opened collar, like someone who had stayed a week too long at a wild party. With his hair wind-blown in a mad-scientist kind of way, the man was indeed the epitome of the phrase "a sight for sore eyes." But something about him was familiar. Mendoza familiar. He resembled her fiancé Rodrigo, but a little shorter. Still not sure, due to the backlighting, she squinted to see better.

Wasn't that Mark Mendoza? And wasn't today supposed to be his wedding? He was obviously dressed for it. The wedding. That was supposed to have happened—she glanced at her watch—three hours ago. But where was his bride? Brianna, wasn't that her name? And why would they be here instead of at their reception back in Austin?

His lost, staring eyes and forlorn appearance hadn't gone unnoticed by diners either, as a subtle hush came over the room while they checked out the stranger. He just stood there looking like an accident that had already happened. Regaining her senses, and needing to tamp down the spectacle, she rushed to her future brother-in-law.

"Mark!"

Completely unlike his usual friendly, easygoing self, he seemed stunned, like he'd somehow wound up here and wasn't sure why. He blinked his dark and sunken eyes, then focused her way.

"It's Ashley. Are you alone?" she said gently as she approached.

He glanced toward his perfectly polished and shined dress shoes, then back up. "Yep."

"Is everything all right?"

"I'm okay."

He certainly didn't look it.

"Did you have a car accident?"

He glanced over his shoulder, outside, toward the parking lot, clearly unsure. "No."

Well, something awful had happened, that was a given.

She quickly glanced around, hoping a table might have been vacated, but knew there were others waiting to be seated even if one had. One thing was certain: she couldn't let him stay where he was in his current state. As she approached, she reached for her cell in her pocket and speed-dialed Rodrigo. It went directly to voice mail. "I need your help ASAP," she said, then she reached for the arm of the usually sunny Mark and felt him tense.

"Let me find a place for you to sit."

Still clearly dazed, he looked around as if just now noticing where he had wound up. "Uh, yeah. Okay. I'm fine, though."

Oh, no he wasn't. "Why are you here?" Her straightforward question was drizzled with sympathy.

"I was just driving around, then wound up here." Sounding bewildered, Mark's voice was hoarse, as if he'd been yelling, and his hair looked as though he'd been driving a convertible all the way from Austin. Which she knew he didn't own.

She found one open seat at the bar. A lone stool

at the far end, which was a perfect place to hide, er, seat Mark until she could get hold of Rodrigo.

"May I ask what happened?"

He made a straight tight line with his lips, obviously not ready to talk about it.

"Never mind. Here, just have a seat, okay? Byron?" She called for the bar manager who happened to be on duty. "This is Mark. My future brother-in-law. Get him anything he wants on the house." Though not with-it completely, Mark was obviously sober.

She turned and tried Rodrigo's cell again, as she heard Mark order a double of something. Rather than leave another message, she texted him, then impatient to make contact called Hotel Fortune's private line and found out Rodrigo was running an emergency errand for Roja, the hotel restaurant, and should be back anytime. So she left another message for him to call her while wondering why he hadn't replied to her text.

"Ashley!" Adam, her cousin and restaurant manager, called out. "We need your assistance in the kitchen."

She'd been in worse situations on busy nights at this restaurant; Rosemary, the chef, could be an occasional prima donna. Mark seemed so lost, but she had no choice. "Mark, I've got to check this out."

He shrugged and smiled in understanding. As she

followed Adam to the kitchen, she looked over her shoulder and saw Mark take his drink in one gulp.

"I'll have another," Mark said from the high stool, leaning his forearms on the long polished concrete bar. He had to give it to Byron, he was attentive and quickly gave him a refill, which Mark immediately downed. He needed to be numb. Because tonight was supposed to be the first night of his honeymoon. And now everything—wedding, reception, flight to Belize—was off. He'd driven two hours from Austin to Rambling Rose yelling and cursing at the top of his lungs over the state of his life. The whiskey burned going down, but the quick, soothing effect was worth the pain.

He lifted his glass again and Byron finally made the pour. The sooner he was drunk and numb, the better. He threw back his head and, while drinking, noticed the corrugated-metal roof, exposed beams and ductwork. Beginning to feel no pain, he was struck by how much he liked the place right down to the metal and blond wood stool he sat on. *Good job, little brother. I approve. Even though you boycotted my wedding. Which, as it turns out, I did, too.* Yeah, he was drunk.

How long had he been staring at the ceiling?

Long enough to put a few things together. Rodrigo had come here last year to help with the opening of Provisions and wound up staying for good after falling in love with Ashley Fortune. A couple of his cousins had married Fortunes, too. And Carlo had married a woman from a secret branch of the Fortune family called the Fortunados. So Rodrigo was apparently continuing a tradition.

And speaking of Ashley, she was obviously worried about him, because she'd come back again.

"Hi, is there anything I can do for you?"

Why was she acting like she hadn't been here just minutes ago? "I'm still fine," he lied as he glanced her way then did a second take. How did women do that? Change clothes so fast, right out of her chic dress into casual dark pants and a light blue sweater set. Man, the booze must be kicking in because he could also swear she'd cut her hair. Before it was long, wavy; now it only came to the bottom of her neck, was stick straight and parted on the side. And the parted side looked longer than the other. *Asymmetrical.* He pondered the word as though it was in the bottom of his glass. Oh, yeah, he was getting blotto. *Say something, be polite, or she'll know you're drunk, too.*

"I don't know how you did it, but I like you in blue. Hair's nice, too."

Ashley's eyes widened, she quirked a brow and crinkled her nose in a typical *huh* expression, then recognition seemed to dawn. Her forehead relaxed and she smiled. "I'm Megan, one of Ashley's triplet sisters. We get that a lot."

Right! There were three of them. Rodrigo was engaged to Ashley. "Oh, yeah, I met you briefly at that party last summer?"

She nodded. The couple on the other side of him stood up to be escorted to their table, so Megan scooted onto the empty stool beside Mark. He didn't necessarily want company while he got plastered, but for some reason, he didn't mind this triplet with the asymmetrical hair sitting next to him.

Ashley had called her at the Hotel Fortune with an SOS just as Megan was about to order a to-go dinner from Roja. Who would've thought she and her sisters would own two restaurants in a little over a year at the ripe old age of twenty-four? Anyway, her presence had been stressfully requested at Provisions. Ashley had said Mark Mendoza clearly needed some TLC and man-oh-man she was right.

From where Megan was sitting, Mark seemed in the early to mid-stage of getting hammered. He also looked like he'd recently been hit by a truck.

She leaned close to the bar and turned her head to catch his attention. "Would you like to talk about it?" Why not start with the obvious.

Staring straight into the huge bar mirror, instead of looking at her, he shook his head, then signaled Byron for a drink. How many would this be?

"Byron, can you bring a couple menus, too?" She turned to Mark. "I missed my dinner." Then back to Byron. "Oh, and some coffee?" Megan said it as though it had just occurred to her, not that Ashley had made her promise not to let Mark get stink-faced and make a fool of himself. So far he seemed in control, but something horrible had happened today to make a successful man like Mark Mendoza, the carefree guy she'd met last summer, clearly want to drown in whiskey to make it better.

Byron placed a bowl of mixed nuts and another of pretzels in front of them, having obviously read her mind.

"I'll have a refill, thanks." Mark also let his desire be known without blinking an eye, which was hard to tell since he wouldn't look at her.

She turned in the stool to face Mark so he couldn't ignore her, then sang the praises of the restaurant's coffee. "You've got to try it. We order it specially from Guatemala, from the fair-trade market, of course, and since I'm the COF, I can guarantee it's still a great deal. And so rich and smooth. You'll love it."

"COF? Is that short for coffee?"

She tolerated his dumb joke because he was tipsy and looked pitiful, and boy, could he use a hug. Not that she'd thought about giving him one, just that she'd noticed how sad he was in that perfectly fitting tux. Or it would have been a perfectly fitting tux if the vest and jacket were buttoned. The shirt collar was open, a look Megan had always been a sucker for, and under the unbuttoned vest, the white shirt clung snug against his abs. She'd noticed that, too. "Chief of finances. I'm the numbers person of us three." She popped a handful of nuts into her mouth to lead by example—eat while you drink. Mark picked up a single pretzel and licked off the salt.

A different bartender dropped off the menus and Mark's next drink. He didn't waste any time before tasting it. Determined to get him to detour toward eating, she gushed about the food at Provisions. "Oh, wow," she said, as though she'd never seen the menu before. "The food is so good here. We try our best to be farm-to-table."

He patiently let her babble on. Which she thought was sweet.

"I always get the lemon and rosemary chicken cutlets when it's on the daily special." She eagerly gazed at Mark for a reaction. Nothing. She checked the day's special. Oh, shoot, no rosemary chicken. "Maybe you'd like Nic's famous fried chicken?" She waited. "It's a closely guarded recipe that will knock your socks off. She started making it here, at Provisions, then when we opened Roja, she got her own kitchen and moved there, but we kept her specialty here, since everyone loves it." The extended explanation made perfect sense to a slightly nervous Megan, who'd been assigned a babysitting job on zero notice for a man who was currently tying one on.

Finally, he turned his face toward hers with half of his mouth hitched up. Granted it was nearly imperceptible, but she'd noticed, and she'd count that as a smile.

"I admire your tenacity," he said before taking another swallow of the amber liquor. At least he'd slowed down.

She had to laugh at that. Silently, of course. But finally, she'd gotten a reaction out of him. "You want me to order for both of us?" She'd just lunge ahead, hoping he wouldn't notice. She intended to get him to eat whether he wanted to or not. "The roasted veggies, all locally grown, are to die for. We can share."

"Sure," he said, clearly resigned.

Progress! As soon as her coffee came, she asked for a second mug and poured him a cup from the carafe. "Try it, you'll like it. I guarantee."

That half smile returned as he took the cup, dropped a good helping from his whiskey glass into the coffee and stirred, tasted, then nodded. "Very good. Yes."

Without giving a thought, she playfully kicked his foot off the barstool.

"What? I tried it."

They laughed and after that, things started to relax between them as they sat side by side at the

crowded and noisy bar. Though he ignored the coffee after that one taste and went back to his drink,
and from the slightly thick-tongued responses he
gave, she figured he was sloshed. Still, he hadn't
asked her to leave him alone. So there *was* that.

She was dying to know what had happened to
him today, but she'd have to be patient if she wanted
him to open up about it. Maybe over their meal, or
after he got some food into him, he'd talk more.

Byron must have pulled some strings because
they got their dinner super-fast. Megan raved over
the presentation. "Don't you love all those colors?"

He lifted his brows and overexaggerated his
agreement. "Oh, yes." He was being patient with
her, she knew it, but that was sweet, wasn't it?

Again, feeling perhaps a little too relaxed around
Mark, she lightly cuffed his arm to let him know
she was on to him.

"What? I'm agreeing with you."

"You're making fun of me."

"I would never do that." He gazed at her for a
second. She could see the hurt in his eyes. "Well,
maybe a little, but only because you're making such
a big deal out of everything."

Appreciating his honesty, and glad to be here
with him, if for nothing more than to be a distraction from whatever awful thing had happened to
him today, she smiled. "I *can* get overenthusiastic."

"And you've been doing a really good job. Now let's eat."

Was he making fun or flirting? Of course he wasn't flirting, and she deserved being made fun of. For whatever reason, she was really glad to be sharing a meal of "Nic's fried chicken" and roasted vegetables with a slightly drunk man at the bar. It was far better than grabbing her to-go meal from Roja and eating quietly in her suite at her family's Fame and Fortune Ranch.

Halfway through dinner, after nothing more than comments about how good the food was, and with Megan practically hand-feeding him roasted asparagus spears and bright red bell peppers, he said something that almost made her choke.

"I thought I'd found the perfect woman. But I was wrong."

Willing herself not to react, Megan went still, because this was a monumental step toward communicating. She hoped he'd continue.

"She betrayed me." He bit the head off the next butter-drizzled and shaved parmesan–roasted asparagus spear and chomped hard. "How could I have been such an idiot?"

Instead of looking at her as he spoke, he talked facing the wall-to-wall bar mirror, where her eyes found his and held tight. For a few seconds they stared at one another from a distance while sitting right next to each other. She was darned if she'd say a word, not wanting to shut him down again. Eventually he turned to her and searched her eyes as though wondering if she were a woman he could trust.

Up close, having turned toward him, looking into his sad dark gaze, seeing the toll the betrayal of the woman he spoke of had taken on him today, Megan sensed his vulnerability. It hurt, too, and her eyes threatened to well up, but she bit back her surprising reaction by taking a sip of the now-tepid coffee.

Betrayal could mean so many things. Did they have a prenup? Was there someone else? Had the fiancée lied about something? It could be anything, but right now one thing was on her heart, and she needed Mark to know it.

"I'd never call you an idiot."

He jerked his head to look back at her. "Thanks."

With that, Megan sensed that they'd just bonded, maybe on the tiniest of levels but it still counted, and she was determined to keep his secret between them.

As they finished the last bites of their dinner in silence, Megan also became aware of the righteous anger she felt on behalf of Mark. It didn't seem possible that someone would dump a guy like him—on their wedding day, no less!

The next thought came from left field. What was up with his taste in women?

Her anger dwindled when it started to take a

turn toward him. Had it been his fault for picking a flake? Or had she fooled him? Obviously that, because he just said he'd thought he'd found the perfect woman. Well, she could have assured him there was no such thing, but they hadn't been friends before tonight. Only distant acquaintances, who would soon be distantly related.

The fact that Rodrigo had refused to attend his wedding spoke volumes. But even if his wedding had been on a fast track to a train wreck and he was partly responsible for choosing this woman, Megan was overcome with sympathy for him. And something more. She genuinely liked him. A drunk guy. A brokenhearted drunk guy, no less.

He could have used what happened today as an excuse to be loud and obnoxious, angry as all getout, but even drunk, he acted like a gentleman. Painfully quiet at times, but overall respectful.

Most of all, she knew his pride had to be wounded after today and the man could use some moral support. If all he needed was someone to sit with him, she'd be that person. Because after whatever happened to him today, he could use some backup.

Megan was compelled to put her hand on the forearm of his tux jacket, but before she could, Rodrigo showed up.

"Sorry to make you guys wait, but I had to deal

with a couple of things back at the hotel. One came complete with an irate guest."

"Oh, no, that couldn't be good." Megan's business mind popped into action.

"Trust me, it wasn't. Their reservations had gotten lost. Somehow. Anyway, it's still a mystery." He put his hand on Mark's shoulder. "Sorry to talk business over you, but anyway, now that I'm here, let me take you home so you can finish sobering up."

"Who told you I was drunk?" He cast a sideways glance at Megan. She lifted her hands, confirming her innocence.

"Ashley. You know, my fiancée?" Rodrigo righted the obvious assumption.

Mark nodded. "Listen, I don't want to put you out. I can get a room at the hotel."

"Actually you can't. Our reservations are a little wonky, and I wouldn't dare use a vacant room in case we have another mix-up tonight."

"I'm just saying I don't want to be a bother." Mark accentuated the "be a bother" part.

Rodrigo's hand was planted firmly on Mark's shoulder. "You drove all the way from Austin in your wedding tux and, by the way, you look like hell, so I can only imagine what happened, and the last thing I'm going to do is leave you alone tonight."

"So you can say 'I told you so,' right?"

"Nah, not tonight. I'll wait until you're sober. Come on. Let's go."

When Mark got off the stool, he glanced at Megan and tipped his head in a humble, gentlemanly manner.

"You've been kind to me tonight. Yes, I'm drunk, so I'm saying it out loud instead of just thinking it. But the point is, thanks for putting up with me, Megan-with-the-Asymmetrical-Hair."

Her hand flew to the ends of her hair, then their gazes united and clung to each other and an odd feeling shot down Megan's center. She'd never met a nicer drunk in her life, but it was more than that. Mark Mendoza seemed genuine, and he made her feel funny, as in really good funny, whenever he got around to looking into her eyes.

"You're welcome, Mark. I enjoyed keeping you company."

"Oh, I'm sure you can do a lot better than me on any given Saturday night," he said as he wandered off with his brother.

"Thanks, Megan," Rodrigo called over his shoulder as they walked out.

Megan stood and watched, letting that interesting feeling linger as long as it wanted to. Because it had been a long time since she'd felt that. Mark had no idea how dead her dating life had been lately. Sure, it had something to do with being married to the job—both jobs—these days. Still, it couldn't be denied. Even if she had been dating, she doubted she'd meet a guy who could cause this kind of reaction— the funny dance-down-the-spine thing. From a man who'd been freshly betrayed today, no less.

Your secret's safe with me.

Chapter Two

Mark pinched his temples with his thumb and middle finger, hoping to stop the throbbing. "How many times are you gonna say 'I told you so'? Because by my count you're up to at least four," he said Sunday morning while nursing his wicked hangover.

From the start Rodrigo had weighed in on what he thought about Mark's rational plans for a marriage. When Mark still blew him off, Rodrigo had made his point by sending regrets with his wedding RSVP. And it stung. Mark couldn't believe it. His own brother.

When he had confronted him, Rodrigo had said

he wasn't going to drive two hours from Rambling Rose to Austin to watch Mark make the biggest mistake of his life. He'd said he wouldn't even drive fifteen minutes to see that. The prediction of doom had felt like a knife in the chest back then and had left a gaping wound. Shaken, Mark had clung to his decision and, though less confident, pushed on. Now, after what Brianna had done yesterday, Rodrigo had every right to read him the riot act. And gloat. But eating humble pie with a hangover was a terrible combination.

"When I'm right, I'm right. Why couldn't you have listened to me *before* you made all those expensive wedding plans?"

"Hey, hold on a second there. You're doing it— making all those expensive plans. Carlo has done it, and so has Chaz, both of them with great success, I might add. Why shouldn't I have given marriage a try?"

"Because you went about it all wrong. You don't decide you want a family, then go find someone to do it with. The point is to find the one person who's right for you!"

Maybe Rodrigo held a grudge because Mark was going to beat him to the altar by three weeks?

"That is so needle in the haystack-y." That was an expression he had never used before, and clear evidence he was still suffering the effects of last night's overkill with whiskey. "And in case you haven't noticed, I don't have a lot of time."

"You're only thirty-five."

"Don't laugh, but men have biological clocks, too. You wouldn't know that because you're four years younger than I am." Mark stopped and assessed his younger brother—how honest should he get? "Look, I don't want to be that gray-haired guy pushing the baby stroller, okay?"

"You don't have a gray hair on your head."

Mark's finger went up. "Yet. But after yesterday, that could change. Probably already has." He'd make a point to check it out after he showered.

"Hey, if all you want is a kid—"

"Kids," Mark corrected.

"You can adopt!"

"I wanted to be married first." He'd always been a traditionalist.

"How many times are we going to have this argument?" Rodrigo dug his fingers into his hair. Now Mark had driven him to pulling out his hair. It was a gift. "It still all boils down to the fact that you don't find the right woman to spend the rest of your life with by making a checklist." Now the veins in Rodrigo's neck were bulging and he'd clearly decided Mark was hard of hearing.

"Dude. My brain can't take the noise." Mark covered his ears with his palms.

He'd thought he'd found the perfect woman in

Brianna since she ticked all the boxes on his list. She was beautiful and vivacious—shamefully, both were right at the top of his list—and she was also the kind of woman who lit up a room. That hadn't even been on his list, but he really liked that about her.

Rodrigo may have gone quiet, but his stare remained intense.

"She said she was eager to start a family and would like to be a stay-at-home mom." Mark had imagined they would have a big family and make beautiful babies together.

"Fine sentiments, but you forgot the most important thing." Rodrigo, taking heed of Mark's hangover, had lowered his voice. "Vitamin L. Love, brother."

Right now, all Mark wanted was some peace.

Could he ever say he'd been in love with her? Even now—well, especially now—he couldn't say for sure. He'd liked her a lot, and he'd had no illusions about Brianna's feelings for him. She wanted security, someone to take care of her. Theirs was more of a mutual understanding than love.

Growing up in the Mendoza household, and thanks to his parents' passionate marriage, he knew crazy-about-you love was the way of crashing and burning. Being friends with benefits was the logical fix to that pitfall, so he'd gone for it. With Brianna. Who he'd found kissing another man while wearing the wedding dress she and Mark had picked out together, on the day they were supposed to get married!

His thoughts may have run wild, but his brother was still talking.

"Marriage is great, but love is never practical. It's when you find someone you can't see yourself living without—someone who changes the way you feel about yourself, about the world. That's when you buy the ring."

"We both wanted the same things." Why was he sticking with this losing argument?

Rodrigo huffed an impatient breath, obviously wondering why Mark was being so dense. "Brianna wasn't the right person for you."

Rodrigo couldn't have known that for sure when he'd first told Mark, but now it was a fact. Mark had been wrong, and little brother Roddy had been right. It stung like a dart in his eye, or maybe that was the raging headache he'd woken up with, but he could no longer deny the truth.

"And you've never had a shortage of girlfriends, dude." Rodrigo wouldn't let up.

It was Mark's turn to sigh, because it was time to be frank, and a man never liked to admit an insecurity. "Now, I'm not sure there is a 'right person' out there for me."

For the first time that morning Mark saw a hint of compassion in his brother's otherwise frustrated gaze.

"You never know when it's going to happen. Have some faith. After Carlo got divorced from Cecily, he found Schuyler. When I finally got over Bonnie I found Ashley. It can happen."

"We'll see." They'd been at it long enough and Mark still hadn't revealed exactly what had happened beyond saying Brianna had betrayed him. All Mark wanted was to shower and get the hell out of there. "Listen, I don't want to impose on you." Or hear any more of his lectures.

"Stay here as long as you want."

"You've got a lot going on—I'd just be in the way. I'll figure something out." Mark stood from where he'd sat on the arm of the couch.

Rodrigo stared him down like a parent with a truant kid. "You gonna tell me what really happened?"

"Not yet. I'm still processing, and my ego's had enough for now." He started toward the guest bedroom door.

"Must have been bad for her to call it off."

Mark stopped and backed up, turned slowly. "I'm the one who left. It was up to her to explain to everyone why the wedding got canceled. I didn't stick around to hear it, but I'm betting she didn't tell the whole truth."

"When you're ready to talk about it, I'm ready to listen." For the first time that morning Rodrigo acted like the understanding brother he'd always been, until Mark had become engaged to Brianna.

"Thanks, man, but just not yet."

They ended on good terms, though Mark still wanted to go off on his own. He had two weeks' vacation, and though Rambling Rose wasn't Belize, it seemed like a pretty little town worth checking out. It was also somewhere he could stay out from under the rest of his family's radar for a while.

As he walked toward the bedroom where he'd fallen completely clothed onto the bed last night— he still wore his tux now, definitely reeking—one sweet face came to mind. The person who'd been willing to sit with him last night and let him wallow. A smile crossed his face. Megan had even gotten him to eat asparagus, something he'd always hated.

That was pretty impressive.

Megan, Ashley and Nicole met for coffee in Provisions' kitchen like they always did on Sunday mornings before they all went off to their jobs. Working Sundays was what they'd signed on for when they went into business together. Since Ashley ran the restaurants and Nicole was the chef, Sundays were a given for them, so Megan showed her support by working, too, even though, being the numbers person, the books could always wait until Monday. But not before they had coffee together.

"Can you believe what happened?" Ashley

started the topic right off referring to the runaway groom. "Did he tell you anything?"

Two pairs of identical blue eyes were on Megan, who wanted to respect Mark's privacy. "Not much. It was obvious he was hurting, though." She stirred the coffee in her mug to avoid eye contact.

"Well, Rodrigo tried to warn him about marrying that Brianna woman. He knew it wouldn't work out." Ashley borrowed the creamer from Megan.

"He struck me as a good guy," Megan said just before taking a sip, then noticing from above the rim, Nicole perk up.

"He was drunk, right?" Nicole prodded.

"Well, not at first, but definitely soon after I got there. Anyway, he could've been rude or angry, or worse yet obnoxious, but he seemed nice, you know? We ate dinner together, and he actually seemed like a sweet guy."

"A sweet guy who got left at the altar," Nicole added, obviously waiting for more.

Which Megan wasn't about to give her. "I'm not sure what happened, but obviously something awful." It surprised her how she wanted to stick up for the man who couldn't speak for himself right now.

"Well, Rodrigo knew the marriage wouldn't work out. That's why he refused to go to the wedding." Ashley added a packet of natural sugar substitute and intently stirred. "He was trying to show

Mark how strongly he felt that he was making a huge mistake. Rodrigo told me when he sent his regrets with the RSVP that he hoped it might change his brother's mind before it was too late, but it obviously didn't."

"Well, if he is a good guy and a sweet man, like you say, Megan," Nicole said, obviously doing her best to piece the puzzle together, "then why leave him at the wedding? Did Rodrigo tell you anything, Ashley?"

"I didn't want to get in the middle of them last night, so I stayed here at our ranch," Ashley said. "I've met Mark a few times more than you guys and he always seemed to have his head on straight. He's hardworking, like all the Mendoza brothers, and he's creative. A marketing expert."

"He's also a gentleman, even when he's sloshed," Megan wanted to remind them. "And I don't think he'd appreciate knowing we're discussing his personal life over morning coffee like yesterday's news."

"Oh." Nicole's eyes got wide. "Someone is being very protective of a guy she babysat last night."

"Well, a whole lot of assuming is going on here. How do we know who walked out on whom?"

He'd told her he'd been betrayed, and there were many ways that could happen, but the second obvious one, after leaving him at the altar, was cheating on him. Still, she wasn't about to divulge what she thought might have really happened on the way to their vows. And this morning, with her sisters, she didn't want to betray Mark's trust or confidence.

"Well," Ashley said, "I'm sure he told you something."

"I don't have any details. Believe me. He's a man of few words."

"And knowing you," Nicole said, "you wouldn't share them with us unless he told you it was okay."

"Yeah," Ashley said. "But don't forget we have triplet telepathy." She made a teasing show of closing her eyes and pressing her index fingers to her temples, as though attempting to read Megan's mind. It achieved what she'd obviously wanted when Nicole and Megan laughed. "Oh, I'm getting something," she said in an overly dramatic voice. "I see my sister being verrrrry protective of Mark Mendoza. Hmm." Her eyes popped open. "What do you suppose that is all about?"

Megan dutifully screwed up her face in denial. "Na-uh. I'm not being protective," she lied. "Besides, you made me do it. So I had dinner with a hurting drunk guy. Big deal. That's not exactly how great romances start out."

"Still," Nicole said, tapping a finger on the table, tilting her head, "I'm sensing something, too."

Ashley and Nicole nodded at each other.

"And I can't believe you used the old *you made*

me excuse," Ashley added, pinning Megan with a playful challenge.

"Well, you did!"

Sounding like kids again, the sisters laughed together.

All Megan could do was shake her head and hope her cheeks didn't turn bright pink because she was a liar. Something odd *had* happened between her and Mark last night. At least on her end. He probably wouldn't remember a thing. Still, no one could tell her otherwise. She'd glimpsed the real Mark, the man behind the put-together facade who, while inebriated, let his guard down. He was hurt to the core by a woman who'd betrayed him. That poor baby needed some TLC.

"Can I ask you guys something?" Megan's thought popped out of the blue. "Would you describe my hair as asymmetrical?"

Later, after Rodrigo had left for work and Mark had showered and eaten a little breakfast, he grabbed his luggage, threw it into the trunk and headed to the Hotel Fortune in Rambling Rose. His brother wasn't around when he entered the Spanish Mission–styled lobby, complete with a liberal use of wrought iron wall hangings and sconces as well as big comfortable-looking leather chairs. His steps echoed on the terra-cotta tiles as he approached the front desk. A young woman offered a wide smile.

Her name tag said Lucy, and she was probably a local kid, since the badge also said "hospitality team trainee."

"How may I help you?" Her smile was bright and cheery.

"I'd like a room for a few nights."

"Let me check." Her fingers clicked and clacked across the keyboard as she dove into the reservations program. Then her brows nearly met. "It doesn't appear that we have a vacancy."

"Really?" Mark didn't want to pull strings or draw attention that he was Rodrigo's brother, but he was tempted.

She canted her head. "I'm sorry. Would you like to leave your phone number so we can contact you if a room opens up today?"

"Sure, why not. Looks like a great hotel."

"It's really beautiful, isn't it?" Lucy's eyes brightened with pride, just the kind of employee he'd want if he ran the place.

He glanced around the lobby again, then nodded. "Well, I'll keep my fingers crossed." As he walked away, he glanced back at the front desk and noticed Lucy with the same expression while holding up her crossed fingers. Now, that was service with a smile.

Later that day at Roja, Megan was lost in the business of tallying numbers for two restaurants when out of nowhere, Mark poked his head around the corner of her small office door. A quick pop of adrenaline hit her chest at the sight of him as he stepped inside. Suddenly, the cozy office felt a whole lot smaller.

The first thing she noticed was his hair was combed, parted and styled, and looked so much better than the finger-in-a-socket version last night. He also perfectly wore pale jeans and a slim-fit short-sleeved navy shirt with a tiny pattern of dots in a darker blue. Wow. He looked straight out of Miami, where she knew his branch of the Mendoza family was originally from, complete with beach loafers and no socks. Yet, though he was dressed for fun, she sensed a deep sadness about him.

"There you are," he said, giving a wan smile, a smile that still lit up her mood. What a change in appearance from last night, if not spirits. There were still dark circles beneath his otherwise gorgeous eyes. He probably hadn't slept well. And, under the circumstances, who could blame him?

"Hi! How'd you find me back here in the dungeon?"

"I've got a brother who helps run this place," he said as he stepped closer to her desk.

"How're you feeling today?" His seacoast and citrus scent had certainly brightened her outlook and was far more appealing than the smell of whiskey.

"My head feels like a rock hit it, my life feels

surreal right now, like something on a reality show, but, hey, I'm alive." He shrugged and half closed his eyes. Wow, some lashes. How had she not noticed those last night?

She made an exaggerated nod of understanding while thinking he looked alive and *fine*.

He exchanged the half-hearted smile for something more serious. "I want to apologize for anything I may have said or done last night that was or could have been interpreted as inappropriate."

"Are you a lawyer, too?" she teased, before going for earnest reassurance. "You were a perfect gentleman."

"Ha! If ever there was a test, right?" He looked relieved.

"Hey, you'd had a lot to drink and I gathered there was a solid reason, so I just looked after you."

"And I appreciate that. I can usually handle my liquor better. Know when to say when, you know? I work at a winery, for crying out loud. But I just wanted to assure you that I don't usually drink that much or get drunk. That's why I wanted to make sure I didn't insult you in any way."

"Well," she said and smiled inwardly, remembering one particular comment he'd made, "you did kind of call out my hair, and I thought, look who's talking." They shared a short laugh, something it seemed he could certainly use.

"Wait, I did what?"

"You said my hair is asymmetrical, and it is, but only when I put it behind one ear, like this, see?" She demonstrated, then released the hair to today's style.

He pinched the bridge of his nose. "Man, I *was* out of it, and I'm sorry if that insulted you."

"Hey, quit being so hard on yourself. I'm just teasing. I thought it was cute. Drunk cute." Which was something, since as the more serious triplet, she didn't ordinarily make jokes. Or admit she thought something a man did was cute. But the guy needed a serious pick-me-up.

He looked relieved. The next few moments were quiet, as if he'd said what he'd come there to say and now it was time to leave. She hoped she hadn't made him uncomfortable. Regardless, something made her reach out. "Will you be staying in Rambling Rose?"

His hands flew to his pockets as he thought. "I had a two-week honeymoon scheduled, so I don't need to be back at work for a while."

She got the distinct impression that Mark appreciated being able to be straight-up with her. After all, she was the person he'd told that his future bride had betrayed him, so he had nothing to hide.

"Then you should check into the Hotel Fortune."

"I already tried—they're booked." His thumb pointed over his shoulder toward the lobby. "But I'm on a wait list."

"Really?" She couldn't recall the hotel being full lately, and there had been a weird problem going on with the reservation program recently. "Let's go check this out." She slipped her feet into her basic black ballerina flats under her desk, wishing she'd had the foresight to dress a little fancier today than her charcoal pin-striped pants and bright blue tailored stretch shirt. Why hadn't she at least thrown on an artsy scarf? Or worn earrings?

They walked congenially side by side to the front desk, and Megan enjoyed getting the sense how much taller Mark was compared to her five feet four inches. He seemed like a substantial guy in many ways.

"So you're the numbers woman, I take it?"

"Yes. Director of finances. You can call me chief or COF, which, by the way you thought was short for coffee last night." Again, they laughed easily together.

He shaded his eyes with one hand in shame but recovered quickly. "I think Numbers Woman suits you better, like a new superhero."

She gave him a dead stare at the absurdity of her with superpowers, as if she thought he was still drunk, but kept her real reaction—she liked his take—to herself.

"I know," he said. "Dumb." Then he proceeded to hum the old *Wonder Woman* TV show jingle.

What wasn't to like about Mark Mendoza?

When they arrived at the front desk, Lucy gave Mark a knowing smile. "Hello again."

"May I take a peek at the reservations?" Megan used her professional tone.

Lucy stepped back, giving her free rein, and Megan, wanting to appear courteous and efficient, did one quick scroll through the computer. "Hmm," she said, discovering a few vacant rooms and wondering why Mark was told otherwise earlier. "You're in luck." Oops, poor choice of words knowing how completely out of luck Mark felt about everything since yesterday afternoon. She hoped she hadn't upset him.

"I can use some of that. Thanks," he said graciously.

"We've got a suite on the fourth floor, or a standard room on the first floor, which has its own outside entrance with a small patio, so that's a plus."

"I don't need a suite, so the standard on the first floor sounds great. Thanks."

"Okay," she said, stepping back to let Lucy do her job. "I'll leave you to get checked in."

"Hey, thanks again," he said, stepping closer to the registration desk. "That's twice you've saved my butt."

"Glad to help," she said, walking out from behind the counter. And if she had noticed correctly in those jeans, he had some butt to save. Though she'd never admit thinking that about Rodrigo's brother even under oath.

"Oh, uh, there's one more thing you can do for me."

"What's that?"

"I'd like to buy you lunch. As a thank-you. After I get checked in and you're done with whatever you were doing that I already interrupted."

Usually, she'd weigh such a proposal carefully, but not this time. He wanted to return a favor and, since they would soon be extended family, they needed to get to know each other. Why not today? "You know what? That would be fine. Is a late lunch okay, though, like two?"

"Sounds good. I'll meet you in the lobby at two."

"Okay."

"Until then."

Megan headed back to her office, unsure how she felt about sharing another meal with Mark Mendoza, while being completely aware her feet felt extra light in her ballerina flats.

Around three o'clock, after a very satisfying lunch on the patio of Roja at Hotel Fortune, Mark sat back and glanced around at the scenery. On the exterior the architect had perfectly captured the feel of a Spanish mission while still injecting a modern touch. He liked that. The red-tiled roof and occasional arch hinted at the past, though step a foot inside the lobby and it was another story. They'd paid homage to the classic style with wrought iron and terra-cotta colors but had modernized it enough to feel like a trendy boutique hotel. Excellent work.

His room, which he'd been told was a standard room, had every comfort a guest could want. It also managed to look chic but feel homey. The classic king-size bedpost headboard was toned down by a simple white duvet with a beige throw, and a rich natural-colored leather bench at the foot of the frame. On top of the matching old-school dresser sat a deep green thick ceramic bowl with bright oranges and apples, and yet again the vintage look morphed into modern by the state-of-the-art flat screen mounted on the wall above. From the understated brown-and-beige fern-patterned carpet to the time-honored burnt-orange heavy drapes, the place seemed effortlessly fashionable. The perk of having a French door outside entry kept the room feeling bright and airy. His mind whirled with ideas how best to market such a place.

Across from him, Megan seemed perfectly comfortable chatting away, and it was a great distraction from the mess in his life. When he was around her, he could breathe easier, and since Saturday afternoon, his chest had been so tight the easy breathing felt like a gift from the gods of Rambling Rose.

"You'd be welcome to look around our new restaurant while you're here," she offered in a rush.

"Since you're a marketing expert, we'd love your input."

The woman loved her coffee and it was showing. He nodded since he couldn't get a word in edgewise, surprisingly interested in the chance to help the new restaurant and hotel in any way. Especially after what Megan had done for him last night.

"My sister Nicole is the executive chef of Roja with Mariana, who runs Mariana's Market, which is another great place you should check out. It's more of a flea market and food truck joint all rolled into one. Anything you want, you can find it there."

He liked the idea of staying away from Austin while things quieted down. The winery, even though he was a co-owner, would be in good hands with his brothers, and they were planning on him being gone anyway. And heaven only knew how much he needed to clear his head. The thought of needing more than two weeks just to scratch the surface of how bad he felt sobered him. And he hadn't had a drop to drink since last night, even though Roja featured many of the Mendoza wines, which he knew firsthand were spectacular.

"I hear you like horses," she continued. He was positive he'd missed a couple topics in between. "There are all kinds of great places to ride in Rambling Rose."

When was the last time he'd been on a horse? There was nothing quite like being on the back of a huge, gorgeous animal, pretending to be in control but knowing you and the horse were a team built on trust. He could use some serious trust injected back into his life right about now, and a horseback ride would be a decent start. Plus, in spite of being the most confused about women that he'd ever been since he was a teenager, he found Megan's earnestness endearing. He already knew she had a big heart.

"You know, that doesn't sound half-bad, but I'll only go if you'll go with me."

The expression on her face was priceless, and she'd finally quit talking. Maybe she needed some encouragement, too.

"I figure if you're here on Sunday working, you probably have Monday off, and I happen to be free tomorrow, so how about it? Join me? Besides, I have no idea where the stables are."

He took her silence, complete with open but wordless mouth, as a maybe.

The next day Mark and Megan couldn't have asked for better weather for a ride. She figured agreeing to come along with Mark was the least she could do when her sister's future relative from out of town came for a visit. Especially under the circumstances with which Mark had arrived. Maybe he'd explain more about leaving his bride at the altar as they trotted around looking at the green hills and wildflower-dotted valleys. Truth was April was a great month for horseback riding.

But on Monday, as it turned out—under the bright Texas sun, while riding the horse paths and getting their daily dose of fresh air—Mark only wanted to talk about superficial things. As though he was still running away from the wedding that never happened. She knew for a fact no one could compartmentalize that easily, and he was using avoidance like a shield.

"I never learned to ride until I came to Texas," Mark said, sitting tall and holding the reins like a pro, even though he wore a bright-colored short-sleeved shirt more fit for a cruise than horseback riding. And he'd had to borrow appropriate shoes from Rodrigo, because otherwise it'd be his beach loafers. Forget about talking him into wearing a hat. Why mess up a perfect head of styled hair?

"Really?" Megan said, after reassessing his wardrobe. "You seem like a natural." Okay, so she was being generous.

"Riding horses isn't exactly the number one pastime in Miami."

His natural quip made her laugh and Megan enjoyed it. Laughter came easily around him, and he seemed to encourage her with the occasional one-liner. When was the last time a guy had wanted to see her smile or make her laugh? Usually they came around hoping to cash in on some of her wealth.

Having the last name of Fortune, with a father who was a tech king in the gaming biz, didn't help either. But Mark knew all about that thanks to his brother and Ashley's rocky start. David Fortune could be overbearing and had proved so when the triplets had started out with Provisions by hiring Rodrigo behind their backs. But all was well that ends well because Ashley and Rodrigo met and now were getting married because of Dad's intrusion.

"Hey, I'll race you to the ridge," he said, pointing off into the distance. "See what kind of a superhero you really are."

"Oh, you have no idea how bad you're going to lose this race," she said, then clucked with her tongue and pressed her legs against the girth of her sleek American saddlebred filly. She'd chosen the breed at the stables for both of them, guaranteeing a smooth ride. She also knew this breed could easily shift from canter to gallop. Which she was about to prove to Mark.

Mark surprised her with a good challenge, but in the end, Megan pulled it out and, man, did it feel great!

When he caught up to her, he held his hand up for a high five, showing no hard feelings. That was another thing she liked about Mark. "You're a good sport," she affirmed.

"That's because being around you is good for my attitude."

Wait, what? For a guy who'd recently been be-trayed, he looked almost happy. Happy?

She pulled her horse to a stop and gave him a smile that started deep inside. "That's the nicest thing anyone has said to me in a long time. Be-sides my sisters."

She wasn't sure if it was because of the sun glare or from her sincere response, but he screwed up his face and looked at her strangely. "Then you haven't been hanging out with the right people."

Mark drove it home to Megan that since opening both restaurants she hadn't been hanging out with many people *at all* outside her family. For a twenty-four-year-old woman, that seemed so wrong. Yet the thought hadn't occurred to her until Mark from Miami pointed it out. That was an aspect of her life that needed to change because today proved how important playing outdoors was. And if he asked her to accompany him somewhere again, instead of sitting in her little office communing with the blue light from her computer monitor, she wouldn't hesitate to say yes.

Chapter Three

Over the next two days, Mark was a frequent visitor to Roja, which, evidently, hadn't gone unnoticed by Nicole on Wednesday.

He's here again. Think of an excuse to walk through the dining room, she texted, interrupting Megan's thoughts while working on a spreadsheet in her office.

How obvious would that be? she texted back.

He looks lonely.

That's because he's on his honeymoon alone.

My point exactly. Come. Out. Here!

Megan made the requisite headshake and eye roll along with her sigh, pretending to be disturbed by Nicole's interruption. Why couldn't her sister just stick to today's specials instead of trying to meddle in Megan's life? But she'd planted a thought, and now, secretly thinking two o'clock was always a good time for a cup of coffee, Megan couldn't let it go. So she stood, smoothed the fabric of her pencil skirt, adjusted the brightly colored scarf around her neck and shoulders—she'd started including accessories when dressing for work lately—and slipped into her faux leopard flats before heading to the restaurant.

She planned to concentrate on the coffee corner and walk with a determined step straight for it— as though she did it every day, which wouldn't be stretching the truth, because she often did. Then, after she filled her mug, she would casually look up and unexpectedly notice Mark. *Oh, hey*, she'd say, or something much cooler than that.

While a little breathy and jittery in her chest, Megan took two steps into the dining room of Roja as planned.

"Megan?" She immediately heard her name in that familiar rich, if not deep, voice.

She turned toward the sound and actually was surprised, because Mark, sitting at his dining table, wasn't going by the preplanned script in her head. "Hi! I was just going to get—"

"Coffee. Right?"

The lunch crowd had thinned out and only a handful of people were left inside. It seemed uncomfortably quiet, like the rare times she had the Fame and Fortune Ranch to herself. "Uh, yeah."

"Why not bring it over and join me if you can. I'm sick of eating alone."

As she poured herself a mugful, she became aware of the prior jitters morphing into what could only be described as nervousness. If Mark was the reason, that wasn't right, and it had to stop. They'd soon be extended family, and he was getting over a bad breakup. The worst possible kind—betrayal by his almost bride. It was ridiculous for her to think of him as anything other than Mark Mendoza, Rodrigo's brother. So that was that. Case closed.

As she brought her coffee with cream toward his table, he stood, like the gentleman he obviously was, and it hit her as she sat across from him. "You are one flashy dresser for a guy eating lunch alone. You sure you don't have a date?"

"Hey, these are the clothes I packed for my five-star resort honeymoon in Belize. It's all I've got unless I drive back to Austin, and that's the last place I want to be these days."

"Well, if you're going to dress so nicely every day, I should show you around to a few of the swanky places in town so you can wear everything you've packed."

"You know what?" He'd gone back to eating what was left of his tri-tip barbecue salad and used his fork to make a point. "I'm going to take you up on that offer."

Once again, Mark had made her lose her thoughts. She'd been kidding, just trying desperately to make conversation with a man who had to be seven or eight years older than her, and who was, from the amazingly handsome picture he made dressed in that expensive shirt and perfectly creased pants, way out of her usual dating league.

"Lunch was fantastic, by the way. I'll fill out a comment card," he continued, since she was still searching for words.

"Great. I'll be sure to let Nicole know. She works really hard."

"I can tell. I've been saying to Rodrigo this place is top-notch. You guys are killing it." He'd finished his meal and sat with elbows on the table, knuckles of one hand tucked into the palm of the other. Such a manly gesture, and one Megan hadn't seen while dating guys closer to her age. Guys who were usually head down, checking their phones every other minute. Mark was the kind of guy who ignored his phone, letting it vibrate away and pretending it didn't exist. Like now. Giving her his full attention. Which was making her squirm.

"Megan? Did you hear what I said?"

Huh? "Oh, yes. Excuse me and thank you." He'd

guided the conversation in a direction she could deal with, a topic she could dig into without getting flustered. "On my end, we're still getting on our feet. The hotel had a few setbacks earlier this year. You probably heard about the balcony issue. What a nightmare to have it collapse during our big party. Thank God, Grace is okay now."

In January, the family had held a private gathering at the hotel, just a few weeks before the grand opening. In the middle of the party—actually, a first birthday party for her cousin Adam's son, Larkin— the balcony had suddenly given way, and the entire thing collapsed. Grace Williams, the first hospitality trainee to be hired at the hotel, had been standing on the balcony at the time and had injured her ankle badly. Thankfully, she was recovering and was now working as the hotel's manager. She was also engaged to the triplets' brother Wiley.

So far, the police hadn't been able to find proof one way or another of sabotage. But Kane Fortune, Megan's cousin who had overseen the hotel project with Fortune Brothers Construction, had reviewed the damage—and his inspection certificates received prior to the accident—and he was convinced the accident was anything but, even though he couldn't prove it. Which left everyone feeling the need to keep an extra close eye on the goings-on around the hotel, even with the security they'd put in place.

"Oh, yeah. Crazy, right? And highly suspicious." From there Mark and Megan went off on an all-business conversation, which suited her just fine. Because it was highly inappropriate to notice all the appealing things about Mark, a guy who, under other circumstances, would be married now.

After a few more sips of her coffee and a lull in the conversation, she made sure not to overstay her invite. "Well, it was nice talking to you, but I've got to get back to work."

"I understand. But I'm serious about your offer to show me around. Just let me know when it's convenient for you, okay?"

He wasn't pressing her, just being friendly, and the thought of spending an afternoon with Mark around town one day later this week didn't sound half-bad. "I sure will. See you later," she said as she made a detour to the coffee urn and refilled her mug before heading back to her office. She was grateful she not only didn't trip on anything but was back to her safe, reliable and unsurprising accounting programs. Okay, so Mark had pegged her right; she *was* a numbers woman, and proud of it.

Somewhere around four, Megan decided to return her mug to the kitchen. But she knew it was a beautiful day, and she'd been inside too long, so instead, she crossed the hotel lobby to put it on the pickup tray just outside the opened double French doors. The weather app on her phone said it would be in the mid-seventies today, which was about right for April, and it hadn't lied.

When she stepped outside, she took a deep breath of fresh air, then glanced around. The term "see you later" spoken by Mark after lunch suddenly took on a whole new meaning when she saw him stretched out on a lounger, poolside. Long, lean and showing off so much of that beautiful olive-toned skin.

He'd chosen a great pair of trunks for his honeymoon, too, a dark turquoise that complemented his complexion. Wow, that flat stomach, which she'd made note of the very first night they'd met, turned out to be all she'd imagined, too. She had to drag her gaze from appreciating it, while admonishing herself. This was wrong, she told herself. She had to keep her little crush a secret. Even from her sisters. *Especially from her sisters.*

The hotel pool was one of the most beautiful spots on the grounds. It wasn't flashy or overly large. Just a perfect-sized crystal-blue pool under a big tree. The red brickwork surrounding the kidney-shaped pool and hot tub was as unique as the local craftsman they'd hired to build it. Mark had chosen a perfect spot under the huge Texas ash tree that her brothers and cousins had had the wisdom to build around instead of chop down when putting in the pool.

She'd spotted him, enjoyed the vision, and the question remained. Now what? Well, from here she couldn't see a drink on his chairside table. And Nicole made the best lavender lemonade, which was perfect for a lazy afternoon by the pool where snoozing may or may not be on the agenda. Why not get him some? On the house, of course.

If she ordered two, Nicole would get suspicious, so she asked for one, grabbed it and left before any questions could be asked. Clearing her throat and standing tall, she gathered her courage to take it to him. The last thing she wanted to be was a sad little puppy dog bounding around a person who really wasn't looking for a pet. God, where had that image come from? Probably from her propensity to rescue strays. Anyway, she walked confidently, with long sophisticated strides, toward the gorgeous man on the lounger as she pretended she did this kind of thing all the time.

"I thought you might like some lemonade," she announced when she was three feet away.

Mark lifted his head, squinting toward the late-afternoon sun. "Megan?"

She stepped closer and handed the drink to him.

"Thanks. Pull up a chair."

She perched on the dark wood Adirondack chair a couple feet from his lounger.

"Get all your work done?" he asked her.

"I did."

"So why aren't you drinking a lemonade with me?"

"Hadn't occurred to me," she replied, even

though she'd considered every angle on the lemonade delivery.

He sat up—which sent a ripple over those abs—and took a drink. "Wow, this is great. I'll have to fill out another comment card."

He made her smile, which helped her relax.

"So tell me something." Since Megan had offered zero to the conversation, Mark stepped it up. "What made an attractive woman like yourself go into accounting? You seem perfect for being a front-of-the-house asset."

"Ah, well, me and numbers go way back. They were always dependable when other things were confusing. And numbers don't lie. You've noticed that, right? You always know where you stand, and if they don't add up, the error can be found and corrected."

"You like order."

"I thrive in it. Nicole's the artistic sister, and Ashley, as you well know, has enough personality for all three of us."

"And your superpower is numbers."

"Yes. But please don't sing that song again." He laughed outright. She was getting good at calling him out. "In my world numbers are truth. They tell me how well we're doing with our restaurants and now the hotel. I believe in receipts and the bottom line."

"And yet I don't get the impression you're all

about being rich or having more and more. Am I wrong?"

"Maybe because I grew up with wealth, I saw early on what it could and couldn't give a person. All I want to do is help my brothers and sisters pursue their dreams and stay out of the red. We might be trust fund babies, but we know how to work hard, too."

Mark looked around the hotel grounds and held out his arms as evidence. "I can see that." Then he relaxed back on the lounger, took another drink. "You're into family, right?"

"Absolutely. How could I not be, coming from such a big one?"

"I hear you." He went quiet for a moment. "That's why I wanted to get married." He leveled her with his gaze. "I want kids. A big family, like the one I grew up in."

"Me, too," she blurted without realizing how her reply might come off or that she'd actually had this desire but never realized it until now.

"Go big or go home, right?"

She nodded fast. "Absolutely. I mean, I'm a triplet." As though that guaranteed a preference.

"True, but that could backfire, too."

"Oh, I got sick of sharing everything, trust me, but I always wanted to be around my sisters and brothers. I love being a part of a big family. I loved that there was always someone looking out for me, or that I could always be there to look out for one of my siblings."

"They have your back," he added. "Even when they bug the heck out of you."

"True." She smiled and glanced at him, soon realizing they both knew exactly what the other was talking about.

His pleasant smile soon turned serious.

"I hope you won't let my horrible experience sour you on marriage."

"Not a chance. Though I wouldn't wish what you've gone through on my worst enemy."

"I'm just going to keep Rodrigo and Ashley in mind."

"Yes," she said, wholeheartedly. "They're wonderful to be around. Makes me…" She held back her true thought. *...wish I were getting married.*

"Makes you what?" He wouldn't let her get away with dropping it.

"Want what they have. Someday." She quickly clarified.

"I may have totally screwed up my approach to it, but at my age—"

"Which is?"

"Thirty-five. You have a lot more time than I do to find someone and settle down."

So she'd been wrong, thinking he was closer to Rodrigo's age. He was over a decade older than her. They were from different generations, for goodness' sake. What could they possibly have in common? And yet, here they were enjoying each other's company. Well, she was, anyway.

"My parents found each other later in life." Megan reverted to overtalking. "After they'd both been divorced and had little kids, and that drove home the point that a person is never too old to find the right one."

Marci Francis, their terrific mom, had married the love of her life, David Fortune, in what was a second marriage for both. The triplets had four half brothers, two from Mom, Steven and Wiley, and two from Dad, Callum and Dillon, and their one big sister, Stephanie.

"Mom had wanted a sister for Steph, because with all those brothers the poor thing needed one. Emphasis on *one*. Instead, she gave birth to triplets."

Megan had been so busy talking she hadn't realized Mark's expression had turned pensive, and though Megan was being honest about her feelings on big families, under his current circumstances, she wished she'd kept that thought about it never being too late to find the right person to herself. Marriage represented failure to Mark.

There was a long pause after that, and Megan worried she'd talked far too much. He finished his lemonade, rolled the glass between his palms, then set it on the poolside table between them.

"So what else do you like?" Mark said after a couple seconds regrouping, making it clear he was ready to change the subject.

Not only was he gorgeous, but he was a man who seemed genuinely interested in her. Not what her Fortune name could do for him. How novel these days.

"Are you prepared to be really bored? Is that what you want?"

"Let me be the one to decide about that, okay? Plus a little nap by the pool wouldn't be so bad, would it?"

If she were sitting closer to him, she might have playfully cuffed his arm like she had in the bar Saturday night. But he wasn't drunk now, nor was he clothed. Was she ready to touch his skin? Heavens no.

As Megan ran down her list of loves, which included music—some he liked and some not so much—reading—they both liked mysteries and thrillers—simple crafts and, of course, dogs and cats, oh, and horses, Mark saw her blossom.

"Oh, and I do have a habit of saving strays, usually cats. And the occasional dog. Oh, wait, there was that squirrel that got hit by a car. But I was only twelve."

"And yet your sister Stephanie is the vet."

"True. Can't stand blood or shots or, well, just

about anything else a vet does. Surgery!" She shuddered.

He laughed at her honesty.

He'd sensed she preferred to stand back in the shadows instead of having the spotlight, and he'd been right. At first, she seemed hesitant when he'd asked her about herself, like she'd rather be in that tiny office staring at a computer, but the more he tossed questions at her, the easier she answered them. All it took was some sincere curiosity.

"I hear you're originally from Fort Lauderdale." He continued to draw her out of herself.

"Yes. And you're from Miami. City boy versus suburban girl."

"Yet look where we both ended up," he said, letting the irony show in his voice.

"Well, at least Austin is a happening place, but a town that begins with Rambling and ends with Rose isn't exactly an epicenter of Texas, like Miami is in Florida."

"True." He nodded, then added, "But it was time for a change. And living in Austin made the transition easier than I thought it would be."

"You're a winery owner."

"Part owner, yes. A businessperson like you and your sisters."

She smiled. "We're working on it."

The glimpse of excitement in her eyes made him envious. He remembered being young and hungry for big things. He still was, and he was far from being old, he reminded himself almost daily. "You're already succeeding."

"Some weeks the numbers say yes, and other weeks not so much," she said with that contagious upbeat attitude he'd noticed about her. "It's all part of the process."

Other than his current outlook on marriage, he tended to be a positive guy, too. After spending a couple days with Megan, he had complete faith in her success.

"Thanks. You're inspiring me to think big and make bold choices. Oh, but what time is it?" She glanced at her watch. "I better be going. I've got a class at the gym in an hour."

"Wouldn't want you to miss it."

"After sitting most of the day, it's really important."

"I get it. In fact, you've inspired me to pay the hotel gym a visit as soon as I take another dip."

They'd both inspired each other today. A good thing.

Mark and Megan stood at the same time, preparing to say goodbye, even though he wasn't completely ready to.

Then, another curious thought occurred to him. "Hey, have dinner with me tonight, so we can pick up where we left off."

"Okay."

That caught him off guard. She hadn't hesitated this time. And since he didn't have the nerve to show his face at Provisions again and he knew only one other place in town that he'd give five stars, he added, "See you at Roja at seven thirty, then."

So they were both from Florida, were businesspersons and had some other basic similarities, except for the cat and crafts parts. They both liked and wanted big families and weren't afraid to admit it. Unlike Mark, it was clear that Megan was still optimistic about love. Maybe if he hung around her a little more, some of that enthusiasm would rub off on him. In the meantime, he'd settle for her giving him the inspiration to haul his ass out of the lounger and go to the hotel gym.

Ashley scampered through the Roja dining room planning to pop into the kitchen and say hi to Nicole. She couldn't help but notice Megan having dinner with Mark Mendoza. They were deep in conversation, and judging by the interested expressions, they were either great actors—Ashley knew for a fact Megan couldn't fake interest if her life depended on it—or they were having a really good time. What was that about?

Her time was limited, and she hadn't seen Nicole in days, plus she didn't want to interrupt whatever The *M*s—Mark and Megan—had going on. Hmm, without trying, she'd come up with the perfect code name for discussing a certain sister and a certain future brother-in-law with her other sis.

She barged into the bustling kitchen and spotted Nicole in chef mode giving orders.

"Hey, I know this is a bad time, but I wanted to say hi in person and ask where you've been lately. You've been ignoring my texts."

"I'd never do that!" She dug her phone out of her deep pocket and must have discovered she'd missed a few before replacing it. "Oops, sorry, but I've been busy planning your bachelorette party with any free time I can grab." Nicole leaned back on the counter, adjusted her jaunty toque and straightened her chambray chef coat, offering her total attention.

"Aww, that's so sweet. What are we going to do? Wait, don't tell me. I know you know all the things I'd enjoy." She did, didn't she? She had to. That's why Ashley had asked her to plan it.

Nicole stood by, letting Ashley ramble on until the next obvious point came to mind. Ashley hiked her thumb over her shoulder. "What's up with The *M*s?"

"You mean the lovebirds?"

Ashley loved it when triplet telepathy saved so many words and explanations. "So you've noticed it, too."

"This is the only place the guy has eaten since he got here. Not that I don't like his business, but he needs to branch out."

"I'm more concerned about him branching out with Megan."

"There does seem to be something brewing."

"And I'm not sure that's such a good thing, what with him running off from his own wedding and whatever was going on there."

"But Megan looks happy." Nicole stated the obvious.

So Ashley needed to play the devil's advocate. "What if he's one of those guys who fall in and out of love easily?"

"I've thought about that, too. Or worse, what if his fiancée comes back and asks for a second chance?"

Like that would ever happen.

They sighed together, but Ashley glanced at her watch and time was of the essence. "Well, now that I've seen you in the flesh, know you're okay, I've got to get back to work."

"Me, too," Nicole said. "It's busy tonight, but don't worry, I'll keep my eye on you know who."

Ashley gave Nicole a quick hug followed by a wink, then turned to rush back to Provisions, which, thankfully, was also busy. She then tried her best not to gawk as she left the dining area for the parking lot.

Megan couldn't go to sleep. She'd had the nicest dinner out with a man in forever. Too bad it had to be Mark Mendoza. The timing was terrible, and it would be the dumbest thing in the world to let the things she was starting to feel for him grow in any way. Yet, she'd agreed to drive him around town tomorrow and give him a walking tour and mini history of Rambling Rose. She told herself it was so he'd be independent and wouldn't need her anymore because he'd know where everything was. That way, things could get back to normal. And she could return to her routine life with spreadsheets and budgets for two up-and-coming restaurants co-owned by her and her sisters. A routine that used to be just fine, thank you very much. But ever since she'd met Mark, she'd begun to feel that maybe there was more to life than work. Maybe that was why she had a bittersweet feeling about taking half a day off from work tomorrow to be with him.

She'd seen how devastated he was on his nonwedding day. A guy in a rut like that couldn't possibly be interested in starting something with someone new. And if he were inclined, it would surely only be a rebound romance. In other words, dead in the water as far as Megan was concerned. But what a nice distraction from the pattern she'd fallen into. As long as she enjoyed herself, what could be wrong with it?

As she rolled over to her side ready to snuggle down for the night, she struggled with something she hadn't had to in a long time. Yearning thoughts and actual interest in a man.

If nothing more, she and Mark had become friends, which was a good thing for future extended family members. The downside was—that was all they could ever be.

Thursday afternoon, as promised, Megan had played tour guide showing Mark all the latest additions to Rambling Rose thanks to the Fortune family. She'd given him the whole spiel about how it used to be a forgotten blue-collar town, but when it was featured in a documentary on public TV several years ago, her brother Callum recognized an opportunity. His company, Fortune Brothers Construction, which he ran with Stephen and Dillon, came in and built up the sleepy little town. She could tell Mark was impressed with their enterprises, too, especially the veterinary clinic where her sister Stephanie worked, the pediatric center, the upscale retail stores and the high-end Paz Spa.

He'd gone wild at Mariana's Market and tried out the food trucks, insisting they both try fried mac and cheese. "Too much goodness" was all she could say about the greasy treat. It was one more thing they agreed on. While there, she introduced Mark to some of the regulars at the Market. Next, sitting at their regular table, four older men were in a heated game of gin rummy. Megan, not wanting

to interrupt, waved and two of the men nodded as
Megan and Mark continued walking. "That's Norman," she said pointing to a gray-haired, lean and
tanned man. He was the most animated of the four
and was currently grousing about his lousy hand.
"Norman and Cotton Head—I think you can guess
which one he is—"

Mark nodded his understanding at the one with
the shock of the whitest hair in the room.

"—and the others are veterans and when they're
not playing cards here at Mariana's, they volunteer
at the food kitchen in Austin. Norman has been
around so long, he's like a fixture here."

Since the Hotel Fortune didn't have a spa, when
Megan gave him a quick tour of Paz, thanks to her
brother Dillon's love, Hailey, being the assistant
manager, Mark took a pamphlet and seemed to seriously consider scheduling a massage. She drove
him by the Rambling Rose Estates, a gated community filled with multimillion-dollar homes, and
he began to see why Callum Fortune had seen the
growth and opprotunities in the small town. Later,
they'd enjoyed a walk around the manmade pond
and park just outside the gates of the high-end estates, then she drove him back to the hotel, wondering how the time had flown by so quickly.

It seemed everyone employed by the hotel knew
Mark, said hello, returned his smile or waved when
they returned. Everyone from Lucy at the front desk

to the house attendants, poolside servers passing through the lobby and the housekeepers. But that was the kind of guy Mark Mendoza was.

"Hey, before you go, why don't we get some lemonade and sit out by the pool for a while?" Mark said, surprising her. She'd certainly enjoyed their time together, but wasn't he tired of her yet?

It had been another beautiful day with temperatures in the mid-seventies and promised to be a lovely evening. She'd done a lot of talking as Mark's personal tour guide for the last four plus hours. Truth was, the thought of lemonade by the pool sounded great.

"Okay, why don't you go grab some chairs and I'll get the lemonade," she said, standing in the lobby and enjoying his smile every bit as much now as she had at noon when she'd first seen him. She stole an extra second to enjoy it. But then, something he spotted over her shoulder drew his full attention and in the next moment his expression did a complete about-face.

He suddenly looked panicked, as though he didn't know what to do, and she'd never seen him like this, even that first night when he'd resembled a zombie.

"Just go along with me on this, okay? I'll explain later," he said, the urgent tone undeniable as the color drained from his face.

Megan was about to skip her many questions

and say *sure, okay*, but she didn't get the chance. Mark's strong hands gripped her upper arms, pulled her close, then his mouth clamped down on hers in a desperate, all-consuming kiss.

Chapter Four

Mark's split-second decision to grab Megan for a major PDA had followed a head-to-toe reaction at the sight of Brianna—the last person in the world he ever wanted to see again—entering the Hotel Fortune lobby. He knew one day he would have to face her, though not this soon. Nowhere near ready to see her, he freaked out and went momentarily crazy. Shaken and desperate, he did the first thing that came to mind.

Now deep in a lip-lock with the unsuspecting Megan, he felt her tense.

He pulled back just far enough and long enough to whisper over her unsurprisingly soft and plump lips. "Please play along. She's here. I'll explain later." Then, when Megan noticeably relaxed, he dove back in for a task that he intended to be all show and hoped would make Brianna suffer. But unexplainably, he found the kiss rattling to say the least, and electrifying to accurately describe it. He'd kissed a lot of women in his life, but this one was power packed. Maybe he should fake-kiss more often.

Megan was either a great actress, or she was enjoying this public display as much as he was, because she'd taken his kiss a step further. She wrapped her arms around his neck and added a few flicks of her tongue to up the stakes. Now the source of his crazy feelings had bypassed Brianna and was thanks to the warm body flush against his and the mouth that knew how to make a guy forget where he was.

Wow.

Someone cleared their throat. Mark and Megan ignored it, kept kissing like they were on a hot date and headed straight to the bedroom. After several more throat clearings and a more conspicuous cough, followed by a sharp finger poking his back, Mark regrettably ended the seriously good and completely spontaneous make-out session. But not before jotting a mental note to pick up where they'd left off at their earliest convenience.

Now all he needed to do was clear his head

enough to conduct a civil conversation with the woman he'd left at the altar.

He took a breath and faced Brianna, who'd torn out his heart six short days ago.

"Brianna," Mark said, keeping his voice level, doing the best he could to cover his true feelings about what she'd done to him.

"I see you didn't waste any time." Did she think she had the right to be offended? That was nuts.

Mark let go a sharp laugh, let his eyes peruse the surroundings rather than face Brianna. How ironic of her when he had waited longer than she had to horse around. But he'd keep that comment to himself because his quick assessment of the area proved the fake kissing and third-person intrusion had caught the interest of just about everyone else in the hotel lobby. Plus, he prided himself on being a gentleman.

"You shouldn't have come here. We have nothing further to talk about."

To her credit, Brianna looked as shaken as Mark had felt when he'd first spotted her entering the lobby. For such a usually proud and self-confident woman, it had to be extremely hard for her to show such humility in public. Maybe his crazy idea to grab Megan had paid off.

"Look," Brianna said, "I know I messed up." Her tone was nowhere near contrite.

"Oh, you went beyond 'messed up.'"

"I blew it. Yeah. But I'd hoped if I gave you enough time to cool off, you might be able to see that we could still have a chance—"

"Hold it right there." He shook his head. "There is no second chance. Not now. Not ever." Realizing he was still holding Megan in a tight clutch, but she didn't seem to mind, he left well enough alone and continued. "I've moved on, and you should go."

It was Brianna's turn to shake her head. "I don't believe you. Look, I know how much I hurt you and I want to make it up to you. Why do you think I came here?" She glanced around at the gathering audience. "To be humiliated in public?" She continued to shake her head as her eyes became watery. "I came here to beg you to forgive me, and I don't plan to leave town until you do."

"Mark and I are together now."

Megan felt Mark's chest tense at the crazy words that had just tumbled out of her mouth. After she'd listened to everything he'd just said to Brianna— the woman who'd turned Mark into the mess she'd first met last Saturday night—she was willing to do what Mark might be too much of a gentleman to do. To take their new fake relationship to the next level.

She'd expected a reaction out of Mark, like, *Well, let's not go that far*, but he smoothly played along. And why shouldn't he since he'd set the stage with that hot kiss?

Brianna's gorgeous face contorted with disbelief. Megan refused to feel judged by her.

"Oh, really," Brianna said with a snotty, dismissive tone that incited Megan—who'd just surprised herself beyond belief—to double down.

"Frankly, we don't give a flying fig what you think." Megan heard the sounds come out of her mouth but couldn't believe she'd said them. Never in her life had she purposely gotten involved in a charade of such proportions. But she possessively kept her arm around Mark and continued. "In fact, I really need to thank you. Mark is the best thing that ever happened to me."

Was this really her voice saying such outrageous words? The thrill spiraling through her almost matched the excitement Mark had just stirred up when he'd kissed her. She would save that confusing thought for later. Now Mark's fingers dug into her waist, which was obviously his reaction to the second bold and surprising announcement coming from his new fake "girlfriend." Maybe she had gone too far. Of course they'd talk all this out later and she'd make sure he knew she was acting. But was she? To quote Brianna, "really?"

Continuing to act out of character, since Megan had apparently shocked both Mark and Brianna into silence, she talked up her relationship with Mark. "We hit it right off and have been seeing each other every day since he left you." Megan ended with a jab meant for what should be Brianna's glass jaw. "What we have is based on honesty and trust."

There was nothing Brianna could add to that, especially since Mark nodded along with everything Megan had just made up. Except for the part about being honest with each other, considering the fake kiss and relationship bit. Obviously, they'd also moved into the trust zone, or he would never have started this ruse with Megan in the first place. He had to trust that Megan would come through for him. Even if only with a crazy prank to get back at the woman who had jilted him. Maybe they *had* become real friends in less than a week.

Having met her match in Megan, who had painted quite a pretend picture, Brianna silently turned and left the lobby. The term *seething* came to mind. Which was good, because that would give Megan a chance to tell the front desk staff to under no circumstances give that woman a room at Hotel Fortune.

"Hey," Mark said softly into her ear since they were still clutching each other for dear life. "Thanks for sticking up for me."

Letting up on her hold, since they still seemed to be the center of attraction in the lobby, she smiled. "I was glad to do it."

"Had some choice words, too. Not just a fig, but a flying one?" His eyes, dark and warm, like a place she could easily get lost in, looked amused. "You're quite the cusser."

All she could do was shrug, which made him smile.

He gazed at her for a long moment as something special passed between them. A bond? Those pretend kisses had gone deeper than either was ready to admit. She felt it and could sense the same in his steady, searching gaze. Mark leaned toward her, as if to kiss her again, and in that second, she knew she would welcome him back. This time there wouldn't be any pretending involved. But something must have made him think twice. Maybe the audience? Because he stopped himself.

Without another word, they stood appreciating each other. This would normally be the time when a high five was in order, but neither of them moved. They both knew the truth, though. When push came to shove, she'd delivered for him, and it was about time the guy had someone in his corner. She was glad to be that person, even if their intimacy was all fake.

Since everyone nearby had clearly overheard the heated exchange, especially about Mark and Megan being a "couple" now, they came forward to offer their congratulations. It finally broke their unspoken standoff. Mark attempted to clarify but was inundated with more congratulations and got nowhere on the explaining. Truth was, if everyone was in on their plan, it wouldn't be long before someone slipped up and Brianna was on to them. He looked at Megan for help. She just shrugged again and signaled with her eyes that they might as well play along. So he did, which had turned out to be something they were both apparently better than good at.

"We should probably talk more about what just happened," he said out of the corner of his mouth, for Megan alone.

"I agree. How about my office?" she replied, also out of the corner of her mouth, while smiling for the hotel employees who were wishing them well.

"Where anyone, including your sisters, can pop in on a whim?"

He made a good point.

"Let's go to my room," he suggested. "We can have complete privacy there."

Mark took Megan's hand and led her out of the lobby, down the hall on the first floor to his corner room, far from the noise and bustle of the lobby.

When was the last time she had followed a man to a hotel room? Uh, never? Sad but true, and this time, even though for fake reasons, it was still exciting as all get-out. He led so naturally, and the man could swagger without trying. Damn. *Fake, fake, fake*, she kept reminding her senses. And when that didn't work, she mentally chided, *Settle down. We're just going to work on our strategy in case Brianna sticks around like she said she would.*

He opened the door to the room, and being a complete gentleman, went right to the French doors and opened them to the outside, giving the room added space and removing a huge chunk of intimacy. But also helping Megan relax about being in his room, just the two of them. Alone. After a world-class kiss. Fake or not fake, this was going to be hard.

"I've got some bottles of water in the minifridge, if you'd like."

Megan's throat was beyond dry and she nodded gratefully. He made quick business of getting them both waters, her only clue that he might feel as awkward as she did. She took the chair across from his bed while he sat on the bench at the foot of the bed.

"Sorry to put you through that," he began tentatively.

"It *was* surprising." In more ways than she was ready to admit.

He looked chagrined, maybe a little ashamed of himself as he stared at the water bottle for a moment. "It's foolish, I know. I'm a grown man, but I needed to get back at Brianna. I just couldn't let her come waltzing back into my life with her big eyes and pouty mouth and think that's all it took to win me back. She needed to get a clear message that I'm not now or *ever* going to be used as a doormat. We're through."

She believed him. And she was also a pragmatist. "I have no idea what I would've done in your situation, but now that we've got everyone around here believing we're an item, I think we're going to have to keep up pretenses. At least until she leaves."

"Agreed. That is if you're willing to disrupt your life to help me out." He sent her a sharp glance, making sure she had a say in whatever happened next. "I realize that's asking a lot."

"As it turns out, this happens to be a good time for me to have a fake relationship." That made him laugh lightly, which made her glad. "Maybe I can parlay it into a date for my sister's wedding?"

"Ha! Yeah. I owe you. You're on."

"Thanks." She crossed one leg over the other and tucked her hair behind one ear. "And I'm sorry if I got carried away. I never realized I could be such a good actress."

Was that a look of disappointment on Mark's face? Brief, but nevertheless, it registered with Megan.

"You were amazing. I almost forgot we were pretending."

As heat trickled up her neck, Megan cracked up. Who'd have ever thought she'd be so good with fake romance?

"So," he said, obviously hesitating to continue. "Do you think you can do it again?"

"Now?" Mark looked perplexed. Oh, my gosh, how embarrassing, that wasn't what he meant. Yet here she was ready to dive back in kissing him again. Why couldn't she have kept her mouth shut for one more second before she figured that out? "I mean for as long as she sticks around?" she said, riding a cringe and covering for her mistake.

"If you don't mind?"

She could insist Mark tell her exactly what Brianna had done to deserve this before she agreed to it, but that wasn't her style. Besides, she had already thrown the idea out there. "Hey, I'm the one who said we were together now. Though I can't believe I said that." She covered her eyes and shook her head, letting embarrassment take over.

"You were great." She looked at him again. Was that admiration in his gaze? "Man, we make a great fake couple."

"I know, right?" Just as quickly her embarrassment was forgotten. They were in this together. Team MeMa. Oh, not that, that was what she used to call her paternal grandmother. MarGan? MegArk. Dang, their names didn't blend well. Which only proved she'd been watching too much *Entertainment Tonight*. And she and Mark weren't a celebrity couple. They sure were good actors, though.

"So," he continued, "I say for the next few days we make a point to be seen all over town, holding hands, stealing kisses, looking all dreamy at each other."

This was surprising coming from a man like

Mark. Though he *was* said to be a marketing maven. It felt more like something Megan and her friends back in high school might conspire to do. Still, it all felt deliciously fun.

Did he just say "stealing kisses"? Could she handle it and not let it or him get to her? "Makes perfect sense." She did her best to sound all business while the cells under her skin were jumping around like Fourth of July fireworks.

"I can't thank you enough." He gulped some water and Megan got the distinct impression he was ready for her to leave. So she stood and he immediately looked confused.

"Uh," he started, "if we're going to be convincing, you can't just take off now." He used the hand holding the water bottle to gesture toward the door. "Everyone in the lobby just watched us come down here. If you go, they'll all think I'm a slam-bam-thank-you-ma'am kind of guy. If we're faking a romance, I want to be convincing."

That angle of the ruse hadn't occurred to her, and his description of what the "audience" out front expected them to be doing right then was an eye-opener. Back came the heat on her neck and up her ears. Plus, he was right. They'd publicly declared their relationship then headed to his room. Right about now they were expected to be in the throes of heated sex. The flush spread to her cheeks, and he obviously knew why, since a teasing smile crossed his lips.

"Sorry if that makes you uncomfortable."

"No, that's okay. And we *were* convincing."

"Why don't you stick around, and we can rent a movie. I'll order room service. Is that okay?"

She didn't have any plans, so why not?

Mark suggested they sit outside the room on the white wrought iron bistro set on his small patio while they waited. Megan understood he was doing his best to make her feel comfortable. She liked that about him. Then, when room service arrived, they enjoyed their dinner outside. Megan couldn't rave enough about Nicole's flatbread pizza with spinach and mushrooms, and a soft mozzarella and parmesan combo on top. She'd asked the kitchen to hold the caramelized onions, though. Mark seemed to be enjoying the chicken he'd ordered from the Tex-Mex menu section. He'd suggested they share some Mendoza triple white wine, too. And it was delicious. The evening was growing cool and fresh, a few stars had started to make their appearance over the low-rising hills in the distance, and Megan hadn't felt this content with a man in ages. Too bad it was all fake because otherwise this would be a very special date.

Later, after they'd eaten, they watched the latest Avengers movie. Megan still occupied the only chair in the room and Mark had pulled in one of the patio chairs. That couldn't have been comfortable for an entire movie, but he was a gentleman through and through and chose not to involve the big beautiful bed in the center of his room.

Halfway through the movie, he checked his vibrating phone. "It's her again. Between my brothers and now her, I may stop answering my phone altogether. You can text or call anytime, though."

"Actually, I don't have your number."

"Really? I've got yours from Rodrigo. Then we've got to fix that," he said, calling her phone.

"What if you get so used to not answering the phone that you never check?" she said, answering the phone and saving his number. "What would the point of my calling or texting be?"

He'd been busy scrolling and tapping his phone since he'd called her. "I'll immediately know it's you because I just assigned you a ringtone."

"You're turning your ringer back on?"

"Yeah. I also changed the sound for Brianna's calls and texts." He played something that sounded like the short, detached violin notes for the soundtrack in horror movies—look over your shoulder! Don't open that door—and it gave Megan shivers. The bad kind. But it also made her laugh, which they did together. "I know, perfect, right?"

"Why don't you just block her calls?"

"Then I wouldn't get to hear this," he said playfully hitting it again.

So he wasn't really ready to completely sever ties with Brianna? The thought gave Megan pause.

He fiddled more with the phone screen and held it up again. "And this is what I've got for you."

The *Wonder Woman* theme song played loud and clear.

"You've got to be kidding me." She was good at pretending to be insulted, too, because seriously, it was kind of sweet.

He lifted a single brow. "After tonight in that lobby? I have proof what your superpower is, and it isn't numbers."

Finally, he'd gotten around to the elephant in the room. Their amazing kiss. So he had felt it, too.

Maybe because Megan knew everything happening between them was fake, it had emboldened her, but she was as surprised as Mark at what came out of her mouth next. "You weren't so bad yourself, honey."

Then in dead silence they stared at each other for an unusually long second or two, before bursting out in laughter. Whew, she'd worried she'd blown it. One thing was obvious: she laughed a lot whenever she was with Mark. It was refreshing and proved they could be good friends. Which brought her full circle to still trying to figure out what kind of relationship they had. The romance part was fake, but maybe the friendship was real?

Then the horror sound of staccato violin strings rang out from his phone.

And he obviously wasn't ready to completely cut ties with Brianna since he hadn't blocked her number.

He made a face for Megan's sake at the horror-movie sound, but read the incoming text. "Get this, she's telling me where she's staying just outside town in some small hotel, and says she won't leave until she convinces me to come back home with her."

She'd already told him that in the lobby, and he seemed eager to read her message. Maybe he wasn't ready to give up on her yet.

"Are you sure you want to go through with this?"

"Absolutely," he said, putting down his phone.

If they were friends, she needed to believe him. "Then I guess we've got our work cut out for us."

He nodded. "We have to be convincing."

"Convincing. Yeah. I'll work on that," she said, tapping her lips with her index finger. Regardless where he really stood with Brianna, it was fun to tease Mark, but his demeanor had suddenly changed.

"You're sure you're okay with this?"

Megan wanted more than anything to convince Mark she could be counted on. "She doesn't deserve you, Mark. She didn't listen to you in the lobby, and she's insisting you go home with her. I'd say we've got a lot of convincing to do. But I'm willing to do it if you're positive this is what you want to do."

"I am."

He smiled that appreciative smile, which was enough to release some adrenaline in her chest. What in the world had she agreed to? "I should probably be going."

"You don't want to finish the movie?"

"I know how it ends. Besides, I've got to brush up on my acting skills. Oh, tomorrow is a big workday, meetings and monthly reports due." Truth was, she needed a recovery day from Mark and their fake relationship.

"Understood. But what about a cocktail by the pool to keep up appearances?"

"After work?"

"Yeah. I'll wait for you."

She'd given him an out, but he'd definitely wanted to see her again. "Okay." Friday nights were usually spent eating takeout and watching reruns of *Friends*.

"So what do you usually do on Saturdays?"

"I hate to disappoint you, but nothing exciting. A little grocery shopping, running around doing errands."

"Well, let's do that. But we'll have breakfast first. Where do you recommend?"

"I like a little mom-and-pop diner on the other side of town. They make great omelets."

"Sounds good. What time?"

With that as a start, they figured out the rest of their evil, but oh so fun, plans for the weekend when they'd put on another great show anytime they spotted Brianna in the vicinity. Then, having decided they'd spent enough time in his room, pretending to do what lovers do in hotel rooms, Megan left through Mark's patio exit.

The minute she put her key in her suite at the ranch, Nicole's door flew open and both sisters' heads popped out. "Were you planning to tell us what's going on?"

Surprising, but not entirely unexpected given the hotel grapevine. Megan grinned. "Only if you pour me a glass of wine."

"Done." Nicole widened her door.

"Get in here." Ashley was impatient. "I stopped by to talk to Nicole and we've been waiting for over an hour and you've got a lot of explaining to do."

The usual Saturday errands had never been so interesting. Even during breakfast, Mark acted like they'd been dating for ages, and after the first time or two, Megan got used to him taking her hand whenever they walked down the main street of Rambling Rose.

Sure enough, across the street Brianna appeared, coming out of The Shoppes at Rambling Rose with a bag in her hand. Had she bought something sexy to help lure Mark back? Megan glanced at her average chest, trying not to let insecurity throw her off her game. She hated to admit it, but the woman was gorgeous.

In an exaggerated manner, Mark playfully pulled her back to the jewelry store that they'd just passed. "Come on," he said, projecting his voice. "Let me buy you those earrings you liked."

"Mark, you're just too good to me." She pretend-protested, speaking much louder than necessary and sounding more Texas than Fort Lauderdale. With that, he tugged her close, then used his palms to cup her jaw, lining up her mouth with his, and delivered their first kiss of the day. The kind of kiss that came with a promise. Oh, man, he could promise her anything and she would believe him right about now. Her average breasts tightened, and she told herself she was a method actress, plain and simple. That Mark was only treating her like she was special to make Brianna seethe. In the process, he'd made her insides sizzle and the backs of her knees tickle.

Oh, and the shells of her ears must be bright red because they were radiating heat. Good thing her hair covered them.

After Brianna got into her car and, obviously seeing them, slammed the door, they ducked into the pet store connected to the veterinary clinic just for fun. She did her favorite thing while waiting to introduce Mark to her sister and played with puppies while her sister Stephanie saw her furry patients.

Megan held a rescue puppy of undetermined lineage next to her cheek. "Stephanie has given her staff strict orders that I'm only allowed to adopt one cat or dog every six months." She kissed the pooch on top of his head, then gave a scrunched-up-nose kind of smile to the dog. "You are a sweetie."

Knockout kisses and puppies—what an amazing day it was adding up to. Could any day with a man be more perfect? And after that, lunch, then later they got coffee.

Once seated at a small table off by itself, sipping their lattes, Megan tried to get Mark to open up more. "I've heard you're a marketing guy with all kinds of great ideas. Rodrigo has bragged about you for as long as I've known him."

"I may know a thing or two."

"How'd you wind up there?"

"Ha, good question. When our family opened the winery, there were a lot of things we didn't know. We're all self-taught, and where there was a need, we filled it."

"I know exactly what you mean. There was so much we didn't realize when we opened Provisions."

"Exactly. Well, I'd worked in restaurants in Miami and saw how they marketed themselves. When we opened, I used what I knew worked, but also added my own ideas."

"So, what would you suggest for Roja and Pro-visions?"

"I'm sure Rodrigo has pounded this point home, and he's using it for the hotel, too. Technology is king. You've got to be easy to find online."

"Check."

"Target the right audience. Provisions and Roja are both upscale, but Roja is a bit more casual, so they may appeal to different groups."

"Yes, makes sense." Mark was setting Megan's mind on fire with great steps to follow through on.

"Also give incentives for people to come, and more importantly, to come back."

She nodded hard. "Yes. Like Tuesday for Two, a special price for two three-course meals?"

"Absolutely."

Before they knew it, they'd talked for a full hour and hadn't even finished their drinks. He'd given her a list of ten things to follow up with her sisters on, and they'd spent an entire day together acting like a couple. Not once did her mind wander to spreadsheets and budgets, except when they were talking business. But the reverse had happened all day Friday. While trying to work, her thoughts kept drifting to him. Nor did he get on her nerves. She liked him. She really liked him. And respected his knowledge and expertise. From his constant attention, she assumed she hadn't gotten on his nerves either.

"After today, everyone we've run into will think we're an item," she casually commented as they strolled the sidewalk.

"And that's exactly what I want, so they can report back to Brianna."

"But no one knows her here."

"So? Word will still travel, tongues will wag about the Fortune triplet and her new guy."

She chuckled and he took her hand again as they walked back to his car. She could get used to this.

It was only a few steps later that Mark whispered, "Incoming."

Brianna was back?

"Let's set this up. I want her to think I'm telling you something very private." He walked her backward to the nearest redbrick wall outside a deli.

Megan relaxed against it as he leaned over her, one hand pressed on the bricks above her head.

"And the purpose of this is?" she said, looking wistfully into his gaze.

"This is where a couple might have a sweet conversation. Say, for instance, if I was your boyfriend."

She couldn't help but smile and fight off a little laugh because it was fun, and a thrill went up her neck when he said *boyfriend*.

Maybe in an alternate universe, but still… "And the purpose of us doing all this is?"

"This is where I tell you something special. Intimate. But sweet. Like how I think your eyes are the most beautiful shade of blue I've ever seen, and I can't believe how lucky I am to get to hang out with you."

"Really?"

She fell out of character just long enough to embarrass herself.

"Perfect response. Makes me realize how darn sweet you are." As her breath hitched from his kind words, he cupped her cheek and leaned in closer. "Now in a totally pretend way, I'm telling you I'm really glad I've met you, and it meant so much to me to have you by my side when I was down and hurting." He stopped talking long enough to draw close to her ear, and Megan hoped Brianna was watching and weeping. But when he nibbled her ear, there was no way to prepare for the onslaught of goodness he'd just bestowed on her. "That since I've met you and have been spending time with you, I feel like a lucky guy. I feel lighter, like a kid again."

Man, she wished he wasn't only pretending. "And if you said all those things to me," she whispered as she lifted her chin more, bringing her lips closer to his, playing along, "I'd want to kiss you, because those were the kindest and tenderest and therefore sexiest words I've ever heard."

Megan's words nearly knocked Mark off balance.

"Cue the fake kiss," he whispered over her mouth

as they joined for the most amazing and tender kiss he'd delivered to anyone since high school. He'd never once kissed Brianna like that, he knew for a fact.

"What is going on here?" Rodrigo's suspicious voice broke the special moment.

"Is she gone?" Mark asked.

"Who?"

"Brianna."

Rodrigo looked around. "I don't see her."

"Good. Then we're done here." And like that, Mark went right back into business mode, Oscar-winning moment over, hard as it was to stop.

Mark wasn't positive what Megan really thought about him, but he sure believed they had something between them. Something undefinable. Something he'd always felt was missing in his relationships. Which made him really like this fake dating, because who knew it could be so emotionally fulfilling?

Since it was no longer necessary, they moved out of the pose and Mark turned to his brother. "We were just putting on a show for Brianna."

Rodrigo screwed up his face and looked around. "Who, as I already mentioned, is nowhere around."

"Really? Could have sworn I saw her again." Mark kept up the deceit, to save face. "My mistake. Sorry, Megan."

She glanced suspiciously at him. "Seriously?"

Mark focused on his brother. "Megan is helping me—"

"I know about the harebrained plan. Ashley told me last night. I just didn't expect to see my accountant and my brother making out in public. That's all."

"Well, I'm trying to get Brianna to leave town and it looks like it's going to take some doing."

Rodrigo shook his head. "Sometimes I wonder which one of us is the older brother."

"You of all people should be glad I'm moving on."

"Pretending to be in a relationship is moving on?"

"It's a start."

"If this is your best plan, then I wish you luck. See you back at the hotel."

After Rodrigo left, Mark glanced sheepishly at Megan.

"You didn't really see her?"

"I thought I did." He hoped he was convincing.

"Oh, you owe me dinner, mister."

With that, Mark snapped his fingers. "And that's what I'm talking about. How about you help me make my infamous return to Provisions tonight?"

They continued their walk to his parked car, holding hands out of habit.

"Sure. As long as we don't sit at the bar, and you don't order whiskey."

"Deal. I promise to smell good, too." He grinned wide as he opened the passenger-side door for her.

"More cruise clothes?" she said as she slipped inside.

He nodded and grinned. This pretending business was really turning out to be fun. And it seemed like he'd picked the perfect woman to help him, too.

Chapter Five

Megan needed to give Mark a pep talk before they walked into Provisions for dinner. She wanted to share the great food from the restaurant she and her sisters launched together last year. Yes, he'd eaten at the bar, while drunk, but she wanted him to experience dining there. At a table for two nestled by the window.

After his infamous arrival one short week ago, he was hesitant to step foot inside again. After spending several days with him, it struck her as strange because in every other way the man oozed confidence. Which she found extremely attractive. Uh-oh, what she meant was, it was a good trait in a

man. And she did sympathize with having to face
the place where everyone saw him at his lowest and
most vulnerable point last week. No one wanted to
be remembered that way.

"Most of the people who were there last week
won't be here," she reminded him. "Sure, there are
a few regulars, and there is the staff. They should
all be the same, but—"

"That's not helping," he said patiently.

"Good point. Okay, then how about the fact we'll
be seated in that window?" She gestured across the
parking lot to the main window for the restaurant.
It was even framed in tiny fairy lights. "If Brianna
is anywhere around, she'll see us."

Since he took her arm and headed straight for
the doors with new confidence, she figured she'd
convinced him. Evidently, he was of the rip-the-
bandage-off mindset, whereas Megan was more of
a one-step-at-a-time kind of person. She'd assumed
they'd wander in, maybe talk to the staff, she'd show
him around—the usual kind of thing. But no. He
walked right up to the hostess and said, "Table for
two under..." He glanced at Megan for the answer.

"Megan? Or Mark?"

"Oh." The new hostess seemed to realize something. "The *M*s."

Huh, The *M*s? It sounded ridiculous, proving
what they were doing was, well, she had to face it,
juvenile. Had Ashley and Nicole already pinned a

nickname on them? Though it was far better than the ones Megan had tried to come up with—MeMa, MarGan, whatever—the nickname still seemed presumptuous.

She inhaled as they followed the hostess to their table with a fresh reminder that everything they did wasn't real. How easily she could forget. Compatible or not, it didn't matter. This was all playacting. The whole purpose being to be seen together to drive a point home to Brianna. Nothing more. Thus the window seating at Provisions. To put them on display. And speaking of display...

He certainly looked fine in his Miami-suave dinner wear. From his pale blue dress shirt with the top two buttons open, and obviously slim fit, to the pressed navy pants and so very un-Texas-like leather loafers sans socks. The rich, almost mauve tone of the shoes matched perfectly with his belt, by the way. The sharp, hint-of-sage linen basket-weave blazer proved the man had excellent taste in clothes. The Provisions hostess certainly agreed, judging by the way she—Megan decided to be kind—*appreciated* his style before and after the procession to their table. Actually it was more like leering. But what could she expect hanging out with such a fine man?

Good thing Megan had also stepped up her game tonight from the usual business casual to flirty and fun. She finally had a chance to wear the new fit-and-flare dress—shorter than she was comfortable with—she'd bought at her cousin's boutique in town. Yet somehow, her navy cardigan with rainbow buttons couldn't compare to his blazer. So she was glad she'd thrown it over her arm instead of wearing it.

And yes, she'd caught Mark checking out her legs earlier. Or maybe it was just the one touch of her outfit that sang out for Texas—her ankle boots. Still, she liked the reaction on his face when he did.

As they sat at their table, she let go of any insecurities by reminding herself everything was pretend. Just have some fun, she told herself. So they did.

An hour later, toward the end of their meal, they were blindsided by Brianna's approach. Her sophisticated little black dress and French perfume were hard to ignore, yet they hadn't seen her coming. Because, instead of looking around, they'd been completely wrapped up in each other. Well, Megan could only speak for herself, but it seemed Mark had been, too. They were already holding hands on the table—Mark had initiated it—while sitting across from each other. Their public displays of affection had become second nature, so there they were when the long-haired, gorgeous surprise arrived.

"Brianna," Mark said, composed for a guy who'd been caught off guard. Her name sounded more like a statement than a hello.

"Mark." She matched his tone. Though her eyes

studied everything about Megan, from how her hair was tucked one side behind her ear to showcase her long silver earrings, to the way she kept her feet under her chair, crossed at the ankles, as though sitting forward and holding hands like that was odd. Well, how else was a girl supposed to sit while leaning across a table to hold hands with her new faux beau?

"I see you're still in town," Mark continued, stating the obvious while Megan's cheeks heated by the close scrutiny of her "competition."

Brianna switched her attention back to Mark and lightly tossed her gorgeously groomed cinnamon hair to prove it. Megan couldn't deny that fact. Brianna was a knockout. Her perfectly manicured fingers played with her delicate necklace. "I'm a woman of my word, and I don't intend to leave until you come to your senses and go with me."

Mark glanced at Megan, as though to gather his patience, then toward Brianna. "Interesting word choice, Bri, 'A woman of your word.' Hmm."

"Everything is perfectly explainable. All I need is some time alone with you." Another glance toward Megan as though expecting her to pop up and take off at her command.

"Not going to happen." Mark, apparently, was of the fool-me-once-shame-on-you ilk. Twice it would be on him, and he was too smart for that. Megan mentally cheered him on as he finally convinced

Brianna to leave them alone. "Now, if you'll excuse us, we were just about to order dessert."

Dismissed, Brianna silently inhaled while dealing with another round of defeat. Her undeniably intriguing amber eyes narrowed a hint as she glanced at Megan, as though her mortal enemy, before she turned and walked back to the bar. The bar. Ha! Was it fate or triplet telepathy that put Brianna there —if the latter, thanks, Ashley—in the exact spot Mark had been seated last week after Brianna had ruined his wedding day?

Later, after that fantastic meal at Provisions and an even better dessert, which they shared, Mark gazed into Megan's eyes. "About that kiss against the wall earlier today…"

"Fake. Don't worry, I get it. I'm not falling for you." *Liar.*

"I have to come clean, though." He sniffed and scratched absentmindedly above one brow. "I wasn't completely positive I'd seen Brianna, just maybe-ish, but I went for it anyway."

She couldn't help but smile and feel complimented. He'd wanted to kiss her? No. She had to be interpreting that wrong. The man was obviously still all shook up about how his potential marriage had fallen apart. "Because you have to make sure Brianna gets the point. No worries. Even if she isn't definitely around, word will get back to her about us. All over town. Isn't that what you told me today? Ha."

"What's so funny?"

"I never saw myself as someone who *wanted* to stand out. I like being incognito, the quiet triplet, the least flashy one. The girl behind the computer. But for some crazy reason, I'm fine with however you want to work this revenge stunt."

He tilted his head and made a face. "I'd rather not think of it as revenge." He turned his coffee cup around in the saucer. "More like comeuppance."

"However you want to put it, I'm fine. Just so you know."

"Then thanks." His gaze settled on her and she let the usual reaction roll across her shoulders like an easy massage. There was something special about his warm brown eyes that seemed to reach inside her and wake up every cell, as though she'd been sleeping her way through Rambling Rose until now.

Brianna's piercing violin alert tone spoiled the moment and ratcheted up Megan's heart rate. He pressed his lips together and looked down long enough to read aloud. "'I'm not giving up.'" He shot Megan an incredulous glance. "The woman hurt me like no one ever did before, and now she thinks she can win me back just by being stubborn."

"More like dense." Though Megan continued to wonder why he just didn't block her calls and texts if he really didn't want to be bothered by her. Which made Megan also wonder who might be denser, her or Brianna?

"Self-centered. I should've caught on to that sooner." He was expressing his feelings and clearly on a roll, so she let him go. "Heartless, too."

Megan sensed his pain, and knew he wasn't exaggerating. She'd seen that all-encompassing anguish firsthand one week ago. The sight of Mark had been etched on her heart ever since. Brianna had done a number on him and she didn't deserve a man like Mark. Always practical, and like the pro she'd evidently turned into in one short week, Megan quipped, "Then we need to make plans for tomorrow."

Or was she taking advantage of the situation?

Seeing his expression change from exasperated to amused emboldened her attitude. "How about tennis in the morning and checking out the local watering hole in the afternoon?" These weren't things she'd ever done before, but they sounded fun. Like something The *M*s would routinely do.

And his smile could only be described as a special reward.

Sunday's tennis match turned into a fiasco in the morning. Megan had pulled some strings with a friend at the chamber of commerce who lived in the Rambling Rose Estates and had managed to get a guest pass for their exclusive tennis club.

Mediocre in tennis at best, Megan happily discovered she was well matched with Mark's "skills" on the courts. Still, they had fun, and fun seemed to be the theme of whatever it was they had going on in their fake romance. They spent more time laughing together and at each other than actually hitting the balls. And neither could remember how to correctly score the matches.

"What match?" They laughed. A tennis game required a volley and it seemed the best they could do was one or two returns at best.

After spending an hour mostly running after missed serves and returns on the courts, they agreed lunch at the local bar and grill sounded ideal. There, they got swept up in the baseball season kickoff game and made an extra effort to cheer on the Rangers. More fun. The kind of fun Megan had never experienced before with a man. Boy, she'd missed out on a lot.

Every time Mark's eyes met hers, he smiled, as though he liked having their secret, which always sent a little sweet something through her chest. Then to keep up the facade, he'd pull her in for a quick hug, or touch her knee when he asked if she wanted another beer. Well, technically, when he yelled at her, because that was the only way to be heard in the noisy bar. At one point, she felt bold enough to put her hand on his neck and tug him over for a quick kiss. Only because they needed to keep up appearances, of course. And he was surprisingly receptive, even though Brianna was nowhere around. But who knew? Maybe she was hiding in the group somewhere.

Yeah, whatever. She kissed him again.

By the end of the weekend, even after having all of Sunday off work, Megan still wasn't ready for Monday. Which was strange because she always looked forward to work. It reminded her how much she and her sisters had accomplished in the last couple years. There was so much to be proud of, and accomplishments required hard work. She'd proved she could do it and was ready for more. At twenty-four she was just reaching her stride. Who knew what the future would hold?

But since Mark had come into the picture, she'd learned about the other side of hard work and pride. Three simple letters: *f-u-n*. The man was definitely that, all wrapped up in an extra pretty package. She'd never been so lucky. Too bad it was all just playacting.

When she walked into the hotel Monday morning, several sets of eyes watched with knowing gazes. Had she mismatched her simple separates? But every person also smiled and waved like she was their friend. Of course she knew all the employees and most of those in the training program, too, but she'd never felt this level of connection before.

When she arrived in her office, she guessed why they'd all had that look on their faces. A huge bouquet of Texas-sized flowers of every color and shape sat in the middle of her desk, filling the small room with a beautiful scent. All of those employees must have seen the florist deliver the flowers. In the center on a tiny plastic holder was a card with Petunia's Posies logo, the local florist, on it that read, "Thanks for the best weekend I've had in a long time. Can't wait to see you again. Mark."

A cascade of chills started at the crown of her head and spread like a waterfall over the rest of her. For one quick second Megan let herself make a wish. Maybe she and Mark could one day be the real thing?

Quickly she came back to reality and glanced at the calendar. This was the second week of his honeymoon for one. By this time next week, he'd be gone.

Mark knew he couldn't run away from reality forever, but he was determined to finish out his scheduled time off from the winery right here in Rambling Rose. Why not? With such great company, he'd be crazy not to. But Megan had a job, and that gave him far too much time on his own to think. The last thing he wanted to do was think about Brianna. That was done. Over. *Acabado.*

Being a marketing maverick, he set his mind to thinking about the potential for Hotel Fortune. According to Rodrigo, their computer system couldn't tell them if they were completely booked or half-empty at any given time, which seriously needed to get worked out. He'd also checked them out on Yelp, as he knew Rodrigo already had, and discovered several disgruntled comments with low ratings because of the booking screwups, and some just nasty for the sake of being rude. Not good. The hotel manager, Grace Williams, had replied to some of the negative reviews, reassuring the guest that they would look into their complaint, hoping they would stay again in the future. She had also thanked everyone who'd placed a positive review, hoping to see them back as well. But what was up with their reservation program?

Some former guests complained that there weren't enough activities to take part in on-site. The hotel had no entertainment organizer, to the best of his knowledge. Brady, the concierge, was a great guy and had been very helpful all week. Maybe he was the one to talk to. Mark understood this was a boutique hotel where luxury and service meant everything, and the hospitality team seemed top-notch, but guests also loved to have a reason to come out of their rooms. He wasn't talking about hotel bingo night, but why not hire a local musician to play in the lobby during cocktail hour once or twice a week? Lots of boutique hotels he'd stayed in around the world offered that. Which, for one quick second, reminded him where he was supposed to be this second week of his honeymoon. If he remembered correctly, he would've been on a snorkeling excursion in the gorgeous Caribbean Sea.

Don't go there. Concentrate on right now.

Or maybe the hotel guests needed more reasons to stay *in* their rooms. Why couldn't the hotel commission the local Paz Spa to send a masseuse here at a guest's request for in-room spa treatments? Seemed like a win-win to him. The wife could have a massage while the husband played golf at the nearest course. Maybe Grace and Brady could arrange a package deal for the spa treatment and eighteen holes of golf. For the more outdoors oriented, there were all kinds of beautiful places to hike. He needed to find out where those places were, too.

Or, to bring in more locals, who would spend money in the bar or restaurant, why not have a theme night a day or two every week?

To keep his mind off Megan, which was getting harder and harder to do, he spent the rest of the morning thinking of possible theme nights, then picked up the phone to talk to Rodrigo about it. And while talking, they discussed the bad comments online, and how some seemed suspicious.

Even then, nothing could keep his mind from wandering to the light blue eyes of his favorite blonde, Megan. She went beyond being a breath of fresh air. She was more like a breezy fresh day that put a person in a good mood and kept him there until she left. Which was crazy for a guy who had intended to be married now with an entirely different, well-planned future. A wife, and children down the line. The family he'd always wanted. But he'd almost married a woman who'd cheated on him before he'd even said "I do."

There went his blood pressure again, so he changed into his running clothes. Then he directed his thoughts to Megan and wondered if she could catch a quick lunch with him after he ran some miles and did some laps in the pool that morning. A smile creased his lips. "I wonder what she thought about the flowers."

Later Mark was disappointed to find out that, though Megan loved the flowers, she would be in a lunch meeting with the staff. She'd said it had to do with their reservation issues. Customer satisfaction being the most important aspect of any business, whether hotels or wineries, he completely understood the need for a meeting. Then, thinking ahead, he asked her out for lunch tomorrow.

Eating room service lunch on his patio gave him time to start thinking about returning home and how to deal with the fallout he'd walked away from last week. His brothers had given him space, which he appreciated, and he was sure Rodrigo had filled them all in about the state in which he'd arrived at Rambling Rose. They'd been good about not contacting him after trying for the first couple days, but he should at least call his cousin Alejandro at the winery and his brother Carlo and let them know what he'd been up to. He also wondered if they knew Brianna had come after him.

Carlo seemed way too understanding about Mark's need to stay away, and he thanked him, then talking to Alejandro, he promised to be back home and ready to work on Monday.

A quick thought of Megan left him with an odd bittersweet feeling and surprised him. He hadn't expected to develop feelings for someone else so quickly after having his heart trashed. But that wasn't the case with Megan. Then again, he'd never really been in *love* love with Brianna—it was more the idea of being married to her and having a family that he'd fallen in love with. He'd definitely loved the family part. His original plan was supposed to be the safe way to go about marriage, well-thought-out and businesslike, and something he could control. Who needed the old-school approach that included love? Major flop!

And how could he think pretending to be in a relationship was anywhere near reality? "The *M*s." Ha! Was that what her sisters and his brother called them behind their backs? *Another great idea, Mendoza*, Mark silently chided himself. *Is there anything you can get right?* Plan a reasonable marriage agreement and wind up duped by Brianna. Fail. Stage a fake romance and fall for Megan. Fail.

You're a piece of work.

He wasn't about to sit around in his room, stewing about the mess of his life, so he threw on his trunks and headed for the pool. Maybe out there he'd get a firm idea about a theme night to pitch to Brady, or Brady could direct him to Grace, the hotel manager.

An hour later, lying on a lounger and enjoying the house lavender lemonade, the *Wonder Woman* alert tone sounded from his phone, which immediately made him smile. He'd gotten a text from Megan.

I see you. That was all it said, and yet it was enough to push off all the dreary thoughts he'd been buried under since that morning and force him to break into a broad grin. He scouted the hotel windows along the first floor but couldn't pick her out. Where was she?

Yeah? he texted back. Well, what are you going to do about it?

Chapter Six

Mark talked Megan into taking Tuesday morning off so they could hike one of the nearby trails he'd found out about online. He'd set up a meeting with Brady for that afternoon about theme nights, and he wanted to have done his homework about other features the hotel could promote. Such as hiking. He couldn't help himself, marketing was in his blood, and if he did say so himself, he was damn good at it. His résumé had a long list of satisfied customers to prove it, which allowed him to include the word *Expert* on his business card.

Right now, he had to deal with the distraction of Megan Fortune in khaki hiking shorts, with a snug yellow tank top and orange bandana tied around her neck. Her well-worn hiking boots with thick wool socks that said I ♥ Hiking proved she liked the outdoors maybe as much as numbers. The point was, she fit well with nature. Not to mention the outfit showed she had great legs. But he already knew that.

Megan took the lead and off they went toward Rambling Rose Springs on the trailhead that was no more than a quarter mile from the hotel.

"The springs are a little-known offshoot of the Colorado River," she said, as she took wide strides on the gravel trail. "There's a waterfall there, too. By midsummer it dries up to a trickle, but since it's spring and we had a wet winter, it should be nice."

"Nice as in okay or *really nice*?"

"You're right, *nice* isn't a very descriptive word. How about pretty? Oh, wait, scenic. Yeah. That's it. Scenic."

"Not willing to commit to *beautiful*?"

"Well, let's wait and see."

"Sounds good. May I borrow your term *scenic* when I talk to Brady?"

"Of course, but why aren't you talking to Rodrigo?"

"As you know, your sister and my brother are getting married in a couple weeks, and they are spending every spare second planning that wedding."

"Sorry you've been stuck with me, but you're right. They're extremely busy these days."

"And Brady is the guy who can take the idea to Grace anyway. I wouldn't want to go over anyone's head."

"Also true." She did a little twirl around to face him and walk backward, and he liked the view. "I love how interested you are in the hotel." He also liked her enthusiasm. That little snug tank top was nice, too. Wait, not "nice" but "scenic." As it turned out, he was interested in much about Rambling Rose, especially his personal tour guide. But walking backward while on hiking trails was never a good idea and she was about to step on a rock the size of her boot, which could twist her ankle. He lunged and stopped her from taking another step.

"Is there a snake?" She stiffened and froze, holding her breath after asking.

"Nope. Just didn't want you to fall."

After breathing again, she went up on tiptoe and left a light kiss on his cheek. "Thanks."

Even that tiny interaction stirred him up. And it sure wasn't fake. But they were here on a business hike. He needed to concentrate on the scenery not his beautiful guide. So he acted like he didn't even notice the thank-you kiss. "Are snakes something for the guests to be concerned about on this hike?"

"Not really. Don't know why I said it. But I freak out about snakes. My sisters used to tease me mercilessly about it."

"Texas has nothing on Florida with snakes."

"I know!" And off she went, happily distracted by the scenery. Was it because she was so much younger than him and hadn't gotten jaded yet? Or could it be her naturally bright nature that made her enjoy every second? He wasn't sure which, but he liked how her upbeat attitude rubbed off on him, and these days he needed all the help he could get.

"What's the round-trip distance?" He got back to business, the whole point of being here, after a few more minutes of silence on the trail where his thoughts seemed to gravitate to Megan instead of the terrain.

"I'd say just short of five miles."

"So packing a picnic lunch would be the thing to do." He had only brought a couple bottles of water for them to share. "Does Nicole make picnic baskets for guests?"

"Gosh, this is our first season open. I don't think we've talked about that."

Mark stopped briefly and made a note on his phone to bring it up with Brady later.

"Would you call this hike easy, moderate or hard?" he asked in full business mode. "So far, for me it's easy."

"Oh, uh, mostly easy." Her natural gait and ease with which she spoke proved the point. "Maybe more strenuous on the last part to the springs."

"So anyone not on the verge of having a heart attack could do it?"

She gave her melodious laugh, the one he'd quickly grown to like. "I'd say so."

"And the waterfall?"

She tilted her head, either calculating the hike or measuring her words. "The thing is, it's not really a waterfall like most people think of. It's a stream that gets bigger in fall and winter and turns into small falls over the bluffs. It's not anything that takes your breath away, but it feeds the springs and it's pretty and kind of a secret unless a person gets out of the middle of Rambling Rose and explores."

"See, that's another plus. Why not call it the 'best-kept secret of Rambling Rose' and get the hotel guests all revved up about getting out in nature and exploring it?" He snapped his fingers. "Or, hey, why not have someone on staff lead a hike there on, say, Saturday mornings?"

"You never stop thinking, do you?"

"It's my livelihood. Marketing to me is like numbers to you."

"I get it. And I'm definitely going to suggest Nicole make picnic basket lunches for our guests."

"Yeah. Nothing fancy. A hearty sandwich and water or that great lemonade." He snapped his fingers again. "Oh, and cookies. A big old honking cookie as the reward for making it to the springs."

"Oh, hey, what about a wine lovers' picnic basket, too?" His enthusiasm had spread to Megan, and he liked how it lit up her eyes.

"Perfect! A 'bread, cheese and thou' kind of thing. Yes. Give them choices. Whether lovers of nature or looking for family fun, there's something for everyone to take to the secret waterfall."

"Now you're sounding like a tour pamphlet."

"Exactly." He liked how she understood his thinking process, too. A lot of women—including Brianna—didn't. Another clue he should've noted *before* making wedding plans.

"If you're interested in selling day trips," she said, sounding breathy on the moderate incline, "there's Rambling Lake ten miles out of town and the Texas Mission twenty miles away. That's where Rodrigo and Ash are getting married and it would be a great place for families to visit, too. It's mostly a museum and tells the history of the Spanish influence in Texas."

"Would you call it educational and fun? Or just educational?"

"It could be called fun." She huffed as she continued to hike. "Especially if the guests bring one of Nicole's soon-to-be-available picnic lunches with some of those big honking cookies you suggested."

See, she got him. He really liked that about her.

"While we've touched on the topic of Rodrigo and Ashley's wedding, will I still be your date?"

"Absolutely. Otherwise, I was on the verge of asking the kid who mows the lawns at the ranch."

His laugh came all the way from his belly. Leave

it to Megan to keep his ego under control. "Then it's a date."

See, he could do this. Keep things at the friend level. He could be a friend with a woman he respected and enjoyed. That was all. Right?

He stopped for a moment to enjoy her final climb up the trail, appreciating how sure-footed she was, while also happening to notice those outdoorsy legs and the sway of her cute hips, then followed. And before they knew it, including the more rigorous last portion of the hike, they'd made it to the waterfall. While it wasn't overwhelming, it didn't disappoint either. The waterfall was small but a worthy destination and decidedly pretty. Kind of like Megan. But he digressed. Take it in, he reminded himself. Be able to describe everything for Brady and sell it. The sound of the falls alone was worth the hike.

"Feel it?" Mark said. "The gurgling, splattering water makes my pulse slow down and my mind relax."

"Gives a person peace of mind."

"Thank you for bringing me here." As natural as could be, he put his hand on her upper arm and enjoyed the soft skin beneath his fingers as she turned to face him.

"Uh, Mark..." Megan's voice went quiet, and with the falls in the background he could barely hear her. "I see Brianna."

"You gotta be kidding me." One phrase and she'd managed to ruin his budding Zen state.

"Don't turn. I think she followed us to see if we're faking or really have something—"

Megan didn't have a chance to get the last words out before Mark moved in. With his back to wherever Brianna was hiding, he wrapped his arms around Megan and kissed her like they were on the big screen. Complete with a little dip. Almost like dancing. Well practiced by this point, and ever cooperative, Megan wrapped her arms around his neck and they continued another mind-blowing kiss with Mother Nature cheering them on. Hopefully much to Brianna's dismay.

And a huge mistake for Mark. He should have stopped at the pretending stage, but here he was going for something that felt far too real to ignore.

Mark maneuvered their embrace a little to the left, then squinted open one eye in time to see a lone brunette hiker, built like Brianna, turning back to the trail. What would it take to convince the woman?

He understood Brianna had been looking forward to being taken care of by him. Marrying part owner of a winery would probably have been a status perk for her. She had a lot to lose when their wedding day imploded. But so did he. Like kids, lots of them. He really wanted a family before he stared down forty. She'd blown it and they both lost out.

Before Mark knew it, the usual excitement of kissing Megan got overshadowed by his mixed-up thoughts. He needed to think clearly from here on out. She obviously felt it, too, because she pulled back and gazed into his eyes.

"She's gone?"

"Yeah," he said, tired of Brianna ruining his plans, and concerned about himself for wanting so quickly to move on.

It was early Wednesday morning when Ashley rushed into Megan's office. "I heard the other woman checked out of her hotel last night."

"Brianna?" What happened to not leaving until she'd made things right with Mark? Wow, maybe their kiss near the waterfall was convincing enough to drive her off? It sure had felt convincing to Megan.

Fingers snapped in front of her face. "Hey, where are you? Did you hear what I said? You two can stop your playacting now."

"Oh! Yeah. Okay. I helped out Mark and now…" Her voice trailed off as she pondered the implications. Would Mark quit coming around?

"Things can get back to normal." Ashley finished the sentence in a way that best suited her.

"Does Mark know?"

"Does Mark know what?" Mark's head popped around the corner of her office, and suddenly three was a crowd.

Ashley said hello to him, goodbye to Megan and, using triplet telepathy, left with a promise to talk more later.

Mark's bright expression didn't change as he watched her go. Did he know? He glanced back at Megan, and she did her best to hide the disappointment she felt. Their game was over, and she already missed it. Dang. Some actress she'd turned out to be, letting herself get all wrapped up in her job. Yesterday's super kiss by the falls flashed in her mind.

"Yes, I know," he said, not missing a beat. "Rodrigo told me."

Where would anyone be without siblings? Or small-town gossip? Her words still weren't coming, so she forced a bright expression, widening her eyes.

"We were very convincing." He clapped his hands together. "And now we have to celebrate. Mission accomplished, right?"

Why hadn't his solution occurred to her? She nodded like a bobblehead figure. "Yes! We did good. Yay." Though her "yay" was totally lacking in enthusiasm. "I feel like I've made a new friend in you." She straightened a penholder on her desk and a few papers to avoid making eye contact. Still, she couldn't help wondering how her phrasing had affected Mark. "Because that's what we are, right?" She didn't think he wanted anything else, and the last thing she wanted to do was misinterpret what they'd done, which would only add to his problems.

But really, was that all they were?

"Right. And to celebrate our mission accomplished, how about dinner at Roja tonight? You. Me. And a bottle of champagne."

He wasn't sick of her yet? The man proved harder to read than she'd thought, and he sure mixed her up. And how could she resist his adorable eyes and happy smile? "Well, I can't very well turn down champagne."

"How about seven?"

Her finger popped into the air. "Can we make it seven thirty?" As silly as it seemed, she didn't want to miss her standing Wednesday night Zumba class at five thirty. The one routine she hadn't thrown out the window since Mark limped into town. A girl had to have some self-respect, especially now when their jig was up.

That night at dinner Mark was still on a high, not because Brianna had left town, but because his meeting with Grace and Brady had gone great. They'd even asked Mark to make a mock Places to See While in Rambling Rose pamphlet as a sample to show the family shareholders when Brady suggested that Grace hire Mark as a marketing consultant. Grace had started the ball rolling to get the local businesses partnering with them before the grand opening, and now agreed it was time for additional outreach. The mutual goal was more customers.

The instant the champagne was delivered they shared a toast. "To success," he said.

"And a bright future, Mark," she said. "You deserve it."

As they clinked glasses and drank, it sunk in how sweet and kind the woman across the table from him was. Megan looked especially pretty tonight, too. Her skin looked fresh and pink, and her asymmetrical hair shone and smelled great, sweet like a field of flowers. He'd caught a whiff when he opened the car door for her in the parking lot. He remembered her gym class and realized she'd probably just stepped out of the shower before their dinner. Now, that put a picture in his head he didn't object to. He sniffed and scratched above his eyebrow. *Think of something else.* How did women get their hair so straight? He'd always had to use product to tame his thick wavy hair into submission. Things had gone too quiet, and Megan had already finished her glass.

"So anyway, after we talked about the pamphlet, and possibly getting hired as a consultant by the hotel, Grace and Brady were all for a weekly theme night, too. They loved all my ideas. Oh, and she agrees that midweek is best, since things get a little slow in sleepy Rambling Rose then." While he spoke, he refilled her glass. "He showed me the second-floor party room, which is beautiful by the way, and suggested using it to accommodate more people than poolside. He'd have some satellite bars set up with steep discounts on drinks, to encourage people to dance." Mark gave a deadpan wink. "Grace suggested a raw bar, fruit, crudités and cheeses made by local artisans. Throw in some mango salsa for the sake of the theme. And what would a salsa party be without music, right? Of course, it would be piped in at first, but maybe down the line, if it's a hit, some live local musicians? You've always got to have a vision of where you want to go with any new company or hotel."

"That sounds fantastic."

He believed her enthusiasm, but something was missing. "Yeah, I won't be around when they start it, but maybe it would be worth a two-hour drive to see the kickoff?"

"Cheers!" she said, starting her second glass of champagne before dinner had even been served. But what else could she do but drink since he was dominating the conversation?

Still, he couldn't shut up. "Would you be okay with me coming back here? Being that we're friends and all." Saying "friends" out loud didn't feel right. But he needed to remind himself Megan should be off-limits. Because he was an emotional mess and had no business getting involved again. He knew it but had ignored the potential fallout his entire time in Rambling Rose with Megan. Fear shot through him. He'd been peddling friendship with her just now, all the while knowing how he really felt—though unbidden and he'd fought it every step of the way, his true reaction was much, much more. Like something his brother had told him had been missing with Brianna. Vitamin L. Nah! Still, the brief thought sent a shock wave through him.

"Why wouldn't it be okay, my friend?" Had she put an extra emphasis on "friend"? "It's your idea, so you should be here." She took another long swallow of the fizzy stuff, then covered her mouth as a tiny effervescent burp slipped out. "Oh, excuse me." Those pretty pink cheeks blushed brighter. Cutest friend he'd ever had. The dangerous thought sobered him. It wasn't too late to save this mistake. If he played it on the straight and narrow from here on out.

Their meal was served, and the waiter did his due diligence refilling Megan's glass of bubbly. Now, as they ate, her cheeks were fully blushed. There was also something else Mark noticed—she wasn't doing any of the usual affectionate stuff he'd grown to expect when around her, because Brianna was gone and she'd obviously shifted into friend mode. He took his own glass and drank. He missed that.

The touching. Not the drinking. A red flag waved in the back of his mind. He couldn't keep ignoring them. This "thing" with Megan was already out of hand. A strong pang of anxiety grabbed his attention.

Throughout dinner he couldn't help but notice Nicole sticking her head out the kitchen door. At first he gave her the benefit of the doubt and assumed she was checking out the Wednesday night crowd, which was admittedly small. Probably needed to gauge how many specials to have on the ready. But after the third time he'd caught her and she'd instantly pulled her head back inside, he assumed she was spying on her sister. And why shouldn't she? They'd spent just under a week acting like newlyweds in every part of town. Now, *ding-dong*, the ex-fiancée was gone, and they didn't have a reason to be hanging out anymore. Nicole must not have gotten the memo about them being friends. Because he liked Megan and thoroughly enjoyed her company. Why should he quit seeing her now? More important, they deserved this celebration together after accomplishing their mission.

He'd grown far more attached to Megan than he'd planned, thanks to her always cooperative attitude when it came to PDA. The thought of not touching her lips again threw a bucket of ice water on his upbeat mood regarding the possible marketing consultation job for the hotel. It also sent a shiver through his heart, because fear of messing up again, this time with Megan, had been growing with each day in Rambling Rose.

When Megan finished off her third glass of champagne, he knew who was driving her home.

Later, after he'd walked her to the front door of the Fortune ranch, he acted the perfect gentleman. But he couldn't let her go without one last suggestion.

"I've got an idea and I'd really like you to take part in it."

"Sure." She'd been the most accommodating date he'd ever had. That's because she was his newest friend. If he believed that was all she was, he could sell himself a big old patch of Florida swampland. Because his feelings were getting out of control. But what about hers? Well, she'd downed three glasses of champagne.

He should end things now, before it was too late, but like a moth to the light he enjoyed being around Megan too much to even consider it.

"Don't you want to hear what it is first?" He laughed, and she self-deprecatingly joined him, because even she knew she was tipsy. "I'd like to suggest one last celebration tomorrow night with music and dancing by the pool." His plan was to make sure it was the last time they saw each other, because his feelings were getting all mixed up and he couldn't trust himself these days. "Will you join me?"

"Dancing by the pool?" It was the first hint of protest she'd given in over a week. "Not in a bathing suit, right?"

"Not if you don't want to. But I can't think of anyone else I'd rather have a private preview with for Salsa Thursday poolside than you."

She glanced down, evidently giving the bathing suit element some serious thought. "You still want to spend time with me?"

"Does that surprise you?"

"Well…"

"I know Brianna's gone now, but as you've reminded me a time or three today, we're friends. Right?" Keep telling yourself that.

She listened carefully to his every word, and when he said "friends" she nodded in agreement. A tinge of disappointment hung around the edges of his mind, but he knew what was best. It had to be for the sake of both of them. Friends was what they would be. He couldn't trust more.

"So, I'd like to hang out with you again tomorrow night. Not because we have to but maybe because we'd like to?" He hadn't been this straight with a woman so early in a relationsh—uh, friendship, and it made him edgy. His desire kept contradicting his brain, which was waving another red flag. Wrap things up. Clear out now.

She went serious as the deep night sky. "Mark?"

"Yes?"

Her eyes didn't waver from his. "I think I see Brianna," she whispered.

On reflex he looked over his shoulder, but quickly understood her meaning. Caution tried to take the lead—this isn't a good idea—but the tenderness that had been building for Megan resisted. When he gazed back at her expectant face, he quit thinking. "Yeah, me, too."

Then he took Megan in his arms and kissed her the way he'd wanted the entire evening. This wasn't a "had to" kiss, it was a "got to" kiss, and no surprise, it was the best one they'd shared yet.

Chapter Seven

Mark texted Megan that he would meet her in the hotel bar first at seven. She would only have a soda this time to make sure she didn't wind up throwing herself at him again. What a mistake last night on her doorstep had been, but the kiss was worth it. Of course the awkward goodbye that followed, where each of them pretended they weren't buzzed by the lip-lock, still had her cringing in her car on the drive over.

When she showed up on time, he was there ordering a pitcher of sangria. Just one glass, she promised. After taking a deep breath for support, she tapped him on the shoulder, and he turned with a smile.

"Hey!" he said, obviously happy to see her, though when he noticed she'd worn capris and a bright patterned halter top made out of a colorful scarf, he didn't do a very good job of hiding some disappointment. "No swimsuit?"

It was in the low seventies, promising to drop lower, but the heat lamps were situated nearby. Still, she had no plan to go swimming. She'd actually brought a matching light cardigan to throw on, just in case.

He, on the other hand, not only wore a loud Caribbean-patterned camp shirt with his bright green trunks, but the most expensive-looking huarache sandals she'd ever seen. No one would want to get those wet, and this time of year in Rambling Rose, when April showers prepared for May flowers, he might have to make a run for it. He'd topped off the ensemble in typical resort flair with an urban-styled panama hat. Short brim and all. Man, Miami Mark looked hot!

"It's supposed to be pretty cool out tonight, and—"

"Hey, that's okay about the swimsuit. I was just teasing. Do me a favor, grab those baskets of chips over there, would you, please?"

"Yes, but first, I need to apologize about last night."

He tilted his head.

"That was the champagne and I don't want to mess up our friendship because I was...well..."

"Spontaneous? That's one more thing I like about you, Megan. You surprise me."

"Well, last night I surprised myself, too."

"Don't worry about it. Our secret's safe. Just grab the chips and follow me."

Well, that was easy, and probably why she brought it up, because Mark was the easiest-going man she'd ever met. So she grabbed the baskets and followed him out to the pool, which they seemed to have to themselves. His grin was wide as he escorted her toward the lounge chairs he'd set up by a small table ready with several bowls of cellophane-covered salsa. Her faux pas was already forgotten, and Mark had moved on to Salsa Thursday.

"I paid a trip to Mariana's Market today," he said when they got closer. "Did you know she has the largest assortment of salsas outside of Houston? That old guy Norman, who plays cards at Mariana's, told me that."

Actually Megan didn't know that about salsa or Houston, or Rambling Rose, but then, she'd rarely shopped for salsa because she had a sister who was a chef and she owned two restaurants that regularly stocked the stuff. "Ah, Norman. If anyone would know, he would. He's been around forever."

Long before they'd gotten to the table, from the other side of the pool, she'd heard the music. One small but mighty speaker was attached to his iPad. Salsa at its finest—smooth, breezy, piano on top with loads of percussion and accented by horns. Exactly the kind of music her Zumba teacher played for the workout. She couldn't help but sway her hips and lift her shoulders to the beat as she walked, until some chips started falling. Oops.

"That's the way," he said. "You know me and my brothers grew up in Miami, right?"

She nodded and put down the majority of chips on the table he'd pulled by their lounge chairs. "Heard that a few times, yes."

"Cuban music was always big. And salsa was popular, too. My parents used to go dancing when they were dating. It's never gone out of style." He set down the sangria and studied her. "Are you ready to dance with me?"

The question shook her to the core. She'd been a nervous wreck all day thinking about facing him after last night. After the kiss she'd flat out asked for. And he'd delivered. Wow, had he delivered. And now, having to embarrass herself by dancing with a man who took salsa dancing for granted. How much more could she endure?

"Dance with Miami Mark?" She shook her head and he blurted a laugh. "Okay, but just remember, I grew up in Fort Lauderdale. Oh, and no dancing until I've had some sangria." Until she developed more confidence, she'd stall.

"That's fine. Here, let me give you a rundown on the salsas. We'll do a taste test, okay?"

"Sounds great." She hadn't eaten much, since underneath her capris and scarf top, she'd worn her swimsuit, and even as she spoke was sucking in her stomach. But if she could help it, he'd never find out about the suit. No way was she ready to be half-naked with him. Oh, man, did that put the wrong image in her already insecure mind.

"Here's the Mexican salsa section." He gestured like a reality show host. "This is the Southwest style, and over here is the Caribbean salsa with papaya, mango, pineapple and cilantro. Mmm-mmm. You've got to taste this one first." He dug a large corn chip into the Caribbean-style salsa and held it out for her to taste.

First he expected her to wear a swimsuit, and now eat from his fingers? She made the mistake of tasting his fingers, too. And wow, everything tasted incredible. "More, please."

That made him smile again, and over the next several minutes they shared various styles of chips and salsa like it was the main course, which it was for Megan. Plus, Roja made a great sangria, and it went perfectly with all the flavors, and especially helped cool down the hot ones. She also couldn't help but sway to the music again. Standing poolside, the thought of jumping in for a swim with Mark definitely had merit. But she still wasn't ready, preferring to think about the biggest challenge—dancing with a man who knew his way about the dance floor.

Mark was as natural as the sunset when it came to hosting a salsa party for two. "Okay, now, time to dance," he said. "You ready?"

Or not. "Please don't laugh." Her hand flew to cover her mouth.

"I'd never do that. You know me well enough to know that, right?"

Her gut told her yes, but she also knew her feet. Mark took her hand in his and put the other one on her hip as light as a butterfly, and she rested her free hand on his arm, never more self-conscious in her life. A solid foot of space lay between them.

"Just listen to the music and follow my lead," he said, pure poetry in motion and extra easy on the eyes as he started with the basic steps. This Miami version of Mark, now with hips swaying and feet keeping perfect timing, not to mention the cool hat, would be implanted in her mind long after he left. Maybe as soon as tomorrow?

She jumped back into the music rather than ruin things with the inevitable—Mark's departure.

"Just listen to the beat for a second," he said, drawing her mind back to more important things like letting her feet move as his were.

She watched and followed, and he turned out to be a good and patient teacher, starting slow and basic. Then before she knew it, she caught on.

"Hey, now you've got it," he said.

She grinned. Yes, she did. "My Zumba classes have finally paid off."

They laughed easily together and continued dancing. Something else she noticed was how fun life seemed since meeting him. Was she the only one who thought that? He sure seemed to enjoy being with her, but maybe that was just part of the charm of Mark, the second oldest Mendoza brother. Always having to find a way to get noticed.

He'd advanced to the twirling stage and she spun whenever he directed her, making it seem natural as breathing. Under his direction she felt she could almost do anything. Turned out they danced really well together, and a secret thought pushed its way to the surface. What else might they do easily and amazingly well together? Her cheeks betrayed her and flushed bright. Miami Mark noticed.

"Let's take a break, grab some water," he said, being attentive and polite.

But Megan hadn't had this much fun in forever. "No. Not yet. Please? That hot salsa got to me, that's all. Let's dance."

He tipped his hat. "You don't have to ask me twice."

They picked up where they had left off and, growing more confident thanks to a great teacher, Megan let her hips do the talking for the next several minutes of Latin dancing. From what she could tell, Mark liked that. A lot.

A few of the hotel guests were drawn out to the pool, unsure at first if it was a hotel-sponsored party or strictly private.

"Have some salsa and chips," Mark encouraged. So they did.

Soon a small group of people had joined them in dancing and Megan had lost their special moment together. But Mark was in salsa heaven because his theme night idea proved to have wings. Or in this case, dance shoes. She could see it in his eyes. He'd clicked from all fun to all business.

"Next time you visit Hotel Fortune, bring some friends and be sure to meet at the second-floor party room for a real salsa party."

At least Megan got to keep dancing with him, but when the hospitality staff came around, the night turned more toward a business meeting, making it easy to slip off without being noticed. At least she never had to show herself in a swimsuit.

"Hey," Mark said, out of nowhere, reaching for Megan's hand. "You can't sneak off without saying goodbye."

"I didn't want to interfere with your impromptu meeting."

"I can talk to them tomorrow." The music had slowed down, and Mark tugged her closer. "One more dance?"

How could she refuse? He eased her closer and did some fancy twirl, which she'd gotten quite good at following. They ended with a complicated move that brought her back to his chest with his arms wrapped around her. Snug. So close. Wonderful. They stayed like that for a few seconds, just swaying to the lovely Latin tune.

"Check that out," Mark said.

He clearly meant the moon, so she did.

"I could've been in Belize looking at that moon tonight, but I can't imagine it looking more beautiful than right here with you." His breath tickled across her cheek, raising the tiny hairs on the back of her neck.

It was a waxing gibbous moon, more than half lighted, and it gave her the craziest memory.

"What are you thinking about?" Mark must have caught on after her silence.

That was the most romantic thing anyone has ever said to me. "Besides thank you? Something silly."

"I'm all ears."

Mark was easy to talk to, yet they hadn't shared much about their childhoods other than both being part of big families and her penchant for taking in strays. Why not go for it?

She took a quick breath. "Every Christmas my Nanny Francis had all the kids watch *It's a Wonderful Life.*"

"I love that movie," he said, an enthusiastic affirmation.

"Cool." Something else they shared. "Anyway, I never understood why George Bailey wanted to lasso the moon for Mary." *Until now.*

"Oh, you *were* young."

A few more seconds passed in thought.

"You want me to lasso the moon for you, Megan?" His romantic words were tinged with hesitation, as if Mark wasn't sure where Megan was going with their new circumstances.

Tell him what you're thinking. "Actually, I wish I could do that for you."

His arms gripped hers slightly more, tucking her closer to his chest. She could feel his breath rise and fall. "I finally get it. It's when you see someone with so much potential that it makes your heart swell, and you want to do something heroic to show them you know how special they are."

"What do you know about me, Megan?" She sensed he was trying to keep her from going further. Everything she knew about him had been based on pretending. Still, she'd seen through that brave facade.

She continued to observe the moon because it was easier to say what she wanted that way. "You're a man who deserves the stars and the moon when it comes to success. I know that I believe in you, and I don't think you should let that mistake with Brianna mold your future. Nothing should hold you back."

This time he sighed. "Thank you. You have no idea how much that means to me. Now I'm embarrassed that the reason I wanted to lasso the moon for you was only to impress you."

They laughed lightly together, as she turned her face over her shoulder, looked up at him and lifted her chin. His dark eyes gazing down at her seemed to glow, as if he'd swallowed the moon and it illuminated through them. His throat lifted in a quiet swallow.

"Are we having a Brianna sighting?" He whispered their secret code.

Oh, yes.

His mouth, so close, came gently down on hers with a tender kiss that promised to explode into something wild in the next second. That special moon glow seemed to seep into her...

"Is Mark Mendoza out here?" A gravelly, clearly Southern accent cut through the night.

"Mark?" another voice, a woman's twang, closer by, repeated. "You out here?"

Their special kiss ended as quickly as it had started. Interrupted from finding its potential. Mark sighed, in an impatient way, then turned, feigning hospitality.

"Who's looking for Mark?" Now back on duty, he let go of Megan and she stepped away from him.

Oblivious to what they'd interrupted, the man continued. "We're celebrating our fortieth anniversary in two weeks, and we'd like to learn to dance the salsa for our party." The man in a Stetson and wearing a Western-cut suit said.

"We saw the dancing from Roja, and the hostess said you might be able to give us a lesson. Is there any way you could teach us a few basic steps?" The woman, accessorized with large jewelry, spoke with a real Texas twang.

With Mark being the gentleman he was, Megan tipped her head good-night at him with a sincere smile, then left.

They'd ventured into unchartered territory and, though partly terrorizing, she'd never felt more invigorated in her life.

Tonight, something crazy and out of left field happened for Mark. The point was to say goodbye to Megan, to put an end to their ruse now that they'd accomplished their goal. He'd kept intending to put on the brakes, to let Megan sneak out like she'd obviously wanted. But fighting the wise side of himself, which seemed to be shrinking with each minute spent with Megan, he went after her. Not ready to let her go. And it scared the salsa out of him.

One minute they were dancing and the next talking about the moon. He'd felt ambushed by that kiss, even though he'd instigated it, then joked it was in honor of another Brianna sighting. But it had nothing to do with his ex-fiancée and everything to do with what Megan had just told him—that she believed in him. The biggest aphrodisiac a man could ask for—to be believed in. And even knowing how dangerous getting deeper involved with her could be, not trusting his ability to handle more, he went for it anyway.

All along she'd been a good friend, putting up with his fake relationship ideas and, tonight, his salsa party whims. It seemed like just about anything else he wanted to do, too. Because that was what friends did. He'd tried to pound that point into his head, but couldn't believe it. Now, after their "lasso the moon" moment, he had proof more was going on between them. Which nearly set off a panic attack. Still, his emotions persisted.

Why couldn't this be the real thing? Some crazy bait and switch compliments of the universe to turn him in the right direction. *Don't marry Brianna. Check this out. Brianna was only for now. This one, Megan, could be for a lifetime.*

Dangerous thoughts.

Yet he and Megan understood the dynamics of a big family, and she seemed to thrive on it, as he did. The next logical step would be for them both to have their own.

Why not together?

These were crazy thoughts from a man under the influence of the moon and Megan, and still getting his bearings after running away from his wedding. He should head for home before he did any more damage.

They'd had to say goodbye prematurely last night because of the Texan and his earnest wife. It was just a spontaneous reaction from some people staying at the hotel, verifying his hunch that theme nights would be good for the guests, and what was good for the guests would travel via word of mouth.

Why not advertise it, too?

There he went again, doing what was second nature and forgetting about an important factor in the last two weeks in Rambling Rose. Hell, Megan was *the* most important part. But having been recently betrayed, the thought of really opening up to someone new so soon seemed impossible. Unadvisable.

But Megan had. Last night. Why couldn't he?

He was looking at going home sometime this weekend, and before he did, maybe he should tell her some of the truth he'd come to understand since meeting her, no matter how much it frightened him. Or how big a mistake it could be.

So, against his better judgment, he made the call to ask her to come back tonight. For a pool party. How much trouble could they get into outside? "Hey. It's me. Sorry about the impromptu dance lesson. Are we okay?"

She assured him they were, so he plunged ahead. "Great, then, if you don't have plans tonight, I'd like to invite you to my going-away event."

She laughed at his having an "event," said she wouldn't put it past him what with all his new salsa dancing friends from last night. As always she was sweet and playing along, because that's what friends did. Friends who believed in each other. And Megan was a great example of a true friend.

"Sorry to disappoint, but it's just going to be you and me. And, oh, bring your swimsuit. It's a pool party."

He got the exact reaction he'd hoped for out of her. She squealed and called him a dirty dog and, as always, they laughed together.

When Mark ended the call, he rationalized that he could keep things under control, even while knowing he'd lost that ability on the hike with Megan, and especially last night. The feelings that had been building against his will since meeting Megan, were running the show now, and it scared him to the core. How in the world could he ever trust his judgment where women were concerned again after Brianna? Especially with someone as sweet as Megan. Someone who wanted to lasso the moon for him.

He needed to get out before he did any more damage to either of them.

The last two weeks in Rambling Rose had been

based on a pretend fling, and tonight should be no
different. He had to drive that point home, because
the thoughts and emotions circling his brain were
anything but fake. And they didn't have to fake anything anymore. Tonight he needed to say goodbye
to Megan Fortune and it would take his best poker
face to do it.

Megan showed up at the luncheon meeting in
the small conference room on the second floor as
everyone had been instructed wearing her director
of finance hat. Nicole and Ashley were there, too,
so she sat by them. Rodrigo Mendoza did not look
happy. She hoped it didn't have anything to do with
the poolside salsa party last night.

Last year, Rodrigo had teamed up with Fortune
Brothers Construction after being invited by Callum Fortune to help develop the plans for this hotel.
He'd worked as hard as any Fortune to make the
hotel a success, but this was clearly Callum's dream
project. Yet from the start there had been problems,
beginning with protests from the community about
the size of the project, and worse yet, in January,
the balcony collapse. That episode had postponed
the grand opening by several weeks, to Valentine's
Day. Now, two months since the official opening
in February they still had new issues cropping up.

Some sandwiches were passed around, the kind
Megan thought would be perfect for Nicole to use

for picnic baskets for hotel guests on day excursions around Rambling Rose. Hiking to the falls. Or short drives out to Rambling Lake or the Texas Mission, where Rodrigo and Ashley were getting married in nine days. She smiled inwardly. Mark had her thinking like him now. But now wasn't the right time to bring it up with Nicole.

"I noticed The *M*s' salsa party was a huge success," Nicole whispered as she leaned in next to Megan. "Everyone eating on the restaurant patio seemed to enjoy the show."

Megan couldn't stop the blush.

"Sorry I missed it," Ashley said as they ate.

To change the subject, Megan brought up her thoughts about the picnic baskets, and thankfully, the topic served its purpose and sent the sisters down another path of conversation. Best part of all, Nicole loved the idea.

"It was Mark's idea." She wanted to give credit where it was due.

"I think The *M*s are onto something," Ashley agreed, rubbing in the annoying couple nickname. Which they weren't. A couple. Not anymore.

Rodrigo had eaten quickly, obviously eager to get the meeting started. He stood and let out a sigh. "I just got off the phone with your dad." He nodded to the triplets. "David Fortune is not a happy camper. The reason? He called to extend his previously made reservations at the Hotel Fortune for our wedding, only to be told his original reservation didn't exist."

Megan shot an incredulous look first at her sisters, then to Grace and Brady, before moving on to the entire hospitality team, who handled reservations.

"I know the reservation existed, because I made it." Rodrigo gave a moment for the significance of his statement to sink in. "Of course, I checked it out. Somehow his reservation had been deleted. And there were *several* vacancies. Yet he'd been told the opposite. So my question is, is it incompetence or have we been hacked?"

"In light of the issues we've had the last couple of weeks and knowing the extensive training we're offering our new employees," Grace Williams said, "I think hacking might be worth looking into."

"Why would anyone want to do that?" Megan asked.

Rodrigo shrugged. "Beats me, but these glitches with reservations have just moved into a whole new territory."

"We can't forget the anonymous bad reviews on those travel websites either," Grace added.

"Exactly. I've been looking into them, and if anything looks phony, they do. Because they all basically say the same thing." He passed around a sheet with some of the reviews he'd culled. "Seems someone wants to ruin our reputation."

Megan had become an expert on faking reality recently, and considering how things were beginning to add up, these reviews she scanned certainly seemed planted. The question was, who hated them that much? "Could it be another hotel in the area?"

"We've been wondering the same thing," Rodrigo said. "All the more reason to check into hacking."

"I know some IT people I can have look into our reservation program," Brady said. "Maybe they can even trace those bogus reviews. If we're lucky, we'll figure out who, or which hotel, is trying to sabotage our success."

"Well, we better find out soon because we're losing good paying customers and this hotel, after all of Callum's hard work, is too beautiful to fail." Rodrigo looked worried, and why shouldn't he be? David Fortune was the last person anyone should want to make unhappy. Not to mention having to grovel to. Megan could only imagine how Rodrigo's conversation had gone with her father.

"And if it is someone from a rival hotel?" Brady asked.

"One step at a time," Rodrigo cautioned. "Let's not accuse without proof."

"Plus we're on great terms with everyone in town, especially since we've joined the chamber of commerce," Grace chimed in, because she was the one who suggested it would only make sense to be part of the town's business network. Megan had wholeheartedly agreed.

"It does seem far-fetched now that we built a smaller hotel, but remember how there were a lot of people in town who resented Callum building in the first place," Rodrigo reminded them. "Brady, get those internet technicians lined up ASAP. Ashley, since your dad's the tech wiz, maybe ask his input? I'd do it, but I'm not sure he wants to talk to me right now." A classic expression covered Rodrigo's handsome face—consternation. "Everyone else, all we can do at this point is be extra careful and vigilant. Double-check every reservation. I want a printout of every single reservation placed each day. I'm depending on Team Fortune to figure this out. Everyone agree?"

All heads around the table nodded.

As Ashley, Nicole and Megan walked together downstairs to the offices, after quickly reviewing what had just occurred in the meeting, Nicole brought up the subject Megan had hoped was forgotten.

"So, last night, I couldn't help but notice the sexual tension between you and Mark. FYI, Ash, it's off the charts."

"What are you talking about? It's all fake. That's what we agreed on." *Not anymore. This is all new.*

"You're telling us, the people who know you best, that everything you've been doing around town is nothing but acting?" Ashley said, with a far-beyond-suspicious look. "I don't think so."

"We only kissed when someone would see it, or when Brianna was around." But to Megan it always felt real, right from the start. She'd never admit that to anyone, though.

"I'm talking about since Brianna left," Nicole said.

"And when did you learn how to dance like that?" Nicole wouldn't let up. "You should've seen her, Ash. You'd think they'd been dancing together forever."

"That's only because Mark is a great leader. That man can dance. And you know I take Zumba."

"Well, there's something else I know, too. It's what they say about men who are good dancers," Nicole teased.

Megan swallowed the anxiety sprouting in her throat. She didn't need to be reminded what she'd already thought. Mark had probably been with loads of women in his life. After all, he was thirty-five. Whereas, even at twenty-four, Megan could count on one hand the guys she'd been with, and a couple of those shouldn't even qualify for "making love."

That man was totally out of her league. But what was another old saying? Fake it until you make it. So she knew exactly what to do. Tonight she'd get to their pool party first and slip into the water, so he'd never even get to really see her in a bathing suit. All she needed to do was keep a towel right by the edge of the pool, and she'd have herself covered and wrapped before he could squint the water out of his eyes when they got out.

No worries. She had it all under control.

As planned, Megan arrived at the Hotel Fortune pool with plenty of time to spare before Mark would get there. She'd even had enough time to stop by the bar and order poolside service of two resort-styled rum-and-whatever drinks with those little umbrellas. On the Fortune tab, of course. The server promised to have them poolside in ten minutes. Perfect.

Where fake relationships were concerned, Mark had trained Megan well. Instead of focusing on his leaving town sometime this weekend, she would continue on with her newfound talent for keeping up appearances. In other words, faking it. She would become a world-wise woman like he was probably used to dating, not her small-town, sheltered rich girl reality.

The April weather had been warm most of the week, and now that the sun was going down, it had cooled to the low seventies. She shuddered when she took off her cabana-style swimsuit cover-up and slipped into the heated pool, cupping her palms and splashing her shoulders, making a point to keep her hair dry. She glanced up to the sky with the gibbous moon they'd watched last night. Could Mark's timing for a pool party, just the two of them, be more perfect?

Soon she spotted him walking from the lobby toward the pool in another resort-style shirt and a new color of swim trunks. These were red. As in red-hot. Yikes, what did that say about…well, anything? Unprepared for the impact of watching Mark Mendoza walk toward the pool, she inhaled a large breath and went underwater. So much for keeping her hair dry.

When she finally came up for air, he stood at the edge of the pool, those expensive huarache sandals at eye level. She turned her gaze upward. He was holding the drinks, which had evidently been delivered while she explored the bottom of the pool. He also sported a typical Mark Mendoza grin. In other words, stunning.

"Hey, sunshine, why didn't you wait for me?"

She ignored the question and mustered some guts. "Come in. The water's great!" she lied, though at least she'd stopped shivering. "Oh, and I'll have my drink now if you don't mind," she said as she hooked her forearms on the red bricks surrounding the pool. Maybe a little rum confidence was just what she needed for the big finale of their fake romance.

Mark studied her in the water, giving her the impression that he liked her with wet hair. Then he handed her one of the drinks and after one draw on the straw, put his on the small table by the lounger. While she sipped through the straw, trying not to poke her nose with the umbrella, he unbuttoned his shirt. When he removed it, he took her breath away, and she nearly choked on the fruity juice with rum. My, my, my, he was gorgeous.

He took his time. Picked up her swimsuit cover-up, studied the wide blue stripes and the deep V-neck. "Would've liked to see you in this, too."

She sucked down more of her drink.

Instead of diving in, he sat on the edge of the pool with his feet dangling in the deep end. There was one other couple in the pool, but they were on the other end in the Jacuzzi. After a few more sips—who was she kidding, gulps—Megan handed him her drink and he dutifully twisted around and put it on the table, giving her an up close look at his abs. Another wow. She hoped she hadn't said it out loud.

How could a person walk around looking that good all the time and not let it go to his head?

Someone needed to keep that man grounded, so she pushed back from the edge of the pool and used her outstretched legs to splash the heck out of him.

Only surprised for one second, Mark grinned. "Oh, now you asked for it. The game is on." Then he dove into the water coming straight for her.

She squealed and swam as fast as she could to get away from whatever punishment he had decided to deliver. Of course he caught up, so she did the only thing she could. She cupped her hands and continued splashing him as he grabbed her toes and reeled her in one body part at a time. Toes. Foot. Calf. Knee. Thigh. Waist.

Too close. Not ready.

She made a breakaway and swam to the other side of the pool. He must have sensed her pulling back, so he casually swam to meet her there, respectful of the distance between them.

"You always surprise me, Megan."

"You mean a water fight wasn't what you had in mind?" Before, the heated pool hadn't seemed nearly warm enough. Now it almost felt boiling.

"I'm not sure what I had in mind. Though tonight is probably the wrap-up for our big fake affair."

"That about sums it up, doesn't it?"

"Not always."

"What do you mean?"

"The other night? On your doorstep?"

Oh, no, he was going to bring up her instigating that kiss. With her fingers on the edge of the pool, she thought about slipping underwater, to avoid the entire topic, but instead looked at him. "The champagne lowered my defenses and that affected my good sense. Should I apologize again?"

With his arm bent and resting on the edge of the pool, he was turned toward her. "Don't even think about it."

Which made her smile, while feeling demure and wishing she had more guts where Mark Mendoza was concerned when they weren't faking.

"Full disclosure," he said. "A lot of times I faked seeing Brianna so I could hold your hand, or put my arm around you, and of course, kiss you, too."

Her inhale was deep, and so was her reaction. Goose bumps came back in full force. It hadn't been her imagination. The realization urged her to be bold, to do something she'd never have the guts to do with Mark unless pretending. Now, shocking herself, Megan put her arms around his neck and kissed him, loving the sensation of being surrounded by water, hearing it ripple and shift as they kissed. He angled his head to cover her lips with his, immediately taking control of what she had started.

He hadn't gone near her yesterday, beyond the dancing, oh, and the spooning under the moon. The kiss that had been sabotaged by the couple. She'd missed their daily make-believe kisses, but this one was so much more. She breathed him in and followed his every lead and when her tongue went searching for his, he ended it. A surprise, but maybe she had gone too far for a hello kiss.

"Let me get our drinks," he said, obviously wanting to slow things down. "We can sit on the steps and relax for a while. Enjoy our moon."

Had she made a fool of herself?

Embarrassed, she sunk under the water, swam

a few strokes, resurfacing a few feet away because she didn't trust being close to him right then. She needed to regroup, to get her confidence back. She spit out some water, squinted her eyes to wring them out, then wiped her face. He was right where she'd left him. To her credit, he looked a little stunned. Maybe she hadn't blown it—so why not go for it? Lay it all out there? The guy was leaving; she'd never have to face him again if this backfired.

"Full disclosure," she said. "At first I thought it was the fun of faking it with you. The excitement of doing something completely out of character. But then after a couple of days, I knew it was *you* who made me feel that way."

His toned arms stroked across the water as he glided toward her in a breaststroke, but he stopped short, treading just out of her reach. "So it wasn't just me."

He was asking for her honesty, and she owed it to him to be open with her other feelings about him, too. "Full disclosure. I think you're still grieving the loss of your marriage."

"And you wouldn't be wrong there. The sting of that is going to take a while."

"Which complicates everything about us. So I've been wondering what this thing is we've been doing. I know about the fake part, but I mean now, since Brianna left town."

He stopped treading, placing his feet on the

bottom of the pool. "Also full disclosure. I think whatever it is we've been doing is great, but maybe dangerous."

She snorted. "Fake dating is dangerous? Well, it was your idea." She hoped she came off authentic, because she already knew how risky it had been for her.

His smile was slow and much too charming. "True. And though I've enjoyed every minute with you, maybe it wasn't one of my best ideas."

Now she laughed outright. "But you're the guy with all the great ideas." Because she had to keep this a game and not let it become real.

She really did like this man, wished things were under different circumstances, but strangely, also wouldn't change what they'd had for anything. Apparently, faking gave her permission to be exactly who she had always wanted to be. Confident. Spontaneous. Fun loving, even. Which, being the mathematician in the triplets, was something no one had called her *ever*. "So we come to the end of our 'fake affair.'" She used air quotes.

He edged closer and, honestly, she welcomed that. "To the end of one amazing, entire fake relationship. Crammed into one short week." He bypassed her and sat on the second-from-the-bottom step, where he'd tried to direct her earlier, his shoulders and head the only thing above water. "It saved me, Meg," he said after he'd settled there, and the words nearly took her breath away. "You saved me from the worst place I'd ever been."

Her gut told her to accept the kindest and sweetest compliment she'd ever been paid, but the words came out by pure reflex. "I can't take all the credit for that. We were a team." She edged away from the side of the pool, moving closer to him, and treaded water, watching, waiting, wondering what if.

"A damn good team."

A meaningful look traveled from Mark straight to her heart. She had to be careful here because, well, she'd never been in a situation like this before, with a man as wonderful as Mark Mendoza.

"I've got one more 'full disclosure' for you," he said.

Her legs stretched down, only her toes touched the floor of the pool, her chin barely breaking water, but she needed the support, then she went still. Waiting.

"I think you're beautiful, and even under the worst conditions of my entire life, I'm glad I met you."

Well, that did it. She lunged through the water and swam to him. He welcomed her in his arms, then looked at her up close. "This has been the best honeymoon I *never* took."

Swept up in the most excellent moment in her life, she couldn't censor herself. "But I have to mention there's been one major thing missing on *your* honeymoon." She kissed him with all the feeling that had been building and that she'd held back for two weeks, until now. The other couple had left the Jacuzzi side of the pool ages ago, so now they had it all to themselves. No one was looking and it didn't have to be a planned PDA. He kissed her in a different way than ever before, on a whole new level.

Getting swept away in that kiss, Megan wrapped her legs around Mark's waist and immediately realized he wasn't faking his reaction to her. Yowza!

He broke off the kiss, holding her face and staring deeply into her eyes, obviously knowing she knew he was aroused. "Any chance you want to make my honeymoon complete?"

And there it was, her chance of a lifetime.

"I thought you'd never ask."

Chapter Eight

Megan had always admired the luxury beds at the Hotel Fortune, but she'd never actually tried one out before. Well, nothing more than sitting on the edge and bouncing a few times, anyway. This crazy, distracting thought broke into her mind as she and Mark walked down the hallway toward his room Now would be her chance to discover how comfortable those beds really were. Her heart pounded when she doubted, under the full attention of Mark Mendoza, she'd notice anything that had to do with the mattress. Only who was on it with her.

Was this really happening?

Their mutual attraction had been playing hide-

and-seek from the beginning, especially growing over the last couple days, since they had run Brianna out of town. Megan had imagined, in the secrecy of her room at the ranch, being with him like this. Many times. It had become her favorite fantasy. She'd never admitted it to anyone, especially her sisters. There was no way she could have predicted how hard her heart would beat in this moment, or how tricky it would be to breathe. How was she going to hold it together to be with Mark?

She hadn't been with many men, and Mark, being a lot older than her, was obviously an experienced lover. He had the moves, the charm, the natural sex appeal. He had it all. So, what would she bring to the table, er, bed? Now her pulse pushed into erratic bursts as adrenaline was added to the mix.

How about enthusiasm? Where Mark was concerned, there was certainly that. She hoped with everything she had she wouldn't disappoint him as he carded his room and pushed the door open.

The hospitality evening turndown service had already occurred, and the shiny silk and cool-looking sheets were ready and waiting for them. The vision sent a shiver through her and she was certain her skin would soon be all lit up with the huge full-bodied blush she sensed coming on.

"Are you sure about this?" Mark asked with a

husky voice, seeming hesitant to step inside until she assured him.

More than a fair share of employees had noticed them walking holding hands from the pool, through the lobby and down the first-floor hall to his room. Talk about her personal life being an open book! Tongues would be wagging all over again. *Was* she sure about this?

Well, so be it. Right now, she didn't care about anything but him.

Megan disguised her quivery inhale as a clearing of her throat. Where was she now? Oh, right. *Was* she ready for this as he had just asked? Her mind sped on with a thousand thoughts. She'd known the man less than two weeks, yet to be honest, she'd felt ready, in her fantasies at least, for the next step with him since day one. And now was the time if there ever was one, to be honest. Because they'd dropped the "fake" back at the pool with those full disclosures, and it didn't get more "real" than making love for the first time. Well, it was now or never, and fear had no business in this room. Why not pretend one last time to be bold and daring and…

She nodded yes to Mark, and to prove her point, once inside the room she let her damp towel fall to the floor.

His eyes lit up. "Finally, I see you in a bathing suit," he teased, obviously enjoying the view, and trying to make her comfortable. Which there was no way of doing under the circumstances. Yet, she wasn't about to let anything—any insecurity or fear—ruin this moment. Onward she would go, faking her way to confidence.

"Not for long," she said, channeling that fake bold self, as she undid her top.

"Hey, hold on. I'm supposed to get to do that." Mark moved in faster than double-struck lightning and did the honors of slipping her straps off her shoulders, creating an instant chill storm. Then his head bent, and his mouth found a spot on her shoulder near her neck to press his lips to. The barely there kiss was enough to send tingles shooting to all parts north and south. It had been a long time, and a recent incessant yearning for this wouldn't let her back out now. No way.

Remembering how Mark took control doing the salsa and, once she'd learned to follow him, how they'd moved like they'd danced together all their lives, she made the wise and snap decision to let his experience take over. Not that she wouldn't jump right in, but just for now, while he broke the ice, it would be all up to him to seduce her. And so far, along with the frisson of anticipation vibrating between them, she was all in and he was doing an amazing job.

First his hand went *there*, setting off a cascade of goose bumps, and the other hand *there*, making her quake. All the while he concentrated kisses on the perfect spot on her shoulder, which guaranteed to drive her crazy. Then she turned into him and her hands got busy, too. Soon his towel and what was remaining of their swimsuits were on the floor.

He looked at her as if she were the most beautiful woman in the world, and right then, she believed it. That gave her courage—no more faking it—to be bold and do what she really wanted. To be with him. He was nothing short of perfection, lean muscled, trim, yet strong and begging to be touched. In seconds she'd put her arms around his neck, and he'd lifted her hips as she wrapped her legs around his waist. The heat they created between them took away what was left of her breath. Her breasts were pressed against his chest, setting off a whole new sensation. Then, while engaged in a full, deep kiss, he walked backward to that big gorgeous waiting bed.

She'd hardly touched the mattress before the solid length of Mark Mendoza's body came beside her and took her mind far, far away to where she had never been before. Not like this. Not this intense. Never this mind-blowing. Ever.

An hour later Mark cuddled Megan close to his body. Fueled by pure desire, he'd ignored the explosion of red flags and had taken her through every fantasy he'd had about her since he'd arrived. She'd come up with a few he'd never thought of, too, but he sure would from now on. Turned out The *M*s had it going on, and he'd never forget this night.

They fit like puzzle pieces, locked in place on the mattress. Damp skin to damp skin. Heat radiated from their entwined bodies. They'd had a staggering workout. She'd surprised him on so many levels, like she had every single day since he'd met her. What was it about this woman from Fort Lauderdale that drove him wild? To sum it up, well, everything. Every single thing about her.

They shared the center of the king-size bed, her soft pale skin pressed against his tougher, brown-toned complexion. He liked the contrast. Her hair was fine like spun silk when he lifted it and let it drop back to her neck. His was thick and wiry. Unruly. Hers lined up in a perfectly straight line on each side of her jaw. And her body... Well, there she was in all her glory right up against him, which felt like heaven on earth. He'd explored and discovered all kinds of things about her, figured out pretty damn quick how to blow her mind, and he knew he was a goner. Because she already had him wrapped around her delicate little finger without even trying.

She dared to move, to gaze with those big baby blue eyes into his, the look of total satisfaction in her slow, naughty smile, which guaranteed a quiet promise of something more. He'd discovered what that promise could be, and he selfishly wanted everything she offered. She sighed in contentment, then lifted her chin and delivered a soulful kiss that set him on fire all over again.

If they kept this up, they might set off the hotel fire alarm.

Several hours later, Mark had finally cooled down enough and confusion set in. What the hell had he done? When would he learn his lesson about getting swept away by his emotions? If the mistake of Brianna hadn't taught him to walk a straight line and be practical, then nothing ever would. Yet he'd just blown the roof off the hotel with the triplet sister of his brother's fiancée, again and again. How messed up was that?

He hadn't been thinking right since the day he'd come up with his foolproof plan—emphasis on the *fool* part—and asked Brianna to marry him. If that wasn't bad enough, he'd definitely lost it when he'd walked away from his wedding. Even for a good reason—a damn good reason. Everything since proved he still wasn't thinking straight and had no right to unleash himself on a perfectly sensible, unsuspecting and wonderful woman like Megan. His very own superhero, which she'd clearly proved to be last night. His hand went to his forehead. What a mistake, albeit an amazing and incredible mistake. But what about the fallout?

The sting of Brianna's betrayal returned, digging its sharp nails into him. Being with Megan suddenly turned dangerous, as he'd suspected all along. He was an emotional wreck, a risk for the long haul, and Megan deserved better. If he couldn't be the man she deserved, then he had no business being with her at all.

He went inward, regretting his spontaneous reaction to Megan. Once it had started, he'd been helpless to control it. By the time she woke up, he'd withdrawn completely, showered and ordered breakfast. His only hope was that she might not realize what an emotional mess he was.

Even then his biggest fear was that she'd feel that he'd used her for distraction. Which he hadn't. That one thing he knew for sure.

She sat up and stretched and it was so hard not to fall in love with her all over again, so he looked away, pretending to look for some underwear.

"Good morning, handsome," she said, sounding smoky and far too inviting.

"Hey! I ordered room service so why don't you hop in the shower before they get here."

That got a cautious gaze. Already she was suspicious. The last thing he wanted to do was act like a man who'd had his good time and couldn't wait to get rid of the woman. "I hope you like French toast. I hear the chef at Roja—I believe you know her—makes the best in Texas." Could he come off as a bigger jerk?

"Mmm, that does sound good. And I can sure use some coffee."

"Ordered a whole pot."

"Well, thank you, sir." She threw back the sheets and took his breath away when she stood and walked to the bathroom. She'd been his all night and half the early morning, to do exactly what he wanted with. She'd freely given herself to him, trusted him to do right by her. Even now, all messed up and searching for what to do next, his body ached for her. His heart wished he'd met her last year instead of after he'd made those stupid plans about how to find the perfect wife with a checklist. But he was living proof of how badly he'd messed up. So, instead of following her into the shower like he longed to, like any sensible man with half a brain would do, he threw on the last clean shirt and shorts he had and chewed the inside of his mouth in frustration.

How could he possibly explain that what they'd done last night—which in all honesty was pure perfection—was also one whopping screwup?

One mistake after another seemed to be the theme of his life for the past year. Until he got his head together, Megan shouldn't have to put up with a guy like him.

Later, as they ate breakfast, mostly in silence,

and he had zero appetite and couldn't hide it, Megan shifted from suspicious to worried. "What's up?"

"Nothing. Just thinking about having to pack and head home." *You jerk, what a horrible answer!* He saw immediately how she'd interpreted his dodging the truth.

"You regret what we did, don't you?" His always pragmatic Numbers Woman couldn't be fooled.

"No." He hoped the extreme headshake would convince her.

She cautiously studied him, and he'd never felt more like a heel in his life, because she could see right through him. Soon she followed down the zero-appetite trail and quit trying to move her food around the plate. "I'm not hungry. Sorry." She scratched her wet, straight hair part, doing a poor job of hiding her true reaction.

If there was an emoji for hurt and disappointed, she'd be it. It cut deep to see her like that, but there was nothing he could do. He wouldn't dare say the words because they'd come off like a pitiful cliché. *I understand.* First of all he couldn't possibly understand what he'd done to her when he couldn't even figure out what he'd already done to himself.

"It's clear we've made a mistake. Should've kept things fake," she said with a deep sigh.

He fumbled through his brain to come up with a response.

"I'm sorry" was all he could say. More sorry than he could ever imagine, sorrier than getting engaged to Brianna.

After that, the silence in the room was deafening as she gathered her purse, slipped her pool cover-up over her cold and still partially damp swimsuit, and headed toward the door.

"Goodbye," she said, so quietly he nearly missed it.

With his feet cemented to the floor, he chewed an even bigger lump on the inside of his mouth instead of running after her like any better man would do. Not because he didn't want to, but because that's how seriously screwed up he still was. And Megan Fortune deserved a better man.

"Megan, open your door," Ashley said through the barrier at the Fame and Fortune Ranch compound.

"Please?" Nicole followed up.

"I'd rather not talk right now." When in Megan's entire life had she ever not wanted to be around her sisters, the people she was closest to?

"We didn't say you had to talk, just let us sit with you." Ashley had always been big on supporting her sisters.

"You shouldn't be alone." Nicole echoed the sentiment.

"I've got Willow keeping me company." If a rescued red tabby wasn't the perfect soul mate for a time like this, no one could help. But she knew that wasn't true. Her sisters were her heart and soul and with Mark gone, she needed them.

It was almost 4 p.m. and Megan had been in her room at the ranch with the door locked for hours walking and thinking, deconstructing the last two weeks. The mathematician had taken over as she'd analyzed her time with Mark. With her gut tied in knots, no way could she eat, but always the pragmatist. "I could use a cup of tea."

"I'm on it," Nicole said, her retreating footsteps proving it.

Megan unlocked the door and let Ashley in. Her arms swarmed over Megan and held her tight. She swallowed a surge of emotion as she welcomed the human contact of her sister. Thank God for family. Hadn't Mark said that once? And she'd agreed wholeheartedly.

"Don't say anything until I get there!" Nicole instructed over her shoulder as her voice grew fainter heading for the downstairs kitchen.

So Megan and Ashley stood where they were and held each other. Thank God for sisters.

Once the tea had been delivered for all of them, they sat on the small sofa in Megan's bedroom suite, Megan at the center. Each sister touched her in some way. Ashley held her hand. Nicole, wanting to give her access to her tea, kept her hand on Megan's knee as her other hand rubbed Megan's back.

Megan used her free and shaky hand to lift her cup. Triplet telepathy at its finest, the tea was chamomile, exactly what Megan had craved.

"Only if you want to," Ashley said. "Tell us what happened."

Several seconds went by as Megan thought about what she wanted to tell them, or how she should go about it. No way did she want to get Mark in trouble with her family. Even now. "We stopped pretending and got real, and, well, it was wonderful, more than I ever dreamed he'd be."

"Wait, you've dreamed about him?" Nicole couldn't hide the surprise, even when she'd obviously seen Mark and Megan together every day for two weeks.

"Beginning from that first night when he was such a mess." She took another sip and noticed her hand was steadying already, and that Willow had barged her way onto Megan's lap. "I've always been a sucker for strays."

Her childhood history of rescuing cats and dogs, continuing into adulthood, proved it. Willow was the most recent rescue, and she'd honestly lost count over the years.

Nicole had thought to bring some soul food, too, homemade shortbread cookies, with a touch of pure almond extract added. The secret touch. Megan took one and ate it in two bites, proving she needed the sugar, plus the presence of her sisters was already helping. There was nothing like family…and pets. She'd also missed every meal, including breakfast today. Which made her remember how horrible that scene had been. How she'd seen regret in Mark's eyes—she'd put it there and couldn't bear it. And just like that, their exquisite night together had been ruined.

She put down her cup and ran her hand along Willow's soft fur. "We'd had this great time in the pool and then he said, 'full disclosure,' and told me things that I couldn't believe I was hearing."

"Like what?" Nicole seemed captivated, and a little nosy. But they were triplets and that came with the privilege of knowing everything about each other. In fact, it had been a little hard keeping Mark and their less fake relationship all to herself these past several days.

"Well, he admitted he'd faked seeing Brianna so he could hold me or kiss me."

"That's manipulating," Ashley said at the exact moment Nicole responded, "How sweet!" proving they weren't always on the same page.

Megan glanced between her sisters, surprised they hadn't agreed but understanding that Ashley saw things more from Rodrigo's point of view than

Nicole did. "The thing is, I'd done the same thing
the night before." That eased the offense in Ashley's
eyes and Nicole cupped her hands to her mouth.

"You *both* double faked?" Nicole's hand came
down on Megan's thigh and squeezed. "So, I guess
a double fake makes it real!"

"Yeah," Megan said, "you know, the way a negative times a negative equals a positive. Right?" The
mathematician in Megan elbowed her sister in the
ribs over the illogical conclusion, by offering proof,
and they all giggled together over the absurdity of
her arrangement with Mark. It did Megan's heart
good to talk about him and what they had been up
to for the last couple weeks. Because it really had
been wonderful. Acting braver than she felt, she
calmly recited as many details as she could remember to prove it, as her sisters looked on in amazement. Especially when she mentioned their sexy
confessions in the pool.

"Did he ever say why he left Brianna at the altar?
I mean beyond 'she betrayed me'?" Ashley's question put an end to the laughter. Megan figured if
Rodrigo knew, surely he'd tell Ashley, so evidently
Mark hadn't even told his brother. Or Rodrigo was
a man of his word. Which Megan knew without
this test. She smiled inwardly, happy her sister had
found such a good man. Suspecting she had, too,
in Mark, but the timing was off.

Megan wasn't quite ready to give up on Mark yet, but she'd never want to be a person he regretted knowing, like Brianna. And that look in his eyes this morning told her all she needed to know. Her stomach roiled again. Then she remembered another look in his eyes when he'd told her something else.

"No, but he told me I was beautiful, and he was so glad we'd had two weeks together." Megan let out a little laugh remembering what he said next. "He said it had been the best honeymoon he'd never taken." How could she not fall for a guy who thought like that?

Nicole's back rubbing became more intense; Ashley squeezed Megan's fingers tighter.

"I was so swept away by his words that I came on to him and he was…" she thought better than to describe his actual state "…very receptive." Her cheeks warmed at the memory. "The whole scene was like right out of the movies. Then something I'd been taking baby steps toward for the last two weeks happened."

Ashley held her breath, and that amused Megan. "I told him if this was his honeymoon that something else had been missing. That's when things went nuts. Before I knew it, we were in his room and I was taking his trunks off."

"Meggie!" Nicole giggled. "You didn't."

"Oh, yes, I did." She ate another cookie, ravenously, then gazed to the right and left at her sisters, whose eyes were wide with silent wonder. The sensible pragmatist of the three had acted far out of character. Were they impressed or horrified? "It was amazing. *He* was amazing. The whole night was like a beautiful dream."

"Wow." Nicole, still single, seemed the most impressed, in an I'll-have-what-she's-having sort of way. Megan hated to burst her bubble, but what else could she do when her own had been exploded to smithereens.

"Then this morning, something had clicked with him. Maybe we got too close and it was too soon after being betrayed by Brianna, but all the tenderness and love I'd felt from him last night had disappeared. It was like he'd put on a space suit. I think he felt guilty for what we'd done, and it was obvious he regretted it. It made me sick and so, so sad." She put her cup down because she'd forced her feelings down all day and now needed a tissue and she had a stash in her hoodie pocket just in case, since she'd been wearing it all day.

"That jerk," Ashley said with conviction.

"He's not a jerk. Mark Mendoza is a great guy, but you saw how messed up he was that first night at Provisions. Brianna had taken him down, and we had no business going from fake to real." It was Megan's turn to grab her sisters' hands. "But I wouldn't change last night for anything in this world."

"Sounds like this morning is the day you need to forget," Ashley said.

"You guys, please don't hate Mark. Last night in the pool, I got him to admit he's still grieving the loss of his marriage. Which includes all his dreams for a family, too."

"He wants a family?" Nicole blurted.

Megan nodded. "Just like me."

"But stopping that marriage was a good thing considering Brianna, right?" Ashley said.

"Right, but he'd really wanted to get married and loss is loss. He needs to face that grief. All we did the past two weeks was run away from that night."

"Oh, Meggie, you're too good," Nicole said.

"We're so sorry things didn't work out," Ashley followed up.

After the long, confusing, frustrating and excruciatingly sad day she'd endured with a stiff upper lip, it now quivered. "Me, too," she whispered. Then four arms locked her tight between them as she melted into the safety of her sisters and finally gave in to what she had been fighting all afternoon. And cried her heart out.

"What in the hell did you do to my future sister-in-law?" Rodrigo challenged Mark late that afternoon in the hotel room as he finished packing his luggage. Mark had also had a few more hours to grow defensive.

"What do you mean?"

"Ashley says she's been in her room all afternoon and won't come out. Insists she's working and won't let them in."

Mark's stomach wound so tight at the thought of how he had tormented Megan, he wanted to hurl. He'd done that to her, further proof he was nowhere near ready to be in a new relationship, and she deserved far more than he could give.

"You've been using Megan ever since you came here."

"That is not true. I'm not the one who sent her to babysit me because you weren't around, and what we did was consensual. I am not going to feel guilty." Except he already did. Beyond guilty, he felt like he'd betrayed Megan's trust, which was the exact reason he'd left Brianna at the altar. What a mess.

"You came up with that crazy idea to have a fake relationship."

"Megan came up with that." To reinforce his defensive attitude, he stood straighter and dropped his hands to his hips. He'd only gotten far enough to pretend to kiss her when he'd spotted Brianna. Megan had taken the game to a whole new level, and he'd gladly played along. Ingenious, he'd thought at the time. Now he wished he could kick his own ass for being a follower.

"You can't even accept responsibility for her needing to help you in the first place." The vein on Rodrigo's forehead was becoming engorged. A sure sign of his frustration.

"I never asked her to do anything she didn't want to, and by the way, the plan worked! Brianna's gone." Like that was all he and Megan had wanted to achieve. Originally it had been, anyway. Until he'd started falling for her and didn't have the guts to immediately take off—to save her from his messed-up life—because he liked her too much! He sniffed and suddenly needed to scratch that patch above his eyebrow. Since he was going down as the villain in this scene, why not double down?

"You should never have been engaged in the first place. Now you're leaving as big a mess here as you made in Austin." Rodrigo had started pointing in the air at Mark. "If you'd only listened to me in the first place—"

If he'd only listened to himself! "None of this would ever have happened." Mark finished the overused sentence for his brother. "Here we go again. Well, listen, kid brother, I'm sorry I've intruded on your little piece of heaven here in Rambling Rose, but I'm going to use your words from when we were kids. You're not the boss of me. Now you don't have to worry anymore. I'm getting out of your hair." He slammed his suitcase closed and zipped it. Then flung it onto the floor. He grabbed his garment bag and pulled the suitcase toward the door, then stopped. "See you at the wedding." Because even as messed up as things were now, Mendozas went to family weddings.

Mark couldn't stand not to make one last dig. "Unlike you, who skipped mine."

"Which didn't happen anyway," Rodrigo said, also hunkering down into the tit-for-tat brotherly verbal sparring match. He stood taller to make obvious his slight advantage in height and folded his arms across his chest in defiance.

"Just do me one favor, then I'll get out of your hair." At the door, Mark stood arms akimbo. "Don't say anything to our brothers. I've got to work with them and I'm not ready to explain anything. I just want to get back home, do what I do best, make wine and market like a madman, and forget about the Brianna chapter in my life."

"Yeah? And what about Megan? Her chapter?"

She'd been the innocent casualty of his running off on his wedding day, and he'd meant everything he'd told her yesterday and last night. Even though red flags had been popping up all along—he was falling for her, knew he was an emotional mess and nowhere near ready for an honest-to-goodness romance—he'd ignored the fear building inside with each kiss and sweet memory they'd made. Then like the cement brain he apparently was, ignored it all! They'd started out faking it but wound up in a whole different place. A beautiful place, one where Mark didn't deserve to go. Not yet. Not ever? He sighed. Who knew?

"Well?" Rodrigo had completely run out of patience while Mark had gone deeper inward.

"Megan is a strong woman who is perfectly able to take care of herself without you deciding what she should or shouldn't have done," Mark finally said. "Just leave things be." *I'll handle this when the time is right. Which certainly isn't now.*

"Sometimes you're a real piece of work."

Hurt to the core that he'd further ruined his already edgy relationship with his formerly favorite kid brother, he still managed to ignore the insult. Instead, he flung the door open and headed out, leaving Rodrigo standing in the room.

Halfway down the hall, he thought of something else. "Oh, and you can return the tux you ordered for me for the wedding." He eyed the bag slung over his shoulder, flashing on all the heartache it represented. "I already have one."

After taking the mess from Austin and transporting it to Rambling Rose, like Rodrigo had dutifully pointed out, Mark couldn't wait to hit the road out of town. He was done here. Well, all except for one person.

Once he got his head back in working order, he and Megan would be continued...

Even now all he wanted to do was run to Megan and explain everything, even the parts he hadn't figured out yet; instead he hit the gas and drove the other way.

Chapter Nine

As predicted, Mark didn't sleep his first night back home. His mattress couldn't compare to the Fortune Hotel's, but the real reason was he couldn't stop thinking about Megan. How he'd second-guessed what they had done, and picking up on his doubt, she'd made it clear they had made a mistake. Not the faking-a-romance part—that had been pure fun. Crazy but so much fun. But the reality, where they both admitted their true feelings for each other, was what had knocked him sideways. It had started that night after dancing together, and built in the pool with their teasing and sexy confessions, then had spiraled to pure passion in the hotel room.

Aside from ignoring every red flag his wiser self had raised, the true danger had come in the quiet of the early morning, while he watched her sleep and came so close to opening his heart again. The fact he had a world of emotions regarding Brianna's betrayal proved he had no business rushing into a new romance, and that had shut him down and made him feel guilty. Because Megan deserved a man who could give one hundred percent to their love.

Still, having her in his arms for even one night should be enough to last a lifetime. As it turned out, where Megan was concerned, he was a greedy man. He wanted more and more. For now, he'd try tearing a page from the Brianna playbook and give Megan some time to cool down, and then try to reconnect and hope for the best. In the meantime, maybe a miracle would happen, and his head would talk some sense into his heart. Or the other way around.

Truth was, Brianna's making out with the head caterer, whom she described as an "old friend" with whom she'd shared "just a little kiss," had done a complete number on him.

Megan wasn't the only one who needed time to cool down. In that moment, seeing his bride-to-be with another man, his world had crumbled. He'd liked and trusted Brianna enough to propose his idea for the perfect marriage. She'd had reasons in her own right for entering into the bargain, and had happily signed on. They wanted the same things in life. It all seemed so perfect. Now he doubted relationships, and everything associated with them.

The dumb thing was, he'd be turning around and heading back to Rambling Rose in a week for Rodrigo and Ashley's wedding. How could one week be enough time to get over the damage Brianna had done, or figure out what to do with Megan? If Megan ever wanted to see him again, that is.

He just had to keep telling himself that Megan was different. Yet, that overly handsy kiss, with petticoats and a lacy garter showing—the kiss he'd walked in on by chance—had managed to shut down his trust for women. If he hadn't caught her, how many more men might there have been over the years? Behind his back. How could he ever believe in any relationship again if one so carefully planned out couldn't even survive? Maybe Brianna thought it was okay to cheat because their wedding had been based on a business plan instead of love. But a contract was a contract, and she'd betrayed her promise.

Yeah, yeah, Rodrigo, get out of my head.

Back at work at the Mendoza Winery offices Monday morning, looking like the dead warmed over, Mark sucked it up and faced his brothers. Expecting the worst, he was grateful to realize that Chaz, Carlo and Stefan were still glad to have him back. Why wouldn't they be? The winery was growing in leaps and bounds, and their La Viña restaurant was catching fire. Fingers crossed his brothers would be too busy to bring up the wedding. A guy could hope, couldn't he?

"If it isn't the talk of the town," Chaz teased when Mark finally showed up for work a half hour late after needing the extra time to mentally pull things together.

Mark shook his head, trying not to imagine how tongues had been wagging. But what could he expect when he'd given everyone so much to talk about?

"Welcome home," Carlo said, the one cool voice of reason. It felt good to know he was always in Mark's corner. Maybe because they were the two oldest brothers and growing up they'd often felt like it was them against the brat brigade.

"Thanks, man." Mark and Carlo shook hands and he saw solidarity in his eyes. "I should've known things were going to get screwed when you beat me at cards at my bachelor party."

They laughed together to lighten the mood, but soon, as in immediately, the subject was dropped because thankfully that's how men handled things, by talking as little as possible about personal matters, and they all got back to the work of running a family business.

Coming from a long line of restaurant and nightclub owners in Miami, the Mendoza brothers were naturals when it came time to help run their cousin

Alejandro's winery in Texas. They'd all bought in, becoming part owners, which made their commitment to quality come from a place of personal ownership. The Mendoza Winery in Austin was also the home of the refurbished, on-site restaurant La Viña. Carlo had personally hired the chef and handled the remodeling and set the stage for the place to become a huge success. Mark liked to think his marketing plan had helped rocket the restaurant in popularity almost right from the start.

Sitting here, looking out his office window, Mark thought the rose and sculpture garden still stole the show. He'd planned his own wedding reception here, not the entire wedding ceremony because Brianna wanted to be married in a church. Ha! That was rich. At the time, he'd thought, yeah, that's the kind of woman I want to marry, a traditionalist like me, and he'd mentally checked off another box for her.

Gazing out the window, he reimagined all the beautiful decorations he'd seen in the sculpture and rose garden the morning of his wedding day, as a queasy wave overtook his stomach. Thinking of his never-ending mistake made him need some fresh air, so he left his desk.

Once outside on the beautiful winery grounds, he walked to the Spanish-influenced fountain with colorful tiles made by a local artisan and sat. Another mistake, because not moving let Megan slip back into his thoughts. Unable to deal with the fall-out from pursuing her the last night in Rambling Rose, he sprang back to his feet almost as quickly as he'd sat, then paced the grounds. Until he felt able to walk back inside and contribute something to the family business, he'd stay outside. Now, after being off for two weeks, was not the time to let his personal life interfere with his job. Maybe working would help numb him to everything that hurt.

Thankfully, Mark had piles of marketing projects to get caught up on. Most of them having to do with La Viña, which was good. He wanted to get word out that their summer menu was in the works with automatic wine pairing suggestions beside each meal. Maybe diving back in would help distract his mind from the girl he left behind. Not the one he'd left at the altar.

Midmorning, Stefan came wandering into his office. Once Mark acknowledged him, Stefan didn't waste a second getting to the point. "You know, Brianna came around the first few days after you took off looking for you. In case you're thinking about mending some fences, I think she's still open to that."

"Uh, I'll pass," he said, using his diplomatic tone. At least Rodrigo had kept his word about not discussing the state of Mark's life with his brothers. But Mark already knew he could count on him for that.

Stefan sat in the chair across from Mark's desk,

looking concerned, obviously wanting more information. "Mind if I ask why you left it up to her to tell the guests the wedding was off? We were all, like, really shocked."

As a matter of fact he did mind, but this was his kid brother, who had spent two weeks wondering what the—to use Megan's creative cuss phrase—flying fig was going on. "She was the right person to do it. Not me."

"You mean, she called it off?"

"No. That would be me. We'd be married now otherwise." Making that statement sent a shudder through him. It opened his eyes and made him privately grateful for small—or in this case huge, humiliating and messy—favors. Who'd ever have thought premarital infidelity could have a positive outcome?

He'd met Megan and discovered, like Rodrigo and Carlo before him, that real love came when you least expected it. It obviously didn't come from checklists. Another major life lesson learned for Mr. Smarty, who thought he'd had it all figured out. Too bad he had such a thick skull.

He ran his hands through his hair and rubbed his scalp to keep his head from exploding over what had occurred to him.

"Well, I can't imagine what she did, but it's not too late. You can still work things out. Guys get cold feet all the time." Stefan, seeing Mark acting this way, obviously had a whole other idea about why he'd walked out on the wedding. Unfortunately, Mark *could* imagine what she'd done, because he'd seen it firsthand.

"If you'd seen her there, tears running down her face," Stefan continued, "looking at the guests that had already arrived, and a bunch more milling around the sanctuary... Her eye makeup was dripping down her cheeks, and everyone was dead silent. Looking so sad and hurt. You'd know she really loves you."

First off, good! Secondly, no! That was not love.

He'd been curious how their family and friends had reacted. That part, leaving them all hanging, gutted him. One day, when his head was screwed on straight again, he'd contact each and every one of them. But since that Saturday afternoon, he hadn't responded to any texts or phone calls from Austin. Not cool but necessary for his survival. Especially Brianna's calls and texts. Her piercing violin strings alert tone, like in horror movies, almost got him to crack a smile. Instead he asked Stefan, "What exactly did she say?"

"How sorry she was to bring everyone out for a false alarm. That, as hard as it was to be so last-minute about it, it wasn't the right day to do it. Not yet. That you'd both agreed on it."

"We definitely agreed." She had no choice. But what was that "wasn't the right day" bit, like her horoscope had warned her off or they'd had a lengthy, unemotional conversation about it? As he recalled, the only thing he'd said was, *What the hell is going on?* Then, *We're done. Goodbye.*

"She said it broke her heart and that you weren't happy either but this was the decision you'd both made," Stefan continued.

The decision *he'd* made, and she had no choice but to accept. And you better believe he was not happy but for a completely different reason than her. "You know what? I'm just going to chalk this one up as a life lesson and move on." He threw out a heavy hint, hoping Stefan might catch on and change the subject or leave.

"But maybe you could still save things?" All of the Mendoza brothers had pleaded with their parents to stay married; maybe this was where Stefan was coming from. "If you want to. I'm just sayin' the door still seems open."

Mentally, Mark had slammed that baby shut so hard the walls shook.

"Here you are," Carlo said, pushing his head around the corner, looking a little frustrated at Stefan. "We've got twenty cases of wine loaded and waiting in the van at the distribution center that won't drive themselves to Foreign & Domestic."

Mark knew Foreign & Domestic had recently spruced up their menu, because he'd suggested it to them when he'd talked them into trying out Men-

doza wine for their customers. He was glad to know
they had reordered. Mark was also grateful that
running the winery and everyday things like wine
deliveries had cut short what felt like an entirely
too long conversation. He loved Stefan and knew
his heart was in the right place even though he was
terribly wrong. Stefan was in the dark about what
really had happened. But he had found out all he
was going to from Mark today about the state of
the canceled wedding.

Before they left, Carlo gave Mark a weird look.
"Fix your hair, man. You're scaring me."

It was going to take Mark a good half hour to
calm down again and get his mind off Megan Fortune. Not Brianna, like misguided Stefan thought.
But Megan. His Numbers Woman. A much more
appealing alert tone came to mind, made him wish
he would hear it, and for the first time that day, as he
used the dark computer screen as a mirror to comb
his hair, he smiled. Though it only lasted briefly
because he'd screwed up beyond all imagination
where Megan was concerned. And he'd probably
never hear that alert tone from her again.

Megan never dreamed being CFO of two restaurants, the job she loved, could be so hard. It never
used to be. Yet over the last few days it felt like
trudging through molasses to balance the books.
Every business meeting left her staring out the win-

dow, wishing she were someplace else. With Mark. Like before. The best two weeks of her life. But, oh, what a mistake that had been. Talk about a sucky ending.

Yet every time she tried to think he had been a mistake she couldn't quite convince herself. What had happened between them for two weeks had been nothing less than magical. Ha! That made her laugh. Yeah, magical all right because it had been all *fake*. And it had disappeared like that. She snapped her fingers to make her point to no one, since she was deep in thought and totally alone in her office.

She hated being cynical, especially with Ashley's wedding coming up, but being hurt by Mark had cut deep. She'd given him her heart and her body and look where it had gotten her.

Fortunately, tonight she had a date with her sisters. Nicole had planned the bachelorette party for this Friday and tonight she'd bring them up-to-date on the agenda. Megan had been assigned the job of gathering something old, something new, something borrowed and something blue.

After racking her brain for ideas, one sleepless night just a few days before Mark barreled into her life, the idea had come to her. As if Nanny Francis had whispered to her from heaven. They'd never been close to Grandma "MeMa" Penny, Dad's mother, but they'd always had a great relationship with Nanny Francis. Unfortunately, she'd passed away a few years back, but had left the triplets something extra special. It had taken a lunchtime trip to the safe-deposit box Monday, followed by the jewelers on her way home, to clean the gift, but Megan was convinced she'd come up with the perfect idea. At least today she had something to look forward to.

Jay Cross, one of the hotel trainees, popped his head into her office, his usual great smile on display. "They sent me to get you," he said with that smooth, deep drawl. He always struck her as handsome and mysterious, not to mention she could listen to him talk all day. There was just something special about him, but not for her, and not anything like the way Mark made her feel.

Yanked out of her thoughts, she wondered who "they" was. She scrunched up her face, clueless.

"The meeting?" Jay prompted. "The IT guys have their report."

How could she forget? She used to be the most organized person she knew.

After the techies got involved, they were still having the occasional reservation glitches, not nearly as big or often as before, but it was still affecting their overhead, and that was not good. With the wedding coming up, they couldn't take their chances on any guest finding themselves without a room. She'd been so distracted lately, Mark being front and center in her thoughts, that the meeting had slipped her mind.

Everyone was on to her situation, which made matters worse. Many of the hotel employees had witnessed that first fake kiss and public declaration of being in a relationship. And more than a few watched her and Mark walk to his room wearing pool towels. How obvious was that? Some may have heard the loud argument between Rodrigo and Mark the day he left. Word had certainly gotten back to her about it. The observant employees also probably noticed how down in the dumps she'd been since Mark had left. Now all she could do was hold her head high and keep her chin up. Yeah, she'd taken one for love, and it had knocked the wind out of her. But she wasn't defeated by it, a Fortune never was for long. She was just still a little unsteady.

Things will get better, she silently chanted following Jay Cross down the hall toward the meeting room. Things will get better.

That evening, Megan looked forward to Ashley driving over from Rodrigo's, where she'd been living since their engagement—though she still kept a lot of her things in her old suite at the Fame and Fortune Ranch. Soon they'd be setting up house as man and wife. How exciting. The first triplet to marry. Given Megan's current state, and how completely wrapped up Nicole was with Roja's menu, it occurred to her that maybe Ashley would be the first *and last* triplet to marry. She couldn't let herself have such bleak thoughts, so she reframed the last words: the last triplet to marry for a long time. Because a Fortune should always be hopeful.

The triplets had been super busy for the last several months, but tonight would be like old times, three sisters meeting up to discuss life and the future. Well, Ashley's future, anyway. Megan had no clue what hers would be. Nicole was kind of in the same boat as Megan, engrossed in work and with nearly zero social life. If that's what it took to get ahead, Megan and Nicole agreed it was worth the sacrifice.

Tonight, they would focus on Ashley, the bride-to-be, and just thinking those words made Megan grin.

As was always the case, the triplets met up in their favorite spot at the ranch, the huge kitchen. It was big enough to include regular living room chairs and a coffee table at the far end, and that was where they sat. Nicole wore one of her hip and colorful tunic tops with bright pink calf-length leggings, and sandals to die for. Ashley knocked them both out with an adorable scalloped hemmed A-line skirt, with a white-and-blue top. The outfit screamed young and sophisticated. Though Megan's only thought was, *How cute! And how soon can I borrow it?* Then it occurred—*But for what?* Since Mark had left, her social life had gone quiet.

Megan wished she'd worn something flashier than her favorite workout pants and ballet-neck maroon top. But she knew she'd end up stealing the show tonight when she revealed the perfect old and new, borrowed and blue tradition for Ashley.

After a group hug and several minutes catching up on the wedding plans, along with two rounds of herbal tea, Nicole started off in her usual enthusiastic manner.

"You guys, we're going to have such fun in Houston on Friday." There would be six of them. The triplets and their sister Stephanie, and Ashley's two closest friends, Cami and Drew, who were also bridesmaids along with Nicole and Megan. Ashley had chosen big sister Stephanie to be her maid of honor. And she was thrilled for the honor when Ashley had asked.

"I've got the limo arriving at ten a.m. with appetizers and refreshments, then when we arrive, we'll go on a museum district guided scavenger hunt for a couple hours, with loads of Instagram moments. So wear comfortable shoes. Then we'll be famished so we're taking a 'bites and sites' walking food tour. Thus the required comfortable shoes."

"This from a total foodie. Why am I not surprised," Ashley said, obviously pleased with the schedule.

"You probably handpicked the restaurants, too," Megan added.

"As a matter of fact, I did. I even used to date one of the chefs. And that's all I'm going to say about that. Oh, and after the tours, it's all about drinks and dancing for as long as we want at Club Tropicana. So bring your dancing shoes, too."

They clapped in excitement and grinned at each other like silly geese, though Megan did her best to hide her melancholy. How could dancing the salsa with anyone besides Mark possibly measure up? Not to mention all the great memories she'd be tortured with. Moments and feelings she might never have again.

"When was the last time we partied together?" Ashley asked.

"Uh, Disney World when we were fourteen?" Megan got a laugh with that memory.

"Wait, what about after we graduated from college?" Nicole couldn't let them forget.

"Oh, yikes, that was a party I'll never forget," Megan said.

"You mean that was a hangover you'll never forget," Nicole teased.

"Hey, I'm the one who held your hair while *you* barfed," Megan reminded.

"You were only returning the favor." Nicole had to mention that one little detail, but it got them all laughing again. A good thing.

Because even the mention of a hangover made her think about Mark. How and when they'd met and she'd known even then that he was special. But tonight was about Ashley and her wedding, and now that the bachelorette party had been revealed, it was Megan's turn to dazzle.

With a coy smile, she brought out the black velvet jewelry bag from her workout pants pocket and watched with satisfaction as Nicole's eyes went big and Ashley subtly licked her lips over what might be inside.

The big blended family they'd grown up in had to be a challenge to keep everyone happy and well-adjusted. With eight kids, Mom had needed backup with childcare and that's where Nanny Francis came in. She was old compared to their friends' grandmothers, but that didn't stop her from getting down on the floor and doing whatever Ashley, Megan and Nicole had going on. She'd always made sure they felt loved for being the individuals they were, and not swept into the three-for-one category. And that was why she'd given specific directions in her will about how to divide the beautiful jewelry set.

"Okay, you guys," Megan began. "We all loved Nanny Francis and miss her." The agreement shone in her sisters' eyes.

"Remember when she got her first cell phone and she paid us to teach her how to use it?" Nicole jumped in with a fond memory from their preteens.

Megan laughed. "I taught her how to text and

from then on I think she texted me at least once a day. Even used emojis."

"Me, too." Ashley joined in.

"Me three. And she always signed off with TTFN." Ta-ta for now. Nicole wore a nostalgic expression and for the next couple seconds they all took a personal trip down Nanny Francis lane.

"I wish she could have seen my wedding," Ashley said, her eyes welling.

"Who says she won't?" Nicole said with conviction.

Being the practical sister, Megan normally wouldn't be inclined to agree, but she liked the pure whimsy of Nicole's idea.

"Yeah, who says?" Megan said, envisioning Nanny Francis looking down over them, but then she immediately worried that if that were the case, Nanny may have also seen the whole Mark Mendoza episode.

"I hope so," Ashley said, as Megan squeezed her forearm and they shared a tender look and she knew it was time for her big reveal.

It was time to put on a brave face and not let her nonstop aching heart keep her from enjoying this moment. The sadness that had chased down her thoughts since Mark left Rambling Rose had to be silenced for now. She took a breath.

"Okay. You know how I like to keep it simple, and when you asked me to come up with something old, something new, something borrowed and something blue, I didn't want to go the garter route."

"Don't forget put a sixpence in your shoe."

Megan smiled at Nicole and nodded. "I've got that covered, too. Okay, so here goes." With surprisingly nervous hands, she loosened the satin strings on the jewelry bag and gently eased out the gorgeous necklace, earrings and ring set that had been packed away and nearly forgotten until a few weeks ago. As hoped for, having not seen the pieces in a long time, Nicole and Ashley both gasped.

"Remember Nanny Francis's blue sapphire set in white gold surrounded with melee diamonds? Well, these gorgeous blue gems were meant for you to wear on your wedding day. Nicole, Nanny Francis instructed that the earrings were to go to you, the necklace to Ashley and the ring to me. So, if you loan the earrings to Ashley to wear with her necklace, we'll have the somethings old, borrowed and blue completely covered."

"That's perfect!" Ashley appeared enthralled with the idea.

"Oh." Megan dug into her pocket again. "Here's the penny for your shoe. I had to search high and low to find a penny made in 1997."

"The year we were born. How cool!" Ashley said, clearly loving the length Megan had gone to for that extra touch. And it sure felt good to know the effort had not been wasted.

"Let me look at that ring," Nicole said, as Ashley reached for the rest of the set, holding the necklace to her throat, and placing one earring beside her head, then batting her eyes.

"They look so new," Ashley commented.

"That's because they've had a trip to the jewelry store for a special cleaning. And the clasp was replaced, so that's your something new. You'll look gorgeous wearing them."

"Did you have them appraised while you were there?" Nicole asked.

"I decided not to." The only thing that mattered to Megan was that these gifts had come from their favorite grandmother. "Don't you think the necklace is perfect for the cut of your wedding dress, Ash?"

"It is. It's beyond perfect, Meggie." Ashley reached for Megan's hand and squeezed it. "More like meant to be."

"Great. Then let's put everything back in the jewelry bag, and we can divide them up again after the wedding." An idea occurred to Megan. "Wait, you know what, there's no reason I can't wear my ring now. You already have an engagement ring, and this will go so beautifully with my bridesmaid dress."

Ashley and Nicole passed side glances to each other, more evidence of that telepathy thing, though Megan wasn't in on this little psychic conversation. What was up with that?

Ashley held on to the jewelry and thought for a

moment. "You're right about the ring, but for now, let's keep everything together for Nanny's sake."

Megan wasn't sure about the logic of "for Nanny's sake," but Ashley was the bride and it was her wedding, so anything she wanted, she should get. Though Megan did look forward to wearing that beautiful ring one day, and she had thought the wedding would have been the perfect place. She'd tried it on when she'd first taken it out of the safe-deposit box at the bank and it had fit perfectly, too. Why they'd all decided to store the gems away when they'd first moved to Rambling Rose, she had no idea. From the great reaction from Ashley, Megan was sure glad she'd remembered them.

"After the wedding, out of respect for and with fond memories of Nanny Francis, we should make a pact to all wear the beautiful pieces every chance we get," Ashley said. "Especially you, Megan. That ring was meant for you."

It was a lovely, if not an odd thing to say, and followed by another secretive glance between Nicole and Ashley, and Megan could not put her finger on whatever it was they were up to. But she was bound to find out.

It had been half a week since Mark had come back and Carlo had never seen his steady brother so unmoored. He found him working late in his office again and coaxed him into joining him in the tasting room. They didn't have an event planned tonight, so they'd have the comfortable and well-stocked location to themselves.

"Come on," Carlo said earlier when he'd suggested they have a drink together. "Keep me company. Besides, we haven't had a chance to catch up."

"Since the wedding that wasn't?" Mark, to his credit, looked humbled by the events from two and a half weeks ago. But it pained Carlo that Mark had paid a huge price emotionally and physically. It was time to get the whole story straight from his brother's mouth. He'd had enough of the gossip.

They arrived at the popular tasting room where the rough-hewn wood door with a brass handle required a key to let them in. Carlo switched on the lights and glanced at the high vaulted ceilings with dark beams, then used the dimmer to keep the ambience inviting instead of feeling like an interrogation room. Even though he expected to get some answers from Mark.

After Mark sat at the marble-topped bar, Carlo reached toward the shelves of corked wine bottles for a recently opened cabernet sauvignon. It was from earlier today when a couple requested a wine tasting for two. The wine had already been breathed, so after Carlo grabbed two wineglasses, he immediately poured. He also opened the mini-fridge behind the bar and took out a premade plate of cheese and a box of crackers on the ready for on-the-spot wine tastings, like earlier. They'd made a point since the very beginning to share the greatness of their wines with anyone who wanted them—to always be prepared. They even joked about being the Boy Scouts of the wine business. And so far, it had paid off. Business, as they say, was booming.

He placed both the wine and snacks in front of Mark, who looked like he could use a stiff drink instead, but tonight, some good Mendoza wine would have to do.

"You seem like something's on your mind," Carlo said, easing into his questions.

"And here comes the interrogation," Mark said. "Turn up the lights!"

"Just a few questions and some observations."

Ever since Carlo had married Schuyler, he'd had to learn to be more sensitive about other people's feelings. It was one of the tough parts about marriage for a guy who came from a house full of brothers. Women were a mystery on every level, and when he'd married his first wife, Cecily, when he was too young and unprepared, he'd had to learn the hard way through divorce. But he and Schuyler were great together and now Carlo realized the biggest part of a successful marriage was finding the right woman. He wished the same for each of his brothers, and looked forward to Rodrigo's wedding.

Carlo understood Mark had taken a more scientific approach to marriage, obviously trying to avoid the pitfalls of a tough adjustment, or all the mistakes their parents had made. Man, had it back-fired. Seeing his brother messed up and looking horrible worried him.

"I can't figure it out," Carlo continued, leaning his forearms on the other side of the bar from Mark, so he could be at eye level with him. "This isn't the brother I know. Is it Brianna? Because she's still coming around, even called me this morning, just to check up on how you seemed. I told her you looked like hell warmed over and your mood stunk."

"Ha, thanks for covering for me," Mark said, with a glint of his old fun-loving self. "Well, I guess you know me. I'm sorry if I've been a pain to be around. I'm just trying to get through every day."

"Maybe you and Brianna should get together, talk things over. Figure out what went wrong. Maybe make it right?"

"The thing is, it's not Brianna who's on my mind."

Now, that made Carlo stand up straight. It also finally made sense, in a crazy, out-of-left-field sort of way. "Well, what's up, then? Was it losing face in front of all your family and friends?"

Mark turned his wineglass around and around on the bar. "Well, there is that. But you want the truth?"

"Always, my brother. Otherwise, why bother, right?" Carlo had been a straight shooter since he was a kid. He took a drink of the smooth and full-bodied wine, as a hint for Mark to join him. Because Carlo expected the details.

Mark nodded but didn't take a drink. "I've fallen in love for real now, and that has made me realize that I never should have proposed to Brianna in the first place."

"Are you telling me that's why you called off the wedding, because you met someone else and had a change of heart?" He pushed the crackers and cheese Mark's way, and they both took a helping of the Gouda and water crackers. Carlo shoved his in his mouth with one bite and washed it down with wine.

"No. That happened when I went to Rambling Rose." Mark wolfed his down and grabbed some cheddar and wheat crackers as a follow-up.

Carlo scrubbed his face, trying to make sense of what Mark was doing a terrible job of explaining. Was it possible to fall in love in two weeks? It had to be a new record for any Mendoza. And completely ill-advised after walking away from his wedding.

Mark took a long drink, then a slow breath. "She cheated on me." Mark avoided Carlo's eyes.

"Brianna?" That news deserved another drink of wine. Cheating.

"Oh, yeah. I caught her a little over an hour before the wedding horsing around with the head caterer. His hands were all over her and, well, I'll spare you the details, but it changed me. I completely shut down." Mark drank more wine. "But you know what? I'm actually grateful now. What seemed like the worst timing in the world turned out to be the best thing to happen. Can you get more cheddar for me, please?"

Carlo did what he was asked and brought out the whole block, then searched through a drawer for a knife and handed both to Mark, who cut a large chunk and forgot the cracker.

"That friends-with-benefits business was a joke," Mark said, after downing the cheese and having the rest of his wine. "How I got myself to buy into it, I'll never understand. Must have been from wanting what Rodrigo had. Love. A wedding. And you know how much I want a family."

"You are a traditionalist."

"But evidently Brianna took friends with benefits to mean *all* friends, and *all* kinds of benefits, and marriage didn't matter. One thing I know now is marriage does matter to me, and it takes the right person to make it work. But it's all pointless now because I've messed *everything* up."

"Hold on a minute. Walk me through this again because you just unloaded a whole lot of information. Who did you find, and where is she, and how did you screw everything up already?"

Mark took a deep breath, reached for the bottle of wine and poured each of them a second glass of cab. Then, to Carlo's amazement Mark tried to explain everything that had happened after he'd met Megan Fortune.

All four brothers were hopping into their cars, along with their wives, to drive to Rambling Rose this weekend for Rodrigo and Ashley's wedding. Something exceptional had happened in a very short amount of days for Mark to claim he had fallen for real this time. Not that Carlo liked crazy stories like this, especially after seeing what it had done and was doing to Mark. Still, Carlo mentally rubbed his hands together in anticipation. It was no secret that he was a fixer who loved to refurbish things. But was this mess with Megan and Mark too big for even him to straighten out?

Chapter Ten

It was hard being lovesick alone. Megan had no choice, though, because her heart wouldn't give up on Mark even though he'd given up on her. Guilt had been written all over his face the morning after they'd made love; he couldn't hide it. Her head was done with trying to talk some sense into her, too. Man, she was worn-out.

From her desk she checked her watch. Uh-huh, right on time. Megan had hit the usual 2 p.m. wall. She called it her daily circadian rhythm slump as one who believed in the order of the universe. So, being the creature of habit that she was, she moseyed over to Roja and the always full coffee urn.

Unbidden, another day and time spun into focus—one afternoon a couple weeks ago when she had snuck over for a coffee and discovered Mark there eating alone. He had invited her to join him in the Roja dining room. It was the week they'd faked their way into honest-to-goodness friendship. The week he'd teased her about being from Fort Lauderdale, and she'd nicknamed him Miami Mark. It was also the week they had discovered they'd been couple-named by her sisters as The *M*s. Also when he'd revealed her special alert tone on his phone. She briefly wondered, if she dared to text now, would the silly *Wonder Woman* tune make him smile or regret ever meeting her? She could use the excuse of checking to see if he still planned to be her date at the wedding—kidding—but even if she wasn't, she didn't have the guts to find out. Besides, he had probably already deleted her as a contact. Bye-bye, alert tone.

Yet she couldn't stop thinking about him. That week and day when she'd come for coffee and found Mark instead was also the week before they'd pretended *not* to be falling for each other. And it had been one week from when they would salsa their way into intimacy…

She had to stop doing this. It served no purpose other than to torture her. Right now was about coffee, nothing more.

First on her quest, she planned to pop into the

kitchen and say hi to Nicole. It was Thursday and tomorrow would be the big daylong bachelorette party in Houston. Megan was excited for the distraction and eager to let Nicole know how much she looked forward to it. But Nicole was in an animated and heated conversation on the phone across the large kitchen. "You are kidding. Rodrigo told you that?"

Well, that certainly perked Megan's ears up as she strained to make out more of the words.

Once Nicole got off the phone, Megan would ask her what exactly Rodrigo had told whom. Though she figured it had to be Ashley that Nicole was talking to. Rather than interrupt, she decided to get that coffee then come back later. Just as she pushed through the door, she overheard Nicole gasp. "So, she's not the only one?"

The only one, what? Megan was on the verge of making an about-face and marching right up to Nicole and demanding to know what she was talking about. Clearly engrossed in the conversation, Nicole now dropped her voice. She had obviously gone into private mode, not wanting anyone to hear her words, even though she had no idea Megan was in the kitchen. Maybe now wasn't such a good time to barge in. But tomorrow, she'd have all day to get Nicole by herself, pester and question her like a regular Harvey Specter on *Suits*.

So she turned back to her original quest, and

there at the coffee urn was a nice surprise. Jay Cross, the guy from the hotel training program. He'd been one of the first who'd signed on when they'd created the program specifically for the locals. It was part of the compromise Callum had made with the town, along with scaling down the size of the hotel to get the approval to build.

"I see we have the same idea," she said, approaching the urn and grabbing a mug from a stack nearby.

"Hey, how's your day going?" he said with that smooth, deep voice.

"Besides needing my afternoon coffee and wondering what big secret my sister is keeping from me, fine."

"Nothing worse than trying to keep a secret in a small town," he said, smiling at the urn.

"I hear you, brother. She may think I'm not aware, but I've got news for her."

"Who?"

"My sister, and probably my other sisters, too. I don't know. Something seems up."

He reached for and filled her mug before getting his own coffee, like a Texas gentleman. "Secrets weigh on people," he said mysteriously as he handed it back.

She poured some cream into her coffee and stirred. "They do, don't they? If I wait long enough, Nicole will probably be dying to tell me."

That got another partial grin out of him, and out of nowhere something occurred to her... "So are you hiding anything?"

His smile shifted to something else and she could have sworn there was a twinkle in those great green eyes of his. "I'd call you darlin' because that's what we do in Texas, but I don't want to be disrespectful of the management."

She swiped the air with her free hand. "You can call me 'darlin'.'" Just because she was from Fort Lauderdale, didn't mean she didn't understand or might be offended by the local Southern vernacular.

He tipped his head in thanks, and she could almost imagine a cowboy hat on that head. "Then, darlin'," he said, "I'll just say, everyone in the world is hiding something." He used his spoon to accentuate his point. After a slow, concealed smile that nearly gave her chills, he nodded and walked away.

Megan drank another sip of coffee and watched his slow, guy-styled saunter as he left the dining room and her with a big old question mark hanging in the air. So everyone was hiding something, and Megan knew for a fact Nicole was. Probably Ashley, too. Megan certainly was.

But what about him? Jay Cross. Suddenly she wondered what his story was.

Friday morning at ten, Nicole met everyone at the stretch limousine in pure tour guide mode. She'd hardly dressed the part, though, wearing a fedora hat with a wide white lace band to top off her cute outfit. As always, her sandals were to die for, and today's looked easy to walk in, too.

Ashley, the star of the day, and part-time drama queen, wore a baby pink satin dress with a tank bodice and a natural flare short skirt. The outfit screamed *Take my picture!* Which they no doubt would hundreds of times that day.

Megan had parted ways with her penchant for separates and found another fun dress at one of the Fortune extended family boutiques in town. She had cinched the waist with a wide leather belt to help give the skirt some flair, exactly like the salesperson at the clothes store had suggested. To keep it simple, she'd decided to wear comfy but always stylish wedge espadrilles that tied at the ankle.

And everyone had managed to wear some sort of statement jewelry to top off their respective looks. What a fine-looking bunch they were.

After a group greeting and ample cheek kisses, before they all loaded up inside the limo, Ashley suggested, "Let's get a group picture before we wrinkle our clothes." All six women moved into formation without the slightest protest.

The perfect hostess, Nicole, gave Megan zero chance to quiz her about yesterday's mysterious phone call. Since Nicole was showering most of her attention on Ashley, who deserved every second, Megan refused to complain.

"Everyone, guess what!" Nicole started right off as the car service hit the road. "Tomorrow at ten we have a group appointment at Paz Spa for massages and mani-pedis. After that, we'll all get our hair done for the rehearsal dinner. This same limo will be right here to take us everywhere tomorrow. Of course, champagne will be included. Oh, and they've promised to have all of us done in time for the wedding rehearsal at four."

The mention of the rehearsal and coming face-to-face with Mark made Megan's tummy twist.

After a happy group clap that Megan only half-heartedly participated in, but everyone else was so excited they didn't notice, Nicole went on to explain what to expect on their excursion to Houston. Again, Megan's thoughts got tied up with a guy from Austin who'd managed to steal her heart. But from the enthusiastic response to Nicole's announcements, Megan figured it would be a great day for all. Maybe even her.

Now all she had to do was keep her mind on fun and off Mark.

The day and night had come off without a hitch. They'd had a great time and were all tired and ready to get home and crash. They'd dropped off Ashley's friends Cami and Drew first at the Rosebud House, the bed-and-breakfast they'd booked. Another reservation glitch at the Hotel Fortune had wrongly told them there were no rooms. Fortunately, none of the out-of-town relatives had run into the same problem after their dad. But that was something else to deal with at another time.

The limousine had gone quiet. Stephanie and Nicole had paired up, talking in whispers. Megan and Ashley sat close and comfortably in silence. There may have been a little too much drinking by a few of them today. Oh, who was Megan kidding, all of them. Including her. And they'd danced like the world would end if they didn't hit that floor with their best moves. Thanks to Mark, she had learned a few new ones to show off. Wasn't that what a bachelorette party was supposed to be all about? Having fun, letting your hair down, laying down the last memories of being single?

Because things were going to change forever for her sister after she and Rodrigo said "I do." In the best possible way, of course!

As it turned out, between museum hopping, food touring and club dancing, Megan never had a second to quiz Nicole about yesterday's mysterious phone call. She knew there wouldn't be any time the rest of the weekend, so she decided to forgo her questions for now. What did it matter, anyway? All she wanted to do was be there a hundred percent for her sister on the biggest day of her life.

Megan glanced down at Ashley, who had laid her head on Megan's shoulder and groaned. "I shouldn't't've had that peach Bellini," Ashley said, her words all running together.

"Which one?" Megan didn't want to be unsympathetic, but...

"Wait. I'm okay." They'd pretty much been sipping champagne all day, but between the walking tours and the dancing, it hadn't really caught up to any of them. Until now, with the pretty little bride-to-be.

"You sure you're okay?"

Ashley nodded, the sour face went away, and she turned serious. "Meg, is it going to be hard to see Mark?" Clearly a bit tipsy, Ashley was blunt.

Megan truly was happy about her sister's wedding, but it was going to break her heart to see Mark again. Ashley was also an ace at reading Megan's honesty meter, so she couldn't lie. "Yes, it'll be hard, but nothing is going to stop me from being completely present at your wedding. Every single minute of it." She took her sister's hand and squeezed, then things went quiet again.

"I've heard he's all messed up in Austin." Ashley may have looked like she was dozing, but she'd obviously been thinking, too.

Maybe there was some justice in this world if Mark was as miserable as she was. At least Megan hadn't been suffering alone. Of course, her suffering was over him and his was over… "He still loves Brianna." She stated the truth she knew. *And he felt totally guilty about sleeping with me.*

"What makes you think that?"

"You saw how beautiful she was." *He never blocked her calls.*

Ashley sat up straight. "First off, looks are over-rated without character. Second, so what? Looks have nothing to do with love. Besides, she *betrayed* him. Turned him into that zombie we met that first night. He'd have to be nuts to still be in love with her."

Precisely Megan's point. Crazy love. Unexplainable love. The kind she felt? Brianna had broken Mark's heart, and that couldn't happen if you didn't love someone. So Mark was nuts. Nuts about Brianna. Sheesh, with this kind of logic Megan wished she had the excuse of having that one last Bellini.

"Oh, and you better not be dissing your looks," Ashley added. Now, not only was she sitting straight, she'd started using hand and head gestures. "Because being your triplet, Nicole and I know we're *hawt*, so you better face up to the fact." Ashley patted Megan's thigh. "You've got it goin' on." Then she folded her arms and pouted out her lower lip. "Because if you don't have it goin' on, then we don't, and that's not happening." She ended her lecture with one firm headshake, left to right.

Megan laughed at her sister's animated, cockeyed logic. Whoever said a night of dancing and drinking was fun could not possibly know how many hard memories the day and night had unlocked for her. She went quiet.

"Oh, honey, what's the matter? You seem so sad."

"Nothing. I'm fine." Megan needed to pull it together quickly. "I'm just emotional about you getting married, that's all. You'll be the first to break our secret sisterhood."

Ashley hugged Megan. "That'll never change."

When they pulled up to Hotel Fortune to drop off Stephanie, Nicole wanted to double-check everything in Roja, where Mariana had sole charge of the kitchen that night. They all stepped out of the car for a quick hug. Megan waited in the parking lot for her turn to say good-night to Steph, whose husband, Acton, was ready to drive her home. She noticed the Mendoza brothers all gathered by the pool, talking and laughing, and having an alternative kind of bachelor party for Rodrigo. Ashley had said it was going to be more of a family reunion than a bachelor bash because that's what the groom wanted. Unprepared, the vision sliced through Megan, making her unsteady. She reached with one hand for the limo to ground her. Like a bad accident, she couldn't look away.

One solemn, handsome man sat off by himself staring at the pool. Megan's knees almost buckled again at the sight. The instant after hugging her big sister, she leaned on the car for support.

The pool was where they had finally found each other. Where they'd dropped the fake dating and got real. That pool had been something she'd been avoiding ever since Mark had left.

Megan's heart sank at the sight of Mark. Every feeling she'd been pushing under, and doing a horrible job of, forced itself back and overpowered her with emotions. Thank goodness the limo was soundproof. She dove inside and let out a miserable groan and pounded her fists on the leather seat in frustration. It was time to face the fact she was the one who was crazy in love.

"Oh, honey, come on, what is it?" Ashley said, joining her in the car.

Megan pointed to the limo window. Ashley looked confused.

"Mark. In that chair. Looking like the long-lost brother from Miseryville. It's because he can't get over Brianna."

"You don't know that. But why should you care?"

"Because I love him." She'd been fighting it, denying it, pretending it would fade with each day he was gone, but her feelings had only gotten harder to bear. Their one night together had changed everything. They were perfect together. She'd given him every ounce of herself and he'd seemed to return it.

They'd certainly proved they were great together. She'd lain with her head on his shoulder, content with the world and allowed herself to dream big. About Mark. About what they could share together. Now, she fought the wave of sadness covering her like a weighted blanket, making it hard to breathe, but she'd run out of resistance. "It's worse than I ever expected," she whispered.

"No, Meg, love is the best feeling in the world."

"Only when it's returned. You and Rodrigo are two lucky people. Mark and I are mirror images of how it looks to love the wrong person."

Ashley gave Megan a worried look, as though she couldn't count on her sister to make it through her big day. "You don't know that for sure."

"He never blocked her calls and texts. And he looks so sad right now."

"That's your proof?"

"Not blocking calls, Ash, it's a huge tell."

Ashley did the one thing a loving sister could do when dealing with Megan's admittedly debatable logic: she stayed quiet and listened while holding Megan's hands.

"I'll get a hold of myself, I promise. It's just… well, look at him!" They both gazed in the direction of the lonely looking silhouette in the Adirondack chair again. The same chair where he'd spent so much time smiling and enjoying himself during his stay in Rambling Rose. "My heart is telling me to walk right over there. To hold him and kiss him." She dug fingers into her hair. "Before I cuss him out for doing this to me." She let go a frustrated squeak. "God, I miss him."

Ashley swallowed hard after Megan's meltdown and looked peaked, as though the whole day and especially their night on the town had finally caught up with her. She grabbed Megan's arm.

"Are you going to throw up?"

Ashley shook her head. "Just promise me you'll forgive me."

"For what?"

As it turned out, Ashley was wrong, she *did* need to barf. Fortunately, the limousine service, having catered to many bachelorette parties, was prepared with a pretty basket complete with a big pink bow on the outside and a white plastic drawstring bag inside. *For your convenience*, Megan read as she shoved it into her sister's hands.

Oh, yeah, now Megan was glad she'd skipped that last peach Bellini toast.

As Ashley did her due diligence into the basket, Megan's eyes drifted back to the pool, and Mark. She was grateful the limo had tinted windows so she could study him surreptitiously. He was the man she loved and missed with all her heart. The man who didn't love her back. Now what she had to do was keep it together for one weekend. It would be the toughest thing she'd ever had to do, but it was for her sister's sake, and the wedding.

Her heartache would have to wait.

Chapter Eleven

"Hey, man," Rodrigo said, pulling up a chair next to Mark by the hotel pool. "You don't look like you're having much fun."

Surrounded by several loud-talking, storytelling men, all in various levels of exaggeration and flat-out braggadocio, Mark was the only standout.

He nearly had to yell his answer. "I'm fine." Except for the fact he'd just watched a stretch limousine pull away from the front of the hotel, and he knew who had to be inside. Was he ready to face Megan again, or would he have to spend the weekend pretending to be an iron man?

"Not drinking?" Rodrigo asked him.

"Not tonight. Sorry."

"Nothing to apologize about." Rodrigo lifted his can of beer toward the rest of the brothers and cousins. "Besides, we're all making up for you."

Mark gave a half-hearted smile. For the life of him he couldn't figure out why he was putting himself through the torture of coming back to Rambling Rose and facing her. But the instant he said it, Megan's face popped into his mind. Then, the craziest thought of all crashed down—he'd promised to be her date for the wedding, and he was damned if he'd let her down *again*.

Somehow, he had to make her understand why he'd done an about-face the morning after they'd made love. It hadn't been because of her. She'd been everything he'd ever wanted, but Brianna's cheating had still had hold of him. He couldn't put the explanation off any longer. He'd thought about waiting until after the wedding, coming back to Rambling Rose at some later date when all the dust had settled, with his heart in his hand. Then, when she didn't have the excuse of being distracted by a wedding, he'd beg her to listen.

The problem was, he honestly didn't think he could survive that long without her. And with each passing day, he feared he might lose his courage. His hands were constantly clammy, like now, and he'd gotten used to the vise around his chest, but how much longer could he bear to live this way?

"I wanted to thank you for coming." Rodrigo looked sincere.

"You know I wouldn't miss it." Mark was past holding a grudge about Rodrigo refusing to come to his wedding that never was. These were entirely different circumstances. Rodrigo and Ashley belonged together, unlike Brianna and Mark. Up popped Megan's face again.

"After all you've been through this month, I would totally understand if you'd decided not to attend."

"I left with some things that needed to be made right. But celebrating your marriage is why I'm here. Besides, Dad would've kicked my ass if I didn't show up."

For one second it almost felt like things used to be as Mark and Rodrigo laughed about their father and the bond they had as brothers.

"He didn't kick mine when I wouldn't go to yours."

"I think he knew, too." Mark didn't need to explain more. Rodrigo obviously knew what he referred to. The huge mistake Mark had been about to make that everyone had seemed to know about. Except him.

Rodrigo's eyes darkened. "Look, I said some crappy things to you before."

"I needed to hear some of them." Oh, Mark remembered the arguments and lectures well. But all he wanted for now and forever was no grudges. From Rodrigo or from him. He had dug himself a hole insisting on marrying Brianna, and Rodrigo had only wanted to make sure he didn't get stuck in it. He'd gone to the extreme of refusing to attend Mark's wedding to make his point. Well, brother, point taken. His only regret was not taking the advice sooner.

"Just so you know, I love you, man," Rodrigo said, leaning forward to get in Mark's face, proving he'd had a little too much to drink at his bachelor party.

"Never doubted it."

With that, Rodrigo gave Mark a handshake and a one-arm hug, nearly falling out of the chair to do so. "Compadres for life."

Mark drank in Rodrigo's sincere emotion, then sent his own honest, grateful feelings right back at him.

"For life." Mark's smile came from his heart as he looked into his brother's face. He loved Rodrigo and his brothers. Only wanted the best for all of them because family always came first. That's why he wanted a wife and a family so badly himself, and at this age, the next step seemed long overdue. Some chances only came once in a lifetime. Had he blown his forever?

"We've got you covered…" Rodrigo stood like

the Leaning Tower of Pisa and walked off before
Mark caught the whole sentence.

What have you got me covered for?

Saturday morning at eleven, after having been
assigned the job of herding a group of hungover la-
dies into a limousine, Megan finally had her turn
on the massage table.

"Oh, you're tight," the masseuse said while working
on Megan's shoulders and up her neck. "Maybe some
aromatherapy will help. I'll diffuse some lavender and
add Roman chamomile to the lotion for your back."

"Wow, that sounds great."

"It's my tension blend. The secret ingredients are
Roman chamomile and frankincense."

Within minutes after the aromatherapy and only
minutes into the massage, Megan had relaxed and
was nearly drifting off to sleep as the masseuse
worked wonders on her aching muscles. She'd had
no idea how tightly wound she'd been lately. "Can
you double up on that Roman chamomile for me?
It's really helping."

"Of course. I'll do one better and give you some
to take home, too. You can use it after your shower
if you're still stressed."

Oh, she would still be stressed thanks to four
little letters: *M-a-r-k*.

Later, Megan made a point to sit by Stephanie
while they had their mani-pedi, since she realized

there would be no time between this and the wedding rehearsal to talk privately. Oh, gosh, all she had to do was think of the wedding rehearsal, and her stomach squeezed thanks to what that meant. She raised her hand and an attendant immediately came to help.

"Could I have a cup of chamomile tea? What would you like, Steph?"

"An espresso. Thanks." Stephanie smiled and glanced at Megan. "Hangover and a baby. Not a good combination. Plus wedding of the decade! Except for my own, of course." Steph was still in party mode and who wouldn't be with another Fortune getting married tomorrow. "Maybe Wiley and Grace will be next."

Megan needed to work on her enthusiasm. "Could you make my tea a double?" *If there is such a thing with herbal tea.*

The repetitive physical response Megan should have been getting used to by now reared its ugly head, drilling down between her shoulder blades. So much for the massage. Between her stomach and stressed muscles, and now the double-strength tea, she wondered if a person could overdose on Roman chamomile. Because she planned to use every drop she'd been given.

Five thirty sharp, Saturday afternoon. That's what the wedding planner had said about the rehearsal. What she didn't know was the difference between Mendoza time and actual time. But at least most of the Fortune side of the wedding party was there. Waiting. Except for her parents, David and Marci. Megan tried not to check her watch. Dreading what might happen when she and Mark finally came face-to-face again.

A swarm of tiny wings seemed to fly right through her. She braced herself by knotting her fingers so tightly together they hurt.

Mark would probably ignore her, which would hurt like the devil but would be for the best. There couldn't be anything more between them when there was Brianna waiting in Austin. Would he bring her? The terrifying thought shot across her, setting off the tiny flapping wings again. Her knuckles were white now. How could she act normally if he did such a terrible thing?

The one saving grace was the fact they'd managed to fake their way through a whirlwind relationship for two weeks. It gave her hope they could, once again, fake their way through Ashley and Rodrigo's wedding. Like nothing ever happened beyond a couple weeks of fake fun.

She'd already planned what she'd say to Mark, if she happened to bump into him. *Quit being selfish. Today and tomorrow are all about Ashley.* Yes. Yes. She needed to keep focused on the one and only reason everyone was here.

And speaking of "here," where the flying fig were the Mendozas?

Megan always assumed Ashley was meant to be married at a big country club. Everyone knew it even when she was a child. Yet, when it came time for her to fall in love and get engaged, she had moved to sleepy little Rambling Rose. More assumptions were made by the family, but instead of having a destination wedding, as everyone had figured it would be, she'd kept things local.

So the former princess wannabe and drama queen, along with her husband-to-be, had chosen the little known but historic Texas Mission twenty miles outside Rambling Rose.

Instead of going flamboyant, Ashley and Rodrigo had gone traditional. Another surprise. The Texas Mission, built somewhere around 1600, was the perfect setting for a wedding. Of course, the old mission had gone through several renovations over the centuries, but never wavered from the original, more simplified, look.

Thick walls, terra-cotta floors, arches all over the place and a high ceiling decorated with colorful Mexican tiles. She couldn't imagine a more romantic setting for her sister's wedding.

Megan wore a spring dress, in periwinkle with cap sleeves. Though she planned to have an updo for the wedding, tonight she wore her hair in the usual way. She blinked remembering how Mark had called her hair asymmetrical that first night, when he was drunk and brokenhearted.

The wedding planner, though dressed like a perfect Texas lady, sometimes gave off the vibes of being a drill sergeant. Mrs. Ketchum was tall and plump with bigger-than-life bottle-blond hair and had a commanding voice accentuated by a genuine Texas twang. At the moment she was checking her watch for the third time and tightening the muscles at her jaw. It was five forty and still no groom.

Oh, no! What if running away from marriages was a family tradition? *Get a hold of yourself.*

Megan was grateful to the masseuse for giving her some extra Roman chamomile oil, which she'd applied liberally to her shoulders and neck after she'd showered. *Come on, Roman chamomile, do your thing.*

At 5:42, another stretch limousine appeared over the horizon, kicking up dust in its wake. Before Megan could blink back the butterflies and body shivers, and everything else that had suddenly gone haywire, Rodrigo and his groomsmen arrived.

One by one the impressive Mendoza men exited the limo. Carlo first, then Chaz and Stefan. Rodrigo got out next, and Megan felt Ashley's grin from six feet away. Man, she was in love with that guy.

Megan's heart tore through her chest, and she wished she had a flask of that calming oil to guzzle when Mark was the last man out. My God, he was stunning.

Her throat went dry and every nerve in her body synapsed with the next, and it was her turn to clench her jaw. How the flying fig was she supposed to hold it together? Act naturally, she kept telling herself as she stood frozen to the spot, her face a mask. Even her eyelids had quit blinking.

Please, someone, slap me!

Ashley and Rodrigo put on an amazing show with a kiss of storybook proportions. The drill sergeant didn't dare interrupt, not even for the sake of her tight schedule.

Megan thought her heart might give out under the excessive pounding in her chest, but so far she was still standing.

Then the mathematician popped in. Wait, five of them, six of us. How did that work for the procession? Now her brain cells were dying out, too, because she honestly could not remember the plans.

Scanning the group as she silently recounted, her eyes accidentally crossed Mark, who was watching her, albeit subtly. And there it went. Adrenaline exploded like scattershot throughout her chest. She'd lied to herself. There was no way she could fake her way through this. One look and even her math skills had gone missing.

Then the silver Mercedes came barreling over that same horizon just as Megan had given up on making sense of anything. Of course, Dad! He'd be walking Ashley down the aisle. And Mom, mother of the bride. Her half brother Wiley was with them. That's right, he was the missing groomsman. Also with them was Rodrigo's estranged parents, who had promised to be on good behavior for the wedding.

Soon there were greetings, hugs and kisses tossed everywhere as the entire wedding party had finally arrived. Even the ring bearers, Toby and Tyler, the cute four-year-old twins Brady was in the process of adopting, were already wrestling with the pillow on which they'd be carrying the rings tomorrow. Still, Megan stood glued to her spot, unable to say hello to anyone, until the drill sergeant—aka wedding planner—led everyone inside.

With her ears ringing, she followed the crowd. Thankfully, no one had noticed her total "systems failure."

"Relax," a familiar and deeply missed voice said, as they passed through the mission doors.

She gasped as though he'd snuck up on her and said "boo." Her body followed suit.

"Hey, it's just me," he said, as his hand lightly guided her elbow into the sanctuary. The mere touch set off tiny explosions over her skin.

Just you? Just the man I've fallen in love with, who still loves the woman he left at the altar? What a soap opera. She shook her head. Obviously, he

was already deeply embedded in their old game of
playacting. Her only hope was to play along. "Hi,
Mark."

"Megan." He whispered her name. "You look
fetching," he said, then once inside he let go of
her arm and turned off toward the groom's side
of the aisle. Megan followed Ashley to the Fortune family pews for further instructions. Gratefully, she sat since her knees were ready to buckle.
Fetching? Speaking of acting, was Mark channeling Cary Grant?

"Are we all here?" Mrs. Ketchum asked, and
Ashley assured her that everyone was.

Mrs. Ketchum glanced at her watch. Again. "So,
we'll forgo the introductions. I'm assuming everyone knows everyone else?"

Her crisp words were met with nods all around.
Slowly, Megan's breathing settled down, and her
pulse felt as though she'd only run a mile instead
of ten.

The wedding planner then placed everyone in
their positions at the altar, where Ashley beamed
like the beautiful bride-to-be that she was. Rodrigo
gazed at her with pure love. Megan swooned for
them.

Doing her best to keep it together, with the help
of little assurances from Nicole, Megan took her
place, as instructed. Her mind was still spinning,
so it was hard to focus, but how hard could it be?

It took every ounce of willpower not to check on Mark again, but she was pretty sure she'd identified his shoes. Who else would wear monk strap shoes with fancy silver buckles and not a scuff in sight? Only Miami Mark.

Mrs. Ketchum clapped her hands. Under other circumstances the gesture would make Megan laugh at the way she treated them like grammar school kids.

Meanwhile, she was still getting over the touch of his fingers on her arm.

"Ashley or Rodrigo? I have a question," Mrs. Ketchum said, scratching the side of her mouth. They both rushed to her side to look over the list she held. "There's been a change," she said quietly.

Ashley answered inaudibly out the side of her mouth. Rodrigo did the same.

Megan couldn't hear a thing with her ears still ringing.

"Okay, let's begin. You here, and you here, and you here," Mrs. Ketchum repeated as she lined up everyone.

It took everything Megan had to act normal, though her nostrils were flaring with severely needed extra breaths. She stared straight ahead, waiting, mentally practicing her walk. Alternating between holding her breath and remembering to breathe, with her eyes cast down, she heard the word "Begin."

She glanced up, catching the silhouette of Mark's hair—which she could recognize anywhere—in her peripheral vision across the aisle. Just as quickly she looked away as her heart fluttered.

A guitarist and cellist played the Secret Garden song "Hymn to Hope." The acoustics in the mission were perfect, and under different circumstances, Megan would be in tears and covered in chills. The music was so beautiful.

Ashley, Nicole and Megan had all chosen that song for their respective weddings when they had been ten years old while playing princesses of England.

Stephanie and Carlo led off the group. Things seemed out of order, but Megan couldn't concentrate on why.

"Next, Megan and..." Mrs. Ketchum checked her notes before saying, "Mark?"

As her heart sunk to the toes of her pointy shoes, Megan didn't need notes to understand with whom she would be walking down the aisle. Apparently someone or "someones" had pulled a switcheroo.

She had been paired with the breaker of her heart, Mark Mendoza.

Chapter Twelve

As terror struck like double lightning, Megan remembered something Ashley had said in the limousine last night. *Just promise me you'll forgive me.* Had she been responsible for the last-minute change to the procession order?

Caught in a whirlwind of emotions, Megan thought she might stumble as her feet tried to move without her.

"I've got you," Mark said, as she bumped into him and he righted her. He gave her a strange look, leaned closer and whispered, "We need to talk." His gaze was quizzical as he sniffed. "You smell like a cup of tea."

Oh, come on. Would've been nice for Nicole to mention that tea part before. And great going, Roman chamomile, for not helping a bit with my stress level!

She huffed out a breath. At least irritation had helped her focus. The one thing she had practiced over and over ad nauseam might actually pay off. Before she thought another second, she needed to get it off her chest. "This weekend needs to be about my sister," she said from the side of her mouth. "We'll just have to act natural, because it wouldn't be fair for their happiness to be marred by our issues."

"So it's back to faking?" Also said from the corner of Mark's mouth. She noticed he'd put his hand on top of hers that rested on his forearm for the processional. Had Mrs. Ketchum said to do that? Regardless, it rattled her all over again. "Does this mean we have to be fake friends for life?"

How could she answer such a crazy question while walking down the aisle beside a man with whom she would never get the chance to explore love? She thought, weighed the circumstances, then tried to see into the future for an answer. After the wedding Mark would go back to Austin and they would begin their roles as extended family from afar. End of story.

"Only for now." It was the best Megan could offer. "Just like before." She missed his touch and still wanted more, but for the sake of the wedding, she would have to deny her feelings for two more days. Then she'd work on it forever.

"Could The *M*s please stop chatting?" Mrs. Ketchum was curt. "Bless your hearts, there will be plenty of time for that over dinner."

Megan tossed Mark a see-what-you-made-me-do glare, and obviously enjoying getting called out more than she had, a flash of the old Mark appeared as he fought back a smile.

Wonderful. On top of feeling humiliated by practically falling into Mark and being the only bridesmaid who apparently didn't know how to walk, now she'd been chastised by the wedding planner. Normally, being a practical person, she would conclude that things could only get better. But the mathematician side knew, under the circumstances, the true odds of that happening. Slim to none.

Mark waited at his assigned seat for the catered alfresco dinner on the mission patio though he had zero appetite. He saw Megan's place card right next to his and a mixture of excitement and fear evened out to mild anxiety. Obviously, he'd shared too much on the state of his love life with his brothers, and someone was playing secret matchmaker. Then something Rodrigo had said just last night registered. *We've got you covered.* Well, Mark hated to disappoint them, but he was the last person Megan deserved. He'd told Rodrigo, Carlo, and eventually Chaz and Stefan the same thing. He loved her, yes, but she deserved better. If his brothers thought they could patch things up by seating them together and having them walk in the procession together, they were mistaken. Because he'd already blown any chance he had with Megan.

Instead of telling her how he really felt when he'd had the chance, the morning he'd headed back to Austin—the morning after the most amazing night of his life, following two weeks of pure joy—he'd doubted himself and left her hanging. Hurting. He'd done this to the one woman who believed in him, hell, who'd wanted to lasso the moon for him. But Megan had held her head high when she left, proving she was not one to be walked on. The memory still tore at his soul. She deserved to be loved and cherished, not hurt or humiliated. Which only proved she deserved better. No man should ever treat her the way he had.

His sorry excuse about still being confused and mistrustful of women from Brianna's stunt had worn thin long ago. He either needed to trust his heart again or live forever in limbo. Alone.

"Oh, come on," Megan said quietly, though clearly out of frustration, when she was led to the table by the maître d' and saw where she had been assigned.

"Would you like to sit somewhere else, miss?"

The older man with silver at his temples and a mild paunch beneath his shiny vest aimed to please.

"No. Thanks. This will be okay." She'd made enough waves for the day.

Instead of fighting the inevitable, having to face Mark again, she slid passively into the chair next to his and cast him a weary glance.

He shrugged. "I did promise to be your wedding date."

This was true, though it seemed like ages since they'd jokingly made those plans.

And anyone who'd been around her this past week knew how down she'd been, so this seating arrangement seemed like another cruel joke.

"Well, it's a good thing we know how to fake it" was all she could come up with in reply.

"It's not like we're enemies, are we?" he whispered, not wanting to grab the attention of their tablemates, who were mostly people he didn't know since the dinner included all the out-of-town wedding guests. Regardless, he worried what her answer might be.

"It's not like we're really friends either," she whispered back, sounding tired, then she quickly distracted herself by starting off passing the rolls around the table. Each couple from the wedding procession had been assigned to a table as hosts, to make sure every guest was happy and enjoyed themselves. At least that was the reason Rodrigo had told Mark last minute on the drive to the mission that he'd be sitting with Megan tonight.

She'd obviously pulled it together since the rehearsal. He was still working on it. She had also stated the obvious. They were great at pretending. Hell, they'd had a whole whirlwind relationship based on pretending. Her mere suggestion brought on an onslaught of memories he recalled at some point every single day just to get by. Right now, going back over those cherished memories made him want to kiss her.

Of course, he wouldn't because like her pulling it together, this wedding was something they'd both have to get through. She'd stated it clearly in the procession line—the weekend was about Rodrigo and Ashley, and they needed to act natural. Except acting "natural" to him would be flirting and kissing and all the things he had missed doing with Megan before, and wanted desperately to do again.

Mark raised his hand for the server who was on the spot. "What kind of whiskey do you have?"

After a short but solid list, Mark made his choice. "Can I order something for you?" he asked Megan.

She seemed a little concerned about him going right for a stiff drink. Well, too bad. She wasn't the only one trying to deal with being thrown together.

"I'll have what he's having," she said, nearly shocking him off his chair. "No, wait. How about a pinot grigio?"

That was more like the Megan he knew. Maybe he should try to act more like the Mark she knew? Oh, but wait, having a whiskey when completely stressed *was* the Mark she knew.

"Anyone else like a drink before dinner?" Mark remembered his role as table host to a group of friends and extended Fortune family who'd be attending the wedding tomorrow. All people he wasn't acquainted with.

Putting on his "duty" face, it was easy to slip back into their easygoing days together in Rambling Rose. Under the guise of faking it, everything became easy. So he'd start like nothing had changed and act, for the sake of the people at their table, like he and Megan were dear old friends.

He began asking everyone their names and to which side of the family or friends they belonged. Megan was helpful explaining that this one was a second cousin or that one was from a side of the Fortune family they hadn't even known existed until a year or two ago. Mark soon realized the Fortunes were as complicated as the Mendozas.

"How's business?" From his left side he accepted the basket of rolls that had made it around the table, then turned to his right and began pretending with Megan.

"Really good." Now that the salads had been served, she slathered butter over half a roll and took a big bite. "Still a few glitches here and there with our reservations, but we're getting there. How's the winery and restaurant?"

"Doing great." He rested his arm on the back of her chair, careful not to touch her. "Our restaurant business has really picked up. Have you noticed which wines your family is serving at tonight's dinner?"

The young male server finally brought their drinks and Megan smiled at the Mendoza Winery label on the bottle when he displayed it and poured a thimbleful for her to sample.

"Delicious. Thank you," she said as the server made a generous pour and she glanced at Mark with her approval.

Mark lifted his glass, promising himself this would be the only drink for the night because he couldn't risk saying something stupid like, *Can you forgive me? Because I'm crazy about you and want to pick up where we left off.* "Cheers," he said, instead.

"Cheers."

Which was ironic considering how down he felt about the mess with Megan. She had made it clear this weekend was about Ashley and Rodrigo, but as Mark watched her lips touch the rim of her wineglass, all he wanted to do was make the night about them and kiss her before begging her to give him a second chance.

"This isn't working," he blurted.

"What isn't working?" She was still deep in the role.

"I'm not feeling it." He spoke quietly. "I've messed things up so much, I can't even fake my way out."

She'd been looking straight ahead while he'd said it, then slowly turned her head toward him with something like a flash of panic in her gaze. "Well, you have to. For the sake of your brother and my sister. If I have to, you have to."

Yeah. He knew that. But how in the blazes was he supposed to do what he had to do with Megan sitting next to him, looking so sweet and pretty? He had to. "You're right again. Let's do this." He broke out into a fake laugh, as though Megan had just said the funniest thing he'd ever heard.

At first confused but soon slipping into her role, she put her hand on top of his hand resting on the table. "I know, right?" Just like the old days. Pure artistry.

From then on, they fake chatted and laughed their way through the rest of the dinner. But this was never going to work. And that was the problem.

Megan had made it through dinner with Mark, and everyone else at the table, which was surprisingly nice once they'd gotten back into their "faking it" bit. It always came so easy to be around him. All she had to do was keep telling herself it wasn't real. This was just their last-ditch effort to survive the wedding for people they loved, without making a scene.

They'd made it through Ashley's and Rodrigo's thank-you speeches, and multiple toasts of goodwill wishes, glancing at each other and nodding their nonverbal Hear! Hear! And every single time they did, Megan winced inside from wanting so much for it to be real. Ashley handled the presentation of small gifts for each person who'd helped plan the wedding. Even Mrs. Ketchum received one, though it had been her well-paid job to do so. During Ashley's toast, she called out Nicole and Megan with the story about how the processional song had been chosen with a pinkie promise when they were ten, and how she got to use it since she was the first to tie the knot, and it made Megan tear up, but she quickly wiped the signs away. She glanced two tables over at Nicole with her glistening eyes. Then she made the mistake of glancing at Mark, who watched her while looking almost as melancholy as she felt.

"Well, guess what," Ashley said to her sisters from the front of the room while looking sly. "I give you both permission to use the song for your weddings, too. Cheers!" and another toast began.

Megan didn't dare look at Mark then, not through blurry eyes about a wedding that would probably be years down the road with some as yet unmet man—who she probably wouldn't be nearly as head over heels for as Mark—when she sat next to the man she loved today. Why couldn't she stay mad at him? It would help speed up the getting-over-him part, and life would be so much easier once she let him go.

Wasn't it time for Megan to accept that Mark would always be her What-If and If-Only guy? Because all the faking in the world couldn't fix the facts. She loved him. But he still lived in a world of hurt thanks to Brianna, which could only mean one thing. He must love the woman.

"If you'll excuse me, I need to go to the women's room," she said after finishing the remaining bite of her dessert and the last drop of champagne in her flute.

Mark stood as she got up. He really was a gentleman. No faking there.

She rushed to the bathroom and made it to the stall before a deep achy sigh escaped her throat.

"Megan? Is that you?" Nicole asked from the stall next to hers.

"Yes."

"What's wrong, honey?"

"I need to pee."

Nicole waited for Megan at the sink, and thankfully no one else was around in the small bathroom. She greeted Megan with a hug. "I'm sorry you're miserable."

"And mad at you." Megan pretended she really was, though it had worn off. "You and Ashley forced Mark and me together and it's been weird."

"It looked like you were having a nice time."

"Of course, because we're the king and queen of pretending. But here," Megan said as she tapped her chest, "in here it hurts to see a man who's so great in every way, and I can't ever be with him."

Because Mark loved Brianna, the math would never add up. In fact, it would be the worst unrequited love triangle possible. The kind where *she* was the odd woman out. The most pitiful kind made even worse because she had never stood a chance.

"Did you hear anything I said?" Nicole didn't often get frustrated with Megan, but right now she certainly was.

"Yes, I did," she lied.

"Then look in that mirror again and tell me you're gorgeous."

Megan looked in the mirror but all she saw was a woman who looked like a hot mess. "When did you start acting like Mom?" she protested.

"I am gorgeous," Nicole prompted. "And wonderful, and any man would be lucky to have me. Come on, repeat it."

"Are you kidding?"

Nicole did her twitchy neck thing that tipped her head one way then the other. Which proved she meant business.

Okay. Megan took a long inhale. Why not give

herself some credit? She'd certainly had it going on with Mark the night after the pool party for two. "I'm gorgeous and wonderful, and any man—"

One of the guests entered the restroom and Megan stopped. The sisters silently washed their hands, but once outside the door, Nicole finished the sentence Megan had dropped.

"And any man worth his salt would be lucky to have you." Nicole was dead serious. After a hug that lasted longer than usual, with Megan understanding how lucky she was to have such a sister, they parted ways.

Instead of going back to the alfresco dining area, Megan stepped out front of the Texas Mission and found Stephanie.

"Just waiting for Acton to get the car," Stephanie said. "The babysitter called and said our little one won't go to sleep."

"Poor baby," Megan said. "First time with a sitter?"

"For bedtime, yes."

So Megan hitched a ride with her rather than return to the table of heartache.

The theme from *Wonder Woman* sounded from Mark's pocket. He hadn't heard that alert tone in over a week and it immediately gave him hope and made him smile. He checked the phone screen.

Just wanted to let you know I'm heading home.
GN Meg

And immediately his smile disappeared and a
small wave of panic set in. He only had one more
day to make things right. He glanced up just in
time to see Carlo approaching and wearing a concerned expression.

Looked like Mark had more explaining to do.

Later, Nicole grabbed Carlo's hand as he headed
toward the back of the mission, since Rodrigo and
Ashley were in deep conversation with person after
person after person. They stood at the temporary
white arbor with plastic ivy vines weaving through
the trelliswork at the front of the outdoor dining
area.

"So what did you find out?" she asked.

Carlo looked over each shoulder before answering. "That my brother is too scared to admit he
loves Megan."

"And I've found out my sister is too stubborn to
do the same. But I'm not giving up. They just need
more time together."

"I think he can't bear the thought of Megan re-
jecting him."

"Well, she's still trying to believe in herself, so
who knows." Nicole shrugged, not wanting to give
up but not seeing any solution to The *M*s' prob-

lem anytime soon. "Hey." She snapped her fingers. "You're the ring guy, right?"

Carlo nodded and patted his breast pocket reassuringly as if he already had the wedding ring tucked inside.

"I've got something for you." Nicole pulled out the black velvet jewelry bag from her purse and untied the satin strings. She fished around inside. Found the ring. "Pretty, right?"

Carlo nodded, hands in his pockets, clearly waiting for further explanation.

"Okay, tomorrow, in case The *M*s work things out, make sure you or Rodrigo have this ring to give Mark." She handed him the beautiful sapphire that went with Nanny Francis's set.

"That's a little presumptuous, don't you think?"

"We've only got one more day for this plan to work, otherwise it could be months before they come to their senses, and just in case it happens tomorrow, we should be prepared."

The next day in the Texas Mission bridal dressing room, Ashley's ivory wedding dress looked like it had stepped right out of the pages of a dream. A corset top with off-the-shoulder neckline was covered with embroidered floral lace that traced across her chest. The lacy pattern continued on the floor-length full flowing skirt to the small train. The sleeves, made all in beaded lace, delicately silhouetted her arms. And Nanny Francis's necklace completed the perfect picture. Her long blond hair hung in waves over her shoulders with Nanny's blue sapphire earrings peeking out.

Megan and Nicole thought it would be a shame to cover her hair with a veil. But Ashley wanted a traditional tulle veil so Rodrigo could lift it for their first kiss as husband and wife. In the end, romance won out over fashion sense.

The bridesmaids all had chosen their gowns, since each person, except for Nicole and Megan, were of varying sizes and shapes. Ashley wanted everyone to be wearing a different pastel color to represent spring with all its glory.

Nicole went for a daffodil-yellow dress with a halter bodice. Stephanie wore blushing pink, a chic one-shoulder style.

Megan loved her mist-blue vintage gown with a tulle bodice and lace-trimmed neckline, and a deep vee back. Simple but elegant, the way she liked.

While Ashley made the finishing touches in the bridal suite in the house behind the mission with the help of Mom, the photographer asked the bridesmaids to line up for a few pictures near the mission. Though distracted by the fact Mark had yet to show up, Megan did her best to smile.

Just before the photos were taken, Mark appeared in jeans and a white dress shirt with the collar open, a garment bag hanging from his finger over his shoulder. The photographer had to take another picture because, without naming names, "one bridesmaid had forgotten to smile." Well, that one bridesmaid was also currently struggling to breathe.

Carlo rushed to Mark. "You better get dressed. The wedding is going to start soon."

Mark looked at his watch. He had forty minutes to pull it together. He'd been in a trance since waking after only sleeping a couple hours, tops. Maybe if he stayed in this out-of-touch, semi-dream state, he could make it through the wedding. All morning little flashes of the days leading up to his own wedding kept popping into his mind. He fought them like a firefighter battling an inferno with only a blanket.

"Did you hear me?" Carlo said. "That bungalow has extra changing rooms. Get going."

Mark snapped out of his trance long enough to acknowledge his brother and head in the direction he had pointed. Once inside the small building, he chose a room at the far end that didn't look occupied.

He'd been dreading this moment since he'd picked the tux up from the cleaners last Thursday. The last time he had worn it he'd had the biggest disappointment of his lifetime and followed that up by the most outrageous response. He'd run away. So not like him.

He took the tux out of the bag and examined it. Clean. Pressed. Ready to wear. Still he hesitated. *Do it for Rodrigo. For Ashley.*

He kicked off his dress shoes and jeans, then took a deep breath as he pulled on the perfectly creased pants, swallowing a wad of what seemed like dry paper in his throat. Man, he needed some water. His skin went hot, and his heart sped up. The worst moment of his life had happened wearing these pants. He put his hands on his hips and paced the small room, head drooping, trying to even out his breathing, fighting more imaginary flash fires with that holey blanket. Brianna. Wedding dress. Church. Crowd.

"This isn't your wedding," he mumbled. "It can't happen again."

He buttoned his shirt, noting his fingers weren't steady, making it take twice as long to finish. Then he put on the vest and had the same issue. He glanced toward the jacket, resisting it with everything he had. Too many bad memories. Unable to forget. So he sat and put the dress shoes back on, then stared at the floor for several seconds, willing himself not to think. If only he could find a nothing-space in his brain and hide there for the duration of Rodrigo's wedding.

He heard some voices outside, women sounding excited and happy. More flashes from his wedding day returned. The bridesmaids gathering, giggling and all smiles waiting for Brianna. Just like out front when he had arrived today. Though he purposely didn't look for Megan, because that would be more than he could take right now.

He'd known he wasn't supposed to see Brianna before the procession, but theirs was an untraditional arrangement. Truth was he'd already started to doubt his genius plan for making a marriage into a business deal to ensure success. He'd needed to see Brianna one last time to brush away those doubts. One more time before he could say "I do" with peace of mind.

The voices outside his door got louder, breaking into his thoughts. "We'll see you out there."

"You look beautiful."

"Let her have some time alone to think." The third voice was Megan's. He knew without a doubt, because the sound rocketed straight to his heart. Megan. "Okay. We'll be ready when you are." Then he heard heels click on the tile floor and dresses whoosh past his door. He flinched at the sound.

For several more seconds he stood, listening until positive they were gone. Then taking every last bit of nerve he possessed today, he put on his tux jacket, smoothed the shoulders with his palms before buttoning it, avoiding looking in the clouded and cracked mirror as he did so.

He took one deep breath before opening the door as the harsh and realistic flash of opening the door to Brianna's dressing suite three weeks ago returned full force.

The door swung open and across the hall the double doors were also open. Inside stood a woman in a beautiful full-length dress, a fairy-tale wedding dress, watching herself in the mirror as she turned this way and that, using her hands to help the full skirt flare. Unlike Brianna, she was alone. For an instant he saw her as Megan and his heart imploded. He grabbed the wall for support. If only she'd been the one that day instead.

"Mark?" Ashley asked, looking concerned.

"Oh, hey." He pretended not to be falling apart as he stared at Megan's triplet. So lovely and full of grace. "You look beautiful. Rodrigo is a lucky man," he said, his throat so dry he was surprised he could get the words out.

"Thank you. You look pretty darn good, too."

He forced a robotic smile. "Thanks. Well, I better get out there. I wouldn't want to be the one to hold up your wedding."

"No worries. I still need some time to pinch myself and realize I'm the luckiest girl in the world to marry your brother today."

"He's the lucky one." With that, Mark left the building and headed for the wedding party lining up for the procession. He'd had the surprise of previewing how Megan would look as a bride, which only served to awaken that longing that had been eating him up since he'd left Rambling Rose. He wanted her for himself but still didn't know how to change things. How to make it right between them again.

With his heart pounding in the veins on the sides of his neck and his ears beginning to ring, he kept walking, fighting off the horrible memories from his wedding day, when the woman he'd intended to spend the rest of his life with, to have babies with, to eventually learn to love, had spit on his dreams and cheated on him.

Megan noticed something was terribly off with Mark the instant he joined the groomsmen. She'd had enough of avoiding their problems. Seeing the man looking tortured—she could only imagine how terrible he felt at this wedding after his had bombed—her instinct was to run and comfort him.

Tearing a page from Nicole's rule book, the chapter on "being worthy," she let confidence be her guide and walked toward the man she loved. The man she believed in. All she wanted to do was help him out any way she could. And it was about time she told him everything she felt, regardless of the consequences.

She pulled him away from his brothers and Wiley in his semi-stunned state, to a quiet and shaded corner on the patio area. "Mark, are you okay?"

He shook his head. Beneath where she had hold of his arm, she felt him tremble.

"Are you sick?" His eyes, which didn't look at her, were glazed and distant.

"Sick and tired of carrying that wedding nightmare around with me."

"That woman never had your best interests at heart. You were her opportunity knocking and she never gave you the love or respect you deserved."

"You don't need to remind me," he said, still refusing to look at her.

She'd started the reality check and she couldn't give up now. "Sorry. But just to make sure, I'll be happy to run down the whole list of why you should forget her, even though I haven't been privy to every detail. All I know is betrayal is about as low as it gets."

His hand went to hers and squeezed, though his eyes focused someplace on her dress. "What I never told you was that when I went against the rules and popped in to see her before we took our vows, I found her getting it on with the head caterer." He finally looked up, as though checking to see if Megan was shocked. Which she wasn't because he'd finally voiced what she'd suspected all along.

"She was wearing the wedding dress we chose together, and there she was with the skirt up and his hands anywhere they wanted to be." He swallowed and gritted his teeth. "That's how little she honored our plans. It ruined me." His eyes drifted away for a second as he thought, then he grasped both of her hands and looked pleadingly into her eyes. "But you've got to know something and understand it. I wasn't then, now or ever in love with her. You've got to believe me."

She fought her growing empathy for Mark, while feeling elated hearing him insist he'd never loved Brianna. Still, wanting only to offer him support, she melded her gaze with his stare. She needed him to know she was here for him. Would always be if he'd let her.

"I never factored in the cheating part," he said. "Or realized how much I really wanted to be married to someone who loved and respected me until that moment. And it was a helluva day to find all that out."

Without thinking, Megan hugged him until she felt his tense muscles relax.

Soon, noticeably calmer, Mark unwrapped his arms from her and carefully put his hands on her cheeks. "I don't want to mess up your hair because you look so beautiful." His thoughtfulness made her eyes well up. "So, so beautiful, but I'm not freaking out today because of what I lost the day of my wedding. I'm freaking out because I'm afraid I've lost my one true love, and I don't know what to do about it."

Confusion set in. Just a moment ago he said he'd never loved Brianna but now he was afraid of losing his true love? Her ever-present need to add things up, to make sense of them, went to work, and it slowly occurred to her. "Wait, you're talking about me?"

He canted his head, relief clearly replacing the tense lines around his eyes. "Only you."

Catapulted to the stars by his confession, Megan reached for Mark's neck, pulled him close and kissed him, making sure he knew how much she cared. A heartfelt kiss tamed by the circumstances of her sister's wedding. At first Mark stood tense as all hell, but she felt him slowly release the tight muscles as she continued the gentle, loving kiss. Soon, he fell into her arms like someone who'd finally found home. She held him and he hugged her close and they stayed that way for several healing seconds.

Before she could speak past the emotion clogging her throat, they were interrupted.

"You guys." Nicole peered around the corner, easily within earshot of what was going on. "It's time." She pointed to the mission sanctuary. "But it's also about time you two admitted it," she whisper-scolded and followed up with a grin and two thumbs up as she walked away.

"Then I better seize the moment and say I love you right now," Mark said, looking relieved and like the old Mark she'd known. "I love you, Megan."

Nearly swooning with joy and her mind abuzz,

she couldn't wait to say the words out loud. "I love you, Mark."

Megan never thought she would see this day with Mark but was ecstatic that this was where they had landed. Finally! Having lived through so much torture lately, their mutual declaration was the sweetest thing she could ever imagine or hope for.

"Rodrigo told me the day after I met you that it's when you find someone you can't see yourself living without—that's when you buy the ring. Considering how hungover I was, I'm surprised I remember." She smiled understandingly at him. "My point is, I know you're The One. No doubts for me," he said. "I know we haven't known each other very long, and I know you're naturally more cautious and methodical than I am, but I'm willing to wait as long as it takes for you to feel confident in me. In us. The way I do."

Knowing their time was limited because the wedding was going to start, she jumped ahead. "Full disclosure. I knew you were special from the start, and I fell in love almost the first time I met you. Not counting the bar night, but also kind of, because your total vulnerability that night pulled at my heartstrings." She stopped, worried she sounded overearnest, which she clearly did, and glanced toward the sky, trying to figure how best to make him understand. "Okay, I'm overexplaining, but that night showed me you were a man who could love completely."

Mark grinned, kissed her again, then, when Nicole reappeared and cleared her throat as a reminder, he put his arm around Megan's waist and guided her toward the others lining up at the doors to the entrance hall as she kept talking. "That night, I saw you for who you were—the nicest guy in the world. A guy with possibilities. A man I could believe in. Someone who deserved to be loved as much as you loved. Not betrayed. That's why I jumped right in that day Brianna showed up."

"And I love you for that, too."

As they walked, Megan noticed Rodrigo say something to Carlo, who nodded and came directly toward her and Mark.

"We've only got minutes before Rodrigo needs to take his place at the altar, but he wanted me to give you this," Carlo said to Mark as he handed him something. "We thought you might be needing it."

Mark opened his palm and Megan saw the gleaming white gold and sapphire piece. "That's my Nanny Francis's ring."

"Is it okay if Mark borrows it today?" Carlo didn't wait for her response before he walked to the front of the line next to Stephanie.

"Ashley's coming," Drew said, alerting them time was short.

Holding the ring, Mark looked at Megan. "Then I better hurry."

Megan couldn't think of anything to say, though she was pretty sure she was about to live her dream. This was her moment, just two short minutes before Ashley's biggest moment of her life. But she'd take it because this was Mark, who'd finally told her *everything* she needed to know.

He stood in front of her and took her hand. "Megan, I've already tried the practical approach to marriage and as you know it backfired. Because something was missing."

So far, she loved everything he was saying, but pressure was building. "You better talk fast because the music is starting," she urged as Mrs. Ketchum took her place up front and Ashley appeared at the back with Dad beside her. Stephanie and Nicole rushed to make sure she was set, Stephanie adjusting the veil and Nicole the train. Megan's heart fluttered with excitement on so many levels she thought she might fly off into the beautiful Texas sky on this most wonderful day.

"Okay." He cleared his throat and regrouped, drawing Megan completely to attention again. They might be standing in line, waiting to walk down the aisle for her sister, but she was savoring this moment, taking in every instant of it. "Now I'm ready to go for it. With you," Mark said. "Because you were my missing link before. You and one other thing. Love. Now I know what it is, and how much different it feels from anything else." He stared into her eyes, driving the point straight to her heart. "So what do you say, will you come along on my dream with me? Will you marry me?"

With chills covering every part of her body, Megan needed to be clear. "You've known me long enough to know it's totally out of character for me to throw caution to the wind, but that's how we've been from the start, right? So, I say yes." She grinned through her blurry vision. "Let's do this!"

Then Mark slid Nanny Francis's ring on Megan's finger. A perfect fit, as she knew, which also happened to be the perfect accessory for her beautiful bridesmaid dress. Just in time.

Nicole, who stood eavesdropping in front of her in the procession line squealed, and Ashley, three people behind her, did, too. Then Stefan and Chaz, who were in front of and behind Mark, slapped him on the shoulders.

When Mark kissed Megan the entire procession line cheered loud enough to draw the attention of people inside the church.

Mrs. Ketchum even smiled. "Well, this seems to be the good news wedding. This bodes well for the bride and groom. Now, bless all y'all's hearts, shall we begin?"

After the kiss, Megan turned and waved at Ashley, who hands down *was* the most beautiful bride she'd ever seen. Ash's veil was lowered, but Megan felt her grin, as she lifted her bouquet and pretended to toss it toward Megan.

Megan laughed just as Mrs. Ketchum said, "The *M*s, on the count of four…"

"That will soon be Mr. and Mrs. M," Mark told the wedding planner as they started down the aisle.

"Congratulations," she said. "But please no talking and walking."

Mark's smile said it all. Megan had never felt anything like this before and was positive she was giving Mark doe eyes. So this was what it felt like when women had that look. And man, was she happy she finally knew it.

"To be continued…" Mark whispered as Megan lifted her chin and Mark planted a quick kiss on her lips as they walked down the aisle, for one second causing them to lose step. But also causing some scattered clapping in the chapel.

"Well, Mrs. Ketchum didn't say anything about not kissing" was all Megan could say on the happiest day of her life so far.

Rodrigo and Ashley's wedding had come off without a hitch. It was beautiful and moving and both the Fortune and Mendoza families had much to be happy about. Who'd ever have thought they'd have two matches made in heaven in the same day?

The joyous day was promptly recorded for posterity by the photographer, who grabbed the entire wedding party for group pictures immediately after everyone exited the mission. Megan was sure she and Mark would forever be the two in the pictures identified by their goofy, ecstatic grins.

Their grins didn't let up, even through the reception at the Hotel Fortune. They kept dancing to the live band, though now, with the bride and groom happily on their way to their honeymoon, and many people having left shortly after them, Mark and Megan had the floor almost to themselves. This particular song was slow and romantic, and Mark took the opportunity to kiss Megan again, something they'd been doing a lot of since the wedding ceremony had ended and the reception had begun.

"I can't believe I almost lost you because I was so messed up. Yet it was like some force physically picked me up in Austin and dropped me in Rambling Rose that night. When I finally understood why marriage could never be treated like a business deal. There I was in your hands." He stopped dancing and looked deeply into Megan's eyes. "We were meant to meet. I'm sure of it."

Megan laughed. "Well, God certainly works in mysterious ways, because you were the sorriest sight I'd ever seen that first night."

He gave a self-deprecating laugh. "I can only imagine."

"And I still fell for you."

A slow smile showed his beautiful teeth and brightened his eyes. "That's what I'm talking about. It was meant to be. You and me." Miami Mark was in true form again, every bit of confidence and swagger back full force. And Megan loved everything about him.

"I can't believe I let insecurity keep me from following what I knew was true." She told her side of their story. "We had something special. But I almost let it slip away because I didn't think I was—"

Mark stopped her from saying *good enough* with another light kiss. "Regardless of what you thought of yourself, I never thought it. You are the brightest star in my universe. You give me so much, I can't believe how lucky I am."

With tingles floating over every inch of her skin, she sighed. "We do have something special going on, don't we." It wasn't a question because she knew without a doubt it was true.

"Oh, yes, we do. So what do you say, when we plan our own wedding, we do everything the opposite of how we would have normally done it back in the days before we knew each other."

"You mean like wing it?"

"Yeah. No firm plans. Except for a definite date. When you're ready, of course."

She was already ready but did her best not to appear too willing. Because wasn't it important for a man to have to work for his goals? "No wedding planner," she said firmly.

"I'm with you on that." They tapped foreheads and smiled up close at each other as they swayed to the music.

"Indoors or outdoors?" She glanced over his shoulder as she lifted the fingers on her left hand and admired her special engagement ring, filled with beautiful memories from Nanny Francis and now with the most amazing promises for her future with Mark. When she looked at that ring, all she saw was pure love.

"Oh, I like how you're thinking. Outdoors?" He ran a finger down her cheek, his eyes sparkling under the dim dance floor lights. "We could get married in a pool."

"In a bathing suit? Never!" She laughed at the absurdity, though loving the idea. "That's where it really happened for us, wasn't it?"

"You know it. That's where I knew I was finally on my honeymoon. With you."

He kissed her again, then led her to the hallway outside the gorgeously appointed hotel party room, where, beside a tall potted plant, he backed her to the wall and kissed her with everything he had.

Memories of their one night together stirred her excitement to a near uncontrollable level. He knew it, too, because he pulled back and looked at her, the same fire in his eyes she'd seen in his hotel room that night that seemed like ages ago.

"Since we're all about seizing the moment now…" He smiled. "Thanks to some screwup with the reservations, the hotel didn't have a single room for me. I offered to stay in my brother's room, but Rodrigo insisted on making it right. So he gave me a suite instead." He popped a quick kiss on her mouth. "Want to see it?"

Megan knew exactly what those beautiful suites on the fourth floor looked like. It also hit her between the eyes that since they'd been extra careful about reservations, this "room switch" probably had more to do with Rodrigo playing matchmaker than any screwup. Along with the way they'd been thrown together in the procession line and at the rehearsal dinner, how the engagement ring magically appeared at the perfect moment. Suddenly, everything came into focus. The Fortunes and Mendozas had been pulling strings in the background to get Megan and Mark back together. Obviously, they'd known better what was right for The *M*s than she or Mark had. Until today, when they'd finally worked it out. She'd be mad at everyone if she wasn't so ecstatically happy.

Since all the agony they'd both been through, she was also all about seizing every moment with Mark, from now until forever. He'd just asked her if she wanted to see his suite. There in the hallway, snug by the wall, her arms were tucked under his, her hands resting on the backside of his shoulders. She ran her palms down his back along the curve of his spine until she put one on each of his gorgeous glutes, then squeezed. "I thought you'd never ask."

His eyebrows shot up and she mischievously grinned. Then she squeezed again.

Mrs. Ketchum appeared out of nowhere looking far less like a drill sergeant than usual, having hung around for the entire reception and obviously imbibing in the ever-flowing champagne. "You forgot this," she said as she handed Megan the bouquet Megan had caught at the toss—since no one else even tried and Ashley threw it straight to her, anyway.

"Thanks."

Once she'd delivered the flowers, Mrs. Ketchum walked off.

Megan looked at the arrangement, especially the red roses symbolizing passionate love, but also the yellow daffodils for happiness, and she couldn't overlook the dahlias, a symbol of commitment. This bouquet said it all and Mrs. Ketchum had somehow known it was exactly what Megan needed to see before she and Mark started their overdue journey together.

This time Megan took the lead, gathering Mark's hand and pulling him along to the hotel elevator. She pushed the up button. When the doors opened

with a ding and they had it all to themselves, she
chose the fourth floor. He pulled her under his arm
and wrapped her close. "Remember that night,
under the moon, you told me you believed in me?"

"Of course."

"That's when I saw our possibilities."

How many more wonderful things would topple
out of those gorgeous lips tonight?

"Well, that," he said. "And after I checked out
your dance moves."

She blurted a laugh and playfully cuffed his arm.
Then, putting her hand that held the bouquet behind
her back, she pecked his lips. "So should we have
our wedding in Austin or Rambling Rose?"

* * * * *

MILLS & BOON

Coming next month

TUSCAN SUMMER WITH THE BILLIONAIRE
Susan Meier

It wasn't right. He was feeling things he wasn't allowed to feel, definitely mixing business with pleasure, when he knew better.

He shook his head. "I could virtually run our multi-billion-dollar conglomerate in my sleep, and your simple family business is breaking all my rules, making me crazy."

She shrugged. Her lips turned up into a smile that stole his breath and made his blood race.

He still held her hand. They stood only a few inches apart. The full moon smiled down on them while the vineyard that was at the center of their problems rustled in the breeze.

But she was smiling. Amused by him.

The humor of it struck him and his own lips rose. "This is crazy."

"There's that word again. You use crazy a lot...especially about yourself."

She really was funny. Fun. He felt like he was getting a glimpse of her as she really was, maybe as she had been before their employee embezzled.

With their gazes locked, everything inside him slowed to a crawl. Warmth suffused him, along with a yearning so pure he couldn't fight it. He inched closer.

The connection between them rose, swelling around him, urging him even closer.

"I think I'm going to kiss you."

Her eyes didn't even flicker with surprise. And why would they? They'd been attracted since the second they'd laid eyes on each other.

"You shouldn't."

Her voice was a soft whisper that skipped along his spine, but she didn't move. Didn't step back. Held his gaze.

Expectantly.

The hum of whatever it was that buzzed between them drowned out his common sense and reasoning. Simple curiosity filled him, as desire surged in his blood and temptation promised fulfillment, pleasure enough to make it worth the risk.

He lowered his head and kissed her.

Continue reading
TUSCAN SUMMER WITH THE BILLIONAIRE
Susan Meier

Available next month
www.millsandboon.co.uk

COMING SOON!

We really hope you enjoyed reading this book.
If you're looking for more romance, be sure to
head to the shops when new books are
available on

Thursday 1st April

To see which titles are coming soon, please visit
millsandboon.co.uk/nextmonth

LET'S TALK
Romance

For exclusive extracts, competitions
and special offers, find us online:

f facebook.com/millsandboon

🐦 @MillsandBoon

📷 @MillsandBoonUK

Get in touch on 01413 063232

For all the latest titles coming soon, visit

millsandboon.co.uk/nextmonth

MILLS & BOON

THE HEART OF ROMANCE

A ROMANCE FOR EVERY READER

MODERN

Prepare to be swept off your feet by sophisticated, sexy and seductive heroes, in some of the world's most glamourous and roman locations, where power and passion collide.

HISTORICAL

Escape with historical heroes from time gone by. Whether your passio for wicked Regency Rakes, muscled Vikings or rugged Highlanders, a the romance of the past.

MEDICAL

Set your pulse racing with dedicated, delectable doctors in the high-p sure world of medicine, where emotions run high and passion, comfo love are the best medicine.

True Love

Celebrate true love with tender stories of heartfelt romance, from the rush of falling in love to the joy a new baby can bring, and a focus or emotional heart of a relationship.

Desire

Indulge in secrets and scandal, intense drama and plenty of sizzling l action with powerful and passionate heroes who have it all: wealth, st good looks…everything but the right woman.

HEROES

Experience all the excitement of a gripping thriller, with an intense mance at its heart. Resourceful, true-to-life women and strong, fearle face danger and desire - a killer combination!

To see which titles are coming soon, please visit

millsandboon.co.uk/nextmonth

MILLS & BOON
MEDICAL
Pulse-Racing Passion

Set your pulse racing with dedicated,
delectable doctors in the high-pressure
world of medicine, where emotions run
high and passion, comfort and love are the
best medicine.